CROWN OF FIRE

BY KATHY TYERS

Firebird
Fusion Fire
Crown of Fire

KATHY TYERS

CROWN OF FIRE

BETHANY HOUSE PUBLISHERS
MINNEAPOLIS, MINNESOTA 55438

Crown of Fire

Cover by the Lookout Design Group, Inc.

Published by Bethany House Publishers
A Ministry of Bethany Fellowship International
11400 Hampshire Avenue South
Bloomington, Minnesota 55438
www.bethanyhouse.com

Printed in the United States of America by
Bethany Press International, Bloomington, Minnesota 55438

Library of Congress Cataloging-in-Publication Data

Tyers, Kathy.
Crown of fire / by Kathy Tyers.
p. cm.
ISBN 0-7642-2216-3 (pbk.)
I. Title.
PS3570.Y4 C76 2000
813'.54—dc21 00-010881

To Maië and Gary,
to Sylvia and John,
and to Kathy and Richard,
wishing you joy unspeakable
and full of glory.

Blessed is the man who perseveres under trial,
because when he has stood the test,
he will receive the crown of life
that God has promised
to those who love Him.

James 1:12, NIV

KATHY TYERS is a bestselling author in the ABA market with earned degrees in microbiology and education. A classically trained flutist turned folk artist, she regularly performs folk music with her husband and also plays with the Bozeman Symphony Orchestra. She and her husband make their home in Montana and have one son.

Kathy and her friends exchange e-mail at lady_firebird@onelist.com

ACKNOWLEDGMENTS

To Steve, Lisa, Amy, Janna, Patrick, and Martha—Thank you for the chances and second chances, for commitment, attention to detail, professional guidance, and friendship.

Mark and Matthew—my models of manhood and excellence. Thank you, too, John and Idessa . . . and my dear Poppa.

Special thanks to Pastor Chris and Pastor Brett, and to the authors, leaders, and fellow students in Bible Study Fellowship who sparked ideas and sustained my growth, particularly Sharon, Sue, Michele, Robin, and Carol.

Thanks to my specialists, General Bob and Doctor Bob, Bill, and Diann. She never could've flown steadily without you.

Cheryl, Kathy, Karen, Chris, Basia, Gayla, and Ed—You held my hand before Firebird won her first wings. Thank you for your patience, ideas, encouragement, and loyalty. Thanks for your friendship down the years.

Sharon, you've been there week after week. God bless.

Tana, you picked up the pieces more times than you know.

Andrew, April, Clint, Greg, Jane, Jo, Harry, Linda, John, Julie, Marlo, Matthew, Peter, Rob, Sigmund, Sylvia, and Wynne, and my enthusiastic friends at lady_firebird@onelist.com—Thank you for letting me draw you into this other world, and thank you for making it so much broader.

Finally, thanks to the holy and merciful One. You give and transcend all stories and songs.

All of the best ideas in this trilogy came from all of you. Any inaccuracies, impossibilities, or accidental perversions of truth are mine alone.

CONTENTS

In this whorl of imagined star systems,
God created not Earth but different worlds.

One world's people lived by false doctrine and death.
Light-years away, faithful exiles awaited
the Messiah of all creation.

On a third world, they met.

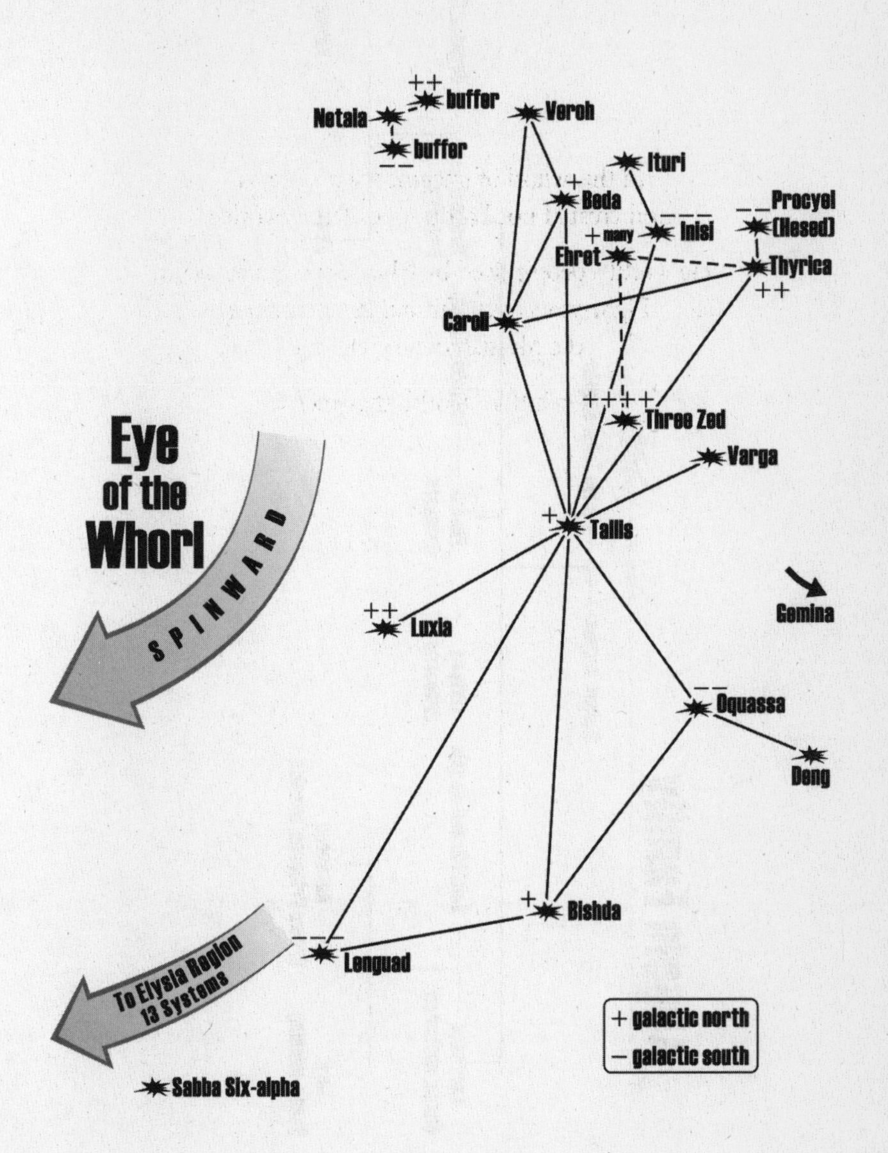

Eye of the Whorl
SPINWARD
Netala
buffer
buffer
Veroh
Ituri
Beda
Procyel (Hesed)
many
Inisi
Ehret
Thyrica
Caroll
Three Zed
Varga
Tallis
Gemina
Luxia
Oquassa
Deng
Bishda
Lenguad
To Elysia Region 13 Systems
+ galactic north
– galactic south
Sabba Six-alpha

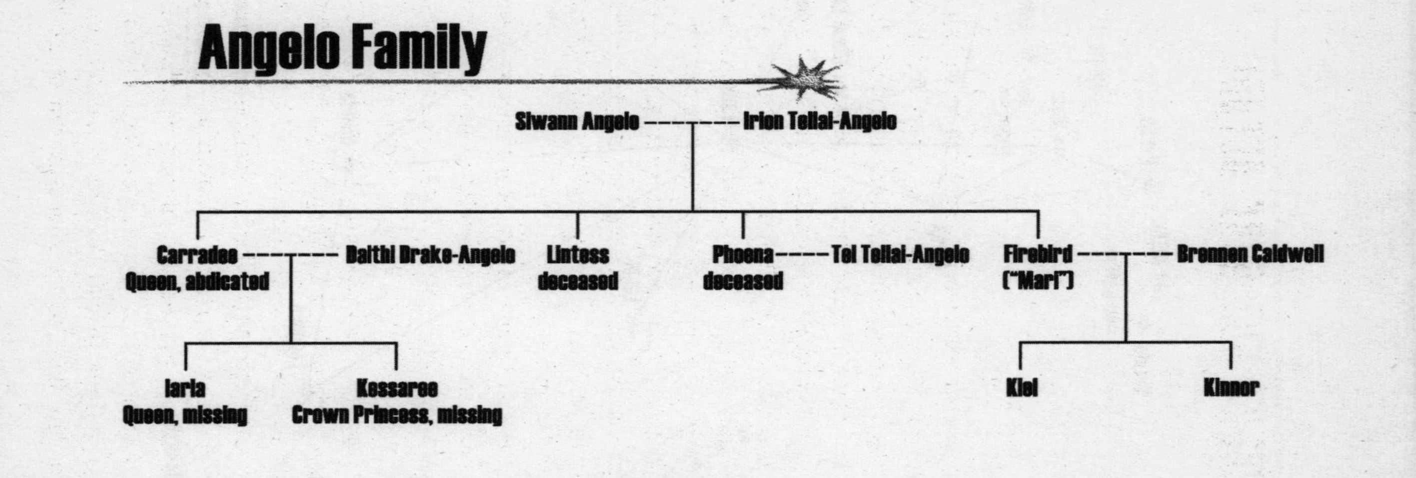
Angelo Family
Siwann Angelo
Irion Tellai-Angelo
Carradee
Queen, abdicated
Daithi Drake-Angelo
Lintess
deceased
Phoena
deceased
Tel Tellai-Angelo
Firebird
("Mari")
Brennen Caldwell
Iaria
Queen, missing
Kessaree
Crown Princess, missing
Kiel
Kinnor

WHAT HAS GONE BEFORE

FIREBIRD

Lady Firebird Angelo was sworn from birth to the service of *Netaia*'s merciless state religion, the nine holy *Powers*, and doomed by her birth order. She was a *wastling*, forced to seek a "noble" death in battle as soon as her oldest sister, *Princess Carradee*, secured the royal succession. Sent to war as a combat pilot against the interstellar *Federacy*, Firebird was captured and interrogated by an enemy officer, *Master Sentinel Brennen Caldwell.* The most powerful *starbred* telepath of his generation, Brennen descended from a people who altered their children's genes to create telepathy. Only two known remnants of this *Ehretan* race survived a terrible civil war: Brennen's people, who called their psi-trained elite *Sentinels*, and a small but powerful group of renegades they called the *Shuhr*, or enemy.

As a prisoner, Firebird watched her own Planetary Navy slaughter civilians and saw her homeland in a chilling new light. Granted Federate asylum, she was sent to safety on the *Regional* capital world of *Tallis*, accompanied by a female Sentinel, *Ellet Kinsman.*

Brennen, promoted to Field General, was ordered to oversee the Federate demilitarization of Netaia. When Netaia fell to the Federates, the throne passed to Firebird's reluctant sister Carradee. Meanwhile, jealous Ellet nearly let Firebird be killed by Netaians who came to Tallis, demanding custody. Ellet then tried to intimidate Firebird, revealing that Brennen had sensed that he and Firebird were *connatural*—perfectly matched to each other at the deepest level of soul and mind. Brennen returned to Tallis to find Firebird in full-defense mode, distrustful of him yet unwilling to let Ellet Kinsman defeat Brennen by subterfuge.

Over the next several weeks, he tried to convince Firebird that Sentinel *pair bonding* was a desirable state, not the dehumanizing continuous telepathy she feared. He also tried to induce her to ask about his faith, the worship of Ehret's *Eternal Speaker*. The Sentinels lived under strict *Codes*, including (as divine discipline for their ancestors' disobedience) a commandment against proselytizing to anyone who did not inquire first. As an heir to ancient prophecies, Brennen knew he must not marry outside his faith.

Back on Netaia, Firebird and Carradee's middle sister *Phoena* and her paramour, *Count Tel Tellai*, schemed to throw off Federate domination and seize the throne from Carradee. Firebird and Brennen returned to Netaia secretly, and against the *Regional command*'s orders, to halt Phoena's research. Firebird was captured by Phoena, her devoted Count Tel, and the piggish *Duke Muirnen Rogonin*. Awaiting a dawn execution, Firebird begged Brennen's one God to show her that such a transcendent being really could exist. She saw and heard a magnificent vision of Him singing the universe into reality. Immediately, she committed herself to Him as the *Mighty Singer*.

Brennen laid out explosives to destroy Phoena's weaponry research lab, then let himself be captured in order to free Firebird. Finally, she realized he would lay down his life for her and that he was worthy of trust and love. Facing execution beside her, Brennen detonated his explosives. They escaped in a single fightercraft. Firebird defeated a Netaian pilot in aerial combat, then flew back to the Netaian capital.

Brennen knew that Firebird had barely committed herself to faith with no real knowledge of doctrine, but after prayer, he proposed marriage and pair bonding. Firebird accepted.

FUSION FIRE

Immediately after their wedding at the Sentinels' sanctuary, *Hesed House*, Brennen was dismissed from Federate service for insubordination. They returned to his home world, *Thyrica*. Eight months later, they were attacked by a Shuhr assailant. Firebird, six and a half months pregnant, managed to give the alarm, but Brennen's brother *Tarance*, his wife, and their three children had been killed. Shuhr had struck the Caldwell family before, leaving only one male heir to a set of mysterious prophecies. Firebird only knew that a Caldwell would supposedly destroy a "nest of evil" that sounded exactly like the Shuhr colony world, *Three Zed*. Brennen could not explain any other prophecies until Firebird was formally consecrated into his faith community.

They retreated to a secure apartment at the *Sentinel College*'s medical center. Firebird was consoled for her loss of freedom by the revelation that her family, like Brennen's, descended from gene-altered *Ehretan* telepaths. At college, she could try to develop her latent abilities, but she was unable to make the most basic mental gesture, *turning* inward to touch her *epsilon carrier wave*.

Brennen's colleagues asked him to help develop a portable long-range transmitter for their *epsilon* abilities. They called the secret project Remote Individual Amplification, or *RIA*. Firebird took up studies in governmental analysis. Sociopolitical-economic simulations predicted that her home world would shortly throw off its oppressive *electors* in a bloody civil war.

On the Shuhr world of Three Zed, the ruling Eldest (*Eshdeth Shirak*) welcomed his grandson *Micahel* back from a training mission to Thyrica, where he had tried to wipe out the Caldwell family and launch the Shuhr on a new phase of planetary conquest. *Testing Director Dru Polar* chastised Micahel for his failure, while Firebird's unexpected Ehretan heritage caught the attention of *Juddis Adiyn*, a genetic researcher.

Phoena was easy prey for a Shuhr agent who suggested that she seek Shuhr aid. She traveled to Three Zed, where Dru Polar made her a prisoner. The Shuhr set about destroying the Angelo family. Phoena's abandoned husband, Prince Tel, came to Thyrica begging for Brennen's help in a rescue effort. Brennen agreed only to house Tel while they waited for Firebird to deliver her twins.

In labor with *Kiel* and *Kinnor*, Firebird finally *turned* and found a flaming darkness inside her mind. Brennen was called to Thyrica's main military base two days later, when three Shuhr-hijacked fighter ships were spotted incoming. As Brennen and other officers scrambled a diversion, disgruntled *Harcourt Terrell*—a Sentinel seduced by the Shuhr with promises of extended life and power—attacked Firebird. When he tried to use *mind-access* to force her to suicide, she unwittingly drew him into her flaming *turn*.

Brennen returned home to find Terrell dead and Firebird near death. He evacuated her, Tel, and the twins as the hijacked fighters plummeted into another Thyrian city, *Sunton*, and blasted out a massive crater.

Back on Netaia, Carradee and her husband, *Daithi*, were nearly killed in an explosion inside the Angelo palace. Muirnen Rogonin had himself named Regent, then turned the Electorate against Carradee, pressuring her to abdicate. Fearing the Shuhr, Carradee sent her young daughters *Iarla* and *Kessaree* offworld. She refused to suicide in the traditional manner but took her injured husband to Hesed House.

Safe at Hesed, Firebird was told that until they understood how Harcourt Terrell died, the Sentinels considered her a threat to Brennen and especially to her twins. The *Sanctuary Master and Mistress, Jenner* and *Anna Dabarrah*, took custody of infants Kiel and Kinnor. Brennen received a dream-summons from the Eternal Speaker, calling him to Three Zed to prevent the destruction of Hesed and most of his brethren.

At Firebird's formal consecration, delayed by the attack on Tarance's family, she learned that Brennen's family was prophesied to produce a holy king who would rule over all worlds and peoples, king of all nations and tongues, eternal and merciful. "In Him shall perfect peace, true atonement, be fully accomplished."

Brennen was captured at Three Zed. Dru Polar tortured Phoena fatally with his *dendric striker*, then boasted that he would force Brennen to torture and kill Firebird in the same way. The Shuhr could then take advantage of Brennen's *bereavement shock* to break his mind.

Prince Tel humbled himself to ask Sanctuary Master Jenner Dabarrah for access healing. Jenner and Firebird worked together to understand the mysterious darkness in her mind, finally concluding she'd been given the ability to see the taint of evil present in every human soul, though all were created in a holy image.

Dru Polar forced Brennen to observe as he tried to "fuse" epsilon carriers with a culled Shuhr youngster. If one carrier were first artificially reversed, Polar theorized, then the superimposition of those carriers should release an explosion of epsilon power. Brennen realized this could explain how Firebird killed Harcourt Terrell. If she had a naturally reversed epsilon carrier wave, then when Terrell attacked her, they could have achieved fusion, amplifying his deadly intent.

Ellet Kinsman arrived at Hesed with Brennen's friend *Damalcon Dardy* in an RIA ship. Firebird and Tel took the ship to Three Zed, hoping to rescue Brennen and Phoena. By now, Brennen had been forced to create amnesia blocks that prevented his access to large portions of his own memory. Firebird found her bond mate tormented by irrational fears. Worse, he did not remember her, though he could sense that she was his pair-bonded mate.

Dru Polar, Eshdeth Shirak, and the Shuhr woman, *Cassia Talumah,* intercepted Firebird and Brennen inside the colony's generator chamber. In a last moment of surrender, Firebird relinquished her will to the Mighty Singer and managed to turn, deliberately linking her carrier with Brennen's to release fusion energy. Cassia attacked, and Firebird remained conscious long enough to draw Cassia into a fatal psiclysm.

In a final duel with Dru Polar, Brennen was nearly vanquished when Polar raised Brennen's own *crystace* over his head, preparing to throw it. Brennen used fusion energy to drive the crystace down through Polar's body into the floor.

Back at Hesed, even Jenner Dabarrah could not heal Brennen. Still, the Federacy reinstated him to Special Operations in return for his attempt to rescue Phoena. He was content in having saved the sanctuary and glad to return with Firebird to their sons.

However, the Shuhr had no intention of simply letting him go.

PRELUDE

Absently smoothing a wrinkle in her snug black pants, genetics technician Terza Shirak pressed her forehead to her scanner and examined a sixteen-cell human morula. She could not allow one microscopic imperfection.

Fortunately, all the visible chromosome divisions proceeded normally. Cytoplasmic proteins were also within tolerance. Terza reached around and carefully returned that culture dish to incubation, then drew the next tiny zygote from its sloshy growing place.

Recently graduated from pre-adult training, Terza worked long hours overseeing these womb banks and embrytubes. Her supervisor, Juddis Adiyn, served the city's new Eldest as a personal advisor. She hoped to be introduced to the Eldest soon, for a vital reason. At her graduation, less than a year ago, they finally told her that Three Zed colony's new administrator, Modabah Shirak, was her own gene-father.

Terza had wondered, during training, if she might be Modabah's offspring. She had his abnormally fair skin, black hair and eyes, and the sharp chin of her half brother, Micahel. She was tall, too, just under 180 centimeters. Still, no subadult conceived in this laboratory knew her parents. The parents never knew her, either, unless she survived training. That objectivity freed the colony to continue its 240-year experiment in genetic engineering. As a named adult, Terza hoped to contribute to Three Zed's strength. To humanity's future.

In such a scheme, there had to be casualties.

Terza stared at the next zygote, then frowned. One chromosome division had stalled, and a delicate chromosomal fibril, which should have divided, dangled through an incomplete cell division instead. The embryo would develop malformed. Absently she inserted a flash probe and vaporized the culture, then removed its entry from her catalog. This no longer bothered her.

Next, she turned to her weekly fertilizations. Fewer than ten percent of zygotes survived to adulthood. The others were culled as malformed embryos or imperfect-response infants, pronounced untrainable at the settlements where they were raised, or killed in training.

As she reached for her touchboard, a barely perceptible temblor shook the ground. Her ancestors had built the Golden City inside an extinct, plugged volcano. The world itself had not quite died.

The tissue-bank list contained her orders for the day, and the first ovum to be fertilized carried the TWS–1 designation. That was her own code—this would be her first fertilization! She sat up straight and flicked black hair out of her face. The odds said this offspring would perish before adulthood, but this was an honor. Her supervisor ordered gene crosses according to hereditary talents and his mysterious ability to predict future events.

Was the cross with Dru Polar? she wondered. The colony's late testing director had been abnormally strong in Ehretan talents. Just last night, her hall-mates on Third South had regaled each other with shivery tales about the trainer who culled so many of their peers. Polar had been found dead twenty days ago, hideously killed, beside Terza's masterful grandfather and another City resident, Cassia Talumah.

Terza grasped her lower lip between her teeth and glanced across the screen, checking her guess. Was it Polar?

No. The ordered fertilization's paternal designation was not Polar's DLP, but the cryptic BDC–5X.

BDC—Brennen Daye Caldwell? Terza clenched a hand. She'd personally cloned that prisoner's skin cells several days before he escaped—but Shirak males made a sport out of thinning his family! According to zealots among his people, a Caldwell would eventually destroy her world.

Terza's people had sacrificed one planet, their home world, to save themselves. Recently, they'd taken a city off the Sentinels' adopted world. They would neutralize the Caldwells if necessary and create more craters, because the timing was urgent. Soon they would be able to offer humanity a gift it wanted at any price: immortality. One world at a time, Terza's people—the unbound starbred—would craft a new human race in a more durable image.

Fortunately, Terza hadn't been involved in selecting the first planetary population to be modified.

She refocused her eyes on her orders. BDC–5X: This would be a female with Caldwell genes, but one who wouldn't carry the allegedly messianic Carabohd name.

This, at least, made sense. Before Dru Polar's interrogations and research ruined him, Caldwell had shown prodigious psionic talent. Maybe her supervisor wanted to create a pool of Shirak-Caldwell embryonic cells. He could tease apart that breeding stock to create a quick second generation.

Whatever he wanted, she must exceed his expectations. She keyed the stasis unit to deliver appropriate cultures. Within moments, the BDC–5X dropped into the micro-injector on her examining cradle.

Because of its dermal origins, the gamete had no whiptail. She confirmed with a glance that it carried the requisite X chromosome, then injected the gamete into the TWS–1 ovum, creating her own first offspring. Instantly, the smaller cell's nuclear membrane started to dissolve, releasing its genetic contents. Flattening her lips, she transferred the new zygote into a dish of nutrient medium.

Maybe her father hoped to duplicate Caldwell's abilities in his own gametic descendants, the ones who might live forever. Or maybe Terza's lab supervisor meant to test her, to see if she'd obey a distasteful order—this one—or else destroy her own fertilization late in its term. Terza did hate culling late fetuses, whose features looked almost human. Gene technology was dangerous work for a woman secretly more sensitive than most of her fellows.

And this one will carry my genes. Half of all I am.

Appalled by the tug of that new sensation, Terza reminded herself that it would also carry the genes of an enemy. She checked her screen for the next prescribed fertilization.

That day's final order sent her to her supervisor's apartment, several levels beneath Three Zed's basaltic surface. Stocky and small-eyed, Juddis Adiyn looked more like a dark-flour dumpling than a leader of the unbound starbred. He slumped in a brocaded wing chair, clasping stout hands in his lap. Adiyn was old enough—152, by the Federate calendar—to need ayin treatments to preserve his waning abilities. That was one reason her telepathically skilled elders normally spoke aloud. "By now," he said, "you are aware of your primary fertilization. An outcross with the Carabohd-Caldwell line."

Terza rocked from one foot to the other. On the near wall, a glasteel case displayed jeweled offworld trinkets against a frothy lava backdrop. Across the ceiling, red, blue, and green threads of light snaked and writhed. Terza found them mildly hypnotic, and she avoided staring at them.

"You're displeased?" Adiyn asked.

Of course, Terza sent silently. A young underling generally subvocalized, speaking mind to mind on her epsilon carrier wave. *I would have preferred not soiling my father's line with Thyrian genes. But this seems appropriate, considering my profession in genetics.*

"Have you made any guess? Any rationale?"

Something to do with Tallis's announcement, she suggested, taking a shot without a targeting beam. Yesterday, the Federates' regional capital had claimed that the Sentinels had developed a new technology. They threatened to use this RIA weapon against her people, in revenge for Three Zed's preemptive strike against Thyrica.

The Federates had good reason to be afraid. Terza was glad to be employed in reproduction, so she would miss the coming horrors.

"You're close," Adiyn said. "It has more to do with your father's scouting trip to Netaia, and with bringing Caldwell back to face justice."

Terza raised her head. Her father gave the fertilization order? She did hope to meet him before the colony moved elsewhere, after a century on this sterile planet. As for Caldwell, he and his Lady stood accused of assassinating her grandfather, the previous Eldest . . . and possibly Dru Polar and Cassia Talumah. No witness to their deaths had survived to testify. A summons had been sent, but no one expected Caldwell to return voluntarily.

Ironically, his people shared her genetic heritage. Because of those psionic abilities, this colony had superb defenses. It had little else, though. Modabah would leave in a few weeks to inspect the chosen planetary system. Netaia had rich assets, estimated at a quarter of the Federacy's. It could be seized relatively easily by altering a few nobly born minds and destroying only one, or maybe two or three, of its cities. Its top-heavy government made it charmingly vulnerable to such a simple approach. There, Terza's people would launch the next phase of their grand experiment. She wanted a pivotal position in that program.

"I assume you've heard that General Caldwell and Lady Firebird will also be traveling to Netaia."

Nudged back to the here and now, Terza nodded and responded, *Some sort of ceremonial.*

"And naturally, your father wants Caldwell back in custody."

She shrugged. Call it justice, or call it vengeance. Eshdeth and Polar had been powerful leaders, poised to destroy the Sentinels' fortress world—

Adiyn raised a hand, cutting off her thought. "Your father prefers to start any operation with several options. If the unexpected occurs, he can be ready."

How true. Down on Third South, her father's love of options had been the subject of some cautious derision.

"Among his options for Netaia," said Adiyn, "is to lure out General Caldwell, preferably in bereavement shock, since he will be there anyway. Modabah requests your assistance."

Terza raised one eyebrow. Bereavement left Sentinels mentally and physically incapacitated, easily seized or dispatched in the following days, because they bonded with their mates at the deepest level of consciousness. But—

Lure him out? she demanded. *A man almost legendary for his ethics?* He wouldn't want illicit power or pleasures.

Adiyn's little eyes focused over Terza's shoulder, toward the ceiling and those eerie light threads. She'd heard that he used them to read the future. "Your primary role will be as messenger, regarding the new Caldwell offspring."

She avoided scoffing, because Adiyn would sense it. *Sir, Caldwell knows we could make him a hundred offspring. A thousand. If we really want to trap him, we should offer him a full case of embrytubes—*

Adiyn raised a gray eyebrow. "Don't display your ignorance," he said tightly.

Terza crossed her ankles. She compressed her lips.

"Sentinels," Adiyn explained, "carry their own young. Apparently, breeding like animals fulfills some kind of psychological need in them." He waved one hand in front of his face. "Caldwell couldn't ignore an embryo that was carried by a woman, particularly a woman highly placed among his enemies. He would try to get her into custody."

Carried by a woman? Custody? "I beg your pardon." Terza spoke aloud this time, dispersing an outer cloud of epsilon static. Normally, she used it to shield her emotions.

"No, we wouldn't let you be kidnapped. We want this offspring for further research and breeding, to say nothing of your own value to your people."

An insubstantial iron band tightened around Terza's chest. He still hadn't explained *carried*. "Sir, you can't mean—"

"If you are unwilling, your father will gladly set you aside and choose another."

The iron band tightened further, and she struggled for her next breath. In colony parlance, "set aside" meant the cold-stasis crypts. There was no escape from that frozen prison, except to a short life as an experimental subject. Modabah wouldn't hesitate to stase one rebellious gene tech, even if she was his own offspring, any more than he would hesitate to order another Federate city destroyed.

Respectfully, sir, she sent, grasping at the first argument that occurred to her, *and I am not saying I am unwilling . . . but if we arrive on Netaia, and circumstances change, the Eldest might not even decide to lure Caldwell out that way. He always has half a dozen options. That would waste . . . my effort. . . .* She could barely imagine the embarrassment, not to mention the discomfort, the blood and pain—

Adiyn clasped his hands again. "Then call it part of your education, Terza. Your contribution to our pending expansion."

CHAPTER 1

TO STRIKE BACK

tema
theme

"And then this is the Codex simulation," said Occupation Governor Danton. "The Electorate sent it down yesterday, demanding that we act."

Firebird pushed long auburn hair back from her face as she leaned forward. Governor Danton's wood-paneled office had two broad, darkened windows and an antique desk, designed to set Netaia's Federate conquerors on equal footing with a snooty nobility. She sat in a comfortable brownbuck chair across from the governor.

Above the media block on his desk appeared an image she would've known from any approach vector: Citangelo, the heart of royal Netaia and its two buffer systems. Between the broad sideways Y formed by the Etlason and Tiggaree Rivers, Sander Hill wore a broad green ring of noble estates, while south of the Y, the central city thrust up ancient towers and shining new constructs. The Hall of Charity stood like a gold-banded cube at the junction of two long green swathes.

Out of midair, a fiery projectile plummeted.

Danton had just shown them an actual recording of the Sunton disaster on Thyrica. Firebird could hardly bear to watch this simulation, but she didn't blink as the projectile—representing a trio of piloted fighters diving from orbit—plunged into the city's southeast quarter near the new Federate military base. It sank through buildings and soil into bedrock. Around it, the city heaved like water into which a stone had been thrown. As the crater blasted two klicks deep, buildings, greenery, and people—everything flammable—coalesced in fire. . . .

"Enough," Firebird muttered, turning away. Muirnen Rogonin, Regent until the majority of Her Majesty Queen Iarla, owned the

Codex newsnet service. Naturally, he'd sent this to the governor's office as a greeting to Firebird and Brennen.

Governor Danton stroked something on his desk top. The window-filters opened, and Firebird took a short step backward. She glanced out at a heartbreakingly familiar view. An ancient arch framed three distant housing stacks and the central-city towers. Closer at hand, a cluster of tinted glasteel terminals had risen phoenix-like out of Citangelo Spaceport's ashes, evidence of its Federate conquerors' rebuilding program. Webs of gravidic scaffolding surrounded a partly finished ten-meter projection dish that was probably part of the new planetary defense system.

Still intact. Still home.

Governor Danton shook his head. "No one actually knows where they'll strike next?"

Firebird's husband, Field General Brennen Caldwell, sat in one of Danton's luxurious office chairs, lacing his fingers, looking just as sober as Danton. A small, whitening scar marked his left cheek, external evidence of his recent captivity. Brennen had taken terrible injuries at Three Zed. In the weeks since their escape, he'd struggled to convalesce. "I'm afraid not," he answered. "That is the real reason we've returned."

"I don't understand," said the Federate governor.

Firebird pointedly picked up a kass mug she'd left on Governor Danton's desk. She forced down a bitter sip, hating the taste but needing the mild stimulant. With her day cycle shifted eleven hours, this was all that was keeping her awake. Her gesture also cued Brenn that she would rather let him answer.

He set down his own mug. "The Federacy asked us to accept the Assembly's invitation," he said. "When Firebird was asked to return and be confirmed as an heiress of House Angelo, we both wanted to refuse."

Firebird nodded. She wanted that made plain.

"But we found good reasons to accept," Brennen said. "Regional command asked us to make the strongest possible statement that the Federacy supports local governments and their customs."

Danton nodded. "No surprises so far."

Brennen pressed one finger to the scar on his cheekbone, a gesture he'd picked up in recent weeks. "This is the crux, Lee. No one knows where the Shuhr will attack next, and my people have no intention of sending an agent back to Three Zed."

Not after what they did to you, Firebird reflected. Vengeance belonged to the One, but in retrospect, she was glad it'd been necessary to kill Dru Polar to escape. He'd tortured Brennen, then tried to force him to kill her—

"They know Firebird and I will be here in Citangelo for the next six days," Brennen went on. "The Sentinel College has publicized the fact that I was injured and reduced in Ehretan abilities. We hope to draw out a Shuhr agent, take a prisoner, and interrogate." He glanced at his bodyguard, the rather dashing Lieutenant Colonel Uri Harris. "We need to find out their plans before they can strike again," Brennen finished.

"That's why you'll be staying in the palace?" Danton asked. "You'll try to take your prisoner there?"

Firebird nodded and said, "That's plan one. Besides, I'm supposed to show that having accepted Federate transnational citizenship doesn't make me any less a Netaian, or less an Angelo." She managed a smile, despite her queasy reaction to the Codex image. "One Shuhr agent might be foolish enough to think we won't be adequately guarded there."

Brennen, recently reinstated into Regional command's Special Operations force, had just sent twelve of his fellow Sentinels to infiltrate palace staff. Sentinel Uri Harris, his bodyguard, was an access-interrogation specialist, as Brennen had been before Three Zed. Firebird's own bodyguard was a weapons instructor at the Sentinel College.

As the Shuhr continued to step up their raids against military craft, Regional command could draw only one conclusion. The decades-long standoff between Brennen's kindred and their renegade relatives was about to fly apart into open conflict.

Regional command had ordered Brennen's new team to find out where the Shuhr planned their next major attack and to prevent it. He carried sealed orders, to be opened if they could get one Shuhr in custody for interrogation.

Firebird's confirmation gave Brennen's team its opportunity. Confirmation was only a formality, and if she did stay here long enough to go through with it, it would convey no actual power—but Netaia had thrived on spectacle for centuries. In one carefully choreographed alternate scenario, Firebird and Brennen planned to walk up the aisle of Citangelo's great, cubical Hall of Charity . . . as bait for the trap.

"And the new RIA technology?" Danton's voice dropped a little farther, and he drummed his fingers on the desk top. Regional command had announced RIA just over forty days ago. Half the Federacy was now screaming for the Sentinels to use it, to attack Three Zed before the Shuhr could destroy one more city. The other half demanded that all trained Sentinels be surgically disempowered, rather than let them dominate the Federacy.

Danton raised one eyebrow and stared at Brennen. Firebird was willing to bet the RIA announcement disturbed him.

"I promise you," Brennen said firmly, "Remote Individual Amplification poses the Federacy no threat. We will only use it against the Shuhr."

Firebird emerged from Governor Danton's inner office into a narrow lounge. Prince Tel Tellai-Angelo sprang up out of a chair. She hurried forward to greet him.

Tel, widower of Firebird's sister Phoena, was their only ally among Netaia's noble class. Flamboyant in a maroon shirt and knickers, he whisked off a feather-brimmed hat. "Firebird," he murmured. "I just arrived." He turned to Brennen. "Caldwell, welcome back to Citangelo. Are you all right?"

Brennen laid a hand on the smaller man's shoulder. "I'm fine," he said, hastily turning aside.

Firebird sensed his sudden shortness of breath. Ever since Three Zed, narrow spaces like this lounge unnerved him. "Shel," he said, "Uri, this is Prince Tel. He's on the short list."

Uri Harris maintained a cultured air, even when walking behind Brenn at full attention. Keeping closer to Firebird, Sentinel Shelevah Mattason was 170 centimeters of feminine power, with pale blue-gray eyes and a strong cleft chin. She rarely smiled.

Tel raised a black eyebrow. "Short list?"

Firebird threw her arms around Tel and translated, "You're not a potential threat. These are our bodyguards."

Tel pulled away, glanced at Uri and Shel, and said, "Good. I hope there are more where they came from."

Two burly men in Tallan ash gray emerged from Danton's inner office. "Yes," Firebird answered. She couldn't inform Tel about the team infiltrating the palace—not out here, where she might be overheard. "And Governor Danton assured us there'll be extra security, plainclothes. One team will follow us to the palace now."

Brennen led down a passway lined with windowed doors. Firebird hung back with Tel, who leaned down toward her. "How is he, really?"

Firebird pursed her lips. "As well as we can hope." Brennen had done the damage himself, creating amnesia blocks to keep his captors from learning Federate military secrets. Eight weeks had passed since their return from the Shuhr, and he seemed calmer, better able to accept his losses. Besides memory gaps, he no longer had the fine epsilon control that had made him a Master Sentinel. That resulted in a shattering loss of status. The college had asked him to give up wearing his eight-rayed Master's star. His Ehretan Scale rating, once an exceptional ES 97, had restabilized at 83. Normally, only those who scored at least ten points higher were considered for Master's training. "Solid but no longer exceptional" was the new prognosis.

She'd seen him powerless and stammering at Three Zed, where one Shuhr had taunted her, claiming that she never could have had him back, not as she knew him. She was thankful he'd restabilized with this much strength.

She glanced up at Brenn's well-muscled shoulder and the new four-rayed emblem. While this mission lasted, he was masquerading as even more dramatically disabled—an ES 32. If the Shuhr thought he was virtually helpless, they might try and strike.

Almost everyone he met these days looked first at his new shoulder star. He'd told Firebird how plainly he sensed their relief. On the pair bond that joined them, she felt his pained attempts to turn embarrassment into genuine humility. He often succeeded.

Firebird quickened her steps to follow him across the new base. It had a sterile feel, bare of trim and almost surgically clean. As they passed an observation window-wall, she could see little of the aging, dignified spaceport she remembered, nor the vast military installation nearby. *Bombed to slag under the Federates*, she realized.

Would the Shuhr try to do even worse here, or had they set their sights on another world? Lenguad, or Caroli, or even Tallis?

"How are the babies?" Tel asked, pacing alongside her.

Firebird pictured four-month-old Kiel and Kinnor, asleep on their warming cots back at Hesed. "Wonderful," she said. "Active. They're changing so fast, we'll be hard put to catch up when we get back."

Tel touched her arm. "Sixteen more days."

Yes. If this trap caught no one, then at least she might return quickly. It would take six days to finish her electoral business, then ten to travel back across space.

On the other hand, if the trap caught a Shuhr as they hoped, then ten days on a different vector would take them back to Three Zed and battle. Brennen's people were determined not to let the Shuhr blast one more crater or slaughter another innocent twelve-year-old and her family in their home.

Firebird glanced at the small black duffel in Brennen's left hand, sent to Hesed by Regional command. There was a sealed message roll inside. Before he could even open it, they had to catch a Shuhr.

"It's not quite that simple," she told Tel.

They emerged at the command building's main entry. Damp winter air pierced her to the bone. She tightened the belt on her woolen coat, a gift from Sanctuary Mistress Anna. A monstrous indigo groundcar stood nearby, its side trunk open, their luggage automatically stacked inside. Uri walked to the trunk and drew a scanning device from his belt. Shel slid into the car, brandishing a similar scanner.

Beside the front door stood a squat man in indigo-and-black Tellai livery. Tel positioned himself alongside the car, then beckoned Brennen closer. He pulled off his hat and offered it to Firebird. "The height of this year's male couture. What do you think?"

Nestled inside lay two tiny handblazers. "I think it's ridiculous," she said firmly, pocketing one weapon. She would prefer to carry a nonlethal shock pistol, but it felt good to be armed again.

Brennen laughed, a hollow attempt at good humor. "I've seen worse," he said. Firebird didn't see the other blazer leave Tel's hat, but when Tel centered it again on his black hair, it rode lightly.

Brennen stared past Tel's vehicle. Returning to this base felt eerie. Danton's office had looked vaguely familiar, but the long hall was utterly strange, full of foreboding.

He did not regret creating the amnesia blocks. He'd saved vital military secrets and brought down two of the Shuhr's most dangerous leaders, saving Hesed House from destruction. He had to believe that someday he would fully understand why the Eternal One let him be disabled.

He'd returned with irrational fears that were clues to the memories he'd lost. Bladed weapons, anything made of gold—he understood why those things stole his breath. He'd returned with a knife scar on his chest, and in accessing Firebird's memories of Three Zed, he'd seen long golden corridors.

But why did he fear pulsing red lights? He remembered little from that place, with one terrible exception. For three generations, a Shuhr family had pursued his own. A Shirak murdered his great-uncle. That man's son killed his uncles, and the grandson . . .

In a black-walled conference room, surrounded by hostile observers, Micahel Shirak had admitted slaughtering Brennen's brother, sister-in-law, and their children. He forced Brennen's mind open and poured in a memory Brennen wished he could forget.

Brennen clenched a hand. This would be a dangerous double game, to protect Firebird Mari while hunting down a Shuhr. He hoped he might catch Micahel Shirak. That cruel braggart ought to feel the anguish of being probed for secrets that might bring down his own people. Micahel's family still threatened Brennen's children, and their children, and theirs. Micahel might have brothers, or cousins . . .

Brennen frowned. If only he could remember! The Shuhr tri-D summons, demanding he return and face justice, showed only Micahel, sitting at an obsidian desk, promising further destruction if Brennen didn't return. Regional command hadn't publicly released that summons.

Laying a hand on the car's fender, he stared at the metal-spiked energy fence surrounding this parking zone. He caught an odd epsilon savor at the edge of his new, limited range. Something felt wrong, almost hazy, as if someone were epsilon-shielding their own presence.

Brennen clung to his masquerade, resisting the urge to react. He had to convince the Shuhr he'd lost more ability than he actually had. He'd planted disinformation in the Sentinel College's records, rating himself barely psi-competent. No ES 32 would notice that vague presence. Hardly daring to hope his trap would bring in a Shuhr this quickly, he gripped his duffel strap and forced himself to play the concerned but unaware husband, depending on Shel and Uri for protection. They knew the real extent of his injuries, of course. Special Operations agents had to trust each other.

Firebird leaned close to Tel, speaking softly. The slight young nobleman was half a head taller than Firebird, and her plain gray traveling suit was an elegant contrast to his gaudy outfit.

Shel grabbed her sidearm. Uri hit an alarm on his belt at almost the same moment. They must have finally sensed the intruder.

Brennen curled his hand around Tel's small defense blazer. A brilliant green energy bolt splattered on the door arch behind him, and a foul presence slid into the edge of his mind. He couldn't resist the probe without compromising his masquerade, and so—as planned—he let it take his arm muscles. Controlled from a distance by a lawless stranger's epsilon power, his own arm swung toward Firebird. His thumb slid against his will toward the firing stud.

He seized his right wrist with his left hand and choked, "Get in, Mari." That was his private name for Firebird. If the Sentinel infiltration team was still in the area, this could be their chance—

Where were they?

He forced his rebel fingers open. Tel's little blazer clattered to the pavement.

Uri, Shel, and the plainclothes guards fanned out. As Firebird scrambled into the passenger compartment, Brennen rose onto the balls of his feet and looked around. From some distance away came a pulse of gloating, of shields dropped to reveal epsilon power, a Shuhr agent tossing down a gauntlet. In that instant, Brennen saw himself through other eyes as an easy mark.

He kept anger out of his surface thoughts, where the Shuhr might sense it, but deep in his heart he answered the challenge. *No. This time, we will take you.* Ingrained habits, such as that confidence, proved how deeply he had relied on his own powers, instead of the One he served.

Uri covered a spot near the gate with his own blazer. *No one's close enough to assist*, he subvocalized into Brennen's mind.

"Who was it?" Firebird demanded. On the pair bond, he felt her tension as she peered out of the car's second door.

"Can't tell," he muttered, scooping up the small blazer. "Uri, Shel. Recognize him?"

"No," Uri answered. "We'll see if we can get him to follow."

Chapter 2

Citangelo

fanfare

a short melody for brasses, used as a ceremonial signal

Firebird tingled with adrenaline as she slid across the seat, making room for Brennen. Tel's chauffeur slammed the car's first door. Tel jumped in front, too, then climbed between seats into the rear lounge. Shel eased around Firebird to take a window seat while Brennen pressed against her side. She hoped she'd acted her role as well as he'd played his. He'd almost convinced her he was helpless.

Uri took another back-facing seat while Danton's men joined Tel's driver up front. "Home," Firebird told the driver, "but not too quickly. We want him to follow." *As if he could lose this monstrosity in traffic!* Danton's plainclothes people would come about half a klick back.

The chauffeur, a lumpish man with shoulders too narrow for his indigo jacket, steered out the base's main gate and turned north on Port Road. Firebird heard a soft trill from the control panel as Central Guidance took over. She almost asked Uri to confirm that the Netaian driver could be trusted, then changed her mind. Tel surely screened his staff. Even if he'd missed a sleeper, Uri knew his job. He'd guarded several high-ranking Federate dignitaries.

She did feel slightly cheated, denied a good view of Citangelo, but she had to get used to moving inside a guarded circle. "Anyone following?" she muttered.

Uri frowned. "No."

One chance lost. Disappointed, Firebird studied Uri's face a little longer. He was Brennen's second cousin, and she saw a resemblance in their fine chins and cheekbones. He had been raised in political circles, which explained his impeccable manners.

Tel fingered a touchpanel on the side console, and the glasteel panel separating them from his driver darkened. "We're privacy shielded now," he said. "What can you tell me?"

Firebird glanced at Uri, then Shel. Shel paused a moment, eyeing her hand-held scanner. "Go ahead," Shel said gruffly. "The car's not transmitting, and the driver didn't react when Prince Tel asked."

Firebird drew a deep breath. "You've probably heard that the Shuhr are raiding again."

"Did Governor Danton show you the Codex simulation?" Tel asked.

Firebird nodded grimly. "Of course. And you do know that the Federacy just announced its new RIA technology."

Tel frowned. "Why?" Tel had gone with her to Three Zed, helping to run an RIA apparatus. Tel already knew most of what the Federacy just revealed—that Remote Individual Amplification would enable a Sentinel to influence other minds from planetary distances, instead of the traditional room's width. It had passed its first combat test when Firebird and Brennen escaped Thyrica, pursued by a Shuhr attack force. Later, it enabled Brennen, then Firebird, to land undetected at Three Zed.

"But RIA was top secret." Tel sounded plaintive. He'd even submitted to voice-command before he left sanctuary, to ensure he wouldn't inadvertently reveal RIA's existence.

Firebird glanced aside at Brennen and caught a glint of keen blue eyes, sober under dark eyebrows. *Do you want to explain*, she thought at him, *or shall I*? Their deep pair bond didn't let them send words, but they were learning to communicate from context and emotional clues.

He opened one hand, gesturing her to go ahead.

She leaned forward on the cushioned seat. "Sentinels have policed the Shuhr for decades," she said. As recently as two years ago, most Netaians hadn't even heard of the Shuhr. There weren't many Shuhr, but it didn't take many to frighten the Federates. "But they've pulled off three raids in the last month."

"Against military ships." Tel glanced up, as if he expected another suicide flight to plunge through the gray cloud cover. Obviously, he'd seen the Codex tri-D.

"Exactly," she said. "They have no military manufacturing. Why bother to build what they can steal?"

Tel nodded again.

"Regional command hopes that announcing RIA might buy us all a few weeks' reprieve. If that slows down their next strike, we might find out where they're headed in time to preempt it."

"Is the Federacy going to attack Three Zed?" Tel asked, looking directly into her face. "Before they can steal RIA, too?"

Again she thought of those sealed orders. She guessed, but she didn't know.

Besides RIA, they would take another dangerous new weapon to Three Zed . . . *if* those were the orders. Ever since Firebird and Brennen escaped from the Golden City, Sentinel College researchers had observed the unique fusion of their epsilon carrier waves. Under certain circumstances, that fusion of mental energy released virtually uncontrollable power. Using fusion, Brennen had sent a swordlike crystace pommel-first from high over Dru Polar's head, down through his body, and into Three Zed's stone floor, blasting out a small crater and filling it with . . . Polar.

Unfortunately, that fusion had sent Firebird into deep psychic shock. The college researchers had also learned that each fusion left scar tissue on the ayin complex deep in her brain, where her epsilon carrier arose. Genetically created by the Sentinels' ancestors, the mental-frequency epsilon wave gave rise to all their unusual abilities.

"I'm sorry," she murmured. "We're not allowed to discuss that possibility."

Tel leaned back in his seat, crossing his arms. Two years ago, Firebird had thought him dull-witted. What sensible person would marry Phoena? In the last four months, she'd seen Tel's courage and intelligence, and his loyalty—one of the highest Netaian virtues.

If the Federacy thought Brennen would lead an attack on Three Zed, why would Tel think otherwise?

She barely smiled at him, then turned aside.

Beneath the shroud of clouds, an elevated maglev rail paralleled Port Road through Citangelo's high-tech manufacturing zone, then bent west toward the fastrans station. Laser-straight avenues and narrow roadways that dated back to colonization crossed Port in the shopping district. An elegant stone bridge vaulted the Etlason River.

"There it is," murmured Shel.

Firebird pressed forward. From this vantage on the Etlason Bridge, she spotted a cubical building at one end of a park: the gold-sheathed Hall of Charity, where her confirmation ceremony was planned.

She might have to leave Netaia before her scheduled confirmation if Brennen made his catch soon enough. Still, if she helped disempower the Shuhr, Netaia might proclaim her a hero even if she left Citangelo prematurely.

. . . Might. There was no predicting the Netaian Electorate.

They passed on into traffic, skimmers and groundcars, mostly controlled by central guidance. Brennen pressed a data chip into the media block on the car's side console. Another half-meter hologram glimmered into existence between the forward- and back-facing seats. Firebird knew every cranny and corridor of the building that appeared. The three-hundred-year-old palace had seven klicks of passways, more than a hundred stairwells and gravity lifts, and two dozen entries. Its governmental and private wings framed formal gardens behind the broad public zone. Behind that columned front, the sovereign—a regent, at present—and other public officials had day and night offices.

Squarely centered between the palace's backswept wings, an elliptical chamber shone off-gold. It was the electoral chamber, heart of power on royal Netaia. Behind it were meeting rooms, galleries, and ballrooms . . .

Firebird glared at the sovereign's night office. In that curtained chamber, her regal mother had given her a last gift—poison, in case she was captured in battle.

Now that Firebird was a mother herself, she could not understand. Back at Hesed, her twin sons were probably fast asleep or enjoying a midnight feeding, Kiel a tiny mirror image of his father, and strong-willed Kinnor with those tight auburn curls, that impish face. How could her own mother, Queen Siwann, order Firebird to poison herself?

Brennen reached into the hologram, creating a double swath of shadow that blacked out several servitors' chambers and the uplevel library. Dozens of small human figures stood inside the two-level image. Nearly all the figures shone the scarlet shade of House Angelo livery, but twelve had been switched to midnight blue. He pointed silently to several.

"You'll have help," Tel observed.

Brennen waved off the media block and retrieved the chip. "That information isn't public knowledge, Tel. I wanted to reassure you."

"Then how do you intend to get a Shuhr in custody?" Tel demanded.

Firebird glanced at Brennen and barely nodded. *Your turn*, she thought at him. Tel had better not hear this from her.

He dipped his chin. "They measure the emotional impact of every action they take," he explained. "As long as they have a chance of catching us in the public eye—"

She sent him a wry half smile. Her confirmation would be public, all right!

He returned a pulse of amusement that only she could feel. "They aren't likely to settle for a quiet assassination," he finished.

Tel dropped his plumed hat. "You're not hoping to lure Shuhr agents into the Hall of Charity."

"To save Netaia or another Whorl world," Brennen said, "we'd prefer to take one quietly, in the palace. But if that fails—yes, Tel. We'll try."

Firebird glanced from one man to the other, hoping Brennen didn't need to put Tel under another voice-command to keep him from inadvertently revealing that information. She hated the idea of violating another person's volition, even for his own protection.

Tel nodded slowly and said, "Now I understand why you came back to Citangelo. The entire Federacy is at risk."

Firebird sensed Brennen's unspoken nudge. "That's part of the reason," she confessed. "There's also the confirmation itself. It is a peacemaking gesture."

Tel smiled wryly. "Well, you've certainly earned it. You've given up more, risked more, for Netaia's sake than any three confirmed heirs."

She agreed, but she couldn't say so. "And I'll be speaking to the Electorate tonight."—Hopefully before the developing Shuhr emergency could call her away!

Tel raised an eyebrow. "I'd thought that tonight's special session was Rogonin's chance to tell you he opposed your return."

"I'm sure he won't miss the chance," she murmured. "But I have more to say than he probably expects."

The car turned north on Capitol Avenue. Fayya trees drooped along the meridian, their leaves winter-dark and rustling in air currents created by traffic. Firebird couldn't see much sky, but she sensed a cold front coming in. It felt good to know she hadn't lost her Citangelo weather sense.

In one way, she hoped the trap didn't spring too soon. If she had to go back to Three Zed, she would love to first rub a few noble noses in her new status as an heir, to face down the young counts and countesses who'd despised a doomed Angelo wastling. She would outrank them now.

It shouldn't matter after all she'd been through, but she couldn't help feeling this way. For all their graceless cruelties, Netaia's noble traditions shaped her life.

On the other hand, she had rejected its strictly external state religion. She'd found mercy in a Singer beyond human comprehension, and she'd seen the evil deep in her own soul, a darkness she could only partially blame on Netaian traditions. That darkness made divine mercy necessary. She hoped she might introduce her beloved common people to something beyond the state-enforced service of Charities, Disciplines, and nine allegedly holy Powers.

"Well." Tel retrieved his hat and replaced it over his dark hair. "I hope you catch your Shuhr and find out what you need to know. But I hope there isn't a pitched battle inside the Hall of Charity."

"It's also possible," Brennen said, "that they might send in an agent who knows nothing important and who could injure anyone who attempted to mind-access him. Or her."

Firebird nodded. They just didn't know enough about the Shuhr's actual capabilities. They needed information on Three Zed's defenses and where the Shuhr hoped to strike. The Federate fleets simply couldn't be deployed to defend twenty-four star systems.

Meanwhile, the new crater on Brennen's home world hadn't finished filling with groundwater. Peaceful, easygoing Sunton, near the single continent's eastern shore, was now a saltwater lake.

Brennen barely swayed with the groundcar's motion, staring as if he were waiting for Tel to speak. He still could sense other people's tension when they prepared to raise uncomfortable subjects. His worst losses were in memory and kinetic skills.

Tel met that stare. "What about Iarla and Kessaree?" he asked.

"Nothing yet," Brennen admitted. Firebird's Angelo nieces—daughters of her eldest sister, Carradee—had been sent away under Federate protection, to be safer from the Shuhr. They never arrived.

Tel frowned and forged ahead. "Some people are concerned that RIA technology could put you people in charge of the Federacy."

Brennen returned Tel's sober frown. Previously, projecting a Sentinel's epsilon carrier wave long-distance could only be done by a planetary fielding team with several rooms full of subtronic gear. Like fielding, RIA's range was planetary. Unlike fielding, an RIA apparatus could be mounted on a single-seat ship.

"People are scared," Tel continued. "After what the Shuhr did to Sunton, every raid is considered a warning. It's that many more suicide ships they could throw at Federate worlds. We need you Sentinels now more than ever."

Firebird wanted to assure him. "The Federacy believes in preserving everyone's freedom. But the Shuhr's freedoms have to end at the point where they threaten other lives. The Sentinels see that as their duty, since they share similar abilities."

Another bridge rose in front of them. To the left and right, hedges marked the boundaries of Angelo property. She sat up straighter as Capitol Avenue crossed the Tiggaree and the chauffeur hit his override. Released from central guidance, their vehicle glided through massive gates tipped with golden spear points.

Firebird bent low to peer ahead as they cruised through a public festival square toward a grand edifice. Six bulky pillars, three left and three right, framed a short flight of wide white marble steps. Two electoral policemen marched down toward the car.

Firebird drew back from the window, almost overwhelmed by her aversion to that uniform. Electoral police, redjackets, enforced the cruel customs that guaranteed the wastlings' martyrdom. Supposedly, she didn't need to dread them anymore.

One tall, crimson-coated man opened the car door on Brennen's side. Freezing air swirled in. Firebird scooted off the seat and stepped onto a white-pebbled pavement.

Half gloved, all in scarlet, black, and gold, the redjacket towered over her. His neckscarved companion shut the car's side compartment. Carrying four large duffels, he strode along the building's front toward an entry in the private east wing.

Brennen followed, carrying that small black duffel.

Firebird's breath glittered as she mounted the steps. At that moment, a tour guide in scarlet-trimmed khaki emerged from the main door, leading a mixed-age troop through the gilt arch. Several reached for pocket-sized camera recorders.

Shuhr? No, tourists. Evidently the palace hadn't tightened security for her visit. She smiled faintly. A few of them smiled back.

Two House Guards in formal red-collared black stood at smaller doors farther on—this branch of service sworn to her family, not the Electorate. Each guard suspended one hand over a golden door bar. Firebird felt Brennen's attentive edge peak, then ebb away. Evidently, the House Guards felt safe to him, but she made it a point to glance around as if she were nervous before she followed Tel into a wide private foyer. Here, especially, they had to make it look as if Brennen had suffered crippling setbacks. Half the palace servitors were probably regency spies. Danton's plainclothes guards entered last.

High overhead, surrounding five ancient chandeliers strung with natural gems, ornate moldings decorated the walls and ceiling with swirls and flower petals. Portraits lined the lower walls. To her right, a staircase curved up to the living quarters. Left, a narrow hall led toward the sovereign's day and night offices.

Shel Mattason strolled forward and took a long look up the office hallway. Her large, wide-set blue-gray eyes did not blink. According to her résumé, Shel held the Sentinel College marksmanship instructors' title, and she was highly qualified in three martial arts. Firebird was glad to have her at right-wing.

Firebird stepped up to the portrait displayed prominently on a screen in midhall. The artfully painted woman wore gold, her dark hair perfectly coifed. Hard lines surrounded her mouth, and her dark eyes had a depth that suggested wisdom. One eyebrow arched slightly.

"Mother," Firebird whispered. There in the eyes, there through the jaw, Firebird picked out her own features in those of the autocratic late queen. *Could I have become another Siwann*? she wondered. If she'd been firstborn, would she have learned to wield power in the Netaian way, disregarding all individuals beneath her station?

Giant white cinnarulias, Siwann's favorite flowers, filled a cat-footed marble table beside the screen. Their scent brought back sharp memories of living here—a proud life, full of pain and desperate striving, and the need to accomplish too much in too little time.

Thank you for taking me away from here, Mighty Singer, she prayed. *But thank you for bringing me back, and for giving me a chance to save my people—from civil war, or Shuhr destruction—*

Quick footsteps echoed along the corridor. A man in Angelo service livery hustled into view. Heavyset with tightly curled hair, he rubbed plump hands together over his white cummerbund. "My lady, let me show you to your apartments."

They followed him up the private stairway, its shortweave carpet muffling their footsteps. Ribbons of gilt edged the banister and floor moldings. A stairwell alcove displayed a bust of the first Angelo monarch, Conura I.

Instead of halting outside the rooms that had been hers as a child, the footman led farther along the balcony, into the crown princess's suite. The high, white-walled entry chamber, with its formal furniture and narrow windows, had been Carradee's sitting room when they were girls. Brennen walked slowly along one wall. She felt how badly he wanted to go to work checking for monitoring devices.

"You will find all the appointments in place," said the footman. "My name is Paskel, of service staff. I live in-house, and you may call for me at any time. My number is six-oh-six." He indicated a tabletop console near the sitting room's door.

The man seemed friendly in a distant, officious way. "Thank you, Paskel," Firebird said. "Should I request dinner a little earlier than His Grace plans to dine?"

"I shall bring dinner up shortly. That will give you time to prepare for the special session."

"Good thinking," said Tel.

The servitor made a full bow. Tel nodded.

Firebird almost laughed. She'd always despised all this nod-and-bow. Definitely, she was home.

"And your . . . personal escort?" the footman asked, glancing at Uri and Shel. "Shall I lodge these in servants' quarters?"

Whether or not Paskel reported to the regent, Firebird wanted it known that she and Brennen were guarded. "No, open the consort's suite that goes with this apartment."

"Very good, Your Highness. Tomorrow, I shall ensure your engagement list is posted to these rooms." Paskel turned toward the door. He closed it silently, without the resounding *boom* so easy to make with heavy doors and ancient, resonant walls.

Firebird stared. He'd *highness*-ed her! She had asked Governor Danton to see that the royal title wasn't used in official releases, but palace staff followed tradition. Was Paskel declaring himself a cautious sympathizer?

Turning his head, Brennen lowered his eyebrows as if he were bitterly frustrated. Firebird knew it wasn't all masquerade. "Uri," he said, "Shel. Please safe the room."

CHAPTER 3

ELECTORATE

promenade

ceremonious opening of a formal ball

Firebird watched the bodyguards walk a slow circuit. Each one paused occasionally, raising a hand toward some innocent-looking object. They passed over the marble firebay and other obvious hiding places for listening and watching devices, reaching instead to touch wall panels, old bits of crystal, a jeweled window-filter. Reaching the far wall, Uri flourished one hand at a priceless, garish South Continent vase, then pivoted on his heel.

Most of those trinkets had been Phoena's, not Carradee's, and now that Firebird considered, that made sense. After Carradee took the queen's apartment, Phoena and Tel had lived in this suite. His Grace the Regent had probably left her Phoena's wardrobe for company.

What did standing in here do to her widower? She turned to eye Tel.

He pulled off his cock-hat and sank onto a pale gold velvette chair. "Here you are, Firebird. The lady of the palace."

Firebird remained standing in the middle of the carpet. She would not sit down until Uri and Shel checked every room. Uri, Shel, or Brennen could also pick up an assailant's focused tension before the attack, so they would have warning of any assassination attempt.

She hoped.

Staying in the palace did make a strong statement on behalf of the Federacy. Even as a transnational citizen, she belonged here.

Or did she? She already felt out of place in her plain gray traveling suit, while Tel's tailored outfit seemed appropriate. "This is more your room than mine, Tel."

"I live in my father's estate. This is a lovely suite, but . . ." He flattened his lips, then spoke again. "You need some time now. I'll be there to support you tonight."

"Thank you for all you've done for us."

Brennen raised his head. "Yes, Tel. You've been a friend where we didn't dare look for one."

Firebird's group assembled in Phoena's second parlor two hours later. The Angelo starred-shield crest decorated both of the study's doorways, and Phoena's furniture seemed oddly placed, with gaps where large pieces had been removed. As Firebird recalled, Phoena had run a resistance movement from this suite before she moved to Hunter Height.

Brennen, Shel, and Uri wore dress-white tunics that made their gold shoulder stars gleam, and the crystaces they normally hid in wrist sheaths rode on their belts. "You look splendid," she assured them.

"You," Brennen said, "look regal." He'd helped select the floor-sweeping skirt and snug velvette blouse, a statement in Angelo scarlet.

She smiled and checked the tiny time lights on her wristband. They should enter the electoral chamber in twelve minutes, at nineteen hundred sharp. Within minutes of that, she planned to interrupt the usual invocation of the nine holy Powers. She must show the electors she was no longer a dutiful wastling. Even the Federacy, which smashed her attack squadron and dismantled Netaia's mighty defenses, had been reduced to waffling against these belligerent aristocrats. Their economic control seemed unbreakable.

Her hand trembled. She stretched it out to show it to Brennen. "I can't look skittish. Touch me with prayer."

He covered her head with one palm. "Holy One, go with Firebird to face these people. Convince them of her wisdom and leadership, and protect her. So let it be." Their eyes met for an instant. "Be wary of pride, Mari."

The name was a private endearment, but she frowned at the warning. He knew what she planned to do. Sentinel College personality analysts had warned her she would always struggle with pride, willfulness, and impatience (Brennen had already known, of course). Still, this was Netaia, and tonight she had to startle the most complacent Netaians of all. "I can't shuffle into that chamber with my eyes on the ground."

"Of course not. Show Rogonin you were born for this. Defy the Powers." Brennen touched her shoulder. "But don't let them tempt you back to the old ways."

She raised her head and strode out.

In the corridor waited another pair of red-jacketed electoral policemen. Beyond them, two uniformed Federate guards waited at parade-rest, Danton's supplemental group. By now, there were probably Sentinels in the kitchens and corridors, looking for Shuhr assassins.

She descended the sweeping staircase, sliding her right hand along a banister and holding her skirt. At the foot of the stair, Paskel stood carrying a servitor's tray. He half bowed as she passed. Despite Brennen's warning, every proud Angelo instinct flamed in her heart and mind. Her adrenaline surged as if she were headed into combat.

Well, she was! Twenty meters along the next corridor, two more redjackets stood at each side of gold-sheathed doors. The doors stood open. Firebird drew a deep breath and walked through.

An elevated, U-shaped table rimmed in gold dominated this elliptical chamber, a room filled with memories. Along one curved crimson wall, beyond a bas-relief false pillar, she spotted a blocked peephole she used years ago to spy on the Electorate. A smooth gold floor medallion carried colder memories. It had felt icy through the knees of her Academy uniform, when she knelt with a redjacket at each shoulder. As a wastling, her birth had helped ensure the Angelo line's survival, but the family's need for her ended when her second niece was born, and so she was ordered to seek a noble death in the name of Netaia's traditions, and for its grandeur. "You are to be praised for your service to Netaia," First Lord Bualin Erwin had intoned the electoral *geis.* "On behalf of the Electorate, I thank you. But your service to this council has ended."

Firebird ground her shoes onto the medallion. She raised her head toward the elevated table.

To be Angelo was to be proud.

Twenty-six elegantly composed faces stared back. The commoners Carradee had appointed were all gone. Ten noble families ruled Netaia as benign despots, treasurers, and demigod-priests for the nine holy Powers of Strength, Valor, and Excellence; Knowledge, Fidelity, and Resolve; Authority, Indomitability, and Pride. Besides House Angelo, there were the barons and baronesses Erwin and Parkai, three ducal houses, and the counts with their countesses. For decades, they had controlled science and shipping, culture and resources, information and enforcement. As Brennen liked to say, their tentacles were everywhere.

At center table, a massive man sat on a gilt chair he'd stolen from her sister Carradee. Firebird half bowed to the regent and Duke of Claighbro, Muirnen Rogonin, but she couldn't keep her eyes from narrowing. "Good evening, Your Grace." *Grace—ha.* His Corpulence was neither gracious nor graceful. All in white with a sash of gold, he glared down through small green eyes.

She nodded left and right. "Noble electors, good evening." Shel remained three paces behind, at the corner of her vision. By protocol, the electors had to allow her one escort. Brennen and Uri remained by the golden door, between Danton's reinforcements and the red-jacketed door guards. The first time she'd seen Brennen, he stood in this chamber as an honor guard. Here they were again!

"Lady Firebird." Rogonin rested both hands on the high table. "You have been summoned by the people of Netaia. Deliver your greeting."

Glancing up, she spotted several miniaturized tri-D transcorders. Black velvette hoods shrouded them. Netaia's three newsnets would not carry this interview.

Actually, that was a relief. She could speak freely.

So could they, of course. . . .

"Your Grace," she called, "Noble electors, I am grateful for the honor of your summons to be confirmed. I am ready to serve Netaia."

Traditionally, that last line ran, *I am ready to serve Netaia and the Powers that Rule.* She expected whispers, and she wasn't disappointed.

Muirnen Rogonin spread his hands. "Then let us invoke the presence of Strength, of Valor and Excellence . . ."

Now! "Before you do," she called, "I have to deliver a warning."

It might not have been the most diplomatic way to get their attention, but it succeeded. Stunned faces glared down at her. Now she spotted Tel, sitting poised and expressionless. "Noble electors," she said, "the Netaian systems are in danger from inside as well as out in the Whorl."

No one answered, and she wondered if these people would ever respect her, under any circumstances. Reminding herself she'd been trained as a soldier, not a diplomat, she plunged on. "On Thyrica," she said, "under a pseudonym, I enrolled at Soldane University. Federate analysts have amassed an enormous database from all twenty-three contemporary systems and several civilizations that fell during the Six-Alpha catastrophe. I have been working toward a degree in governmental analysis."

Count Winton Stele, son of the Duke of Ishma—Dorning Stele had been one of her commanding officers at Veroh—cleared his throat. "What were your motives, Lady Firebird?" Count Winton managed to make her wastling title sound like an insult. "Your Academy education was in military science. We need the military now more than ever."

She frowned up at his sallow face. "I enjoy learning, Count Winton. Federate society embraces many local governments. Each one has a slightly different structure, suited to its own culture."

Bennett Drake, Duke of Kenhing, pressed to his feet. He resembled his brother Daithi, Carradee's husband, though Kenhing wasn't quite as tall. His hairline had the same widow's peak, and his face was almost as round.

Kenhing was also one of the few electors who insisted on being called by his old-style title. When fully dressed, he usually wore a gold dagger on his belt. He wore it today. "Well answered, Lady Firebird," he called. "However, we are most concerned about the danger from this world they call Three Zed. Did Governor Danton show you the Codex simulation?"

Surprised by Kenhing's compliment, Firebird felt her shoulders relax infinitesimally. *See?* she asked herself. *Tel isn't the only elector with some humanity.*

"Yes, he did," she answered him. "Twenty-three other worlds are also desperate to find out where and when the Shuhr will attack again. Several Special Operations teams have been deployed to find out the Shuhr's intentions." *Including this one*—but she couldn't say so. Instead, she returned to her previous topic. "The movement of governments from feudalism to populism has been widely studied," she said. "When I discovered the topic, it intrigued me. The more I learned, the more I worried, because wherever that progression toward representative government has been delayed by force, the downfall of feudalism came by force."

Without pausing, she recited the histories she'd studied: star systems bloodbathed by civil warfare, nations subdued by outside forces . . . *that* gave her a chance to tie the Shuhr threat back in. She used every story-telling skill she'd studied at Hesed House, trying to make those tales compelling, explaining how the Federacy's Regional command could not intervene in cases of internal conflict. She wished she could add music. Mere words didn't convey the terrorized heartbreak of decimated worlds.

"Our people," she said, "appropriated Netaia's ancient mythology and made it a state religion. We adopted a strict caste system and penal laws and called it stability. We set up traditions that perpetuate the transmission of wealth and authority inside a few privileged families. The system has not failed. Our world remains rich in culture, heritage, and resources."

A few heads nodded. Other faces reminded her of blast gates, shut and shielded against her—Wellan Bowman, and young Daken Erwin. The elderly senior baron creaked to his feet. Netaian nobles wore youth-implant capsules under their skin, so First Lord Erwin's hair remained bushy and brown, but even the finest medical technology couldn't forestall aging forever. His formal blue nobleman's sash sagged on a stooped body. He cleared his throat.

That was her cue to stand down, and now she was pushing their tolerance. Instinctively she knew that if she relinquished command of the situation now, she would lose it for good. "For an independent project," she pressed, "I entered cultural and governmental variables regarding Netaia's current situation into a set of equations designed by Federate sociologists, economists, and political analysts. I ran the simulations dozens of ways, altering variables such as subpopulation movements, materials shortages, and shifts in standards of living. Please let me tell you what they predict."

First Lord Erwin made a show of raising both thin eyebrows and spreading his hands. He sat down.

Relieved, Firebird lowered her voice to a confidential tone. "There is a high likelihood of civil war here on the North Continent." Now that Erwin had ceded her the floor, she gave them a moment to picture the crisis. "Disenfranchised classes could take control of the military and our Enforcers, plunging our systems into a period even darker than the Six-alpha catastrophe. Soon. Within months."

"We assume," the regent called, sneering, "that you will now claim that the Federacy can save us."

"No," she said. "You control Netaia's fate, the Electorate here seated." Whispers followed her sweeping gesture around the table. "Without a miracle, there will be war. But you can create the miracle. According to simulations, cultural holidays such as my confirmation tend to preserve cultural unity for a while. But after as little as half a Netaian year, the rising could come. If that rising distracted the Enforcement Corps, Three Zed could seize this world."

"Your husband's kinfolk," said a shrill-voiced countess. "What are you—and he—doing to combat that menace? And where are your nieces? The queen and the crown princess?"

"The Shuhr," Firebird answered, "would threaten Netaia whether or not I had married General Caldwell." She couldn't let them sidetrack her even further, talking about Iarla and Kessaree. "Listen to my proposal. It is incomplete in many ways, but it could give you a framework for your own more thorough designs. You could save Netaia from anarchy, exactly the way our ancestors saved it thirteen generations ago."

The whispers quieted. Really, they couldn't expect her to know where Carradee's daughters had gone. Rogonin, as regent for Iarla, probably hoped they would stay missing.

"For decades," Firebird continued, "the Netaian sovereign has been a legal figurehead, standard-bearer for this Electorate. I propose that all electoral seats gradually become figureheads. Advisors. Do this by stages. Shift control of our navy and the Enforcers to the elected Assembly." Judging from the way several leaned away from the gold-rimmed table, they already disliked her idea—as she'd expected. "The Assembly would remain answerable to the Electorate, but if you . . . shift . . . fifty-percent veto power out of your own hands and to the Assembly, voluntarily, that would show unprecedented faith in your people. You would retain checks on the Assembly. I have also proposed that the noble houses be compensated for this loss of influence." Firebird beckoned, and Shel stepped forward to hand her a recall pad. "I encoded a timetable, along with other aspects of the proposal." She'd spent most of the last two months, while Brennen convalesced and retrained, recording every possible simulation and developing the final document. Over a year ago, she'd made the Federate Regional council a silent promise: spare her life, and she would do all she could to bring Netaia into the Federacy. The time had come.

Rogonin clenched his hands on the table, not into fists but into claws.

"You've been given half a year's reprieve," Firebird said. "Please, for our people's sake, use it wisely." She shifted her weight under the long skirt, hardly believing that she had dared to speak to the electors this way. She almost hated to give up her recall pad and let them commence tearing her ideas apart.

"And who," Rogonin demanded, "would compensate our Houses? Does your considerable influence with the Federacy extend to demanding funds to buy out our seats and our ministries?"

"I have no influence with the Federacy at all." *And you know it, Your Grace*, she wanted to add. "That is one of many details that remain to be worked out. But this is your chance to escape the destruction of a world's way of life. Your estates, your families—the Shuhr would love to take them away from you."

No one plunged into her silence this time. She hoped they were picturing their grand homes plundered, their children carried off to Three Zed or subjected to unimaginable genetic experiments. "You could guide Netaia through a difficult transition," she called. She dropped her voice. "Or you could all die in a terrible bloodbath."

As wretchedly as they'd treated her, she didn't want that to happen. She laid her recall pad on the gold-banded table.

Rogonin eyed it, pursing his lips with obvious contempt. "If civil war threatens," he said, "we will raise additional troops and build more prisons to hold any rebels we choose not to execute. Netaia's strength is Netaia's future, Lady Firebird." He lowered his voice. "You are dismissed."

His arrogance raked her. He didn't care squill for the common people. No surprise there either, really. Still, she'd hoped . . . "Listen to one more request, noble electors—"

"Dismissed, Lady Firebird." The regent raised his voice.

Incensed, she pitched hers to match his. "For the love of your own children," she called, "do not conscript those troops. If you do, they will be the ones who slaughter you—if the Shuhr don't arrive first!" She whirled toward the door, flaring her long skirt. *Dear Singer, don't let them choose destruction!*

She wanted to say so much more. To tell them Netaia's common classes had every reason to revolt. That they deserved privileges that most Federates called rights—the right to earn a decent, stable living, to conduct commerce with other Whorl worlds, to sleep unafraid that city Enforcers might imprison whole families for one member's indiscretions.

But she'd probably said too much already, too forcefully . . . too willfully. Politically, she had probably been utterly ineffective. But maybe a few hearts had listened.

Shel stepped in front of the Netaian door guard. Brennen's eyes flicked back and forth, watching behind Firebird. Uri led out.

Firebird walked with her head upright and her shoulders relaxed, as if she'd chosen to leave, instead of being sent away.

She retired early, exhausted by the time shift, but memories haunted her into the night. Carradee had invited her into these rooms many times. This had been her mother's palace. She lay on her sister Phoena's bed.

It was good to know that Phoena would never torment her again.

She stared at the curtained ceiling, examining the sensation of relief. Finally, she could think about the middle Angelo sister with some objectivity. Despite Phoena's scheming and cruelty, she'd been a sharp stone grinding at Firebird's heart, honing her steel to a sword's point. If Firebird hadn't battled Phoena for so many years, she might not have found the strength to fight Brennen's enemies, or the evil that invaded her own soul.

Her eyes suddenly ached, imagining Phoena trapped at Three Zed. She wondered if at some point, Phoena finally realized that the Shuhr would not help her, that they would take her life and give back nothing at all.

By the Word to Come, she actually pitied her sister.

Shocked, she swallowed. She rolled off the bed and hurried out into the dressing room, where her tears wouldn't disturb Brenn. She caught Shel pacing along the high windows, several meters away.

"It's all right," Firebird managed. "I'm just—finally—grieving my sister."

"Princess Phoena." Shel stared out one window. "I understand. I'm also recovering."

Firebird wiped her eyes and stared at her bodyguard. This was the first information Shel had volunteered since they met, back at Hesed. "You lost a bond mate?" Firebird guessed.

Shel nodded once without turning around.

"How long ago?"

The Sentinel's voice softened. "Six years."

"I'm sorry." Firebird had been told that bereavement shock was devastating. Half of all Sentinels suffered it. Brenn had said it took his mother two years to recover. Still, Shel was young. "Some time," Firebird said hesitantly, stepping closer, "I mean, I would—"

"No," Shel answered. "I'd prefer not to talk about it."

Six years later, she still was tender in a tough line of work. *Shuhr*, Firebird guessed. Many of the Sentinels killed in action were taken down by their distant relatives, by Micahel Shirak and his compatriots.

Then setting this trap was personal for Major Shelevah Mattason, too. Firebird took a few more steps toward her bodyguard, wondering if some gesture of comfort would be appropriate. Shel didn't respond.

Firebird really didn't know whether she hoped they would catch a Shuhr and attack Three Zed, or return to dig in and defend Hesed. Even with RIA, attacking the Shuhr stronghold would be perilous. The last time, she and Brenn had arrived separately, stealing past Three Zed's fielding satellites with single RIA ships. This time they would have to attack in force. They would face the full terrors of Three Zed's fielding technology.

Even at the Sentinels' sanctuary world, fielding defenders could drive off any intruder by directly producing fear in the intruders' minds, and Sentinels followed high moral standards. She didn't like to think about what a Shuhr fielding team might do.

Shel still didn't turn around. Convinced that the Sentinel preferred to keep her grief private, Firebird tiptoed back to bed.

She paused to touch a tri-D cube at her bedside. That touch made it glow with internal light. Her babies might be waking now—Kiel with that squared Brennen-chin and hair that was thickening to Brenn's light rich brown, and Kinnor with his chin pointed like a sprite, his face scrunched in an impish pout. In the tri-D, Brennen's arms wrapped her shoulders, and their hair mingled in a wind that blew out of the rugged mountains around Hesed House. Staring at the cube, she could almost smell kirka trees—

Brennen pushed up on one elbow. "You're all right?"

Firebird slid beneath a silken cover warmed by soft, embedded microfibers. "I am now," she said. "I've buried Phoena. But I can't sleep." If she ever lost Brennen, could she hope to recover? *Please, Singer. One of us must die first, someday. I know this is selfish, but let it be me! Brenn is stronger. He could bear it.*

She couldn't bring herself to relate Shel's story. "I should've asked you to tuck me in," she told him. "Would you help me get to sleep?"

She sensed epsilon energy focusing at one of his fingertips. When he touched it to her forehead, her stressed alpha matrix uncoiled instantly. She sighed, relaxed against his chest, and slipped into dreamless peace.

INTERLUDE 1

"Mistress Anna," said Carradee Angelo, "this is not the innocent request you seem to think. Of course the Shuhr have no sense of honor. I'm not averse to embarrassing them. Who knows, they might even cooperate."

Hesed House's skylights had faded, and silver strands in Sentinel Anna Dabarrah's waist-long hair glimmered by candlelight. Anna frowned deeply and answered, "Even if they offered to help, the Federacy would refuse. No one would work alongside a Shuhr search team, even if they honestly didn't harm your daughters—and I doubt that."

Carradee had let Netaia's Federate governor send Iarla and Kessaree to safety on another world, but they never arrived. Not knowing their fate . . . that was the hardest part. Even now, Federate teams were searching for them.

She pursed her lips. This candlelit dinner table stood near the sanctuary's underground lake, and her husband's mobility chair had been pulled close by. A student-apprentice Sentinel, a *sekiyr*, cut Prince Daithi's umi steak into small bites. Daithi worked manfully to spear them with a fork attached to his hand splint, taking obvious joy in keeping up with his nephews' physical development. Carradee no longer worried whether he would recover from his injuries.

Mouth full, he didn't respond to Anna, so Carradee stared out over the underground lake. Forced to abdicate in favor of her vanished daughter, she'd slid gratefully into the sanctuary's pastoral lifestyle. Sometimes Hesed House seemed far more elegant than the palace where she'd grown up.

When she arrived here, she hadn't understood why even the evil Shuhr would attack her innocent daughters. She'd learned so much since then, about the Shuhr . . . and her sister Phoena.

The events that followed Phoena's departure from Netaia—the explosion that injured Carradee and nearly killed Daithi, their daughters' disappearance—supported only one theory. Phoena had tried to enlist Shuhr help in a grab for the throne. According to what Brennen's captors told him, though he couldn't remember witnessing it, Phoena had paid for her crimes in agony.

The Shuhr must not be believed or trusted. What had she been thinking? No wonder Rogonin deposed her. "Carradee the Kind," she'd been called, and "Carradee the Good."

"Carradee the Hopeful Romanticist" might be a better title. She arranged a cloth serviette on her lap. One of the Shuhr's announced fields of study was genetic research, and Firebird had proved that one of the Sentinels' distant relatives married into the Angelo line, several generations back. So maybe the Shuhr—

Not even the healing blocks that Master Dabarrah had graciously placed on her grief could strengthen her to finish that thought. She could not envision her precious daughters as research specimens. She would not rest until someone found them. A demand for information had been sent to Three Zed but not answered.

Master Dabarrah leaned over the table. Carradee had grown quickly to respect this psi-medical specialist. He and Mistress Anna supervised Hesed's student-apprentice Sentinels, who in turn helped Carradee care for Daithi and her nephews. This was all the realm she really wanted.

Daithi swallowed his mouthful, then spoke up. "'Dee, Mistress Anna is correct. The Shuhr would be no help. Let the Federates keep their promise. They will find whatever clues can be found." Daithi's diction had almost normalized, thanks to Master Jenner's treatments. He and Carradee often read to each other from the Sentinels' holy book, *Mattah.* That way, they could research their host family's faith while he practiced enunciating.

Back on Netaia, after being injured, Daithi had been under electoral pressure to suicide, leaving Carradee free to marry again. Saving him had been her justification for abdicating. Here, without the pressure to conceive more heirs, they could celebrate each day's millimeter of progress.

Seated on her other side, in side-by-side transport chairs, the Caldwell twins were reaching for bread bits but not quite grasping them—Kiel's fair hair fluffed on one side and Kinnor with a smear of bread crumbs along one flushed cheek. Carradee nudged a bread bit closer to Kiel, who promptly mashed it, then mouthed his hand.

"You're right, of course," said Carradee. "Something about this place makes me too hopeful, I think."

"It was a lovely fantasy," Anna murmured, "but we have no dealings with Three Zed. They are perverse and deceitful. We would attack them in force, except that the Eternal Speaker commands us to hold back until He calls us to destroy them."

Carradee ignored Anna's gloomy analysis and the sideswipe at Brennen's current mission. Anna obviously disapproved of the attempt to trap a Shuhr. She claimed that the God they served would provide enough knowledge and power to destroy Three Zed when He issued the call. "Very well," Carradee said softly, wiping Kiel's face with her serviette. "I will wait. But it is hard. I want to hold my own children again."

Chapter 4
Mirrors

courante

a quick dance in triple time, with rapidly shifting meters

Fifty-four days had passed since Juddis Adiyn injected the Caldwell-Shirak embryo into Terza Shirak's womb. Waking from a fitful sleep, Terza rolled away from a shipboard bulkhead and pressed one hand to her stomach. *I could almost wish that the Sentinels' god existed*, she moaned silently. *I would order him to smash Juddis Adiyn into sub-biological particles. He owes me. They all owe me.*

She pulled a cover over her head. Darkness held off the inevitable queasiness. It would catch her once she moved, but she didn't want to choke down breakfast while the crew watched and smirked.

If Brennen Caldwell had simply died on Three Zed, this never would have been suggested, even as one of her father's infamous options. The implanted embryo and its supportive membranes couldn't be safely removed, except by childbirth.

She kept to herself on board her father's transport. Beautifully appointed, it might have served the Federacy as a luxury transport before her people took it. From the opulent, enhanced-wavelength shimmer of its corridors to the generously appointed stateroom where she ate and slept, it was a magnificent craft.

On this morning—ship's time—before they were scheduled to arrive on Netaia, she stood for most of an hour inside her vaporbath cubicle, stroking water across sore and swelling breasts. She despised the symptoms that developed as her body adapted to this new role as a container. All her glands seemed to be responding to the half-foreign tissue graft. She'd already learned an important lesson in her chosen field, that the womb-bank was an unspeakably wonderful gift to womankind.

She finished bathing and slipped into formfitting civilian shipboards in a subtle charcoal gray. Superbly ventilated, the shipboards clung to her like a fond dream.

They wouldn't flatter her figure for long.

Abruptly overcome by the completeness with which her life changed with one tissue injection, she dropped onto her bunk and let herself cry silently behind her secret inmost shields. Cursed with the reflective temperament, Terza felt the loss of her freedom, the loss of her few friends at Cahal and in the City. She might have—no, she *would have* been culled in training for her temperament, if not for those inner shields. Even Director Polar hadn't detected them. Discovering them had been an accident, when as a seven-year-old she'd been in danger of severe discipline.

She ought to report them to Juddis Adiyn, who was always looking for new epsilon abilities. He bred them carefully into the next generation. Still, self-preservation was mightier than scientific curiosity.

Her door buzzer sounded. "Go away," she whispered, but it buzzed again.

She rocked to her feet. She checked her dark hair, pulled conservatively into a holdfast, in a freshing cabinet mirror. Then she touched a tile that opened the door.

Her half brother Micahel, cleft-chinned with strong cheekbones, shoved something that looked vaguely edible into her hand. *Come*, he ordered subvocally. *Father wants to meet you.*

That thought no longer delighted her. Terza shoved the doughy lump into her mouth. *Why now?* she asked in the same way. *I'm barely awake.*

His eyes, like her own, were so dark they nearly looked black. She and Micahel also had the same extremely fair skin, but his hair made a thick cap of curls on his head, while hers hung limp over her shoulders.

He smirked. *You have an order. Better come.*

She followed him up the ship's shining passways to a guarded door and stepped into an enormous stateroom. All its walls—she couldn't think of these as bulkheads—were mirrored, reflecting endless rooms in all directions. The ceiling reflected images, too. So did the floor, though it yielded like soft carpet as she walked forward.

The tall man she knew from tri-D images as her father, Modabah—barely gray at his temples and oddly stooped—stood at the crux of a row and a column of reflections. Terza inclined her head and dissipated her habitual epsilon-energy shields, proper signs of submission. *I am honored to meet you, sir.*

He returned the gesture, dropping his own shields. She expected him to speak aloud. Instead, a blast of epsilon power gusted through her. Something in the smell of that wind was familiar and self-like. Something else came across as unbalanced, insane, inhuman. As she cowered against the assault, discontinuous images flashed through her mind—scenes from unfamiliar military bases—satellite images of a world she knew as Tallis, the Federates' regional capital—

Voices surrounded her, too. Her father's: "No feints, this time. Cripple them before they can use RIA anywhere except Thyrica or Hesed." Her brother, answering: "I've said it all along. Kill him. Kill the whole family." Her father again: "After we find out how they escaped." His voice drew closer. "Lure him to us, little Terza. Bring him in."

Threads of her mind tore loose. The presences scrutinized and rewove her thoughts and memories. Their otherness thrust deep into her mind. She screamed, and screamed . . .

Terza looked up, disoriented, not sure whether she'd fallen on the mirrored floor or still stood upright. Her father and brother hovered over her. She felt their probes thrust through her again, examining their work. . . .

Then another probe, like a garrote, choked her memory. It squeezed off the moments she'd just experienced. She struggled, but she didn't dare think about using her inner defenses. The memory danced away, faded, and was lost.

Her father helped her onto her feet, gently holding her shoulders until she felt steady. "You must have fainted," he murmured. "Have you eaten breakfast? This room has an odd effect on many people the first time."

Sorry, sir. She nodded respectfully. Her father's epsilon shields seemed to sparkle in the mirrored cabin.

You have accepted all my requests, he subvocalized, spending epsilon energy in a formal greeting.

As . . . willingly as can be, she answered in the same way. She felt oddly weak, dizzy, as if something more than the strange mirrored room had struck her. Something had just happened. Something strange—something she ought to remember . . .

The tall, handsome man raised a dark eyebrow.

I serve our people, she said, *as you do.*

"Show me your thoughts," ordered her father.

For some unremembered reason, Terza felt that his probe ought to feel like a wind. Instead, it pierced like a knife, stabbing through her alpha matrix, cutting multiple breaches.

She struggled to keep looking his way, focusing on his real face instead of his many reflections. She slowed her breathing and straightened her back.

She scarcely remembered returning to her cabin and falling onto her bunk. Hours later, she awoke sick and dizzy again.

She lay on the broad bunk and stared, shrouding her despair and humiliation under a layer of hatred, but hatred only amplified the gnawing pain in her gut. She must have missed a meal. She couldn't do that anymore.

She swung her legs over the side of her bunk and waited for lightheadedness to pass. Like it or not, she carried her enemy's genetic offspring between her hipbones.

Her enemy . . . her prey. She almost pitied him. Like Caldwell, her destiny had been determined before she was born. Her life had been choreographed by others, and now even her body wasn't her own—or her mind! What had her father just done to her, there in his stateroom? She knew enough about memory blocks to know one had been placed. She dug as deeply as she could manage, wishing she could escape this predicament.

A new thought brought her head up. What if the disquieting new theory was true? RIA technology was disturbing enough, but another rumor had surfaced just before they left Three Zed. It was suggested that Caldwell had developed some terrifying new epsilon skill, something that killed Testing Director Dru Polar. Now it wasn't just justice that required them to take him down. There was also fear—

But that rumor couldn't be true, to her way of thinking. Caldwell had already been epsilon-crippled by the time Director Polar died . . .

and besides, it was dangerous to harbor seditious thoughts and fears. Her father might send quest-pulses up and down the corridors, checking the thought life of others on board.

But would Caldwell help her escape? The idea would not go away. What if somehow she could shield her fetus from her supervisor's inevitable experimentation, even deliver it offworld? Give it—give her—a life in some other place, where she might grow up happy and unafraid . . .

Her? That disgusting fifty-day tissue *blob* had become female in her mind?

Stop! she commanded herself, panicking. *Don't even think such things!*

The Shiraks' landing shuttle set down in a rural area not far from Netaia's capital, three hours after local midnight. Within two more hours, Micahel Shirak stalked into Ard Talumah's topside apartment and took a good look around.

Netaians did not live underground. Outside Talumah's windows, stars glimmered, distorted by a blanket of air. It wasn't as thick or as moist as Thyrica's, but it still looked eerie to Micahel's senses. Inside, poorly cured duracrete was daubed with orange paint. The apartment smelled musty and was furnished with cheap sling chairs.

At least it was half a klick away from the elegant midtown flat where a dozen of his father's lackeys were unpacking. As soon as they arrived, one of Modabah's crewmen called Talumah to get a preliminary report, since he'd been living on-site. Couched in his answer was the offer of a spare room, and after eleven days in close quarters with his father, who was constantly dithering about his half-made plans—and too close to that pitiful, pregnant half sister—Micahel jumped at the offer, even though he barely knew Ard Talumah.

Micahel's late trainer had called Micahel a renegade, with unpredictable tactics that made him almost a liability. Maybe he shouldn't cultivate Ard Talumah, but he didn't care shef'th about the long-standing ill will between his and Talumah's families. Talumah's deep mindwork specialty put him outside the Shiraks' chain of command. That made them more or less equals.

As for this survey mission, those ludicrous options, and the shifts in policy from his grandfather's regime to his father's, Micahel only cared that he would see Brennen Caldwell stripped of any RIA intelligence he still remembered, or had relearned, and then killed in a creative manner. He prided himself on artistry.

He glared at an electronic ceiling grid. "What's that?"

Ard Talumah waved a hand, dismissing his concern. "It's taken care of." He pointed at a subtronic device that sat on a scarred table. "Local enforcement looks in now and then. This shows what they want to see." To Micahel's surprise, he used the Federate trade speech, Old Colonial.

"They spy on their citizens?" Talumah was probably right to use Colonial, in case someone might be listening. The rich, ancient tongue of Ehret could give them away.

Talumah nodded. "Here in Citangelo, they do. They can only check one in ten thousand, but the risk is enough to keep some people in line. This way is the kitchen."

Micahel followed Talumah into the last room, with a servo area along one wall and a table on the other.

"I've taken in lodgers before." Talumah backed away from his servo, holding a slender blue bottle. He had the long face of many Ehretans, with a pouting lower lip and long, nondescript brown hair. He sat down on a high stool, opened the bottle, and sipped. "Help yourself, if you want. The local wines aren't bad. I recommend the joyblossom."

Micahel shook his head. According to Modabah, Ard Talumah had lured the local princess Phoena to Three Zed. Traveling as a trader in rare commodities, he had also fired the blast that ripped open a certain missing shuttle as it emerged from slip-state. Queen Iarla Second and her infant sister, Kessaree, were as dead as deep space. For now, Modabah forbade releasing that information. Keeping information from his enemies gave him more options.

Modabah's dithering kept him paralyzed, to Micahel's way of thinking. It was time to take the next bold step. The Carabohd family was his rightful prey, and this pair humiliated him at Thyrica. His most vivid memory of the late director Dru Polar was a scornful subvocalization: *Undone by a pregnant woman. Shame, Micahel.*

They had disgraced him again at Three Zed, escaping before he could return from Cahal to the Golden City. There would be no third escape.

"So." Micahel took a sling chair. "You've lived here a year—"

"Two years," interrupted Talumah.

"What do you think of Netaia?"

Talumah pulled on his bottle. "Open air. Resources to waste. We've survived for a century taking goods from the Federacy. Why not take a planet?"

"Well put." He liked Talumah's practicality. Adiyn and his aging cronies could babble about serving humankind by giving them immortality, but their starbred ancestors created the superior genes. Their own kind would rule the new civilization.

Talumah gestured toward the cold cabinet, and Micahel shook his head again. The unbound starbred did not trust their most gifted young people. Only a few potential leaders were ever conceived, and they learned not to turn their backs. Until he felt sure he could either trust Talumah or dominate him, he would avoid recreational depressants. He dug into his duffel and pulled out a scan cartridge. "I assume you saw this?"

Talumah loaded the cube into a tabletop viewer, read a few lines, and laughed. "Oh, dear," he exclaimed. "Tallis promises military retaliation . . . unprovoked attack on the Federate world of Thyrica . . . Sunton destroyed . . . new technology . . . Micahel, you're famous."

Another scoffer. "Evidently you didn't read the part under 'new technology' carefully enough."

Talumah waved a hand. "Believe me," he growled, "I've read every release on RIA technology. I could quote them all."

"We need to get it. And stop Tallis from using it."

Talumah shrugged. "I think we can take Netaia peacefully, from inside, without leaving a single crater. We'll have to discipline Tallis, though." He sent Micahel a subliminal nudge, replete with respectful undertones.

Micahel smiled slightly. Talumah respected his methods? Maybe that was why he offered the room.

"After that," Talumah continued, "we can give each Whorl world a choice when its time comes. I don't think you'll have to waste too many suicide ships."

"It's a good time to be coming into our own." The Whorl only had two real powers, and Micahel believed he and Talumah would live to see that reduced by one.

"Well," said Talumah, "now that Caldwell scores thirty-two instead of ninety-seven—"

"I won't believe that without better evidence."

Talumah shot him a tolerant half smile. "Berit, on their campus, cracked the data base, and I got a shallow probe into him yesterday as they left the governor's camp. I can tell you Brennen Caldwell is no longer that kind of threat."

"Really." Micahel grimaced, glad for the information but resenting Talumah's success. If Dru Polar could've kept his prisoner semiconscious in the interrogation lab, too drowsy to focus on complex tasks like amnesia blocking, they would've had RIA from him—and now he would be dead.

"And the lady," said Talumah, laying down his viewer, "is a seventy-one, according to Berit. Nothing remarkable. So Polar must have been blasted by something else, something new. Did your people turn up any more clues as to how they escaped him?"

"No." Micahel frowned. "But I never liked the theory of Polar destroying himself. Polar was too smart."

"I agree," said Talumah.

Micahel rubbed his chin. The Sentinels refused to breed for talent and even married outsiders. Over recent decades, his own people had grown measurably stronger while the Sentinels declined. Polar had reported that their strongest Master was easily dominated. Debilitated by his own amnesia blocks and drugged to the gills with the epsilon-blocking drug DME-6, he shouldn't have been able to escape.

Talumah widened his eyes and let his face slacken in an idiotic expression. "I know!" he exclaimed. "Their all-mighty god has finally gotten mad enough to slap us down!"

Micahel ignored the mockery. "I'm less interested in Ehret's god than Netaia's regent. You have contacts on his staff, don't you?"

"Yes. I could call—"

"Not yet." Micahel paced to the window and stared out at the unsteady stars. "First, I want to test Caldwell's other defenses, his reinforcements. To see what I can scare up, with a feint."

Chapter 5
Conspirators

allemande
a stylized dance in moderate duple time

That same morning Firebird steered a small, unmarked skimmer up a ramp into a residential block's parking stack. Tel's town apartment was half of an impressive granite-block complex, and they'd agreed to meet him early. Followed by Brennen at one hand and Shel at the other, she sprinted up the steps and touched the door. Uri came last. Danton's uniformed team followed in another vehicle.

The first meeting on today's agenda had nothing to do with the Shuhr. Firebird had already delivered a vital message to the noble class. She hoped to send one more to the rest of Netaia, to people she'd known in downside Citangelo, huddled in back rooms together—her fellow musicians and the people who passed on their songs.

A tri-D image appeared on the door's central panel. "Come in," said a woman wearing a stiff blue apron. The door swung open.

Firebird spotted movement behind Tel's servitor. Shel swept around her, one hand grasping the butt of her blazer, and stared up the paneled hall.

Tel strode into view, dressed in casual slacks and a natrusilk sweater. "Come in, come in." He led through a wood-and-stone door arch. This long room had a massive stone firebay at its center, surrounded by deep chairs and loungers. Firebird's feet sank into longweave carpet.

A woman stood up quickly. "Lady Firebird," Tel said, "this is Clareen Chesterson, a versatile bassist and arranger who sings like a brook sprite."

Firebird clasped the woman's hand. Gold-blond hair waved around Clareen's shoulders and fell to curls near her waist. She wore a floral tattoo under one eye. Her grip was strong, with rough fingertips.

"Clareen," Firebird said, "I'm honored to meet you."

"And you," said Clareen. "And General Caldwell." She turned to Brennen, offering her hand again. "I was raised on Tallis," she said. "I'm a consecrant and deeply honored to meet you, sir."

Brennen bowed slightly over their clasped hands. Firebird backstepped. She'd asked Tel to find a competent performer and arranger, but she hadn't specified "Netaian." She'd assumed . . .

"I've lived on Netaia almost a year," Clareen told Brennen. "I've been trying to get a Chapter room established or a house built. I hope you might help me negotiate the legal tangle."

"I wish we could," said Brennen. "I can at least contact Shamarr Dickin with your request."

"That would be a help. These people are desperate for mercy."

"I know," Brennen said, and Firebird felt the gentle warmth of his pity on the pair bond.

Clareen released his hand. When she became a consecrant, Clareen would have been told about the prophecies regarding Brennen's family. Besides destroying a "nest of evil" that sounded strikingly similar to Three Zed, some Carabohd descendant would wield the creative power of the One who sang all worlds into existence. In that person, the Mighty Singer would complete a reconciliation that none of His other servants could attempt.

Firebird still didn't understand all those prophecies. She suspected they weren't meant to be fully comprehended until after the fact. Still, she liked Clareen's sense of priority.

Brennen sat down on one arm of a long lounger and motioned the musician to a nearby chair. Firebird took a seat next to Brennen. "Clareen," Brennen said, "you must understand that we need to check your intentions."

Here we go again, Firebird thought glumly. "This isn't deep mind-access," she explained. "It isn't interrogation. Sentinel Harris—Uri—can simply make sure you don't mean to betray us. He can make sure you won't, too," she added, trying to sound lighthearted. Voice-command, the violation of another person's will, was no laughing matter. "But as for prying into your secrets, that's just not done. It's only . . . uncomfortable," she admitted. "The first time someone did it to me, it turned my stomach."

Clareen frowned and sat down. "Since I'm one of your fellow believers, you might simply take my word. I am on your side."

"Certain parties on Netaia," Firebird said carefully, "would consider this kind of music seditious. If you're suspected of involvement with us and questioned, voice-command will protect you. You won't be able to incriminate yourself." She flicked back her hair. "Believe me, I understand how most people feel about mind-access." She barely resisted shooting Brennen a glance.

His amusement came through, though, followed by a rueful sense of apology.

Long forgiven, she thought at him. *Don't worry about me. Clareen's our concern at the moment.*

Clareen folded her long, slim hands in her lap and exhaled heavily. "I should have known. Your lives are at stake, aren't they?"

"I'm afraid so," Brennen said softly. "I do apologize. My people have been made stewards of abilities that many of us dislike. We try to use them responsibly."

"Then you have my permission, General."

"I can't," Brennen insisted, but Firebird felt a ghost of his former self-confidence. He'd lost abilities, but nothing could change his standing as the Mighty Singer's eldest heir. "Will you permit my bodyguard, Lieutenant Colonel Harris?"

Clareen's lips tightened, but she said, "Of course."

Uri moved a second chair close to hers. Firebird hardly knew where to look as Uri gave Clareen basic instructions—to get comfortable, try to relax, look into his eyes. While the silent mind-access lasted, an ancient clock ticked over the mantel between a pair of beautifully executed portraits. She suspected Tel had painted them, though she didn't recognize the subjects. On the pair bond, she felt Brenn focus tightly. Again, he had to rely on someone else's abilities. Firebird faintly sensed his frustration.

Uri broke the silence. "Thank you, Clareen. I don't need to go any deeper." His voice sounded slightly fatigued. "Welcome to the conspiracy to give Netaia back to its people."

It was exactly the right touch. Clareen smiled weakly, wrinkling the floral tattoo. "A lofty goal. Very Federate." She turned back to Brennen. "All right, General, Lady Firebird. How may I help?"

Firebird reached into a pocket of her loose, blue Thyrian skyff and pulled out an audio rod wrapped in bio-safe cloth, which she passed to Brennen. Without touching the rod, he pushed it onto the arm of Clareen's chair, then pocketed the cloth.

"I've put together several songs," Firebird said. "Some are better than others, but I think the melodies are catchy—"

"Wait." Tel remained standing, close to his massive firebay. "You put them together? You wrote them?"

"Yes, but I don't want that known. They're about Netaia, Clareen." She pulled one leg up on the lounger, trying to recapture the casual, cordial air they'd lost by insisting on an access check. She explained to Clareen that she'd written them carefully, including lines about seeking freedom in the right way and giving it to others. Most freedom ballads were spark in tinder. She wanted to prevent a war, not start one.

"Prince Tel told me about your presentation to the Electorate," Clareen said somberly. "I came here hoping to research popular ballads like you're describing. I'm particularly interested in the Coper Rebellion period."

It was Firebird's turn to smile weakly. Two centuries ago, Tarrega Erwin—regent for the infant Queen Bobri—had killed eighty thousand people, putting down that coup attempt. Two young noble offspring had led it, and Netaia's wastling traditions began shortly afterward. "I know those songs," she admitted. They'd been some of her favorites, years ago. " 'Northpoint,' " she suggested. " 'The Bridge of Glin,' and 'Bloody Erwin.' "

"Yes!" Crossing her ankles casually, Clareen raised the audio rod. "What would you like me to do with these?"

"That," said Firebird, "is a recording of chords with a synthesized voice. The songs can't be traced this way, but no one would change her political views from listening to them. They have no soul. Still, I think—I hope—that the melodies have broadcast quality. I have to trust your judgment. If you don't think they're up to par, destroy the rod. But if you think they might influence people, can you record . . . can you release?"

"If they move me," Clareen said soberly.

"Perfect." Firebird touched her hand, relieved, suspecting Clareen would deliver a quality performance or none at all. They discussed instrumentation, Firebird suggesting a double conchord, a wide-necked instrument with four pairs of strings, two pairs tuned an octave apart. It put a soul-digging "chunk" in every note.

Clareen pulled back her hair with one hand. "Is there a chance you could make an appearance this week? You'll change more minds and win more friends with one live concert than a dozen recordings. People who have sat in the same room bond to you."

"They do." She knew it well. Her secret performances, years ago, showed her how much a wealthy but doomed wastling had in common with poor laborers. But security had to take precedence.

"And you don't want to encourage an uprising?" asked Clareen. "I think you should. Songs can only do so much. If there's no other way of getting Rogonin out of office, there has to be violence—"

"No!" Firebird's stomach churned at the thought. "No more Coper Rebellions, Clareen. You've seen the Codex simulation of what a Shuhr strike could do to Citangelo? A civil war would do worse. The Coper ballads make warfare sound noble and exciting. It's brutal. Good people die in horrible ways." *Eighty thousand of them . . .*

Clareen stared at her. "I respect your point of view," she said. "You have been in combat. You . . . don't want the regency ended, either?"

Firebird laughed. "I'd love to see Rogonin tossed out. But someone else should take the regent's rod. Someone who could cooperate with Governor Danton and gradually shift power away from the Electorate. Slow changes tend to be permanent."

"But if you became queen—"

"That won't happen." Firebird spread her hands for emphasis. "I'm being confirmed as an heir, but that's just for show. The Electorate controls the crown. They wouldn't give it to me, and I wouldn't take it. Anyway, Brennen and I expect a transfer back to Regional command on Tallis as soon as we finish here." He *had* been reinstated to Special Ops. "I hope to set up a cultural exchange program and work toward covenance there."

The woman toyed with the curling end of one long blond lock of hair. "Don't worry, Lady Firebird. General. I won't let you down. And I would never betray the Carabohd line and the Word to Come. General," she said, "maybe you're the one who'll end the Shuhr threat. I hope it happens soon. People are frightened."

Brennen opened his hands. "I wish it could've been ended before they killed my brother and his family and Firebird's sister. Don't look to me, Clareen, but remember us in your prayers."

"From this day on," Clareen declared.

As his servitors escorted Clareen to the door, Tel swept an arm up the other hall. "Would you join me for an early lunch? My staff prepared a meal. Nothing fancy."

"That would be wonderful." Uri and Shel had tested the palace-delivered breakfast, and Firebird's biological clock had been ringing "dinnertime" ever since she rolled off Phoena's bed, but she'd barely touched the palace meal.

Following Tel's gesture, she strode into a timber-beamed dining area. At its far end, double doors hung open into a kitchen. High curtained windows let her see Citangelo's streets. The inlaid wooden floor would have cost a high-commoner two years' wages, and this was only one of the Tellai family's Citangelo holdings.

Uri and Shel walked slowly around the room, and then Shel took a parade-rest stance near the hall door while Uri moved behind Brennen. A servitor laid out steaming dishes. Though Tel insisted the meal would be modest, Firebird found familiar foods well prepared, their flavors a cauldron of memory: pied henny baked in a tender crust, crisp multicolored slivers of marinated vegetables, and the traditional steaming mug of sweet, spicy cruinn.

She attacked this target with enthusiasm.

"Firebird," Tel said gently, "if you would ever want lessons in, ah, diplomacy, I would be delighted to assist. Waiting for the right moment to speak last night might have won you more allies than shouting down Erwin and Rogonin."

Amused, she washed down a bit of pied henny with a sip of cruinn. "Tel, they remember seeing me kneel on that floor and agree to go out and die nobly. I had to prove that I wasn't their wastling anymore. I'll be more respectful in the future."

"They already know you're no wastling." His dark eyes gleamed—fondly, she thought. "But to get people to really listen, sometimes you have to speak in the right way, at the right time."

Pride, willfulness, impatience. There they were again—

"Thank you, Tel," she said, trying to sound gracious. "Maybe we will have time to get together again."

Brennen sipped his cruinn and made a face. He'd never liked the sweet, spicy Netaian beverage, which was fine with Firebird. She barely tolerated the ubiquitous Federate kass.

The servitor brought a soup course, then disappeared into the kitchen. Tel leaned close to Firebird and murmured, "Firebird, Brennen, it's my turn to bring you into sedition. Don't tell people you would not take the crown. There is a growing alliance to restore the monarchy, mostly among high-commoners. Something must be done to get rid of Rogonin. I feel strongly about this. Better you were on the throne . . . than him."

She'd been half afraid Tel felt this way. Something at the back of her mind adored the idea. She sat on it. Hard. "Tel, if I took the crown, I would try to change one thing immediately. No one would worship the Powers, even though people could still respect them as attributes. Do you want that?"

"Service to the Powers has never been a matter of faith," he said. "Only action."

"Be careful, Tel. You almost sound like a heretic."

He smiled broadly. "I am. I want an Angelo in the palace again. Danton's reforms make sense, but a low-common rabble cannot run our government. As queen, you would have the support of many of the noble class—"

"Tel, they despise me. And not all low-commoners are rabble—"

Tel's blue-aproned servitor hurried back in, and they fell silent. On the woman's tray, three mounds of granular white powder burned orange on individual dishes. "Flamed snow!" Firebird exclaimed. "Tel, it isn't Conura Day." On that holiday, Netaia's nobility celebrated the accession of the first Angelo monarch, who freed Netaia from out-Whorl invaders.

Tel arched one eyebrow. "You've missed Conura Day for two years."

The serving woman slid a plate, still flaming, onto the tapestry tablecloth. "The trick to eating this," the woman told Brennen, "is to keep it alight. Blow out each bite just before you take it into your mouth."

"I see," he said dubiously, trying to spoon into it. He lifted the bite, and it extinguished.

A faint bell chimed behind Shel's back. She stepped aside as Tel's servitor hurried up the hall.

"Do this." Firebird slid a spoon into the center of her portion, let granules spill in, then carefully raised the bite, still flaming.

The blue-aproned woman reappeared beside Shel. "Your Highness? Crosstown link."

Tel pursed his lips. "Right in the middle of dessert. Wouldn't you know?"

"I'll make you another, sir," the servitor said as Tel brushed past her. She remained in the room, eyes averted from Tel's guests, so Firebird didn't speak. The sweet, rich dessert had a perfumy taste.

Less than a minute later, Tel returned, frowning. "Evidently," he said, "they really want to speak with you, Firebird."

"Who?" she asked, glancing at Shel.

Tel folded his hands. "He didn't give a name."

Frowning, Firebird followed him to his crosstown station. A featherweight headset dangled from a wall panel that could display a caller's face, amplify a voice, or show informational displays.

Shel's footsteps came close behind.

Tel lifted the CT headpiece. Firebird hooked it over one ear as he hurried back to the dining area, and then she made sure his link wasn't set to transmit visuals. "Hello," she said toward the blank wall panel.

"Lady Firebird." It was, as Tel said, a male voice . . . and no face appeared. The caller hadn't set to transmit either.

"Speaking," she answered.

"Greetings from Three Zed. We've missed you."

Firebird's blood turned icy. She whirled to lean against the wall and stare into Shelevah Mattason's blue-gray eyes. As Shel pulled a subtronic tracing device out of her tunic pocket, an epsilon probe slid into the back of Firebird's awareness. The sensation made Firebird wish she'd eaten less—and made her sympathize with Clareen Chesterson. "Go on," Firebird said, not bothering to turn her head. The pickup was omnidirectional.

"So you dislike idle talk, too. Good. Are you familiar with a phenomenon called the *shebiyl*?"

Firebird thought back to something Brennen had once mentioned, a practice forbidden in the older holy book, *Dabar*. "Alternate paths of the future," she said crisply. *Keep talking*, she urged him as Shel held her device close to the CT unit. Danton's plainclothes agents had been assigned to cruise this neighborhood in a second car. Shel would alert them.

"Very good. We have seen on the shebiyl that your presence could lead to Netaia's destruction. We've seen this world as a cold cinder spinning in orbit. If you really care for your people, you should leave quickly."

She silently cried, *Liar!* but the mental image made her tremble, especially after watching that Codex simulation and hearing Tel make plans on her behalf. Could she live with herself if she caused—

Could *she* spark the uprising?

"Nothing to say, Lady Firebird?"

"Who are you?" Was this Micahel? Whoever had emerged from the shadows, Brenn needed his location. They also needed to know how the Shuhr tracked them here.

"You wouldn't know my name, Lady Firebird."

Disappointed, she said, "Go back to your own world. This is mine."

The voice laughed. "Yours? I believe it belongs to your countryman, Muirnen Rogonin."

Firebird rolled her eyes. Shel adjusted her device.

"Do enjoy your visit home. And your bond mate, while you have him." The connection clicked off.

Chilled, Firebird dropped the headpiece onto its hook. *While you have him?* "What did you get?"

Shel cradled her tracer on one palm. "Frequency, range, heading, and a voice profile. He's close, maybe half a kilometer." She reached for the CT link. "I'll relay this to base and our auxiliaries. Maybe we can take this one."

Firebird marched back toward the dining area. Brennen stood in the hallway, Uri at his shoulder. Firebird wondered how much they'd heard. "Shuhr," she murmured, "and Shel says he's close. Half a klick. She has the base trying to trace the call." She slipped back into the dining room and sat back down. With one puff, she blew out her dessert. "Tel," she said, "we just had a call from one of the Shuhr."

Brennen followed her in. "Governor Danton will get you a guard in minutes," he told Tel. "Meanwhile—"

Tel's expression darkened, and he lowered his eyebrows. "Not necessary, Cald—"

Shel emerged last from the hallway. "I've got a trace on the call. The auxiliaries are on their way."

Tel glanced up. "I have a bodyguard of my own, uplevel. I gave him some time off while your shadows take care of me." He touched a control on the table's edge.

Brennen blew out his own dessert, a smoldering cinder. An image sprang into Firebird's mind—Netaia, blackened like that burned-out dish of flamed snow.

Liars! They couldn't be trusted, but the image wouldn't leave her mind.

A liveried man appeared in the hall doorway, imposingly square-shouldered, impressively quiet. Tel turned to him. "Paudan, the threat is outside. Watch the front door."

The big man half bowed and slipped out.

With a sweep of double doors, Tel's servitor pushed through again, three more dessert portions gleaming on her tray. "Let's try this again," Tel said cheerfully.

Shel moved to the window and stared out, resting one hand on her holster. Before the servitor finished setting down the desserts, Shel murmured, "There he is. That's no pedestrian."

CHAPTER 6

THE BEST ANSWER

galliard
a vigorous dance with repeated leaps

Firebird sprang up and followed Brennen to the window.

He'd already pulled an interlink off his belt. "Tel," he said, holding the link aside, "how many entries do you have?"

"Three." Tel pointed toward the kitchen. "He seems to be headed for the service entry. Side door's in the firebay room, and there's the front way, where you came in."

As Brennen relayed Tel's information to his other forces, Firebird pulled Tel's small blazer from her deepest pocket. Brennen drew an oddly shaped weapon, designed to be concealed in his palm. It contained ten tiny injector darts, each loaded with two drugs. One was a rapid sedative. The other, a chemical called DME-6, temporarily blocked all epsilon abilities. Brennen had refused to touch the darts but let Danton's nongifted aides load his pistol. Firebird, who'd struggled with a needle phobia all her life, literally could not carry the weapon. "Don't get separated from Shel." Brennen touched Firebird's elbow. "You two, firebay room. Tel, can you and your man handle the front door?"

"Yes."

"All we need to do is keep them busy until Danton's reinforcements arrive." Brennen turned to Uri. "We'll take the service entry." He loosened his crystace in its wrist sheath, then glanced toward the back door.

"What makes you sure there'll be more than one of them?" Tel asked.

True, she thought at Brennen. *He came alone that night at Trinn Hill.*

Brennen shook his head slightly.

All right, then. Brennen, at ES 83, was still better equipped than Tel and all his servitors to deal with Shuhr until reinforcements arrived. *And what about windows?* Firebird wondered.

Following her bodyguard, Firebird hurried back up Tel's hall, past the link station and into the room where they interviewed Clareen. Now she saw it with an eye for defense. Its windows faced downhill. Across from the windows loomed the massive stone hearth, and then one more heavy wooden door beyond the hearth, at the room's end.

"Watch the window," Shel said. After propping the inside door and examining the outside door's palm-lock, Shel took up a position against the firewall.

Firebird eased toward the outer wall between window and door and peered through the edge of the glass pane. Or was it glasteel? Would it hold until a Sentinel force arrived? There were more ways into this apartment than through doors. Her stomach tightened on Tel's "modest" food.

She saw movement outside. A bony, dark-haired man—she didn't think it was the assassin she'd glimpsed at Trinn Hill—mounted Tel's steps.

He hadn't gone to the service entry after all, but straight to the door that no Sentinel guarded.

"Shel," she whispered, drawing back. If she could see him, he could sense her by her individual tang of alpha-matrix energy. More than ever, she wished she could shield her mind against the gifted. She'd only learned to turn inward and touch her epsilon carrier, and unless she coupled it with Brennen's, she'd only managed to kill two assailants who attacked her psyche. She prayed she would never again get that close to a Shuhr.

The door chime rang.

The ancient mantel clock's pendulum swung in slow arcs. On one side of the firebay, a covered canvas lay on an easel, probably one of Tel's projects. Traffic hummed in the distance.

The caller knocked lightly at first, then harder. Just inside, beyond the propped parlor door, Tel squared his shoulders beside his broad-shouldered shadow. Firebird wiped moisture off her palms, cringing. Brenn hadn't wanted to involve other non-Sentinels in their trap.

An eerie wail started overhead. Shel's head jerked up, her blazer wavering between door and ceiling. As the wail grew in volume, Firebird jammed a finger in her left ear. Sonic weaponry? Or—

Down the chimney came a rattling shriek. *More ways in than the doors!* Simultaneously, something slammed against Shel's side door. *A second assailant, attacking while we're distracted.* Shel crouched, shutting her eyes and flattening her palm against shuddering dark wood.

Out of the hearth burst a shrieking flock of black saucer shapes. Spinning and sputtering, they scattered. Firebird dropped to a crouch, steadied her little blazer two-handed, and tracked one saucer. She fired. The saucer exploded, scattering metal fragments over a narrow radius, showering Tel's longweave carpet and some of the furniture, and piercing the covered canvas with a *pop.* She tracked another saucer and fired. They had to be close-quarter drones, the kind that adhered to a victim and then exploded. If caught midair, they wouldn't throw much shrapnel—

Three of them whirled toward Shel. Two more whizzed at Firebird. Her blazer quivered in her hand. She got one, missed one . . . ducked . . . caught it as it spun back toward her, then picked off the others.

Tel shouted a challenge from the entry. Had she missed another saucer? A hasty glance back showed Shel still crouched at the side door, left hand raised in voice-command. Someone had to be outside that door, pitting his epsilon strength against hers. *Mighty Singer, where are those reinforcements?* So much for their assumption that the Shuhr would wait to attack publicly!

There *was* another saucer in the entry, diving at Tel. Tel's servitor fired, missing Tel by centimeters, too close to hit the swooping drone. Firebird tracked the drone and fired again. Metal exploded with a flash that seared afterimages on her retinas. Tel fell back, one arm flung up to cover his eyes. His other servitor huddled in a corner, holding her sweeper aloft like a weapon.

Outside, an engine roared up and stopped. Shel shouted through the parlor, "They're here!"

The clock's ticking seemed to grow loud again. Firebird listened hard. Running feet and shouting voices passed by . . . outdoors. She blinked, trying to clear smokelike puffs from her vision. A weird chemical smell filled the hallway. Shel pulled an instrument off her belt. "Nothing toxic," she assured Firebird. "Just explosives."

More light footsteps ran through the dining room. Brennen and Uri appeared in the hall. Firebird felt Brenn relax when he saw her unharmed.

Tel lowered his arm. Two short scrapes oozed blood on his forehead.

"Are you hurt?" Brennen asked.

"Scratched." Tel frowned as the door chime rang. "Do we let these men in?"

"Yes." Uri reached for the interior lock panel. The front door swung open. "Did you—?"

A uniformed Sentinel shook his head. "We were too late. Couldn't pick up a trail. How many—?"

"Two of them," Shel broke in.

Leaving Shel with Firebird and Tel, Brennen and his cousin walked four new arrivals around the apartment's perimeter. Tel's manservant biotaped his scrapes.

"I'd heard you were a good shot," Shel murmured, smiling. "Well done."

Firebird shrugged, wishing Brenn's reinforcements would have arrived three minutes earlier. He and Uri would be restraining an epsilon-blocked Shuhr for interrogation in Tel's parlor and sending Shel back to the palace for those sealed orders.

Tel inhaled deeply. "Ventry," he said, relieving the serving woman of her sweeper, "could we possibly try, one more time, to eat a quiet dessert?"

Firebird thought she heard the woman groan.

A carload of Sentinels escorted them back to the palace, then remained on watch, parked in the public square.

Firebird's afternoon commitment to the elected Assembly wasn't for two more hours, and she knew she'd better consider every trip outside these walls as a perilous opportunity. Brennen put Shel to work on the voiceprint, tracing calls through the crosstown network's memory banks.

Brennen was also making plans to fly a search grid, hoping to spot those Shuhr agents by their stray flickers of epsilon energy. Firebird doubted he would try such an overflight more than once, if at all. Flying surveillance would be risky and difficult.

She decided to make one pilgrimage inside these walls before her Assembly appointment. Shadowed by Shel, she padded up the private hall and around a corner. She palmed the locking panel on her old rooms. The door didn't budge.

Unsurprised, she stepped back to look around. Down the stair, a servitor hurried across the wide hall—and she recognized him. She'd heard Brennen assign this blond-bearded Sentinel to kitchen staff, back at Danton's office. He was one of their undercover agents. "Hello," Firebird called down. "Good afternoon."

The young man paused. "Good afternoon, Lady Firebird," he answered stiffly, mimicking palace-staff decorum.

Not bad, she observed. Following protocol was his best chance of going unnoticed. Higher-ups on the staff, having served together for years, couldn't be impersonated—but lower-echelon servitors came and went regularly. If this Sentinel diffused his epsilon shields, he would sense her approval. "I'm sorry to bother you," she called, "but I would like to look in on my old suite."

He turned away. "I'll find someone to deactivate the lock."

Five minutes later, Firebird stepped into a sitting room she could've crossed in the dark without stubbing her toe. Shel followed, silently shutting the door.

The furniture remained, but otherwise the sitting room had been scoured of all evidence that Firebird ever lived here. Her parlor and bedroom were just as tidy and soulless.

Still, her mind saw a row of Academy trophies, a stack of tri-D souvenirs, and her brownbuck flight jacket flung over the ornate desk chair. This suite reappeared regularly in her dreams. She stroked a tiny pit in the stone wall, then traced a mineral vein with one fingertip, letting the sad sweetness of actually standing here roll over her.

She'd lived simply at Hesed and liked it. She wondered if five days in-house would leave her a spoiled aristocrat. It occurred to her that she'd been raised wealthy, never lacking anything she really craved. *Except faith, except security, except love*, she realized. Even her first clairsa was the work of a master instrument maker. The family had paid for her Academy training, knowing Netaia would never recoup that investment.

Maybe it would. Maybe she would serve her people better than her mother ever dreamed, steering Netaia toward Federate covenance and the Ehretans' faith.

She pushed open the last door. Her music room, a narrow chamber with only one window, had been utterly stripped. Not even the high stool and transcriber table remained.

Shutting her eyes, she leaned against the marble wall and wrapped her arms around an imaginary clairsa. She'd written her first songs on this spot, sitting here with her transcriber running. She'd collected other instruments, enjoying the challenge of learning to chord or pick out melodies.

Sighing, she opened her eyes and turned to leave—

And looked into her own image beside the door. For one instant, her brain registered it as a mirror. Then she recognized the portrait. Painted when she was sixteen, seated in a royal wastling's pose, the portrait showed her wearing a smaller diadem than the one she would accept in five days. The artist had somehow created an odd, haunted sadness in the eyes, contrasting with the proud uptilt of her chin.

Who hung it here? Firebird wondered. Carradee must have done this, consciously leaving a ghost of her presence in the one room where she'd dared to hope she might survive a wastling's fate in the songs she left behind. Even Rogonin's staff must've felt it appropriate to leave the portrait here, or else they simply hadn't bothered to take it down.

"Nothing has changed," Firebird whispered. She still hoped to touch her people's hearts—not the detached, unflinching electors, but the people who truly were Netaia.

Would anyone listen? She was a convicted criminal. She wished she could ask for a fair retrial, besides her gubernatorial pardon. After covenance, maybe. Before the Assembly instead of the Electorate.

She stared at the picture, grateful for one more of Carradee's kindnesses. Mentally, she retraced her route through the portrait hall. She couldn't recall seeing Carradee's image. When Carrie abdicated, they must have removed her portrait from the entry, replacing it with Siwann's.

If anyone ought to have pride-of-place down there, it should be Carradee's daughter, Iarla Second. Surely the four-year-old's portrait had been painted before she vanished.

Firebird hung her head. Almost without question, the Shuhr had found Iarla and her sister. If they were alive, anywhere, surely they would have surfaced by now.

But if the Shuhr had destroyed them . . . then with Carradee abdicated and Phoena dead . . .

Firebird pushed away the thought. The electors would continue their mockery of a regency for decades, if necessary, to keep her from ever coming back.

She pushed away from the wall. Shel, standing against the door, raised an eyebrow.

"Nothing, Shel. I've seen enough. We have work to do." Firebird felt half-complete when Brennen wasn't close, bad enough without adding a burden of memories. She turned away from this place that once vibrated with music. Leading her bodyguard, she hurried back to the crown princess's suite.

When they left the grounds headed for the Assembly, two small, dark cars pulled up alongside their limousine, and she saw midnight blue uniforms inside. A phalanx of Citangelo Enforcers surrounded that unit and delivered her to a hall in the central city. For most of a glorious hour, she sat in a balcony listening to a re-creation of the vote that brought her here. To override the inevitable electoral veto, she'd needed ninety percent of the popularly elected representatives.

She took ninety-four. This time, the Assembly representatives also made short speeches, praising Firebird for entering the single "nay" when the Electorate voted to attack Veroh, and demanding pledges that the Federates would protect their cities from Shuhr suicide attackers. Firebird answered with assurances, then delivered her cultural-exchange proposal. That drew polite applause.

Afterward, an ice-mine director, a metals stamping robot operator, and a woman who operated heavy machinery by virtual remote—all of them elected to represent working constituencies—joined her in a small private room.

Firebird tried to explain Federate covenance and the process by which free elections would lead to an application for Netaia's membership in the Federacy. By careful questioning, she learned a little about postwar living conditions on the North Continent. Metal and technology items had become scarce with so much manufacturing destroyed. The rich weren't suffering, but low-common and servitor classes pieced together a harder existence.

The pale, dour ice miner asked about Federate wages and rights.

Firebird admitted, "I've seen the Federacy make mistakes. I can't say covenance would end everyone's troubles, but living conditions would improve."

The ice miner lowered her voice. "Under Rogonin?"

Firebird longed to say she'd love to boot Rogonin out of her mother's office and over one of the moons. *Diplomacy!* she reminded herself, but lyrics danced into her mind, set to an old bugle call. *He's back, Bloody Erwin is back. . . .* She hadn't recorded *that* composition for Clareen Chesterson.

The other woman kept her arms crossed. "Governor Danton," she said, "sends inspectors. He makes promises. But so far we haven't seen anything change. We're almost as fed up with him as we are with the Electorate."

"He has only peeled away the surface layer," said Firebird. "This system has lasted for two hundred years. There will be more changes."

The ice miner spoke softly again. "If there's rebellion, the Enforcers will be key players. They're electoral employees, but they're mostly low-common. What would it take—"

"War is never the best answer," Firebird insisted, shaken by this proof that already Netaians were bracing themselves to rebel. The Enforcers, whom Federates would call a hybrid between police force and standing army, maintained order in the cities. What would it take to get their loyalty? Rogonin's wages fed their families. Idealistic songs wouldn't soften them. *Could* she enlist them, if—

What was she thinking? She could not, would not lead an uprising!

The door opened slightly. Shaken by her own thoughts and how easily they turned to war, Firebird reached for the ice miner's hand. "I think we're being told that this meeting is over. Contact me through Danton's office if you have other questions about Federate covenance."

That evening, the Assembly's Pageantry Committee filled the wood-floored west dining hall, applauding and drinking the regent's wine . . . or was it hers? She suspected Rogonin would bill every possible expense to her modest new heiress's allowance. She managed to greet all eighty-five guests, mostly high-commoners. She followed their conversations, depressed by the class prejudices that colored their attitudes.

Interstellar diplomacy, she'd found, also revolved around money, pride, and influence. Class differences just weren't as obvious out there—or as permanent.

CHAPTER 7
ESMERIELD

gavotte
a dance in moderately quick quadruple time

"The Countess Esmerield Rogonin of Claighbro has passed the main gate," intoned Tel Tellai's footman, "with an escort of her House."

Tel paused at an indoor trellis, halfway across his estate's dining balcony, and stretched out a hand. "Cutter, Gammidge."

A gardener in black-and-indigo livery handed Tel a small laser cutter.

Tel whisked six buds from a jantia vine's tip. "You've let this runner try to support too many blooms."

His bodyguard, Paudan, remained at the town house, supervising cleanup and interviewing two dozen muscular commoners. Tel could afford to increase a security force for his properties. With Phoena gone, overseeing his homes and their landscaping gave him something to care about.

It no longer mattered whether the other electors approved of him. As he told Firebird this morning, Netaia needed an Angelo ruler. The figurehead role, on behalf of the mighty Power of Authority, had been passed down for thirteen generations. It was a psychological need of this culture. Really, though, he'd never cared whether the Powers, Electorate, or Assembly kept Netaia prosperous. His worship had gone to Authority and Excellence, in the person of Phoena Angelo. . . .

Since returning from Three Zed and Procyel, Tel had required his servitors to keep the Charities and Disciplines whenever possible, but he no longer felt like a representative of the Powers.

He handed off his shears. "Dismissed, Gammidge."

Straightening a gold-trimmed blue sash over his pale blue sateen tunic, he walked to the dining balcony's edge. He'd dressed for Esme Rogonin's protocol visit. They both had postponed this to the last possible evening before her presentation ball. By tradition, the head of each noble House must be invited to a debut ball during an informal dinner.

A man in Angelo scarlet plodded out of the gravity lift at one end of the dining balcony. He had Rogonin's size, but not his figure, and a black cap tucked into his belt over a crimson tunic. Rogonin's eighteen-year-old heiress followed. *Using a palace redjacket as Escort of the House!* He might be entitled, but this was another deliberate affront to the Angelos. Regardless, Tel had to stand and bow. "Countess Esmerield," he intoned.

"Prince Tel," said the young woman. She pushed past him to his table.

Tel's butler pointed out a place to the redjacket, who seated Esmerield and then stood behind her. Tel took his own chair, glanced out through stately gold-framed windows toward the gardens, then back to the countess.

A final growth spurt had stretched green-eyed Esme, giving her attractive proportions and making her almost as tall as he. As soon as the butler poured tiny glasses of gold-white Southport wine, Tel toasted her.

The green visiting gown made her eyes shine like emeralds—or poison, which was a better comparison, considering her father—and like the regent, she eyed everything as if she either despised it or wanted it. Without waiting for Tel's staff to lay out their first course, Esmerield flicked a rolled and beribboned paper up the table. "My father bids you come to my debut ball tomorrow night, as head of your House."

Efficiently done! She could leave now, if she wished. He didn't often think of himself as the head of House Tellai, but when Phoena had been absent for two years, he would be ordered by the Electorate to remarry and start producing Tellai heirs—wastlings, too—so the line would not die out.

For now, Tel missed Phoena too badly to feel any interest in remarriage. He would honor her memory by fighting for her sister's rights, though Phoena would not have found that appropriate. Counseled and healed by Sanctuary Master Dabarrah, he'd come to realize his late wife was selfish, ambitious, and cruel. . . .

But regal and proud, and breathtakingly beautiful. She would have made a better goddess than queen.

He would've begged her not to go to the Shuhr if she'd stopped to say good-bye. His last memory of Phoena framed her sitting on their octagonal bed, knees to her chest, fuming over Firebird's dishonorable pregnancy—wastlings were not allowed to marry or bear children—while he drifted, frustrated as usual, toward sleep.

Mustn't let my mind wander this way! "My thanks to your father," he answered Esme, "and the House of Tellai will most certainly be represented."

Having concluded that business, Tel reached for his fork. The first course, a rich and beautifully constructed soufflé, had arrived while his thoughts skipped back.

"As I hear it," Esme said, "our current discomfort began at the United Session, when the Assembly voted for Firebird's return."

So she meant to stay a little longer? Tel glanced up at the redjacket before he answered. The big man stared back. Tel didn't feel threatened. One of his own bodyguards sat in a hidden observation room, controlling several remote security devices.

He had nothing to lose now. He would not be Rogonin's flunky anymore. "Originally, Countess, I only presented Carradee's request to restore Lady Firebird's Netaian citizenship. The Assembly took that issue a step further. Carradee might have made a capable monarch," he added, "in time, if things had gone differently." Tel would still serve an Angelo queen, gladly. But not Muirnen Rogonin, never again.

"Time." Esme tapped her plate's edge with her fork. "Netaia has little time, Prince Tel. In a year and a half, we could be absorbed by the Federacy. Meanwhile, their occupation taxes are ruining us."

He knew that Esme only echoed her father, having no opinions of her own yet. Tel wanted to remind her that the nobles' taxes were rebuilding defenses that the Federates shattered in response to an unprovoked attack on Federate space, and that the Federates were paying fifty percent of that expense. By the time Danton's engineers finished rebuilding, this world would be better defended than ever. He hoped they hurried.

"We must walk a careful path," he said, deliberately oblique. Rogonin had to be deeply displeased about the timing of Firebird's return.

Her confirmation was overshadowing Esme's festive debut. Protocol demanded that she and Caldwell attend the ball.

"Why," Esme demanded, "don't Caldwell and his mind-crawlers just fly to Three Zed and eliminate those people? Why are they wasting time here?"

So that's what she wanted. He could answer part of her question. "Three Zed has defenses that even the Sentinels can't pass easily. Unless they do it right, it would be suicide."

"Obviously, the Shuhr don't hesitate to fly suicide missions. Losing most of the Sentinels wouldn't bother me at all."

He considered telling her about voice-command, and how a Shuhr pilot could be forced to act against his or her will. That, he decided, would only encourage her hatred and fear of Sentinels. He held his peace, finished the last bit of his soufflé, and sat back. Servitors removed his plate and brought sherbet glasses of tart eden fruit, round and pink, seeded and syruped, to cleanse their palates for the next course.

"Thank you, but I'm quite full." Esme raised one finger at her escort. The redjacket drew back her chair.

Fine. Leave. Tel dismissed her mentally but not without a twinge. He did sometimes miss the placid assumptions of his youth—the lifestyle he'd been raised to expect and the absolute certainty that a nobleman was a superior being. Rising, he bowed again. "Please convey my thanks to your father," he said, "for the pleasure of your company."

Esme's cheek twitched. She dropped a half curtsey and bounced down the balcony stairs without bothering to ride his lift.

Esme's father, His Grace the Regent, sat in his night office and watched two strangers stride past his uniformed door guards. Bypassing the enormous, internally lit crystalline globe of the home world, the wiry young black-haired man stared malevolently. His long-haired partner, slightly shorter, looked vaguely familiar.

Rogonin frowned down at them.

"Thank you for receiving us, Your Grace." The second man made a full, courtly bow. He spoke with a throaty accent so deep that his *R*s almost gargled. "I am Ard Talumah. I have worked on Netaia for some months as an independent trader, representing a non-Federate concern. My colleague, Micahel Shirak, arrived on Netaia early today." His glance darted toward the taller man. An instant later, Shirak bowed, too.

Muirnen Rogonin's stomach gurgled, and he covered it with one hand, pressing through folds of flesh. These people had demanded an audience on one hour's notice. He wouldn't mind if the Shuhr ejected Occupation Governor Danton and all his ilk from Citangelo, but not by destroying the base, as in the Codex simulation. He had no intention of dealing with a mind-crawling, gene-fixed, offworld trader. Not long ago, offworld trade had been strictly illegal. "Whatever you have to say, you will listen to me first. Any threat against Netaia, or any of my subjects, will not be tolerated. Am I understood?"

Talumah spread his hands. "I give you my word, Your Grace. We have designs on only one of your subjects—Mistress Firebird. Why in all the worlds is she being honored in Citangelo?"

"Not honored. Only confirmed." Rogonin balled a fist. In principle, he approved of the confirmation of wastlings if tragedy struck a noble family. That was why they were born. Each privileged family had to raise wastlings along with its heirs and instill a willingness—even eagerness—to die for Netaia's glory as soon as elder siblings secured the succession. That system, coupled with strict isolation, had kept Netaia stable for decades.

But the notion of restoring Firebird Angelo Caldwell to the royal succession soured his digestion. She'd proved herself poisoned by Federate ideals. Last night she'd shown how eager she was to poison others.

Talumah took one step forward. Rogonin watched him closely. One more step and the offworlder would feel a House Guard stun pistol.

"Despite our political differences," Talumah said, "we are also a people who do not bow to the Federacy, and we are deeply concerned with justice. Firebird was found guilty of treason, was she not?"

"Treason," Rogonin pronounced, "sedition, and heresy—but what do you know of the nine holy Powers?"

"Strength, Valor, and Excellence," recited Micahel Shirak. "Knowledge, Fidelity, and Resolve; Authority, Indomitability, and Pride. Laudable attributes, Your Grace. They should be served by those born to represent them. Such as—her."

Rogonin raised an eyebrow. Maybe he'd misjudged the young man. "That is correct. But I can deal with Lady Firebird without outside help." His greatest fear, after losing his family's position, was the danger of Federatization. Netaia's high culture, directed for centuries by a knowledgeable elite, could drown in a sea of low-popular influence. He would hate to see his people reduced to the homogenous culture of other worlds while others carried off Netaia's wealth. Obviously, Firebird was cooperating with those forces.

"Reconsider." Micahel Shirak's voice sounded brittle, even icy. "The Netaian systems are preparing for pageantry. Would you find it satisfying to substitute a state funeral?"

Rogonin's eyes narrowed. He wanted to ask if Princess Phoena really had died on their world, or if that was Federate fabrication. He'd admired Phoena. Still, she was one more Angelo, and she would have stood between him and his new personal hopes. "I don't need your help," he repeated. "My legal agents—"

"You must understand," Talumah interrupted, "that when it is necessary to take a life of public significance, the event should be arranged to bring the maximum benefit. Firebird Caldwell's death could guarantee permanent Netaian independence from the Federacy."

Rogonin frowned down at the long-faced man and his icy compatriot. Independence . . . permanent . . . As the words circled each other in his mind, he linked his fingers again. Could these people break Netaia's Federate chains and dispose of the dangerous wastling without implicating him? After all, those reports of the Shuhr threat to Citangelo came from Federate sources.

Maybe he'd misjudged that, too.

He waited to see if they would react to his shift in attitude, even before he spoke. Caldwell had shown they could read his emotions.

They gave no sign of having probed him. After several seconds, he accepted their apparently respectful silence (and mentally cursed Caldwell, who had forced mind-access on him twice). "You interest me," he admitted. "But you, too, have your own resources. You may threaten, even dispose of that Netaian subject, but do not implicate me, and do not come back to this palace again." He started to raise a hand, gesturing to his guards. He glanced at Talumah's eyes.

Something warm, like good brandy, threaded through his brain. It lulled and comforted away his desire to see them gone. *What harm in hearing if they have anything else to offer?*

He laid down his hand.

Shirak seated himself on the grand desk top, dangling a leg. "Your Grace, what is your present military strength? We assume the Federates have done pitifully little to help you rebuild."

What harm in letting them sit? Rogonin reached for his touchboard and called up data. As he read it off, Shirak shook his head.

"That," said Talumah, "is disgraceful. They have left you virtually helpless."

"But we will never bow to them."

"Neither will we, Your Grace." Talumah jerked his head to one side, and Shirak slid down off the desk. "Our people's goal is to save humanity. Civilization barely survived the first Six-alpha catastrophe. If that binary emits another radiation storm, we will all be better prepared."

Rogonin raised one eyebrow.

"But the Sentinels oppose us. The last thing they want is for humankind to become immortal. They want us all to settle for life after death, if such a thing exists."

Immortal? They had his attention now!

Shirak gave the crystalline globe a spin. "We started testing Caldwell's defenses this morning, at Prince Tellai's town home. Since we are sharing information, you may want to know he and Lady Firebird are defended by at least three plainclothes remote teams."

Rogonin laughed shortly. "I saw two this morning myself."

"Now you know of another," said Talumah. "And there are more. Here, inside the palace."

Rogonin jerked up his head. He eyed the House Guards at his doorposts. "They wouldn't dare."

"They wouldn't dare come here without bringing assistance, Your Grace. I would suggest rescreening all palace employees. We could help," Talumah said softly. "We know *them* when we see them."

With his daughter's ball impending—should he?

"No," he said. That would be collaboration. "Thank you for the information, but my security staff will investigate."

"As you wish, Your Grace." Shirak chuckled.

His laughter shattered Rogonin's temporary languor. He sat upright. "I can spare no more time." He flicked his fingers in dismissal.

Talumah bowed and turned away, but Shirak stood his ground. "Do you remember," he said, "that General Caldwell's brother and his family were murdered?"

Drawn oddly to the man, Rogonin answered, "Of course. That came over Federate newsnets. Though we distrust the sources, we did use Caldwell's bereavement as an occasion to open a case of old southern wine. Is it true?"

Shirak crossed his arms. "I killed them. I will kill again, this time for you. Set aside a case of old southern wine to drink with me. When *she* is dead."

Rogonin raised an eyebrow.

Shirak pivoted and strutted to the door.

Rogonin watched until the massive gold panels shut them out. Yes, he decided, Shirak looked like a murderer and a braggart. Deciding to have him tailed, Rogonin reached for his desk pad.

Oddly, the screen glowed with military information. He didn't remember calling that up.

He frowned, blanked it, and tapped out an order to Enforcement.

Chapter 8
Quest

sarabande

a dignified dance in triple meter

Early the next morning Brennen's interlink gave off a soft tone. Firebird rolled aside as he retrieved it from the nightstand. "Caldwell," he said.

"Good morning, Caldwell," she heard. "Danton. Nothing new on yesterday's callers to Tellai's house, but one of your quiet help reported suspicious presences last night. There's a chance the Shuhr have tried to contact the senior authority."

Firebird blinked. The interlink channel was supposedly secure, but neither Brennen nor Danton would refer to Sentinel infiltrators in the palace.

"No changes to our staff? We'll have a quiet morning and an afternoon fitting. The Rogonin ball is tonight."

Firebird sat up, and Brennen's amusement followed her delight like an echo. He had no intrinsic interest in meeting that protocol requirement. She, on the other hand, might have been tempted to interpret protocol a little too strenuously for the chance to dance a triplette in his arms—

But as their second most public appearance, it was one more chance to draw out a Shuhr agent without endangering too many civilians. There would be thousands in the Hall of Charity. Already, their palace-staff infiltrators would be jockeying to serve on tonight's shift. Her own assignment was simply to be as visible as possible, and the dance floor would serve nicely.

"We'll be ready," Danton said. Brennen thumbed off the interlink.

The "quiet" morning would give Firebird one more chance to prepare herself, mentally and spiritually, for the days ahead.

First, she spent half an hour at her studies in *Mattah*, the Sentinels' holy book. She'd been battling with the issue of atonement. Self-sacrifice was something she'd always understood—but for her full and final justification, according to *Mattah*, she must trust in an atonement the Eternal Speaker would make . . . someday, in the Word to Come's time. That was less clear.

After reading several chapters of the historical Second Confessions and one in the meatier Wisdom of Mattah, she set the book aside. Again, she'd found more questions than answers—but Brennen had gone out. Intellectually, she could understand the idea of substitutionary death, of escaping the consequences of her own actions thanks to someone else's sacrifice. She knew that the Singer had laid a covering over her so she could stand in His presence. Still, in her heart of hearts, she felt that if a sacrifice needed to be made for her full and final cleansing, she must make it. Herself.

This was progress. Back when she honored the Powers, she'd had to be the sacrificial victim.

She took a fast turn in the vaporbath, then settled in Phoena's parlor with Shel. After months of effort, she'd learned to touch her epsilon carrier. It was the first skill all Sentinels learned.

This was pathetic progress, but because of her oddly polarized epsilon carrier, it allowed the unprecedented explosion of power they now called epsilon fusion. RIA alone wouldn't guarantee their safe passage through the renegades' fielding net. They would need her—and fusion. College researchers had all but proved that she'd killed the Shuhr who attacked her by fusing carriers and amplifying their deadly intent.

The researchers had also measured considerable scarring to the ayin complex in her midbrain. The more she practiced fusing carriers, the sooner she would destroy it altogether. That made her more determined than ever to learn how to shield her mind from attack.

Shel sat in a straight-backed waiting chair. "Try this," she suggested. "Think of the air around you as neutral, uncharged. With your carrier, you want to charge it positively, so it will repel other positive energy. Can you think at the electrical level?"

"Perfectly," Firebird answered, "if it's pertaining to a shipboard console."

"Go ahead, then."

She quieted her thoughts and forced herself to relax. Turning inward, she first faced the flaming darkness, the taint in her soul that surrounded her epsilon carrier. She no longer felt compelled to find an intellectual explanation for its existence. She was learning to focus on the Mighty Singer instead, and to be grateful He could use her flawed gifts. Cautiously, she touched the carrier itself.

Colors suddenly brightened, while common sounds developed a deep, eerie music. Holding that mental posture, she tried Shel's suggestion, envisioning air molecules charged with energy. She tried imagining them turning different colors. She tried shifting them into sound waves.

Nothing happened.

She let go of her epsilon turn and drooped against the back of Phoena's deep chair.

Shel shook her head. "I can't tell if you have the idea," she complained, "not when I have to stay shielded this way."

Firebird understood the danger. If she and Shel accidentally created fusion, Shel might be killed. Cassia Talumah and Harcourt Terrell had died this way, according to the Sentinel College's current theory.

"I understand," Firebird said. "I'll try again."

Several attempts later, while holding the depth of her turn, she remembered the visualization she'd first used to find her carrier: the stone wall surrounding the Angelo estate at Hunter Height, where Phoena nearly executed her. In her vision, that barrier walled a perpetual inner darkness away from conscious perception—and with it, the carrier.

What would happen if she tried to take part of the wall down?

She imagined herself drifting alongside, considering its lichen-crusted strength.

What if she imagined a crack?

Wanting to find it, longing to find it, she wasn't surprised when a crack appeared some ways ahead, between stone blocks. She forged a firm link between her point of consciousness and the convoluted cord of energy behind her. Grounding herself in that power, she thrust at the crack. Thrust, again—

And fell back in her chair. "I almost had it." She shoved hair back from her forehead. "Did you feel anything that time?"

"No," Shel admitted, "but if you felt that was progress, try again."

This time, when Firebird shut her eyes and rested back in her chair, Shel Mattason dispersed her shields. Like most Sentinels, she'd picked up her basic skills without weird visualizations—but Firebird was notoriously unique. Shel had been warned to avoid creating any situation that might produce the potentially deadly fusion, even though the masters' research reassured everyone that Firebird could now control whether or not fusion occurred.

The faintest tendril of epsilon presence touched her. Instantly, Shel shielded herself.

Firebird had gone stiff again, her hot brown eyes open wide. "What was that?" she exclaimed. "Something happened."

"I don't know." Startled, Shel sat back down. She didn't remember standing up. "It was no shield, but I think it was almost a quest-pulse. Could you do it again?" This time, she shielded heavily.

Firebird shut her eyes. This time, the only outward sign of her effort that Shel could see was a bead of perspiration that trickled down her forehead, along her left eye, and then down the edge of her cheek.

She was trying. Desperately. She couldn't make it happen again. Eventually, she gave up.

"I think," Shel murmured, "you're too tired to go on. Do this, though—remember what you did the first time. Let me watch you remember. Just don't pull me into your turn."

"I won't." Firebird felt the weird otherness of Shel's epsilon probe slide into place. As soon as she knew the Sentinel could observe, she touched her epsilon carrier. She recalled the effort of thrusting at the chink in that everlasting wall, battling until a tiny granite chip split off its surface. She was through! On the outside, she felt the slightest echo of another epsilon presence.

She opened her eyes.

"That," Shel pronounced, "was a quest-pulse. Not very strong, but it was real. Well done!"

Firebird cocked one eyebrow and barely smiled.

"Take a minute to let your carrier rebuild, then try again while your memory is fresh. Do it over and over, until you can do it under consistent control."

"What good is it? That slowly—that weakly—I need to be able to shield, Shel! To put out fifty times that much energy." And to hold on to consciousness after fusion. She hated the thought of sparking fusion for Brennen, deep in enemy territory, and then falling unconscious.

Shel frowned. "Sometimes, the Holy One gives us only one skill for a number of months. It's like His call on our lives. We don't necessarily understand, but He'll give us whatever we genuinely need, and always in time."

Firebird gripped her armrest. Coming from the bereaved Shel, that encouragement carried considerable weight. Surely these infinitesimal achievements wouldn't feed pride, not the pride she would feel if she saved Netaia, even if achieving that glory cost her life—

Whoops! Again, she caught herself in Powers-based thinking. She could not shake the idea that if any sacrifice had to be made for her sake, then she must be directly involved or it would count for nothing. It was a virulent Netaian sort of pride, the exact opposite of the future atonement taught by her Path instructor, in Second Confessions, and in the Wisdom of Mattah.

Intellectually, she had almost grasped it. Obviously, she still believed otherwise.

"So practice," Shel said. "You'll build speed that way."

Firebird pushed away her theological reflections. "What good is a quest-pulse, Shel?"

"Controlled, it can be used to find a person whose mental savor you know, or to send energy in small packets, or communicate your presence. Brennen will be delighted," she added. "And sorry he wasn't here to see."

Brennen was engaged in his own struggle. In Uri Harris's elegant parlor in the adjoining consort's suite, they both sat in straight-back chairs. Brennen was relearning to remotely lift simple objects—starting with a shoe, then his crystace. They'd progressed to nudging pieces of furniture away from the walls and then back. Even the precursor skill, focusing epsilon energy in his hand's long nerve bundles, no longer came consistently. Once, all this had been so easy that he could control his own rate of fall.

Now it felt like trying to fly through syrup. His spiritual father had recently said, "Rarely do we experience a true spiritual victory without afterward being tempted to believe we have lost something precious. Other temptations will come, too, because the Adversary tries to avenge his losses. You won a great victory at Three Zed. Do not forget that."

Brennen exhaled heavily. In one way, it was a relief to lay down some of his ancestors' burdens, the psi powers that resulted from unconscionable gene tampering. His losses, and his new fears, must strengthen his faith. He must focus his reliance on the Holy One.

That wasn't easy for a gifted man. He had to sympathize with Mari's struggle against the pride that kept her from dying to willfulness and being fully used by the Eternal Speaker. As the Caldwell-Carabohd family's eldest surviving heir, he had to live by that highest standard of humility. He'd been tempted by a conqueror's pride, back before he lost so much epsilon ability.

Guide me, Holy One. Help me walk this new Path.

Uri rested his chin on one hand. "Before we try springing this trap at the ball," he said, "you and Lady Firebird ought to try fusion again. Shamarr Dickin was firm about being prepared. All this, everything else we've tried, strikes me as avoiding the real issue."

"And no one has heard the call," Brennen pointed out. It had been decades since Sentinel forces found the enemy's stronghold, and still they waited. Previous shamarrs, speaking on behalf of the Holy One, had warned them to hold back until the chosen moment.

Uri nodded. As commissioned officers, they should obey Federate orders, even to a premature strike, if there was no overwhelming moral reason to disobey . . . but Special Ops had already warned Regional command that sending a Sentinel force too early might result in losing it.

Brennen hoped his orders might include a discretionary provision. That could be granted under extraordinary circumstances. Assuming they gave him command, he might have several hundred lives resting on that judgment call. Uri, for example—the son of parents with ES scores too low to qualify for training—really hadn't wanted to become a Sentinel at all, but acquiesced to his parents' wishes. Brennen might have to decide whether to risk Uri's life.

"Hiding our gifts," Uri said, "is one way of misusing them."

Brennen rested his head against the wall behind his chair. "So we have the Codes." He had only to look at the Shuhr to see what his people would be without those restrictions on using their skills. "I wonder," Brennen said, "if they are already cloning offspring from Phoena's cells. If she inherited a reversed carrier, too, that might give them fusion-capable warriors in just a few years."

And my own cells? Would there be Caldwell offspring among Three Zed's next generation?

He must not think about that.

"And passive fusion-partners even sooner, if they manipulate development." Uri stroked the side of his chin with two fingers.

If the Shuhr attacked Federate worlds using RIA and fusion, they could take anything. Everything.

They *must* catch one Shuhr. Maybe then they would be called. This, not Mari's inexplicable passion to try dancing with him, was the real excuse for attending Esmerield Rogonin's ball.

"If I could wish," Brennen said, stretching the kinks from his back, "I would wish there were some way to show mercy. To win them to truth. To show we could destroy them but would rather hold back." He'd toyed with one perilous idea. If Three Zed's fielding could be taken down, he might go in under a flag of truce and try to negotiate, even knowing he might be killed by his own forces if the Shuhr refused to cooperate and the Federates had to attack. He hadn't forgotten disobeying Federate orders to go to Hunter Height. That incident had put a count of insubordination in his master file.

But if the true call came, he would not disobey, even to save his life. He couldn't save it, anyway . . . only lengthen it. *Let a door open to mercy,* he prayed, *or else show us your will. Plainly.*

The bedroom door opened, and Brennen peered through. "Are you ready?"

Firebird frowned. "Not really." Brennen and Uri had interrupted her session with Shel, reiterating the urgency of practicing fusion before tonight's potential encounter. She'd demanded ten minutes to rest and pray.

"Uri and Shel will wait in the next room, shielding." Brennen sat down on the bedside, casual in a skinshirt and trousers.

Firebird dropped her copy of *Mattah* on the bed. She was learning to tell when Brennen would not back off, and he was right about this.

"Let's get it over with," she grumbled. "Do what you can with the excess energy. See if you can restore any of those lost memories."

"I'm going to try," he said, "simply to keep you conscious."

"I need to do that myself. After all—"

"The longer we procrastinate, the more frightened—"

"Yes." She shut her eyes. She envisioned the granite wall and pushed her point of consciousness inside, irked as always by her slow-motion turn. At the heart of the flaming blackness, she spotted the glimmering epsilon nebula. She felt a smoky-sweet presence follow. That had to be Brennen, already holding a turn.

Help, Mighty Singer!

She touched the nebula and then latched onto Brennen's epsilon presence. For one moment, she felt herself as an explosion, expanding at horrific speed, blasting through everything around her. She was a compression wave, or the gas shell of a star going nova. She was Sabba Six-alpha, flinging energy storms into space, atomizing every molecule for light-years. She . . . was . . .

She was a small woman, struggling to open her eyes. Finally, she focused on a blur that became Shel Mattason's face. Uri and Brennen stood close.

She drew a deep breath. "Brenn, are you all right?"

"He's fine," Shel said curtly. "How do you feel?"

"Dizzy. How long was I out?"

"Twenty-six minutes."

The best yet, but still pitiful. "Did you need to bring me back? Out of psychic shock?"

Shel nodded.

Firebird bit her lip. She hadn't yet revived without help. "I'm not going to be much help in a crisis."

"Yes, you are. You're the key we've been given for this time. Everything is falling into place," said Brennen.

Glittering gold tracery hung from the ceiling high overhead. The tour guide's ludicrous white gown had tripped him twice, and Micahel thought it might tangle the simpering fool's legs again momentarily.

Rogonin's Enforcement tail had been pitifully easy to lose.

"The nave, of course," whined the guide, "dates from the late second century of settlement. Notice the exquisite parabolic arches, and how they meet delicate ceiling tracery at precisely calculated angles to create the impression of an infinite golden distance."

Micahel stared upward, paying attention to detail that surely gratified the tour guide. Following those arches, Micahel imprinted every angle on his trained memory. Among those gaudy traceries, he should easily find a sniping loft.

The Hall of Charity was really three halls. He stood in the central nave. The North Hall, with its separate entrance, tight seating, and low ceiling, was normally used by the low-common class. Similarly, the South Hall accommodated servitors who cared to worship their oppressors, the noble electors, in their capacity as priestly demigods. The high-common class was entitled to enter the nave, in sight of the "holy" electors.

The mincing guide led his troop up the nave's long aisle. At the front, five steps led up onto a stage ringed by curved seating. "Here in the sanctum," he intoned, "the noble electors take their places. On the left, the Houses of Tellai, Drake, Gellison . . ." As he spoke, he touched a tri-D projector. A host of ghostly images appeared, holographic portraits of long-dead electors who stood wreathed in heavy floral incense.

Still staring at the ceiling, Micahel jostled a frowzy-haired woman. High rafters crossed the main arch. According to his diagrams, he thought he'd seen . . .

Yes. Near the left pillar, at the sanctum's edge, a gilded beam protruded, concealed from all other angles.

Back at Talumah's apartment, Micahel studied detail maps of the nave, palace, and Federate occupation base. "Borrowed" from Rogonin's files, the first two maps had the look of antiques, printed in two dimensions on thin, brittle wood-pulp paper.

Long-faced Ard Talumah hovered near Micahel's shoulder. He hitched one hip up to half sit on the table. *Did you ever meet our would-be monarch, lovely Phoena?* he asked.

Struck by the way one portion of the map nudged his memory, Micahel matched a balcony-level overlay of the nave to its lower story, running one finger along ceiling beams, studying scanner angles. From beneath, it seemed to vanish. *Yes, Ard. I saw her so-called execution.*

What does Adiyn mean to do with her? Talumah demanded. Dark brown hair drooped onto his forehead, almost into his eyes.

"Keep her in stasis," Micahel muttered aloud. He'd spoken Old Colonial so much lately that he was starting to think in the trade language. "She's just a gene specimen."

Talumah followed his shift to vocal speech. "How seriously damaged was she? Really?"

He shrugged. "If Adiyn ever revives her, it won't be out of kindness. There's not much left of the mind when the body's gone through that." Sipping his kass, he eyed the map again.

"I met Phoena," Talumah rambled, "at the queen's birthday celebration, here in Citangelo. Caught her alone for one moment, proud and angry, superbly open to suggestion . . ."

The thought nudged Micahel out of his concentration. Tonight there would be another ball.

Talumah paused. "What?" he demanded. He must have sensed Micahel's turn of emotion, but he knew better than to probe uninvited.

"The debut tonight. Caldwells are required to attend, aren't they?"

"By protocol, yes. Anything less would be an unforgivable insult to the Rogonin family."

"Then tonight, we'll find out which so-called palace servitors are actually Sentinels. They'll all be there, protecting that pair." Ten or twelve Sentinels, two of them. Acceptable odds. Caldwell's high-ES bodyguard would recognize him, of course. There should be a microsecond's delay between the guard's warning and Caldwell's reaction, if Caldwell really were disabled.

The Sentinels might even try to grab him.

He smiled at Talumah, envisioning Caldwell sprawled on a restraint table, stunned by bereavement shock. That had been the plan back at Three Zed.

If Caldwell's imitation palace servitors attacked him, he might take one down. Violence at the regent's daughter's ball would guarantee an interstellar incident. It might even spark a war. His people could step in, becoming Netaia's saviors. He was willing to bet Modabah hadn't thought of *that* option.

Yes. Tonight, he would dare Caldwell to go through with his mate's mock coronation. He would scare them and slip away. He'd enjoyed the outcry over Sunton. Publicity went to his head like a drug.

He wanted more.

Modabah Shirak's rich apartment, on the other side of midtown, had too many windows for his gene-daughter's taste. Seated on a lounger near an inside wall, Terza listened to voices speaking Colonial in her father's room. He often closed her out. For a while she'd hoped that by impressing him she might advance her career. He scarcely talked to her, closeted with on-site agents or poring over travel documentaries with other members of the crew that had brought them here. Apparently, Netaia was all he had hoped.

A youth of fifteen or sixteen scurried past her, carrying a carafe of fresh kass. Terza kept her shields steady. She didn't want to feel the youngster's fear. She'd been a subadult too recently, and the sensation might bring back her nightmares. Her father, or any adult of leadership status, could order a trainee sent back to the settlements—or culled, if she were judged inept or dangerous.

Then was Terza, even as a named adult, only a specimen to be sacrificed for others?

Never!

She tightened her inner shields to stifle that cry, then picked up a primitive data desk. With no work to occupy her, she had accessed the Federate register and researched the Carabohd family. She understood Micahel better for it. Terza couldn't fantasize with her father around, but whoever destroyed Caldwell would enjoy unusual pleasures. He would obviously try to die faithful to his god. That kind's despair, as death and defeat sucked him down, should be sublimely sweet.

So she'd been taught. Now even that notion was losing its appeal.

Other details in Caldwell's biography intrigued her. Unmarried until he was thirty by the Federate calendar, he must've been unable to find a connatural Sentinel mate.

Terza wondered what set him apart. Speculating kept her from utter boredom.

And nausea. Always, the nausea.

Chapter 9
Regalia

pavane
a court dance in slow duple meter

A different kind of duty took Firebird downstairs that afternoon to a windowless first-floor room in the west wing. She vaguely remembered a diplomatic reception here years ago. Four meters by five, it was adequate for this purpose.

Brennen sat quietly, almost invisibly, in a chair against the wall. In the end, he'd decided against flying that surveillance grid. There was simply too small a chance for success compared with the risk of being shot down.

Three women bustled around boxes piled on chairs and tables at the room's opposite end. These women were genuine palace staff, too highly placed for Sentinels to impersonate. Shel stood at one heavy wooden door, Uri at the other, twin midnight blue shadows in a chamber frosted with gilt. Brennen wore his uniform, as he'd done during every public appearance, as if he too were on guard duty. He also needed to show off that four-rayed star.

He shifted on his chair as someone hurried past Uri's door. They'd insisted on a room with two entries for this fitting. Though it might be less private, it would be easier to escape . . . in case. She sensed that Brennen didn't like its closeness, nor the number of strangers. His dislike fell short of phobic panic, though. She wondered which one of the Adorations he was silently reciting.

"Over here, please, my lady."

Startled by the chief dresser's contralto voice, Firebird walked her direction. One helper dragged a spiral-legged table underneath the room's central chandelier. The stout dresser gently laid down a box, lifted its lid, and drew out a garment of shimmering pale gold.

Firebird felt Brennen's tension focus. He was already bracing himself to face the gold accouterments in the great Hall of Charity.

"Undertunic, my lady," said the deep-voiced dresser. "If you won't mind slipping out of that skyff, we'll check its fit. If this hangs well, we won't worry about the gown for tonight. It's not quite finished."

Shel and Uri stepped out through their doors and shut them, leaving Firebird alone with Brennen, the dresser, and her assistants. She appreciated their concern for her modesty.

In the middle of undressing, Firebird glanced back at Brennen. He leaned forward on his chair, hands clasped over his knees, watching intently. She knew his attention had nothing to do with watching her disrobe. He would be entirely open to sense her mood. She wondered if the ceremonial significance of these garments had started to mean anything to Brennen. His upbringing was so different.

His bird-of-prey medallion dangled down her chest as the tunic slithered over her shoulders. At her sides, the assistants pressed seams together to fit it.

Firebird smoothed the undertunic's front and lifted one heel to eye its length. The long-sleeved garment rippled to her ankles.

The stout woman brought up a second parcel. "When your sister Phoena was confirmed," the woman huffed, "we had to try these six times. I do hope you're easier to fit, my lady."

"I doubt the problem was your workmanship," Firebird muttered. Phoena had terrorized palace staff.

The dresser twisted one corner of her mouth upward. "If you wouldn't mind stretching out your arms, my lady."

Three women draped a sleeveless crimson gown with open side seams over her shoulders, then girdled it with a belt crafted of interlacing emblems, finely worked in gold, a relic of the House. Each emblem symbolized an heiress confirmed more than a century ago. "We've kept this regalia under all-day watch," said one woman. "Several small but valuable pieces are missing from the state treasury."

Another said, "Some people say the Federates are stealing things."

Firebird frowned. "I doubt that. But I wouldn't put it past the Shuhr." She fingered the belt while a length of crimson fabric, fastened with a gold brooch to each shoulder of the gown's open neckline, was dropped behind her and draped. The emblems stood for her heritage, her responsibilities, her rights as an Angelo heir.

She looked around for a mirror and found none. She was surprised by how much that peeved her.

The woman pursed her lips. "The overgown seems to fit," she said. "I'd have thought we might have to let it out again. You should be proud, my lady. You've had twins."

Firebird straightened her shoulders. She hadn't worked to get her figure back. She'd lost all that weight worrying while Brennen was a prisoner.

The dresser's attendant brought up a final box, smaller than the rest, made of dull metal. The stout dresser touched its latch and lifted out a tiara sparkling with large, square-cut rubies—at least a hundred of them—and a single diamond drop, dangling at center, to touch the wearer's forehead.

Archivists called it the Crown of Fire, more delicate than the heavy, jeweled Crown of State, the dressy goldstone Iarla Crown, or any of the others. Phoena had worn this tiara, an elegant nine-year-old with her chestnut-colored hair elaborately coifed, her small chin high and forward, when seven-year-old Firebird witnessed her confirmation.

The woman set it on Firebird's hair, far forward, then eased it back toward the crown of her head. It squeezed uncomfortably. The diamond drop tickled her brow.

The woman backed away.

Firebird took a tiny step to her right, facing Brennen. *I used to want this desperately*, she thought at him. *How silly do I look?*

He stood up. On the resonance of the pair bond, she felt an uneasy concern. He paced around her, clasping his hands. "She'll wear low shoes, like these?" he asked the dresser.

"It's been fitted for low shoes," she answered. "The costume's normally worn by a preadolescent. She's small for an adult, so it suits her."

He paused in front of her, looked her up and down, then extended a hand. She took it, not quite sure what he intended, or what bothered him.

He raised her hand and kissed it formally. Then he touched one fingertip to her forehead.

An image flooded her mind. With Brennen, she stared up and down at herself as she stood in the costume, taking in its rippling scarlet train, the disquieting shimmer of golden undertunic snaking down the gown's open sides, and the high-waisted fit of the belt. He stared longest, for her sake, at the ruby confirmation tiara, its diamond drop glittering over her forehead.

She was still lost in that image when she and Brennen took an early dinner at the Tellai estate. Tel had invited several local dignitaries, but after Firebird managed a few words of thanks and greeting, those people engaged each other in conversation, excluding her . . . to her relief.

She'd fulfilled every wastling's dream. She'd survived to be confirmed, and tonight—just for tonight, she promised herself—she would bask in this pleasure, here at Tel's reception and later at Esme's ball.

Shel remained at one door of the indoor dining balcony, Uri near the other. Tel's staff paraded past, serving a light soup garnished with fresh herbs sprinkled on floating dollops of set cream.

Firebird spotted one uniformed Federate turning aside to speak into an interlink. Two minutes later, the woman beckoned.

Brennen still seemed oddly distant. He pushed back his chair. "Excuse us for a moment, Tel."

Tel made some polite reply that Firebird scarcely heard as she sprang up and followed.

This aide wore the khaki uniform of Carolinian forces. "Another raid," she said somberly. "Two picket ships got too far behind a trade convoy from Beda to Inisi. Inisi is investigating."

Two more ships! Firebird glanced back toward the table. Several of Tel's other guests had fallen silent, staring in this direction. "This isn't classified, is it?" she asked.

The Carolinian shook her head. "It's going out over the newsnets."

They returned to the table, and Brennen relayed the news to Tel and his guests. Firebird went back to eating, watching faces turn sour lipped and narrow eyed as Brennen spoke. As soon as he finished, Tel's clairsinger ran his fingers lightly up and down his instrument's strings and took up a prim art song about picking herbs in springtime.

Netaia! Firebird fumed silently. Sabba Six-alpha could blast out another radiation storm, and most of these people wouldn't even notice. They clung to their ways like limpet mines to a destroyer.

Yet all these things—the balcony, the art song, the servitors—were part of her heritage, like the small Crown of Fire. "I could help Netaia. I could," she murmured over her soup. She could accomplish things here that she never could do out in the Federacy, and be honored for them. She had every right to wear the Crown of Fire.

"You could." Tel folded his hands on the tabletop across from her, then glanced aside. The dignitaries remained busy with their own conversation. "You must consider your people, Firebird."

"I could at least help them wake up."

Tel plucked a fragrant purple jantia blossom from the nearest table bouquet. "Don't ever give up on us." He leaned toward Firebird with it. Then, appearing to change his mind, he handed it to Brennen. She felt a flicker of surprise before Brennen passed it along to her.

She glanced from one man to the other, unsure of what had transpired.

Neither of them explained.

Back at the palace, Brennen took her coat as Shel and Uri disabled a new set of listening devices. "What was that with Tel and the flower, Brenn?"

He laid her coat over a chair. "He wanted to give it to you. He decided that might not be appropriate."

"I can take a flower from a friend. He's just trying to court me for the . . . no, don't tell me he's . . . no," she said, disheartened. "No, Brenn. I know I look like Phoena, but Tel's too intelligent to mix me up with her."

"He admires you for what you are." Brennen slid an arm around her waist. "Mari, be careful. Pride has no place in our hearts. You are lovely, and regal, but—"

She laughed sharply, realizing what had been bothering him. "It's only a costume, a role. I'll take it off when that day's over and never wear it again."

He raised one eyebrow. Then, to her surprise, he leaned down and kissed her forehead.

She shut her eyes and pressed toward him. Brennen's lips almost pulled away, then pressed again, as a smoky-sweet presence hovered at the edge of her mind, enjoying her sensations, amplifying them. "I really am looking forward to the ball," she whispered, kneading the small of his back. He particularly liked that. Now his pleasure, too, echoed in the bonding resonance. "Dance one triplette with me, just one, as soon as we get there. If we're supposed to be visible, let me enjoy it before anything else can happen."

"I don't know the triplette," he murmured against her ear. He'd pulled off his coat, and a faint scent of leather clung to him. In an hour they would bathe and dress to go downlevel. In the ballroom, their kitchen infiltrators would coordinate every supply run with rotating door guards and footmen, to ensure security coverage at all times. Shel and Uri would run the actual intercept if possible, allowing those Sentinel backups to remain inconspicuous in case they were needed again.

"We can easily create the illusion," she answered. "A little mind-access on your part, a little reminiscing on mine, and you can anticipate anything. The court will be so impressed."

"Using mind-access," he said softly, tangling his fingers into her hair, "to create the appearance that I know how to dance, falls very close to 'capricious or selfish' use of epsilon abilities."

"Not selfish," she insisted. "It's not for you, or even me. It's for the mission." He couldn't argue with that. She tilted her chin, wordlessly asking to be kissed on the lips.

Instead, he reached in through her hair, stroking her throat with both palms. "And for us, my lady."

"Don't tease," she murmured.

His voice turned solemn. "This intercept," he said, "could be the riskiest moment of our trip."

"Second riskiest," she whispered. "There's also Three Zed—"

The crosstown link chimed before their lips could touch. Scowling, Firebird reached for the receiver.

Brennen raised a hand. "Shel?" he called through the marble wall.

Firebird waited silently, wondering if Shel heard the sensuous huskiness Firebird felt in Brennen's voice. Guarding a pair-bonded couple must be torture for a bereaved Sentinel.

Brennen walked to the room's end and opened the door.

"Good evening." Firebird heard Shel's voice, then silence.

Standing just inside the archway, Brennen raised one eyebrow, and then he frowned. "No one there," he relayed to Firebird, his sweet physical tension fading.

The CT chimed again. Irked, Firebird joined Brennen in the door arch.

Shel held the earpiece on one side, her wide-set eyes cold. "Good evening," she repeated. Firebird waited a slow ten-count, then Shel jabbed a key to break the connection. "Would you suggest calling palace security?" she asked Firebird.

"It could be palace security, harassing us. Redjackets, or House Guard. Or other friends of His Grace."

"Or Shuhr," Brennen said.

"By now, they could be working with him," said Firebird. "Nothing Muirnen Rogonin did would surprise me."

"It occurred to me," he admitted. "Rogonin has tried nothing against us. He could be waiting, collaborating—"

"If he's caught collaborating, the Electorate will throw him out. That's treason—"

Chime, again.

"Shall I?" Firebird moved toward it.

"Let me." Brennen extended a hand. "Yes?" he asked the wall-mounted pickup.

. . . nine, ten. Brennen switched off.

Chime—

Brennen lifted the earpiece, keeping it away from his head. "If you have a message for Lady Firebird, I'll relay it." He stared at the floor, glacial-ice blue eyes gleaming. "Nothing." He hung up.

"I'm going to bathe," Firebird said firmly, glancing over her shoulder toward the master room.

Brennen held the earpiece, looking ready to originate a call himself. "I'll come soon."

She undressed, then lay down on Phoena's bed. The Shuhr were flaunting their invulnerability, she guessed. Much more of this, and protocol or no protocol, appearances or no appearances, she would move out of the palace and down to the base, with its better security.

Not that she wanted to! She'd been homesick out in the Federacy. Netaia wouldn't like her moving out, either, unless some incident proved she was in danger.

Maybe that was why Rogonin held back. Maybe he knew he'd get only one shot at her, so he'd better take a good one. If only he knew how easily she and Brennen could destroy him!

She closed her eyes and turned inward. Holding her epsilon carrier, she probed the visualized wall, looking for that flaw. She grasped the carrier, looped it around her point of consciousness, and thrust at—not through—the tiny crevice's edge. A new crack appeared. She beat against it, widening it by a millimeter. If she hoped to really use the quest-pulse, she had to learn to create it without using this visualization. She had to—

Gasping, she relinquished the turn. Brennen's voice filtered through the wall. He paused, then spoke again.

She centered her next thrust at the enlarged breach. The carrier's eerie gleam dimmed momentarily, and she thought she sensed a warm, smoky presence. When she opened her eyes, Brennen stood inside the doorway, clutching the hem of his shirt. With a smooth motion he pulled it off. "You called?" She heard delight in his voice. She felt it in her soul.

Progress at last! "What did you find out?" she asked. "Who did you contact?"

"House Guard. The calls originated outside, but they didn't appear on their switching monitor."

"So the House Guard claims."

Brennen sat down on the edge of the bed, then stretched out beside her. "Yes. So they claim."

Micahel Shirak smiled as he reentered his apartment. For now, it was enough to know that this afternoon, without any manipulation, Rogonin had provided the correct CT number for Firebird's rooms. The information itself was unimportant. More vitally, Rogonin was starting to cooperate. If he seemed to support them before they took his volition, the change in him would be less noticeable.

Micahel did hope he hadn't frightened the Caldwells out of attending tonight's ball. He'd found a wonderfully garish outfit.

Nineteen hundred arrived. Firebird tugged the shoulder seam of an electric blue gown, almost wishing she'd taken the couturier's suggestion and hired a personal girl to help her get it on, but she'd dressed herself for almost twenty years. Even when the Angelo fortune supported her, she hadn't rated a dresser. No ball gown was going to defeat her.

Finally, tonight, she would dance with Brennen. She matched her shoulder hems before setting the bodice stays. This really would be the perfect time to get a Shuhr in custody. Then she could enjoy her confirmation uninterrupted.

But one slip of attention tonight could leave her lying dead on a black marble dance floor. Danton would send half a dozen auxiliary plainclothes guards. She wondered how obvious they would look in a ballroom full of aristocrats in full finery.

She adjusted the chain of Brennen's bird-of-prey medallion around her neck. Shortened just . . . so . . . it dangled dramatically, several centimeters over the gown's neckline.

A muffled step caught her attention, and Brennen's image appeared in her mirror. He looked princely in dress whites with the red-and-blue Federate slash on his chest, even with his plainer shoulder star. Before their marriage, she'd observed that he moved with a dancer's grace. With him, she'd done a hundred things beyond her childhood hopes . . . but this would be their first chance to dance together.

His more moderate sense of expectancy dimmed hers. Like Uri and Shel, he'd concealed his crystace and a dart pistol under his uniform. "Stay close to at least two of us," he reminded her, "until they make a move."

She slipped Tel's little blazer into a deep side pocket. If she managed to carry it in past door guards, who ought to be wearing weapon sensors, she could encounter others there who might be armed as well. "We'll do this," she said. "I intend to live to see Kiel and Kinnor again."

Behind her, Shel peered through the near arch. Shel had consented to wear one of Phoena's gowns, sorting with Firebird through still-full closets until they found a pale blue creation less formfitting than most.

"I'll be just a minute." Brennen headed into Uri's rooms, probably to finalize plans by interlink.

Firebird walked out to the study. Pausing in front of a mirror, she pulled her shoulders back to carry off the ball gown's draping. When she'd been younger, she had always felt more comfortable in her Naval Academy uniform than in fancy dress, and she often tweaked tradition at gala occasions. But tonight she represented the Federacy, Brennen's people, and even the Mighty Singer. She'd tried to gown up properly, had even called the palace tresser and submitted to a hurried coifing.

She stood a moment longer, studying the effect. *Just for tonight*, she'd told Brennen . . . but playing this role felt fabulous. With the red-brown waves of her hair chemically controlled, whisked up at the crown and swept low across her right eyebrow, she might have been mistaken for Phoena. It had happened more than once when Phoena was alive.

Guilt made her slump. What would seeing her like this do to Tel?

"Ready, Mari?" Brennen's image appeared beside hers, his shoulders broadened by his dress whites.

She smiled and whirled, trailing her stiff blue skirt on marble flooring.

Uri entered with Brenn, matching him in dress whites. Poised in his posture, urbane in his slight smile, Uri looked a noble escort to Shel, who wore Phoena's heavily embroidered gown with surprising grace. Shel's usual gait had no female sway. Firebird guessed that normally, if unconsciously, she tried to repel male attention.

Brennen looked hard at Uri, then Shel. "Stay with us until you spot a target. We'll draw him on. Don't be afraid to signal the backups for help. That's why we have them."

Uri nodded gravely.

Firebird took a last glance at her party. A thousand snares of etiquette awaited, but she couldn't drill them in inconsequential nonsense. Tonight was their first serious chance to catch a Shuhr. "Don't worry about fitting in," she said, drawing on her pale blue gloves. "You're expected to behave like offworlders. As long as you make it obvious that you're trying to observe the niceties, you'll please anyone who's willing to be pleased. There's nothing we can do about the rest of them."

A whiff of festive spices blew through the hall door. Paskel stepped through. "My lady, here is Prince Tel." As Tel strode past him, Paskel crossed the formal sitting room in his inimitable palace-staff strut. Tel swept off his indigo-plumed hat and bowed, holding the pose long enough to confirm Firebird's apprehension. "I'm sorry," she said, adjusting her gloves. "I can't help looking like her."

Laughing weakly, Tel drew a hand cloth from one pocket and dabbed at his face. "No, you can't," he said. Pocketing the cloth again, he straightened the ends of his gold-edged sash with a gesture so automatic she envied him. He replaced the cock-hat, then offered Shel his arm. "Are you ready?"

Firebird linked her hand around Brennen's arm. "Tel," she murmured, "there could be some excitement tonight."

"Again?" he asked, raising his head.

"Possibly," Brennen said. "Just be ready to dive out of harm's way, in case our visitors come back."

"Paudan will be there," Tel assured them. "I'm covered."

Paskel held the door open.

Arm in arm with Brennen, Firebird strode out the door, along the balcony, and down the long curving stair toward the main ballroom. Soft footfalls behind her assured her that Shel, Tel, and Uri followed.

Chapter 10

One Triplette

valse noble à cinq

waltz in the aristocratic style—for five dancers

Firebird paused as Tel left his hat with a scurrying servitor in the portrait hall. After that, rank and decorum decreed she must lead into the ballroom. A footman announced them, crying first, "Lady Firebird Angelo Caldwell and General Brennen Caldwell."

A hundred stares turned toward the door like targeting lasers. Firebird walked one step ahead, directly down the right side of widening stairs carved from gold-shot black marble, as the footman announced Prince Tel Tellai-Angelo, Major Shelevah Mattason, and Lieutenant Colonel Uri Harris.

His Grace the Regent stood at the foot of the steps, resplendent in a fully formal white brocade jacket, with his House insignia of three stacked platinum triangles pinned at his throat. His thin eyebrows arched regally.

Mindful of the press cadre, Firebird composed her face to respectful solemnity. *Here we are*, she thought at Rogonin . . . and the door guards. *Get a good look.*

No one moved to take away her blazer.

Muirnen Rogonin looked broader than life in brocade. Dark blond Esme stood at his side, a rich spring green gown artfully revealing her flawless shoulders. Until this trip, Firebird had only seen the girl from a distance. Her father's round face was softened through Esme's cheekbones by her mother's Parkai blood. Duchess Liona stood third in the receiving line—

Parkai . . . Chilled, Firebird realized she had killed the girl's granduncle at Hunter Height. It had been accidental, in self-defense, but no one here believed that.

It galled Firebird to curtsey to Muirnen Rogonin. Still, she dropped a full one, forehead to her knee, before bowing to Esme. Out of the corner of her eye, she saw Brennen give a full bow behind her. As she rose out of her obeisance, Rogonin smiled down with an expression she'd last seen on Dru Polar, testing director of the Three Zed colony—a greedy, deadly hunger.

"My lady," he said, clasping her gloved hand. "Let me ask privately, what are your plans for Netaia? Will you stay with us beyond your confirmation?" Through his white gloves and her blue ones, his hands felt unclean.

"I've come back only because the Assembly called, Your Grace. My future is with the Federacy."

"If Netaia covenants to the Federacy, all your troubles will end. Am I correct?" His breath already reeked of liquor and spiced hors d'oeuvres.

"I will never put my own convenience before my people's welfare. The risk of civil war is substantial. I would have sent my proposal, even if I couldn't have come in person."

Rogonin glanced past her right shoulder, and his eyes narrowed. She felt Brennen's disgust for the man who had twice tried to kill her.

The regent seemed to be enjoying himself, though. Still gripping Firebird's hand, he lowered his voice. "My Lady Firebird, if you will sign something for me, I will personally see you protected during the length of your stay, and I will ensure that you leave Netaia safely."

Was that a veiled threat? "What do you want?"

"A pledge. A promise that on your honor, and despite any public statement you may make, you will use your influence to free the Netaian systems from all Federate influence."

Her diplomatic resolve had almost run out. "Your Grace, that would be a disaster. The Shuhr would devour Netaia like a choice morsel if the Federates withdrew—"

"And who destroyed our defenses, Lady Firebird?"

"My mother did," she snapped, "by attacking Veroh. My pledge to you is that I will not interfere with the peace of your lawful rule." She turned her head and looked pointedly at Brennen, who stood waiting to pay his formal respects. She curtsied again, feeling too angry to offer any more pleasantries. The prim opening strains of a gavotte fell into her silence.

She shuffled to her left, gave Countess Esme the ritual kiss, and whispered, "Congratulations, Countess. You are beautiful tonight." She curtsied again and stepped to her left. "Duchess Liona."

Esme's mother glared.

Shel murmured in her ear, "Go ahead and move out. I'm at your back." She plainly felt Brennen at full-defense readiness. Glad to show the Rogonin family the gathered back of her skirt, she took Brennen's arm and led into the room. She sensed Uri and Shel falling in behind, each slightly to one side. *Just like flying in formation.* Were the Shuhr here yet? Were they watching?

As she walked she stared around the ballroom. Beyond the mural of Conura First's coronation, ranks of crimson curtains stood open. Brilliantly lit formal gardens showed beyond the porticoes, between lawns where she once played touch tag with other wastlings. The palace orchestra filled the dais, its conductor wearing the gold-trimmed black of a servitor assigned to public performance. His graying curly brown hair was caught back in a tail. The tip of his baton flicked toward Firebird in midsweep. He nodded a greeting.

She let her stare travel clockwise, picking out one of Danton's plainclothes people, discernible by his conservative clothing and less arrogant face—and then recognized two Sentinels in Angelo livery, balancing trays full of wine goblets. They played the servitor's role surprisingly well.

Quadruple doors at the far end stood open. They admitted more tray-pushing, liveried servitors and a heavenly aroma. Glancing over the shoulder of one "servitor," actually a Sentinel she'd met shipboard, Firebird saw a refreshment table laden with crystal plates and bowls, and she spotted several of her favorite delicacies. Red gem tartlets, nut wafers, pastry wings with various spiced fillings . . . her mouth watered.

Not yet. She stepped away regretfully. *Maybe not even later.*

Slowly she crossed the ballroom, pausing to curtsey and exchange a few words with the nobles and high-commoners who were willing to tolerate her. Only one group tried to extend greetings into something like conversation. "Lady Firebird, is there any news at all about Carradee's daughters?"

"No news," she admitted, "but there are eight teams searching the Inisi system and surrounding space. The Federacy is committed to finding them."

The high-common woman flicked a strand of hair out of her face. "How long do they think that will take?"

"Frankly," Firebird said, "in an area that large, even if they can be found, it could take months or even years."

At an uncrowded spot near the tall windows, she was hailed by a man and woman, both tall and extremely thin, who carried themselves with aristocratic poise. Curtseying, she wracked her brain. She could have sworn she knew every member of all ten noble families. . . .

"Cometesse Verzy Remelard," the woman introduced herself, "and my husband, Comete Noche. Our home is on Luxia. We are ambassadors to Tallis."

Firebird had heard of the Luxian nobility, but these were the first she'd met. "Welcome to Citangelo," she said solemnly.

"Thank you. We have come to see you confirmed and to acquaint ourselves with our peers in the Netaian systems."

"You've had an opportunity to meet the regent, then," Firebird guessed. "As you entered."

They turned to each other. "Yes." The comete's mustache waggled as he spoke. "We weren't quite snubbed."

The cometesse turned to Brennen. "Has anything been heard about Her Majesty Iarla or Princess Kessaree?"

Distracted by a change of music, Firebird let Brennen answer. She seized a goblet of water from a passing servitor's tray. From this spot near the windows, she had a good view of the celebrants. Besides the occasional Sentinel infiltrator, she recognized many young nobles who had posed hazing threats to a wastling child. She had never felt truly safe from them until she enrolled at the Naval Academy. Heirs left military wastlings strictly alone.

The conductor's reedy voice caught her attention. "Noble electors, honored guests. We play tonight for His Grace, Regent for the Crown, and for Countess Esmerield . . . a lovely young girl, and this night—a woman."

As a triplette began, and Firebird reached toward Brennen's arm, a huge man passed between Firebird and the conductor. Firebird set down her goblet and stared. She had never thought to see long-faced Devair Burkenhamn again. Once the First Marshal of the Netaian Planetary Navy, he'd stood as a witness when she vowed away her allegiance to Netaia.

He had also signed Netaia's surrender.

He headed straight for her. "Marshal," she said softly, half curtseying. She felt Brennen and Uri ease closer. Taller than anyone else in the room and heavy with muscle, Burkenhamn projected disciplined power.

He grasped her hand and spoke softly, though his posture never loosened. "My lady, welcome back. His Grace will not be pleased if he sees us speaking. Call on me in person tomorrow, on base, for a few minutes. My secretary will admit you at any time." He strode on toward the refreshment tables.

Dumbfounded, Firebird tracked him. She had admired Marshal Burkenhamn, and he always treated her with respect. "We need to talk to him," she told Brennen. Even if Burkenhamn gave her a dressing-down for her failures at Veroh, he might help their present cause.

She felt Brennen's amusement rise.

"What?" she asked.

He inclined his head toward the dance floor.

Out on the glimmering marble surface, Esme Rogonin minced through the triplette's sweeping steps, engulfed in her father's arms. He moved ponderously, without regard for the beat. "Rogonin couldn't dance a triplette if he had three legs," Firebird muttered.

To her surprise, the couple finished their triplette near Tel, who lingered with his sister Triona and her husband, Count Winton Stele. Esme and her father bowed and curtseyed to each other, then turned simultaneously toward Tel.

"Do you think Tel needs help?" Firebird pivoted half aside, not wanting to stare, not wanting to lose sight of them. Rogonin laid Esme's hand on Tel's arm and backed away. The orchestra started a bourrée. "What is he up to?"

"Fishing," Shel suggested.

Brennen's eyes darkened. "Tel is under full voice-command," he reminded them. "He's safe from any 'fishing' attempts."

Firebird stared around the ballroom. Fifteen-year-old Grand Duke Stroud Parkai took the dance floor with Winton Stele's sister, Countess

Alia. Lace cuffs drooped over the young dandy's hands, and a matching jabot cascaded down his shirt front. Near those two, the elegant Duke of Kenhing swept his duchess into his arms. Firebird glimpsed Kenhing's dagger, this time with the slightest shudder. Muirnen Rogonin had tried to bring her just such a dagger when she'd been in protective custody on Tallis and the electors expected her to suicide.

She glanced over her shoulder at Shel. "Ready?" she asked.

Shel barely nodded.

She touched Brennen's arm. "The next triplette?"

He pursed his lips, then said, "You really want to do it this way."

She laid her gloved hand on his shoulder. "More than even you can imagine."

"All right," he said gently. "The next triplette. Until then, we need our backs to a wall, not a window."

Firebird nodded. She led the group to a section of floor between windows, again with a good view of the dance floor and Esme Rogonin.

Poor Tel.

Brennen winked, dimpling the scar on his cheek.

Tel couldn't escape the evening's honoree. This was too high an official obligation.

But perhaps it was a chance to chip at Esme Rogonin's shell, or at least to see how thick it was. He held her small hand with detached firmness.

She took his lead well, following through the bourrée's quick, light steps. After half a minute, she blurted, "Your Highness, may I ask an impertinent question?"

Now he was glad for the secret moments with Caldwell. "I will answer if I can," he said, smiling to himself at the double meaning.

Her lips crinkled. "You probably think Father ordered me to ask half a dozen questions."

"It occurred to me."

"Oh, he did. But I know you won't answer any of those. When we spoke last night, I should have asked if those mind-crawlers ever did anything to your brain."

Tel raised one eyebrow. A sort of fatal curiosity gripped Citangelo's nobility, but no one else had dared to ask. He liked Esme's courage. "I assume you mean General Caldwell."

She nodded. Her steady gaze assured him she really wanted to know . . . had Tel's mind been violated?

Thinking back almost five months, he steered her out of the path of Kenhing and his full-figured wife. "When I first arrived on Thyrica," he said, "General Caldwell was naturally afraid that I might have come intending to harm Lady Firebird. He did examine my intentions. He is . . . was . . . highly skilled."

"Mind-access," she said, frowning.

Tel nodded.

"I'm told it's uncomfortable."

"Certainly that." But unavoidable.

Esme glanced toward the Caldwell party, virtually ostracized between the tall windows. "Is he really as badly crippled as we've been led to believe?"

"Yes." Tel couldn't expect her to understand how tragic that was. "The Sentinels aren't evil, Esme. They are committed to serving other people, just in an unusual way. Just as you and I both are committed to serve Netaia, though we have different opinions about how best to do it."

Esme's hair, loosely coifed, rustled as she tossed her head. "Lady Firebird seems civil enough. Father says she killed Grand-Uncle in cold blood."

"Accidentally."

"Of course she says that."

"I'm convinced," Tel said.

"You've seen her in battle, I'm told. Does she enjoy killing people?"

"Not in the least."

"Hmm," Esme said. Her skirt swirled on the polished floor. "But wastlings are all a little unbalanced, aren't they?"

"If they are, Countess, we made them that way."

Her nose wrinkled in perfect court coquettishness. "Perhaps you've hurt wastlings. I've done nothing."

"If your conscience is clean, Esme, count yourself fortunate. Mine gives me no such peace. By refusing to insist on their safety, I am as guilty as . . . others," he said, squelching distasteful memories. "What are our true motives in demanding their deaths? Have you spent time with your little sister and brother? Do you want to see them die?"

"I have been taught to look the other way," she said tartly, "and so have you. That is only common decency."

The bourrée had nearly ended. He steered her toward the refreshment table and her father, glad to escape, wondering if he'd accomplished anything.

Scarcely pausing after the bourrée, the conductor swept up his baton and directed the opening chords of Firebird's favorite triplette. Those chords sang irresistibly. *You belong here. You are one of us. You were born to this.*

She seized Brennen's hand and tugged him toward the dance floor. "I assume," she murmured, "you watched the first triplette?"

His arm slipped around her waist, warm and steady, and he gripped her hand. "And I assume you haven't forgotten how."

"Not at all."

"Then close your eyes. Visualize dancing with someone very smooth."

The smoky-sweet tendril threaded into her mind. She back stepped onto the floor as if Brennen were leading. She felt him follow, felt his warmth press close. In her mind, he led her left in an arc (*Watch out for other couples, Brenn!*). His legs moved close to hers, perfectly synchronized.

Was this a dream, or was it really happening? Her eyes flew open, and she felt her cheeks cramp with the effort of smiling so broadly. Other couples had taken the floor, but several backed to the edge, standing, watching them.

"Concentrate, Mari," he whispered.

She grinned.

Shel didn't have to use Sentinel skills to see the rapture on Firebird's face. Her own memories wrenched her. She was no dancer, but years ago she and Wald had joined an open-hand drill club. Already pair-bonded, they relished the grips and the throws, the strikes and blocked punches. It had been very much a dance—

A newcomer distracted her. This young man, wearing velvette

knickers and cascades of ruffles on his pale green shirt, seemed ostentatious even for a Netaian aristocrat.

Then Shel caught a momentary blurring of his aquiline features.

Without hesitating, she sent Brennen a cautionary quest-pulse.

He paused in his dance step and followed her pointing finger toward the stranger, now standing at the dance floor's edge.

For one second, Shel clearly saw the intruder's curly black hair and a sharp, cleft chin—and the startled look in Brennen's eyes. Clutching Firebird's hand, he backed off the dance floor.

Shel picked a path that positioned her between Firebird and the newcomer. She reached into her ball gown's wide belt, seized and palmed her dart pistol, and slipped closer. Deadly risks didn't bother her. When the inevitable happened, she would simply join Waldron.

Brennen's pulse thundered. Cringing like a helpless ES 32 facing his executioner, he shielded his mind, and Mari's, with minimal energy.

It wasn't hard to fake panic for Micahel's sake.

Firebird clung to Brennen's hand. Uri sprinted toward them, and several women craned their necks to watch Uri. Two false servitors set down their trays and headed for exits, cutting off someone's escape. Brennen's handclasp shifted to a vise grip. He backed toward one of the windowed doors.

As the orchestra played on, her pulse did a full symphonic accelerando. *Where?* she thought at Brenn. *Where is he?*

Uri whipped an interlink from a pocket. Firebird followed Brennen's stare. At the back of her mind, his emotions had gone to knife-edge. With Muirnen Rogonin stood a thin young man in elegant knickers, staring back at her. He smiled, showing teeth. He didn't seem to see Shel, edging toward him around knots of socialites, or notice the servitors who had moved to the glass doors along the colonnade.

"Micahel Shirak. Side door. Now." Uri's hand went to Firebird's waist.

Aghast, she hustled to the nearest open door. This was the man who had murdered her niece—her nephews—their parents. She let Brenn tug her out into a chilly evening, but her hands clenched into fists. He led down three marble steps off the porch, then aside, out of the brilliant lumibeams on a glistening lawn. Uri took up a post near the door.

Over here, she urged silently. *This way, Shirak. One good shot with a dart pistol, and we have you.*

"You're not going back in there," she muttered to Brennen. "Not until somebody gets blocking drugs into him."

He drew his short-barreled pistol.

"Stay out here, Brennen," said Uri.

She seized Brenn's hand. "He'll shoot to kill, Brenn. It's your family he attacked."

A gust of wind tossed the fayya trees as Brennen pulled his hand out of her grip.

"If you go back, I'm going with you," she declared. "If he attacks, we might have to use fusion."

Finally, Brennen focused on her. "We can't do that in public."

She shook her head. "If your life's at stake, your orders mean nothing to me."

Firebird felt an unspecific rumble she'd learned to interpret as Brennen thinking quickly. Then he said, "Come on, then. Both of you."

Firebird eased along the exterior wall, back toward an open glass door. Capture if possible, kill if necessary. . . . *Come on, Shirak*, she thought at him. *Here we are. It all comes down to this.* She shivered.

Uri's shoulders went stiff. He shook his head and looked to Brennen.

Shel hurried out the door. Instantly, she turned toward them. Brennen backed against Firebird as if hiding her behind his body.

Shel reached them a moment later. "He got away," she said. "He ran out through the main entry, and we lost him."

Firebird drew a quick breath. "Did our people miss a door?"

Shel shook her head. "One's down. Shock pistol."

Was Micahel doubling back, then? Behind the curtained windows, richly dressed silhouettes stalked back and forth. "Hiding?" Firebird whispered. "Or gone?"

Straining to listen, she heard the soft buzz of small hovercraft approaching out of the south, probably more reinforcements from Governor Danton.

Uri stepped into the lights and held perfectly still.

"I can't tell," Shel said flatly. She turned her back and stared out into the night, on guard.

Firebird flattened her lips in frustration, then seized her skirt. The hem had turned dark with moisture from the lawn. Her feet felt clammy. "Good try, Shel," she said.

Brennen caught her hand. "Now we know they have camouflaging skills. We only suspected it before. We'll be able to seal the Hall of Charity better than this."

"He didn't even try to attack," said Firebird. "So what was he doing here?"

The hovercraft descended toward the festival square on the palace's south side. "I suspect," Brennen answered, "he came to check on me. On my disablement. The last time I saw him—"

"And you were dancing," she interrupted. "Linked with me. A thirty-two could do that."

"Ye-es. I didn't notice him until Shel alerted me," he admitted. To her surprise, she felt embarrassment behind his irritation. "If he was testing me, I probably passed—thanks to you."

She wriggled her damp toes, which were growing painfully cold. "We should report this to Danton's people. For us, the ball is over."

"We should do more than report." Brennen glanced up at the white marble facade. "This is no good anymore. Too many entrances, too many spies. We've made our statement. You do belong here, but I think they've found out we're too well guarded. Staying here any longer would only put you in unnecessary danger from Rogonin."

"You're right," she admitted, though it made her feel wistful. "We'll go back to the base and stay there—until tomorrow afternoon's rehearsal." She glanced up at the private wing's windows. She couldn't bear to walk past her old doors once more, knowing it could be the last time. "I'll have Paskel send over our things."

INTERLUDE 2

Light-years from Netaia on the Sentinels' sanctuary world, Carradee Angelo grasped her nephew's round little hand and counted off fingers. "One, two, three." Three days ago, Master Dabarrah had sent her request to Three Zed, diplomatically couched as an offer to open talks at a neutral site. Assuming it reached that system, and assuming someone might deal with her request, how many days would it take for a response to come back? Transport time, minimum, from here to Three Zed, was reportedly nine days. "Well, Master Nearly-a-Prince Kinnor Caldwell, it looks as if we shall need your toes." She reached for one foot. He shrieked with laughter, kicking and kicking.

Anna was probably right, though. Any response to her request would probably be deceitful.

Oh, my Kessie. Little Iarlet. Is someone holding you tonight? Do you sleep in medical stasis somewhere . . . or are you holding an angel's hand, exploring the hills of paradise? Every day the searchers found no trace, it was easier to believe there'd been a tragedy.

Little Kiel sat in the crook of Daithi's arm, nestled in the adjustable bed. Today, the scanbook gleaming on Daithi's lap was *Mattah*, the Sentinels' holy text. "'Dee," Daithi exclaimed, "listen to this. I've found another triple name for the deity. 'The Wisdom, the Love, the Power,' " he read. "How does that match the Shaliyah?"

Mistress Anna had spoken of the three ways God showed himself. "The Speaker . . . I suppose that would be Wisdom."

"I got that far," said Daithi. "But the other two don't fit quite as well."

"Power," Carradee mused. "That would have to be the Voice, wouldn't it? But that would leave Love as the Word, and . . . no, I think I have those backward. The Word they expect—the personal incarnation—is supposed to come in power. Some of their teachers say He will destroy evil wherever it exists. Some of them think the prophecies refer to more than one person, but one in particular." What a tremendously complex, majestic entity this god of theirs seemed to be. There would be no end of learning about Him, even if she lived forever.

Kiel gurgled loudly and reached for Daithi's chin.

"What would you know about that, little man?" Daithi asked his nephew.

Kiel babbled again. Carradee laughed, heart-happy. Like her girls, these babies spoke in full, unintelligible sentences long before their lips and tongues could form words. "Daithi," she said, "everything we've read, everything they've said about this deity rings true, even when I don't understand. There is a magnificence here, a grandeur beyond anything mere humans could have imagined." She laid Kinnor on the bed. Instantly he took off, scooting toward his brother and uncle. "They say there's a leap to make, trusting and blind," Carradee reflected. "I feel like leaping today."

Daithi dropped the scanbook on his bed sheets in time to save Kinnor from a tumble. "So do I," he said. "So does Kin, obviously."

Carradee pulled Kinnor back to her shoulder and rocked to her feet. Kin gurgled and kicked, demanding to be set back down. "I'll speak with Master Dabarrah," she said.

"Aaaaah!" That was Kiel's voice behind her.

She turned around quickly. "What did you do to that child?"

"Nothing," insisted Daithi. "He just bellowed. I don't think he's in pain."

Carradee eyed her nephew. The little boy did look blissfully happy. She smiled at her beloved husband and daredevil nephew. These twins were exceptional . . . something about them, perhaps their latent psionic abilities. *But no one will ever take my girls' place—except, maybe, you.* She found it amazingly natural to talk to someone she couldn't see, couldn't even comprehend. "We'll be back in a few minutes with Master Dabarrah," she told Daithi and Kiel. "Won't we, Lord Kinnor?"

INTERLUDE 3

The Inisi system, near the counterspinward edge of the Federate Whorl, had collected the usual amount of debris—long-dead prospecting probes, defunct satellites, and trash jettisoned by uncaring freighters or passenger haulers. Second Lieutenant Aril Maggard slipped into her seat on *Babb*'s crowded bridge and entered a tick mark at one corner of her com console. Major Charin Dunn had just relieved another search ship. Her crew of eight was buoyant, expectant. The diplomatic shuttle that Governor Danton had sent to Inisi, with the little Angelo girls and their servants on board, had carried emergency supplies for several weeks. Even after this long, it was quite possible that the transport crew and its passengers were alive, stranded by a malfunction, unable to answer hails.

Babb lurched as her pilot fired braking thrusters. "Almost on sector," he announced.

Aril activated her scanners and leaned over her tracking board. "Hang on, little ones," she whispered. "We'll find you."

Chapter 11
Ria

cotillion impromptu
a complex ballroom dance, with improvisation

Esme Rogonin lingered, watching musicians pack oddly shaped gear. Her father strolled back down the short flight of entry stairs, having seen their final guests through the doors. When she last checked the time, it had been just after three hundred. She hated to see the evening end. This had been almost pure pleasure. Even the Caldwells' indecorous exit kept her blissfully entertained.

Her father took her hand. "You were lovely tonight, Esme, and so gracious. Your mother and I are extremely proud."

She patted his arm. "I hope you got what you wanted from Lady Firebird. Dancing with Prince Tel was not what I came for."

Smiling, her father kissed her fingertips. He looked so grand in white. "We shall see," he said. "She disrupted a triplette for no reason I ever saw, and she has not returned to her rooms. Furthermore, we seem to have picked up a number of false servitors. The House Guard will be busy tonight, checking records."

Esme couldn't be bothered by servitor problems. She yawned. What a grand night—even her formal introduction to Netaia's most notorious wastling, a woman still technically sentenced to die if she lingered in Citangelo. Esme couldn't wish death by lustration on anyone. "I thought she was actually quite civil."

As rain spattered the tall windows, her father leaned back in a tired stretch. "She's biding time. She'll live up to her reputation, child. You'll see."

"She's pretty." Esme sniffed. "And spirited. I almost like her."

"She stands between us and the life we cherish, Esmerield. Between you and a fortune."

Firebird blinked hard. Why was the bedroom window over *there*?

Then she finished waking up. She lay beside Brennen on a bed half the size of Phoena's, in a bare off-white room. Late last night, base staff had escorted them to a small apartment with a view of the new Memorial Arch. This really was necessary, she guessed. Their first attempt to catch a Shuhr had failed. Their enemies were moving, and it wasn't difficult for starbred individuals to infiltrate palace staff.

She stretched, then looked across the pillow into Brennen's blue eyes. "Good morning," he said. "Could you manage an early start?"

"Something urgent?" she asked, feeling bleary. She could use one more hour of sleep, even though she had promised to drop in on Marshal Burkenhamn. "About last night, I suppose."

"Governor Danton wants to speak with me." She felt his regret like a warm cloth wrapped around her shoulders. "I suspect his call woke you up."

Firebird yawned. The electoral schedule makers had decreed that she should rest this morning, and for once she liked their choice. This afternoon there would be a rehearsal for her confirmation. "Ask for extra guards today." She heard Shel and Uri talking in the front room.

"I'll do that."

She threw off the gray bedcover and dropped her legs toward the floor.

Brennen busied himself in the freshing room. Firebird gazed out toward the spaceport and a rain-washed winter morning. An early passenger craft roared in, one of the flattened-oval Federate landers—dropping toward the field, bringing more people into Citangelo.

And more Shuhr?

Frowning, she fingered the coarse curtain. Defeating the Shuhr at Three Zed would require fusion, RIA, and everything else the Federacy could throw at them. Fusion still was the weak link in that chain, and she hated being the weak part of anything. While Brennen spoke with Lee Danton, she intended to sit in a lounge and do some more experimenting. Then they could speak to Burkenhamn together.

A guard waved their shuttle to a parking area near the new three-level command building's entry. As Shel steered into a slot, Brennen spotted the massive projection dish he'd seen on their first day on

Netaia. The scaffolding had been peeled away, revealing a honeycombed parabola, part of a new civic particle shield. *One more response to the Sunton catastrophe*, he observed. Downtown and in the suburbs, Danton's people were building more projectors.

Was Three Zed also bracing for war? he wondered. He left Firebird in a lounge, and an aide took him into the occupation governor's office.

Lee Danton stood at the side of his desk, in front of one of the broad windows. He rolled a cross-space message cylinder between his hands. An auxiliary bluescreen gleamed alongside his memfiles, and its glow cast a bluish light on the right side of his angular face. "Come in," he said.

Catching an uneasiness, Brennen dropped his epsilon shields. He and Danton had worked together during early occupation. He'd foiled four attempts on Danton's life before the angry Netaian separatists realized it was no use trying. He and Danton respected each other. Now either the governor believed in Brennen's disablement or he wasn't trying to hide his tension.

Pretending ignorance, Brennen took a wide stance at midfloor. "Good morning, Governor. Tell me how I can serve you."

Danton dropped the message roll onto his desk. "Sit down, Brennen. You can see I'm somewhat nervous."

Brennen took a side chair near the memfiles. "I hope I can reassure you."

"Mm." Still standing, Governor Danton touched the message roll. "Four hours ago, my aide received a scan cartridge by special courier. According to cover information, the original was sent to Regional command from Thyrica."

Now he was thoroughly puzzled. "Yes?"

"The cartridge contained an eyes-only memo concerning research that has been conducted at Hesed House and at Sentinel College, regarding a phenomenon they're calling 'epsilon fusion.' "

Caught off guard, Brennen reached toward Danton's auxiliary bluescreen. Then he saw the pulsing red light on its control surface. He jerked back his hand.

"What is it?" Danton stepped closer.

Embarrassed, Brennen inhaled slowly. "Forgive me. I came back from Three Zed with some illogical fears. Red light is one of them." At the back of his mind, he was already thrusting down wounded pride, examining his mental state for too much self-confidence. *Power and might are in your hand, Holy One. No one can stand against you.*

"I could cover the panel."

Unshielded, Brennen felt Danton's embarrassment like a fainter echo of his own. "No, I'm all right. It just startled me." *My peace is in you, Eternal One, and you are my power.* Sentinels were trained in emotional control.

He placed his thumb over the indicator light.

The memo was indeed eyes-only, thank the One. "It's our best chance to strike back against Three Zed," Brennen said after skimming the address and heading codes.

"You and Lady Firebird."

"Yes."

Danton took a step closer. "Now I see why you both might have to leave on a moment's notice. Go ahead, read. Then you'll know what we're free to discuss."

Brennen scanned quickly. The memo explained that the fusion phenomenon seemed to rise out of Firebird's oddly polarized epsilon carrier wave. It did not say she'd killed two assailants, but it mentioned concern that the Shuhr could have taken genetic specimens from Princess Phoena, and that they might breed individuals capable of this kind of fusion.

That research was one more reason Brennen dreaded those sealed orders. In light of those programs, he might be ordered to sterilize Three Zed down to bare rock. His ancestors had already destroyed one world.

He turned back to Danton. "You didn't call Firebird in."

Danton stroked his chin. "I'm half afraid to."

"It doesn't happen accidentally." Brennen pointed out the paragraph that explained its near-fatal effects on Firebird Mari. Missing was any mention of the scar tissue accumulating cell by cell inside the ayin complex at the middle of her brain. Naturally, the Federacy worried less than he did . . . about that and about the self-focus that had seemed to infect her when she put on that confirmation costume. He'd paid dearly for his own self-reliance. He wanted to spare her from that kind of disciplining.

"I would hope," said Danton, "that by using RIA, coupled with this other development, the Federacy can move quickly against Three Zed."

"As soon as we know how to take down their fielding team, we can get close enough to slip effective payloads past their particle defenses."

"Finding that out is half of your mission here, as I recall."

"Besides getting a handle on their long-range plans."

"And appeasing Councilor Kernoweg's crusade to see Netaia covenant to the Federacy. I don't suppose your Shuhr hosts exactly took you on a tour of their fielding unit," Danton observed.

Brennen heard and felt the good humor creeping back into Danton's mental stance. "If they did," he confessed, "I've forgotten."

Danton winced. "Understood. I was hoping that your disablement is . . . somewhat less than is being publicly reported."

It wasn't really a request for information, and Brennen didn't volunteer any. Until they had a Shuhr captive, he would not tell one more soul his actual ES rating. "Thank you, Lee. I wish I could tell you I'm fine, but I'm not . . . as you just saw." He slid his thumb off the pulsing red light.

Danton stroked his chin. "With the kind of power this fusion report implies, no other authority in Federate service will be able to control you and Lady Firebird. Some will want to separate you."

"Lee, the same vows that protect you from capricious use of an RIA apparatus—"

Danton cut him off. "Sometimes those vows are no control over your people. You do swear loyalty to your kindred above loyalty to the Federacy."

Brennen studied the governor's face, feeling no hint of sympathy. "That is the vow," he agreed.

Silence dampened the air. The Federacy barely trusted his people. That had been one major argument against revealing RIA to the Federacy, and this new development made him and Firebird, personally, into potential threats.

"We could demonstrate fusion at your convenience."

The governor exhaled. "Thank you, that won't be necessary. How can I facilitate your strike at Three Zed?"

Brennen relaxed into his chair. "My orders are sealed. I'm assuming they are to strike, but I will open them only when we have that prisoner."

Danton stared off into space for several seconds. "Is Lady Firebird fighter-rated for Federate ships?"

"No. She and I would fly together. Thyrian fighter-trainers are notoriously underpowered, but—"

Danton leaned toward his com panel. "Maybe," he said, "I could give you one more option." He touched the panel. "Major Harthis, give me Marshal Burkenhamn's office."

Firebird sat in the third-floor observation lounge, ignoring the view. She was distracted by wondering what Governor Danton wanted with Brennen.

Hearing footsteps, she looked up. Beyond a cluster of angular, upholstered chairs, a man came striding up the corridor. He wore Netaian cobalt blue trimmed in red. In the next instant, she caught a red glitter on his collar, the ruby stars of a first major—her own former rank in what seemed like another life. She'd been so proud to wear that uniform.

He marched into her lounge. Shel sprang up.

Firebird rocked onto her feet. Even if she'd been in uniform, she couldn't have saluted. She'd been dishonorably discharged as soon as the Netaian Planetary Navy learned she was captured instead of killed at Veroh. She was lucky they hadn't court-martialed her, too. Evidently her electoral trial sufficed for all offenses.

"Lady Firebird," said the major, "Marshal Burkenhamn wants to speak with you. I'll take you downlevel to his office."

Shel stepped forward. "Is that office secure, Major?"

"Yes. You're also welcome to escort her, naturally."

Firebird glanced from one to the other. Of all places on Netaia, this base was probably the safest for her. Still, it was good to see that Shel took nothing for granted.

They rode the lift back downlevel. As she walked up the corridor with the major on one side and Shel on the other, she composed a formal apology. If ever she felt guilty about betraying Netaia during the Veroh war, Burkenhamn's was the face she'd seen. At Tallis, he had helped save her life by refusing to endorse a proposed execution—and she'd promptly snubbed him by taking Federate transnationality.

He'd accepted a position under the occupation government, so maybe he wasn't entirely anti-Federate.

A windowed door, lettered NETAIAN FORCES—MARSHAL BURKENHAMN, slid open. "He'll see you immediately." The major stroked a panel on the clearing room's desk, and a second door opened.

Firebird glanced at Shel, squared her shoulders, and walked in.

Behind a red-grained leta-wood desk, Devair Burkenhamn was rising to his feet. Something whirred on his desk top, spewing hard copy. The silver fringe of hair behind his ears seemed thinner than before, and she saw deeper lines between and over his eyes. He extended a huge hand, and she clasped it over piles of scan cartridges, chip stacks, and more hard copy, the typical flood of administrative busywork.

"Good morning, sir. You asked to speak with me."

He sat down, and as she took the opposite chair, she flattened her hands in her lap. Marshal Burkenhamn must make the first move in this new, awkward game. She'd always been his student and very junior officer.

Though he was one of the few Netaians whose body couldn't tolerate anti-aging implants, he remained superbly trim, his broad shoulders looking as solid as ever. "Lady Firebird," he began, then he paused. If he'd addressed her as "Major," she might've expected a reprimand. But calling her by her title seemed conciliatory. "I said this last night, but I mean it sincerely. Welcome back."

She hated to humble herself like this, but she had to. "Marshal, the last time we faced each other, I—"

Burkenhamn waved a broad hand. "I wish to discuss the future, not the past. Would you be so kind as to say nothing about previous events?"

Relieved, Firebird sat straighter. "As you wish, sir. I would like to be numbered among those who support you wholeheartedly."

Burkenhamn smiled sidelong. "That is refreshing to hear. I tried to help with the . . . disturbance last night. I'm afraid I accomplished nothing."

She hadn't read a follow-up report yet. "Thank you for trying, Marshal." Oh, the memories this man's long face and rich baritone brought back! "I'm sure you made an impression."

He spread his broad hands. "Please, let me explain why I called you here."

She nodded formally.

"Governor Danton has just asked me to offer back your fighter-rated status in the restored Planetary Navy."

He couldn't have immobilized her more effectively with a shock pistol. After four or five seconds too long, she found her voice. "Marshal, I'm . . . I have commitments. I couldn't accept a military position here."

"I'm not sure I understand Danton's request." Burkenhamn half smiled. "He asked in confidence, and I must assume your bodyguard is also sworn to silence."

"Yes, but—"

"Your husband's name was also on the request," said Burkenhamn. "Governor Danton implied that this has something to do with our general assumption that Sentinel forces are being assembled for a possible strike."

"Oh," she said softly, and her mind whirled forward. If she were fighter-rated, she and Brenn could each fly into fielding range. That would give them the combined power of two RIA units. "Maybe the Federates would like to have all Federate worlds represented, even an occupied one, in any case," she suggested. She couldn't confirm his guess. He wasn't directly involved, and officially, no such order existed yet. "What fighter, sir?"

"The governor sent down simulator training materials for something called a Thyrian Light-Five. Are you familiar with it?"

"I've seen them. Federate cockpits are engineered to standard specs." But every fighter would respond differently. She would need sim time.

"Very well." He rested his elbows on the desk. Old habits made her answer his gesture by coming to seated attention. "I would also like to take Danton's request one step further. I want to offer you a field promotion . . . an honorary title, more or less. If you accept, it will become public knowledge."

One of her hands did an involuntary flutter in her lap. "Go on," she murmured.

"Your discharge has already been canceled, by my order. I want to offer you the rank of second commander, subject to eventual approval by the First Naval Council."

She felt her eyes widen. That was a full rank, probably three years of service, above the first majority.

"I will present it to the electors as a symbolic gesture." His stiff back relaxed. "If Netaia can only send one soldier against Three Zed, we should be proud to send our best. Firebird, you acquitted yourself honorably at Veroh."

"Sir," she managed, "thank you, but from the standpoint of Netaian honor, I failed miserably at Veroh."

"I disagree." He leaned away from her. Trying to look casual, she guessed. "Governor Danton only asked that I get you rated for that particular fighter, which would automatically make you Federate personnel. If you prefer, you may accept the rating at a lower rank."

Firebird took a closer look at his cobalt-blue uniform. Sure enough, the Federate slash had been added over his breast. "You know me too well for that, Marshal."

"Yes, I do. You were one of the few high achievers who consistently gave more than necessary. If you accept my offer, that will only improve Netaia's standing with Regional command. As a transnational citizen, you will represent both Citangelo and the Federacy."

How thrilling! But . . . *This promotion feels like a temptation, Mighty Singer. Is it?* "Appointing me commander of whom?" she asked carefully. "Sir, I have family commitments. I will not choose to leave my children to serve a tour of duty." Leaving them for a little while was hard enough.

Burkenhamn leaned against one armrest of his chair. "You've seen heirs take honorary positions."

"Well, yes." Here on base, she had trouble thinking of herself as an heir. Heirs who wanted to wear a uniform were given an empty rank and a few speeches to make. Wastlings trained at the Naval Academy. They saw front-line combat and died.

"Your real experience would be valuable in a training and liaison capacity . . . and, yes, in our reserve defenses. Tallis is letting us reestablish an active force, but I'm only a figurehead. You'd be more effective in that role, especially after your confirmation. I've made arrangements for heirs' occasional reserve schedules. I would find it a pleasure to do that for you."

Firebird's mind sprinted ahead. What if civil war erupted? With a military rank, she might actively shorten the conflict. She could only imagine the ballads that might be sung about the wastling who saved Netaia.

"Marshal Burkenhamn," she said solemnly, "for two years, I've suffered whenever I thought of you. I owe you a debt of honor."

Burkenhamn extended his hand. "Then you accept?"

His fingers surrounded her palm. She gripped the edge of his hand with her fingertips. "Yes, Marshal. Thank you." *Second Commander.* Picturing three gold moons on her cobalt blue uniform collar, she couldn't help smiling. *Commander Caldwell!* Or would they call her *Angelo*?

Terza Shirak sat at a servo table, staring out the window, feeling like a neglected pet—or a breeding animal. Her father's apartment had several sleeping rooms off a short hall, but she spent much of her time in this south-facing dining area. Her appetite had returned with a voracious vengeance. Ever since leaving the Golden City, she'd done nothing but swell. Others might not notice the signs of her pregnancy, but to her they were becoming obvious. She felt like one of the ceremonial kiprets that her overzealous ancestors used to fatten and then butcher for sacrifice. She missed her station in Adiyn's laboratory, her wombbanks to tend, her cultures to fertilize and check. She had loved achievement, exercising her own small control over the next generation. She missed the Golden City.

She glanced down. The only visible mark of her . . . pregnancy (she still hated the word) . . . was the tight fit of her clothing, especially her shirts. But its chemical effect on her brain astonished her. Though her father still frightened her, she felt a growing sense of familial identity, of pride to be called by his father-name. If he'd shown any sign of returning that pride, she would be sleeping easier. Also, the mundane touch of human skin had become almost a fetish, the softest, most appealing texture imaginable. She kept close control on that notion. Preoccupation with the physical was vulgar.

She pressed both hands to her middle. For all the discomfort she would have to endure, she wanted some return . . . some assurance that her embryo would thrive.

Her embryo? Half the chromosomes, maybe. But the zygote, like all subadults, belonged to Three Zed colony.

She felt less certain of that every day. Making a gestational mother of her had been Modabah Shirak's mistake, if he hoped to maintain her objectivity.

Maybe he didn't. Maybe he meant to sacrifice her. Again she thought of the half-witted creatures her ancestors took to Ehret's great temple.

Cautiously, she looked around the dining area and lounge. One of her father's dozen lackeys bent over the servo, ordering a preprogrammed Netaian specialty. Another stood close to the view window, reading something on a recall pad. Across the living area, on a long animal-hide lounger, her father sat with another stranger, who was describing Netaia's cultural museums.

If the man could have guessed Modabah's intentions for the contents of those museums, he might not have come to this apartment. But once inside, under voice-command to speak freely, he might as well deliver the artworks.

She frowned, pitying all Netaians. Juddis Adiyn had remained on Three Zed, but he would travel here sooner or later. Once her people had the Sentinels' RIA technology in hand, they could take control of Netaia's resource base.

Then Adiyn could expand his staff and set about modifying the planet. Three Zed retained centuries-old genetic weapons that had already sterilized one world of human life, but her grandfather's long plan had been superseded by Adiyn's. Here, Terza might be ordered to assist in the release of other agents, viral organisms that would infect all Netaians, turning them into carriers for whatever genes Adiyn selected.

Early die-off would come first, naturally. Their altered descendants wouldn't need to fight another war, like the one that devastated Ehret. That had been a hard lesson.

Brennen Caldwell, who would give them the key RIA technology, had been carried in some starbred mother's womb. Lady Firebird had been a noblewoman's child, though not a cherished offspring. How could these "nobles" sentence their own named youths to die, simply to preserve their wealth? It was bad enough in the Golden City, where inferior or dangerous youngsters *must* be eliminated.

Mustn't they? Now she wondered if she could still approve even that. Infecting an entire world's population, even with an eye to their descendants' immortality, no longer sounded generous.

She had to hope Micahel succeeded in the Great Hall and took Caldwell down. If that option failed, her father might use her next—to dangle as bait.

Micahel reported to his father's apartment after stopping midtown for a noon meal. Netaian food, fresh and varied, did impress him.

Modabah sat slumped over the servo table, eyeing its inset bluescreen. He must have sent Terza and his crewers away. Only Talumah sprawled on the lounger.

"So," said the Eldest, "no fatalities reported at the Rogonin ball. Did you have an off night?"

"I accomplished what I set out to do." Micahel straddled a stool, putting the sun at his back. "I tested his defenses. They had more support than I expected."

"What about Caldwell's powers?"

"He actually reacted as a thirty-two would," Micahel admitted. "I could have killed him. He didn't even see me arrive. He was *dancing*," he sneered. "Making love in public. If Talumah had gotten closer, he'd be ours."

"So it's Talumah's fault?" Modabah swept one hand over inset controls, darkening the bluescreen. "I'm still surprised you didn't leave a few bodies."

"Too much support," Micahel repeated. He'd been grabbed by a huge Netaian man—a long-faced, balding military type—and flung bodily toward a wall. He'd barely stopped his flight in time to keep from being knocked senseless. He had fled, irked to find Talumah outside and unhurt.

"How did they stop you?"

He would *not* mention the big Netaian. But he would have revenge. *All right, I had an off night.* Micahel switched to subvocal speech, with its implied subservience and layers of emotional overlay. *They were waiting for us. They were prepared.*

"They'll be prepared at the Hall of Charity," his father pointed out.

There, we expect them to be prepared. A kill is easier than a capture.

You could wire the headpiece, Ard Talumah insisted from across the room. Micahel glanced toward the lounger. Talumah hadn't even opened his eyes. All along, he'd wanted to redesign the confirmation tiara with miniature explosives, sensitive to body heat. Blowing the woman's head off by remote would terrorize Netaia. With Sentinels so nearly involved in its government, that could throw all sorts of suspicions. Possibly set a large Federate element against Thyrica.

"No," Modabah called over his shoulder. "Not the tiara. Standing close, Caldwell could sustain injuries."

"She's mine, Talumah." Micahel shifted. Sun on his back, even weak winter sun, felt strange. "With the lady dead and Caldwell in shock, with the side entrance covered . . . we'll take him." The public press could be counted upon to sear images on the public mind, images that would prepare Netaia for its regent's capitulation to Modabah. Micahel grabbed a bottle off the servo counter, poured a glass of joy-blossom wine, and raised it. "And this time, we'll keep him."

Talumah sat up on the lounger. "Then I have another contribution. One of my suppliers just dropped off a multifrequency disruption grid. I think you could use it."

CHAPTER 12

PERFORMER

ballade

a composition suggesting the epic ballad

Firebird's simulator screen faded to gray, and she exhaled hard, relieved to know she hadn't lost all her reflexes.

Someone stood beside her booth, and she felt a welcome presence. She refocused her eyes on the real world.

"Second Commander," Brennen said gently. "Congratulations. Marshal Burkenhamn reported back to Governor Danton while I was still there." He extended a hand, and she grasped it, leaning on him to unfold herself out of the booth. "What are your orders?" he asked.

"For the moment, I'm only rated to start training again." She hadn't wasted a minute, either. She pulled her hair out of the catch at the nape of her neck. "But step by step," she murmured, "we're getting closer to Three Zed."

—And its planetary fielding team. No matter how thoroughly she trained, fielding operators could attack the areas of an interloper's mental matrix that responded with the deepest torments of fear.

Still, she had some confidence in her ability to endure terror. She'd already faced the darkest side of herself. What was left to fear?

Firing on friendly forces, for one thing. Or if they couldn't terrorize her, they could try to drive her insane. If she had to lay down her life there, so be it. But if they stole her sanity . . .

Better not to think about that. She peeled out of the heavy life suit Danton's people had issued for sim use. "And you?" she asked.

Brennen reported on Danton's fusion memo.

"Sounds to me," she said as she returned the life suit to an adjoining locker, "that he took it rather calmly."

"He's nervous." Brennen glanced out the nearest door. Beyond several other sim booths that were closed down for use, Firebird spotted one of their plainclothes guards.

"The Shuhr haven't missed a chance," Firebird said. "It could be an exciting rehearsal."

"They haven't seriously tried yet," Brennen answered. "When they do, we'll know."

She frowned. "I want a bath before the rehearsal."

He slid one finger under his collar. "Actually, so do I."

They hurried back to the apartment.

Shortly, a large car with base markings pulled up outside the housing unit, and Shel and Uri escorted them to the vehicle. Four Tallans in ash gray uniforms, sidearms prominent on their belts, rode along this time. Two additional cars served as outriders on each side. Brennen sat silently, watching the roadside pass.

He'd sent a decoy car ten minutes ahead. Along Port Road traffic flowed smoothly, with no sign of any disturbance.

He frowned. His agents still had no luck finding the Shuhr's nest. Shirak and his compatriots could hide and shield themselves too well to be found that way. They must be lured in.

He glanced up at the clear sky. There was probably enough Federate force deployed here to prevent a suicide strike, even if more Shuhr arrived with an attack group.

No, the confrontation would be personal, and he guessed he knew when it would come.

At the Hall's security blockhouse stood a line of groundcars, their doors marked with House insignia. From several vehicles marked with the crimson Angelo-starred shield, staffers unloaded long, stiff bundles, covered trays, and crates and boxes of all sizes. Uniformed security guards examined the bundles.

Firebird stepped out of the base car between Shel and Uri. A line of servitors steered laden carts toward the tunnel entry while Enforcers in city black stood sentry. The servitors stepped aside and let her group board the lift.

As an inquisitive child, Firebird had explored the downlevel tunnel while others thought she was obediently discussing Charities with her

Discipline group. She hurried along, sensing Brennen's disquiet as they passed storerooms, sacristies, and vestries. He too must be badly distracted if the narrow tunnel was bothering him.

Up a stair, through the broad narthex, then down a long straight aisle. Nearly thirty people already stood at the foot of the sanctum. She didn't see Muirnen Rogonin, but she did spot midnight blue figures at several stations.

"Good." First Lord Erwin straightened slightly, and his voice rang out in the nave. "Here you are at last. Gather close, please."

Shel led to the front. Firebird mounted five steps to the stage-like sanctum, then glanced back again. Servitors worked in teams, using telescoping booms to hang wide streamers of scarlet velvette from the sloping side balconies and spiraling them around gilded columns. Twenty-two of those pillars lined the side aisles, then pierced the balconies, to split treelike and form limbs of gold tracery.

Other men and women, at least twenty of them, sat and watched the servitors. More Federates, she realized. *Thank you, Governor.* Shel and Uri had unquestionably dropped their shields to listen for any hostility, too. But in Brennen she still sensed the faint underlying panic.

Gold, she understood. The nave was full of it.

Memories leaped out as if they'd hidden between pews, images that had remained lost to him until this moment.

. . . Golden corridors, with ceilings that arched close overhead. A lanky, black-haired man with lashless eyes walked at his elbow. . . .

. . . A tiny black room with pitted walls, its door a glossier black shadow. A single white lamp hung over his head, and he lay on a narrow black shelf. . . .

. . . Another face, younger, eyes brimful of hate. A firm mouth, a cleft chin . . .

Micahel.

His throat constricted, and breath came hard. He'd studied chapters and chapters of scripture that he once could've called instantly to mind. He'd come across one that must have been a favorite, from the number of marginal notes he'd made:

I will be with that remnant.

I will refine and test them as meteor steel
And make them a sword in my hand.

Loose sword, he found in his own penmanship, *useless. Effective only in His hand.*

He had to fall into the Holy One's power when terror unbalanced him. He could not fight these irrational fears alone. Deliberately, he relinquished himself—and the situation—to One whose strength was broad and deep.

Then he could breathe more easily. He eyed the high golden ceiling with a practiced eye. During this rehearsal, his own forces would run a final surveillance from assigned positions—at exits, or seated where they could wield scanning imagers, behind tapestries.

He would have that ceiling, those tapestries, and every individual who entered the Hall thoroughly checked. Intercepting an assassin "in-coming" would be the ideal scenario.

Catching one during the ceremony—an agent with enough tricks and abilities to penetrate his perimeter—might be dramatic, but at this point the idea had considerably less appeal.

Firebird faced forward again. Ornately carved seating boxes surrounded the sanctum's main stage. Behind them, in corners along the front wall, two musicians sat at banks of keys, panels, foot pedals, levers, and sliders. The Hall's organum wall could drown out a full choral orchestra or fill the nave with soft, meditative strains. She wished she'd been consulted on the choice of music. . . .

Then she changed her mind. Distracted by a favorite march or air, she might stop paying attention. It would take only a moment to unbalance their fragile trap and let Micahel Shirak take his bait.

She sidestepped closer to Brennen and frowned up at the statuary. She couldn't remember, because she had never noticed, how much of a part the graceless Netaian faith had played in Phoena's confirmation. It hadn't mattered back then. Centuries ago, the Netaian government deliberately corrupted its people's faith. Now it mattered very much.

The stooped first lord read a few lines, then set down his recall pad. Firebird listened, reluctantly impressed, as he recited her lineage from Conura I to her mother without glancing at the pad. ". . . who bore to

Netaia four daughters: Carradee Leteia Authra, Lintess Chesara Solvé, Phoena Irina Eschelle, and Firebird Elsbeth, Lintess and Phoena now deceased."

Firebird barely remembered Lintess. The family had lost her in a childhood accident, but even then, Firebird suspected Phoena. If only she'd been stopped as a youngster and disciplined. How might their lives have been different?

Firebird would never know. *Only one Path*, her instructor had said, *can be walked or understood.*

First Lord Erwin turned to her, and she shook off memories. "You who stand in the sanctum to be confirmed, tell your name and your lineage, and your right to stand here."

She cleared her throat and raised her head. "I am Firebird Elsbeth," she said, "and you have told my lineage."

"Yes, good." The ceremonials director stepped forward. "But keep your body straight ahead. Try that again."

Firebird compressed her lips, came to military attention, and repeated her line.

"Better." The director stepped back. "All right. Continue, Baron Erwin."

"At this point," he said, "I make a rather long speech that my writers haven't finished. I end with the big question, Lady Firebird. Here it is. Will you stand ready to serve, should the high calling to which you are now declared an heiress ever fall to you?"

"And I answer," Firebird said firmly, "I live to serve Netaia." A five-year-old could master that declaration. During the ceremony, though, she meant to change a few words. From *live* to *hope*, and from *Netaia* to *Netaia's people*. She *hoped* to serve *Netaia's people*. Small words were important.

"Then I reach around," said the director, "to the table, for the tiara. You will kneel."

Firebird back stepped into a deep curtsey. She took it deeper yet, then dropped one knee onto the carpet. Once steady, she dropped the other knee. This would be awkward in costume.

Baron Erwin pantomimed laying his hands on her head, sliding the tiara into place over her hair.

"In the holy names of Strength, Valor, and Excellence," intoned the baron—

Firebird jerked her head up. Baron Erwin droned on, asking a complex blessing in the names of all nine holy Powers. To Firebird, it sounded like a curse. She'd spent much of her life flaunting insignificant Netaian traditions. This no longer seemed insignificant.

She must speak with Baron Lord Erwin. Surely he could be reasonable about shifting a word here and there.

He finished.

"Questions?" asked the director.

Now, urged a voice at the back of Firebird's mind. *Object!*

She hesitated. She'd already disrupted Esme's ball. If she spoke up now, there could be a loud, unnecessary fight.

No. Now.

"May we talk about that blessing?" Firebird stared hard at the baron. "Later tonight?"

He nodded slightly, pursing his lips. "And I have a question for you, Lady Firebird. Do you intend to disrupt this ceremony and disgrace us, or have you finally accepted your role in Netaian society?"

"If there are disruptions," she said carefully, "they will not come from me or the Federates."

He glared at Brennen. "General, I demand your word of honor that your people will not use this solemn occasion to further their own agenda."

"The Federacy," Firebird interrupted, "asked that I accept this invitation. They will not—"

"General," snapped Erwin. "Your word."

Brennen's hand clenched down at his side. "I will protect Lady Firebird with my life if necessary. Otherwise, I will be silent and decorous. You have my word."

"See to it."

And maybe, just maybe, the Shuhr wouldn't show up. Brenn had mentioned putting a decoy team in the motorcade to the Hall.

The director stepped forward, clasping her hands over the front of her white gown. "After the recessional, we will motorcade back to House Angelo. There will be a formal luncheon. Lady Firebird, you will be given your heir name and make gifts to your chosen charities."

She nodded. Heirs had two middle names, and the second usually honored one of the Powers. She hoped the pageantry committee had been kind. She'd requested *Mari* instead.

"There will be time for all celebrants to rest after the luncheon," the director continued. "Dinner in the main hall for electoral families—"

Firebird was not looking forward to that.

"—and the day will end with the confirmation ball."

Finally, finally! Compared with other concerns, this was insignificant, but she still hoped to finish that dance with Brennen before heading to Three Zed. Let this trap spring successfully, and Rogonin wouldn't dare accuse her of sedition. She'd be a hero.

Don't forget, she reminded herself. *Only the Electorate can save Netaia.*

Riding back to base, she spotted five Enforcers on street corners. She'd never seen so much patrol activity.

Maybe His Grace was nervous.

She leaned against Brennen's shoulder. "I suppose they expect me to retire early that night, exhausted."

"You will be," said Brennen. "Or else you'll be shipboard."

"I wonder," she murmured, still later as she eyed a stack of luggage, delivered to their four-room apartment on base, "if our exalted ceremonials director or Lord Erwin have any idea who really might disrupt the ceremony."

"They'll be warned tomorrow night and informed of our precautions. No point frightening them any sooner than necessary."

Twice during Firebird's evening session with law advisors, who read her every regulation that concerned her conduct as a potential elector, she halted the proceedings. She hurried to the base lounge's CT link, called House Erwin, and asked to speak with the baron. The first time, he'd gone out to dine. The second time, he'd gone to bed.

At nineteen hundred? *His youth implant must've expired*, she fumed as she returned to the briefing room. Brennen raised an eyebrow. She shook her head, then turned to her second counsel. "Go ahead," she said. She still had all day tomorrow to reach Erwin.

When the counselors finally finished, she flicked the CT board again and found a call from Clareen Chesterson, the bassist. "Firebird," the singer said, "there's a sing at Nello's tonight. Can you get away?"

The message ended.

"Nello's?" Brennen raised a dark eyebrow.

Dozens of memories rushed back. "Most nights, it's a factory warehouse. But a group uses it for impromptu concerts, very much frowned on by the noble class. Wonderful music, with the heart of a world in it. Exactly the kind of place where . . ." She halted. Really, there was no use hoping to do this. The Shuhr had proved they weren't waiting for the ceremony. "I used to go to Nello's every chance I got," she said wistfully.

"You'd like to go tonight."

"Of course. But it would be foolish." She could've been among real people, common folks. "There's no point trying to make it a trap, though. Too many bystanders, too little advance warning."

She felt his amusement.

"But there might be one thing we could accomplish," she realized, and suddenly the risk seemed worthwhile.

"What?"

Firebird leaned against the windowbar. "I've discovered something more profound and real than the nine holy Powers—"

"Mari." Brennen frowned. "I know you haven't been vested, but it's still not allowed to proselytize, unless someone inquires—"

"I'm not even Thyrian—"

"You have Ehretan ancestry. You've been consecrated in the faith, and you have epsilon powers—"

"What powers? I can barely quest-pulse."

His eyebrows lowered. He covered his mouth with one hand, and she felt his intense disapproval. "You and I, together, have an ability that—"

"I want to help my people, Brennen—"

"Of course you do. How do you think we feel about other Thyrians? Even some of the Shuhr probably aren't beyond redemption. But we are commanded. If others inquire, then we can tell them what we believe. Otherwise," he said, gently prodding her chest, "you would have heard plenty before you ever set foot on Veroh."

Irked, she stood staring at him, working one finger against the side of her thumb. Even when she experienced his emotions, she didn't always agree with them.

His voice softened. "If you cannot obey our codes, we cannot train you. Obedience is all that sets us apart from the Shuhr. This command will change, one day when we've learned patience."

"I could sing to them," she insisted. "There's no commandment against performing an old ethnic hymn. Is there?"

He shook his head, still unsmiling. She could almost feel him thinking, *Pride, willfulness, impatience.*

She did recall how patiently he had waited for her to ask about the faith. He hadn't broken his codes, not even for her sake, not even when he desperately wanted her to ask.

She ought to feel honored, by an honorable man. Still, she would like to have known more—sooner.

Maybe she could arrange for Clareen's Chapter house to be built in Citangelo. She would soon have an heir's allowance.

Abruptly, she realized that Clareen would be there tonight, and Clareen was under no prohibitions.

Getting off base proved simpler than leaving the palace. Brennen enlisted a Federate aide, who drove a midsized groundcar to a quiet street, then parked and walked back to the base. Five minutes later, Firebird pulled off the blanket that covered her and looked around from the backseat. "We're clear, Shel. I'll direct you from here."

In an urban area that smelled of industry, at the back of a brown-brick commercial plant, Uri softly voice-commanded a watchman to turn aside. Firebird led the way in.

Two hundred people, most of them dressed in drab, working-class coveralls, sat in chairs or on the floor, surrounding two singers and a lutenist. They were performing a love song Firebird hadn't heard in two years. Months and light-years retraced themselves. Now she marveled at how well the lyrics described Brennen. Some of her irritation with him flowed away.

She edged toward a short stretch of standing room along a wall. The cavernous room smelled of sweetsmoke and sweat. Shel's eyes didn't stop moving, and Brennen's emotions were at fever alert. They couldn't stay long.

The song ended. As the last chord faded, a man jumped to his feet. "Firebird!"

Again, the stares were like targeting lasers . . . this time, friendly ones. Shouts of "Welcome back," and "Sit here," and "Introduce your friends," echoed through Nello's back room. Someone tugged Firebird to the trio's chairs. Shel squeezed forward with her and sat down. Uri and Brennen—dressed in black civilian clothing—stood thirty degrees apart, along the wall. A high-headed small harp was passed hand over hand to the front.

"Introduce your friends," somebody called again.

The place stilled. Its high, smooth ceiling gave it a lively, bright acoustic presence she remembered well.

Most of these people had seen few offworlders, and never a telepath. "This is Shel Mattason," Firebird said. "She's . . . well, I don't go anywhere without her this week."

Laughter bounced out of one corner. Someone asked, "Can she sing?"

Shel glanced left and right, looking no less intense in her casual white pullover than in uniform. "I have no sense of pitch."

Uri extended an arm, calling, "I don't sing, either. But I enjoy listening—and it's my job to watch."

"And this is my husband," Firebird said steadily. Brennen took a short step away from the dark gray permastone wall. He *could* sing. She loved his light, pleasant tenor. Her musical training intimidated him, though, and he rarely sang in her presence . . . except at Chapter. "Brennen Caldwell saved me from a wastling's death. He has given me hope, and love, and shown me how very much more there is to the universe than I found inside palace walls. We have two beautiful sons." What else, what more could she tell them? Brennen had been Danton's strong man, lieutenant governor for the occupation. They'd already formed opinions about him. "I owe him more than I could ever repay," she added, and the truth of that statement washed away the last of her irritation. "And no," she said, "none of them can read your minds without your being aware of it."

Old Tomm Shawness pushed away from a nearer wall. Tomm had taught Firebird some of Netaia's best historic ballads, and though his singing voice creaked, his interpretations always drew cheers. "Sentinel

Caldwell," he said, "if all she says is true, then we owe you a debt, too. On behalf of us all, thanks."

To Firebird's delight, most of the others applauded.

"Iarla!" Clareen's voice came from the floor, near her feet. "Firebird, give us the Iarla song!"

Wondering where the Tallan researcher turned up that two-year-old ballad, Firebird placed her hands on the clairsa's strings and played a few experimental chords. This instrument was painted with stylized vines twining up its bow and upper arch, leaving the sound box plain. She tweaked a sagging bass string, then sang her ballad with only one pause to clear her throat, and after the applause settled, she led a boisterous chorus about working conditions in places like Nello's front rooms, adding a few nontraditional chords to keep things interesting. Ballads that had survived the passage of time were anything but ordinary. The real workers sang along. Behind them, Brennen leaned back, appearing to relax.

It was too bad she didn't actually want to incite a rebellion. It could be so easy. A song from the Coper Rebellion, a short speech—

Was there a chance, after all, that her destiny lay along musical lines? She could almost feel energy coursing into her, drawn from her audience. If it hadn't been for her wastling fate, she might have pursued this kind of career. Now that she knew a mightier Singer, this almost felt like a call on her life.

She glanced down at Clareen, then over at Brennen, determined not to waste this chance at center stage. She fingered a soft arpeggio and said, "I want to tell you something wonderful, from beyond the Federacy."

Brennen raised a dark eyebrow.

"But I can't," she said. "Here's a woman who could. Clareen?"

As if she'd been waiting for just such a chance, the bassist sprang up. "There is something much better than the Powers," she said. "They're only personality traits." Someone hooted from a dark corner.

"Your electors are only people like yourselves." She touched Firebird's shoulder.

"Most of them are a lot worse than she is." That from another corner, near a gridded ventilation chute. Catcalls answered it.

"But all this"—Clareen's long hair rippled as she gestured toward both sides and up toward the sky—"came from somewhere. An infinite being is Sovereign over everything that exists. There wouldn't be time tonight to tell you about Him . . ." She looked toward Firebird.

Firebird pulled the clairsa against her shoulder. "Here's a song from the Thyrian tradition."

She tried to focus her heart on the original Singer, praying even while her lips formed lyrics. *Let these images catch in their memories. Let me bring mercy and light to my people.*

Before the long dreams of eternity flowed
He stood matchless, alone and sufficient
And out of the Word of His speaking
Made light, life, and time, made all things
So that over all living
He might justly command our obedience.
He is beyond time, more brilliant than light
In Him is no darkness at all.

Shackled by our selfish lust to be gods
We stand powerless, alone and despondent
And only beginning to fathom
The majesty and flawless power
Of this highest of judges
And His right to condemn us to sorrow
For we disobey, and we smother the light
And the darkness falls over all.

Holy One who made time and the light and all things—
Brilliant paradox, transcendent judge
Who promises undeserved mercy
To your servants, flawed as we are!
Holy Speaker, Shaliyah,
With your own hands lift us past sorrow
To your land beyond time, where you are the light
And there is no darkness at all.

The hymn translated jerkily into Old Colonial, but Firebird was glad that the translators had aimed for textual accuracy instead of forcing the lyrics to rhyme. For several seconds, the room remained silent. Firebird carefully avoided looking at anyone, but gave them time to reflect on what they'd heard.

Then out of a corner, someone asked, "Would you sing it again?"

Firebird did, gladly. Then, nudged by Brennen's growing unease, she handed off the clairsa and touched Shel's shoulder. "Let's go."

"Escort," ordered a small, middle-aged woman near the door.

Instantly, the people nearest the woman surged out into the night. Others surrounded Firebird as her group emerged. She felt Brennen's confusion, then his amusement, as servitors and low-commoners preceded, guarded, and followed them, ten deep in places. It was an honor they'd accorded her before, when they were concerned for her safety. This way, she couldn't see a potential assailant, but he couldn't see her either.

As they approached the door, one woman slipped into the open space around them, glanced at Shel, and kept a cautious distance. "I would like to know more about the Thyrian hymn tradition," she said. She blinked small brown eyes, then added, "And that transcendent judge."

I told you, Brenn! I told you! Firebird turned around, rose onto her toes, and pointed back into the room. "Do you know Clareen Chesterson, the bassist? That woman with the long blond hair? She can tell you more."

"I will ask. Thank you." The mob moved forward, hiding the woman once more.

Shel stayed close as Uri steered the mob to the unremarkable base groundcar. Netaians lingered while he activated the engine, and a sea of Netaian faces parted only a few at a time as he steered through the workers' parking zone. Others surrounded the gates. Uri emerged from the crowd to join traffic.

Firebird craned her neck, staring back at the crowd. "Now you see, Brenn. Now you understand why I love these people. These are the ones Rogonin sees as subhuman. These are the ones Carradee and Danton have tried to help. The people," she added as Uri turned the car out onto Port Road, "who would die in a civil war."

"And you see how little interest most of them showed in the truth."

"They listened," she said. "They were silent. That is a wonderful hymn from an artistic standpoint, too." Still, he was right. The Sentinels' Ehretan ancestors had disqualified themselves to proselytize when they gene-altered their children. She did share that heritage.

She shook her head as a maglev train sped past, one long white streak in the darkness. She couldn't help basking in the sense that she'd done something splendid. "I'm sure Clareen will talk with that woman," she said. "And they may attract others."

Brennen rested one hand on her leg. "The time will come," he said, quoting, "when truth will come in like the tide. No one will be able to deny it in that day."

In Kiel or Kinnor's time, maybe. His family would ride the crest of that tidal wave. Dozens of prophecies said so, and now she was part of that magnificent heritage. "Maybe that time is now." She stroked his hand. "Maybe the place is here."

INTERLUDE 4

Carradee opened her eyes and peered up at a skylight. At last, she and Daithi would begin Path instruction today. She rolled onto her side and eyed his therapy bed. He snored softly under a long regeneration field projector, one of Hesed's few concessions to modern technology. The twins slept in an adjoining room, which she'd vacated to move back in with Daithi.

Today.

She hadn't waited for Path instruction to start praying, though. *Eternal Speaker, Firebird's day is almost here, too. Bring her and Brennen safely through danger. Save her from the unholy Powers.* It felt wonderful to say that, even silently! *Save her from her enemies.*

Then a more personal plea. *Guide the searchers to find my daughters' real fate. Protect Hesed and everyone who lives here. Lead Netaia out of darkness. By the power of the Holy Word to Come, let it be.* Then, *Go on healing Daithi* . . . His body was starting to respond in surprising ways.

She slipped into a nightrobe, laid one hand on the regenerative projector over his bed, and kissed him awake.

He opened his eyes and said, " 'Dee. I've had an idea."

She raised the projector and stroked curly brown hair off his forehead. "You wake up so quickly. I envy you."

"I read something yesterday that stuck in my mind, about the power of prayer, illogical as it seems. If the Speaker truly wants us involved in the workings of the universe, we should ask everyone here to fast tomorrow. To fast and to pray that Firebird's confirmation will proceed safely. It could be urgent."

"Tell Mistress Anna at breakfast," she said softly. "That is an excellent idea."

The strangest sensation came over her, a sense of approval and rightness. *Is that you, Speaker?* she asked, delighted. *Are you truly here in this room?*

Dust motes sparkled under the skylight, as if the sun were directly overhead.

INTERLUDE 5

Juddis Adiyn strode through Three Zed's central meeting chamber, hardly sparing a glance toward the vaulted ceiling, barely looking into the volcanic depths beneath the chamber's transparent gray floor. Onar Ketaz, commander-in-chief in Modabah Shirak's absence, had called him to the fielding station across the colony from his apartments.

The city ran smoothly in Shirak's absence. Adiyn had seen a marked decline of wisdom and focus in the Shirak family, despite his lab's best efforts. His young tech, Terza Shirak, had seemed stable enough, but Modabah had informed him Terza would not be returning, and the shebiyl confirmed it.

He did not like or trust Micahel. No longer sure the Shiraks could lead an assault on the Federacy, he might have to repair the strain or remove it. He would not order his techs to breed Micahel a son. The next namable Shirak would come from Micahel's grandfather's banked gametes.

As he passed his laboratory, he glanced in. A security lamp gleamed, lighting rows of womb-banks and embrytubes. Behind its locked inner door, in a vast cold room, lay dozens of stasis crypts—Golden City residents awaiting medical treatment, subadults culled for experimentation—and a few gene specimens, including the faithless princess who had briefly graced Three Zed with her presence. Smaller cold cases held specimens taken from Phoena's nieces. Unfortunately, no one had taken samples from the sister Firebird. No one thought she would leave here so suddenly.

So rarely was a new Ehretan family line found that Adiyn's senior staff had focused on decoding the Casvah-Angelo genes. He did have the feeling that something vital could come from the reunion of Caldwell-Carabohd with the Angelo-Casvahs . . . here, in his laboratory. He always attended to those feelings.

At 152 years old, Juddis Adiyn had reached his productive middle age. Three Zed's bioscientists had almost given this people immortality. Unfortunately, epsilon powers still deteriorated, and this laboratory's day-to-day concern was to provide injectable tissue suspension for revitalizing the ayin . . . hence the embrytubes. He'd had a few flickers himself recently. He was due for a fresh treatment.

Beyond and beneath the cold room, a deeper lava chamber housed his ancestors' biological weapons. Though his ancestors destroyed the non-Altered residents of Ehret along with most of their own kindred, his people were now humankind's best hope of survival. The trade worlds had barely survived the first Sabba Six-alpha catastrophe, when that binary star spewed radiation storms out into the Whorl, disrupting travel and trade, destroying technology. Adiyn's people couldn't prevent further storms, but their potentially immortal descendants would be compelled to solve that problem. In time, they would become gods. Their servants-elect on other worlds would be altered over generations. On each world, the first new generation's genes would be manipulated to ensure die-off as soon as the second generation came to maturity. A second generation could carry any gene he chose to introduce. In the truest sense, they would be his own people's descendants.

He did hope he would live to control that phase of the experiment. After death, he expected nothing. Bliss, the Speaker's Country, and all other "spiritual" hopes for eternity were the hopes of a short-lived people, sops to their outraged sense that there ought to be more than a hundred or so years of existence.

He could do nothing for them. For Onar Ketaz, he needed to check what seemed to be a manifestation of the shebiyl.

He backed out of his lab and strode on.

The City was silent tonight, except for low voices here and there. His people wasted little time with sonic entertainments, and infants conceived in his lab lived in distant settlements until subadulthood. The Golden City was no place for youngsters, whose budding epsilon potential made them more nuisance than use.

He found Ketaz in the fielding station, not far from the main north airlock. Inside a ten-sided chamber, teams of three sat in five rounded wells, wearing gray-green shipboards and headsets, watching vast fields of space projected on ten continuous overhead panels.

Ketaz strolled toward him. Square-faced and stocky, the man was about to celebrate his ninetieth birthday. He looked forty by most worlds' standards, another triumph of Golden City genetics.

"Adiyn," he said. "I was simply standing here, watching the screens. I saw two large ships and half a dozen small fighters coming in. When I looked again, they'd vanished. The mass detectors picked up nothing."

Only a few were born with Juddis Adiyn's exceptional ability to foresee the future, along branching paths or streams of alternate reality. He could also tell, with ninety-nine percent accuracy, whether another individual's seeming shebiyl experience was genuine.

He had not bred himself any descendants. He didn't want any potential rivals yet.

He took the seat Ketaz offered.

Ketaz scattered his epsilon-energy static, and Adiyn focused a probe. Ketaz brought up the memory. Adiyn watched, second-hand, as the ships appeared to approach. They had Federate markings . . . Thyrian, in fact.

The vision flickered, looking lifeless and two-dimensional. His own glimpses had the texture of reality. This must be an illusion, created by fear and excitement.

"No," he said. "You were right to call and have it checked, but this is false. You are under stress, and the colony needs you at peak objectivity. I relieve you."

Ketaz narrowed his eyes.

"Report to second-level south," said Adiyn. "I'll call ahead."

Adiyn sensed that Ketaz wanted to object. At Second South, the colony's medics could readjust brain chemicals to ensure peak performance. He'd had it done once. Unsettling, not at all like the multisensory blast of ayin-extract injections.

Tomorrow, he promised himself.

CHAPTER 13
CRUX

subito fermata
sudden stop

For Firebird, after the excitement at Nello's, sleep came slowly. Midnight passed, and then one hundred . . . two hundred . . .

She lay awake in the dark, not wanting to nudge Brennen and ask for a calming touch. Behind her eyelids, black-haired Micahel Shirak stalked up their hallway at Trinn Hill . . . and this time, she imagined waiting for him with a dart gun.

This would be her fifth day on Netaia. Not today but tomorrow, the ceremony—then she'd have one day to conclude her charitable obligations. After that, she might fly back to Hesed and her sons, or on to Three Zed.

Actually, she'd half expected to have that fielding information by now.

She reached over the edge of the bed and touched her tri-D, wondering if Carradee thought about her as often as she missed her sons. She hoped she would return to them with the best possible gift, an end to the Shuhr menace.

She slept a little.

Her schedule had been left empty, this last day before confirmation. Tel called early and invited her and Brennen back to his estate, mentioning his newly expanded security force. She leaped at the chance to get off the sterile, unfamiliar new base—but at Tel's, she had trouble settling into any one room, and soon she regretted her choice. At the base, she could have been logging sim time.

Brennen had notified Danton of their whereabouts, and the steady hum of low-flying surveillance craft did nothing to settle her nerves. Guards in Tellai indigo and black stood at every door and sat on Tel's rooftop. She only had to stay calm and let time pass.

Impossible.

Her old palace physician, Dr. Zoagrem, arrived at ten hundred. He diagnosed stress and imminent exhaustion and insisted that this laid her open to several mutant respiratory viruses making the rounds.

If she got sick on the way to Three Zed, she could have trouble using her epsilon carrier. She had to let him give her a series of three lung-strengthening injections, an hour apart. Only Brennen's epsilon touch helped her sit still for a needle. Even Brenn had been unable to help her overcome that old phobia. They'd never dug deep enough to find its cause.

She spent the last morning hour closeted with him, locked away from Tel's hovering servitors, trying to develop a shielding visualization. Again, the quest-pulse was all she could muster . . . and it was weaker than before.

"Distracted," he observed.

"Well, yes." She rubbed her sore arm.

She tried calling Baron Erwin from a CT station surrounded by bubbling fountains. *Still in bed*, she was told, but she no longer believed it. He knew what she wanted. He refused to cooperate. Like it or not, she would have the Powers' blessing.

Brennen sent out another decoy team, and between taking their reports of a disappointingly uneventful day, he heard her recite the first quarter of her second codebook. He corrected her stumbles with uncanny patience. They nibbled exotic sweets that Tel's servitors brought on trays. She even locked herself away with a clairsa lent by Tel's staff clairsinger, but after she loosened her fingers with long-memorized scale and arpeggio exercises, nothing she played expressed anything but discordant tension.

So she ate and paced and explored the grounds with half a dozen of Tel's stiff-backed new guards. Behind her, one of them quizzed Shel about Federate training techniques. Tel walked beside Firebird like a gallant out of some old story, paying court to her ego, trying to revive old dreams of the Netaian throne.

He was almost succeeding. She could accomplish so much if she stayed here. Halting beside an artificial waterfall planted with exotic silverthroats and trailing oncidia, she turned to him. "Tel, remember what

I told you. If some combination of circumstances put me on the throne, I would do everything in my grasp to introduce an alternative to Powers worship. Could you support that?"

He glanced back and aside at his guards, then crossed his arms. "I ask my servitors to keep the Charities and Disciplines. I've never punished one for neglecting them, though. Their spiritual status is their business, not mine. I simply want an Angelo in the palace again." He half bowed and then stalked back up the lawn toward the estate house. Two of his guards followed. The rest stayed with her.

She trailed one hand in the chilly cascade. She hated to think of Netaia's future resting on her shoulders. It was a weight she didn't want to carry. Still . . . maybe the Mighty Singer had brought her back to show Netaia the difference between faith and legalism, and to save her people from civil war. Maybe she was meant for the throne.

One of Tel's guards struck a pose at the top of the two-meter falls on a newly landscaped artificial hillside. Two more stood down on the lawn, while one remained close, with Shel.

Suppose she did stay on. She would need a personal security force. The Electors had their redjackets, and every noble House had its House Guards. She should've asked for more Sentinel escorts.

A vague suspicion nettled her. Brenn wouldn't like to catch her entertaining these thoughts. He'd accuse her of the usual offenses.

But she could do so much here. She was capable. She was trained. She had the common people's support.

Hearing a step at the library door, Brennen turned around. He didn't shut the leather-bound volume he'd been scanning. Tel stood framed in the doorway, hands behind his back.

"Thank you again for the invitation," Brennen said. He reached for a velvette page marker, then closed the book, using that time to dissipate his shielding cloud of epsilon static.

Tel raised one eyebrow, curious. Brennen showed him the biography's cover. It was *Iarla of Citangelo*.

He'd enjoyed Firebird's singing last night, and he'd felt surprisingly comfortable in that warehouse after cozying up to too many swaggering nobles. Her sweet voice had carried him up and out of the demands of his mission, into a Hesed-like realm of contentment with the eternal.

Still, she must obey the codes. She must not put herself above those laws, or according to all he'd been taught, the One himself would bring her down. He needed to speak with her about pride, too. That subtle glow after the fitting had grown stronger.

"I had that out for research." Tel moved toward a long ebony table. "I've been painting Iarla First. A confirmation gift, though I suppose Firebird might not have room to pack it back to Hesed House." He lifted a cover from a large canvas square.

Brennen eyed the image underneath. The dark-haired, fiftyish woman wore Angelo scarlet, and her eyes glimmered, with amber sparkling through brown. Brennen knew little about painting, but the image impressed him as lifelike and lively. "She'll love it."

"Can anything more be done to ensure her safety tomorrow—and yours?" Tel moved closer and glanced at a long indigo lounger, but he remained standing.

"We'll have guards at every imaginable station, and new equipment, but security is stretched. The best we can do is to ensure tight protection right around us. Like this." Brennen gestured toward two corners of the estate. "Thank you again. We appreciate this deeply. It is much more pleasant than base housing."

Unclenching his hands, Tel leaned forward onto the table where Brennen had laid his book. "I'm beginning to feel responsible, to wonder if you two should have come back to Netaia at all." Tellai's sincere concern gave him a twinge of sympathetic worry. "What about the new technology, the RIA? Can you use that to defend us?"

It still felt strange to discuss RIA publicly. "Yes, but you—and everyone you can convince, on the Electorate and in the Assembly—can do more than we can to bring stability," said Brennen. "Only a unified Netaia can defend itself. Remember Firebird's simulations. Even without Shuhr interference, there's a strong possibility of civil war. Firebird's confirmation came through on the equations as a stabilizing event."

Tel shook his head, frowning. "I hadn't forgotten. I'm glad she came. I'm amazed by how little I care if the Electorate approves of me now."

"You were a follower," Brennen said. "You're emerging as a leader."

Tel chuckled. "I doubt that."

Brennen backed away. Several other portraits lined a shelfless stretch of Tel's wall. Aristocrats all, from their haughty faces and blue sashes. Brennen wondered how many Tel had collected and how many he'd painted.

That couldn't distract him for long, either. They had failed to capture a Shuhr at the palace, and the decoy groups had been ignored. Tomorrow he must be ready to step into Micahel Shirak's targeting scope. *Holy One, protect us. Take us home to our sons.* He'd half expected Firebird's physician to diagnose him, too, as stressed.

"I love her," Tel murmured, his head bowed. When he raised his chin to meet Brennen's sudden glance, he exhaled. "I assume you know that, Caldwell. I have, since—"

"Don't." Brennen tried to say it kindly.

The nobleman snapped his mouth shut.

"I knew. It will go no further."

"Not to her."

"Never to her," Brennen said, knowing Firebird had already guessed. "I've been burdened professionally by many secrets. I have reason to sympathize with yours."

Dinner started as a quiet affair, spent watching news at lap tables in defiance of court etiquette. Rogonin's network, Codex, used the occasion to chronicle the few production quotas that had declined under occupation. There'd also been high-common class protest against Firebird's return, mostly in southern cities and out on Kierelay Island. Codex reporters accused the Federates of complicity in Iarlet and Kessie's disappearance. One netter smilingly detailed an accusation that Firebird murdered Phoena herself, that her half-alien husband was using her for mysterious purposes, and the story that she'd birthed sons was fabrication. Where were these mythical princes?

Firebird glanced aside as one of Tel's servitors brought in a carafe of cruinn. "Still no luck, my lady," she murmured as she poured for Firebird. "His Grace must have gone to the country for a day."

Firebird frowned, and then the tri-D caught her eye again. A woman in drab worker's dress was speaking out against the aristocratic tradition that would spend so much money, waste so many worker hours, on one day's pageantry. "I can't believe Codex carried that," Tel said from the depths of a brownbuck chair.

Firebird agreed, but next, the announcer skipped to four men and women who wondered aloud how much of the Angelo fortune would fall Firebird's way, and how much would be hers to take offworld, after her confirmation.

She tossed a lounger pillow idly. They *would* worry about that. Frankly, she wasn't counting on a torn credit-chit after the bills came in—but it would be gratifying to build that Chapter house.

If only she'd demanded that First Lord Erwin change his blessing right then, at the rehearsal when that small Voice prompted. Now she was trapped, with no escape except to try counteracting Erwin's wretched invocation with her short speech afterward.

The other newsnets—Affiliated, a public corporation, and Drong, which had been family owned for centuries—were making a gala out of anticipation, interviewing souvenir hawkers and running old clips from Firebird's adolescence. On screen, she relived her triumph at the Naval Academy's war games, where she'd been nominated for top graduate. She felt Brennen's pleasure as it ran—and his amusement to learn that her all-Academy flight simulator record still hadn't been broken.

Then Marshal Burkenhamn, interviewed live, announced her re-commissioning in the NPN. Newsnet analysts took off from that in all directions. One called it "another step toward the Federatization of Netaia."

Tel laughed. "Congratulations, Commander," he exclaimed, attempting a salute.

She grinned.

Another spin-off showed the Hall of Charity's interior, with guards at every entrance. That image metamorphosed unexpectedly into another newsnetter. "There have," he said, "been warnings that Second Commander Angelo's confirmation ceremony might be disrupted by offworld elements, despite all assurances from the Federacy. As a result, the Electorate was polled by CT. Our holy electors will not observe from the sanctum, as scheduled, but from the adjoining North Hall. His Grace the Regent wishes to inform ticket holders that tomorrow's ceremony will be segregated not by class but by preference. To accommodate all comers, the Hall will open at seven hundred tomorrow morning."

"Oof," Tel exclaimed. "No electors in the sanctum? They're scared, Firebird."

"Didn't they call you?" she asked.

"No," he said grimly. "Obviously, they know I'll be there. Did you notice how quickly they picked up on Marshal Burkenhamn's announcement?"

"Yes." Firebird glanced at Brennen. "And if we can pull it off, do you realize what this means? We could have a nave full of people who actually care what I'm doing." A nave full of sympathetic witnesses, if they managed to capture one Shuhr. Those witnesses would tell their children, and grandchildren, about watching Firebird and her security force catch a terrifying enemy. *Second Commander Angelo.* It sang at the back of her mind. *Commander, Commander, Commander*...

As Brennen discussed the early Hall opening with security people, Firebird called the palace and asked for six-oh-six. Paskel spoke softly. There'd been talk of delaying the ceremony one day, he admitted, but all parties—even Rogonin, consulted via interlink—decided to go ahead as planned. Paskel believed that Rogonin was anxious to see the ceremony concluded and Firebird sent back offworld.

She spent the silent ride back to base rehearsing her lines for tomorrow. *Commander.* Now that it had been announced, it felt real. She hoped Burkenhamn kept his promise about making it temporary.

As she climbed under the bedcovers, she felt a disquieting tension in Brennen. "Mari," he said softly, laying his arm over her. "Don't let all this distract you from the real call on your life, and your responsibilities. Not even catching a Shuhr is as important as one immortal spirit. Our humility is crucial, before the One."

She yawned. "Can we talk about this in the morning?" she mumbled. She rolled aside before he could answer.

She felt as if she'd barely fallen asleep when her dreaming mind was snatched into a reality more vivid than life. She sat on a gilt chair, suspended from space over Citangelo—except that it wasn't Citangelo, but an eerie transmutation of the metropolis, built over a basalt mountain that reminded her of the Shuhr's Golden City.

A Voice sang from everywhere, a Voice she'd heard like this once before, flinging the worlds into existence. This time, it addressed her, singing deep and sonorous, *Strength, Firebird. Whence your strength?*

She trembled at the solemn sound. "My strength is from you, Mighty Singer." Her feet dangled over thousands of meters of empty space. It would be easy to fall to her death.

The Voice rose one note of the scale. *Valor, Firebird. Whence your valor?*

"From . . . you." Her own voice sounded pitiful, breathy.

One by one, the Voice thundered the Netaian Powers. Each time it spoke, it ascended one note of a modal scale like the Sentinels used in worship.

Silence rang in the heavens with one Power left. Firebird clenched both arms of the gilt chair . . . her mother's chair. Her sister's chair. The chair Muirnen Rogonin had stolen from them.

Now the Voice sang in a whisper, all notes of the scale and the half steps too, a dissonant tone cluster. *Pride, Firebird. Whence your pride?*

Other voices sang a chorus out of her memory, her own thoughts and words.

Pride, impatience, willfulness.

To be Angelo was to be proud.

The pride she would feel if she saved Netaia . . .

If only Rogonin knew how easily she and Brennen could destroy him!

She could only imagine the ballads that might be sung about the wastling who saved Netaia.

Let me *bring mercy and light to my people.*

She could accomplish so much if she stayed here.

Maybe she was meant for the throne.

Commander, Commander, Commander . . .

And she'd turned away from Brennen tonight when he gently tried to warn her.

Of all the nine Powers, Pride was the only one *Dabar* and *Mattah* rebuked. It was her birthright and her burden. It was the Adversary's claw, caught in her soul.

—By her own permission. She'd forsworn too much of her upbringing to cling to that as an excuse, when it came down to pride.

"From myself," she admitted. The relief of honest confession balanced her pain. Maybe pride fueled that flaming, dark taint on her soul.

Pride brought you here, my child.

He did not disown her. He still called her His child.

Silence rang, a grand pause deeper and longer than Firebird could bear. She whispered to break it. "Forgive me, Singer. I wanted to save Netaia myself. I wanted—I still want to catch the Shuhr who murdered my niece, Destia." And there was more. "I want to be seen and admired, and respected . . . saluted." She'd explained to everyone that she came to serve Netaia's people, but deep in this dream, her buried reasons clamored for recognition.

Without truth, said the Voice, *you are vulnerable.*

"And . . ." Would this dream never end? She couldn't bear this. "You may have called Brennen here to get the intelligence he needs, but you didn't call me. I . . . wanted . . . I still want," she managed, "revenge. For Destia and her family."

Revenge is mine, sang the Voice.

"But I do want to help my people," she insisted. "I want to save them." She knew what she must add. She resisted. Disappointment hung in the heavens, so keen and loving that she couldn't hold back. ". . . Myself." She let it out, almost choking on that admission. "I want to save them myself, without giving anyone else the chance to do it."

The sky rejoiced again, billions of molecules dancing to music she could not hear.

"But, Singer, you brought me into this royal family. You gave me this longing to achieve and the abilities I would need. I could help the common people. Truly, I could." As she argued, her chair rose higher, and loftier, until the sky around her darkened toward black. The fall, deadly before, now looked twice as terrifying.

Pride, sang the voice, *brings a long, long fall. But never so far I cannot catch you. You are mine. Forever, I have called you. The final price is mine to pay.*

But the consequences are yours. I shatter the proud heart, so that you may wear my image.

Slowly, the gilt chair tipped forward.

But I give grace, and true peace, to the humble and contrite. To the obedient.

The chair kept tipping. Firebird scrambled around to seize its ornate back. The farther it tilted, the harder her cheek pressed against the starred-shield Angelo crest. Her body slid, first a few centimeters, then farther. "Singer!" she pleaded. "Help me!"

Know this, sang the Voice. *Even in tragedy, I am God. I am not surprised.*

She woke in a puddle of sweat.

Brennen lunged for the nightstand, where he'd concealed a blazer.

"No," she groaned. She touched his arm. "It was a dream."

"Mm," he mumbled into the pillow. Then he rolled over. "You don't feel," he said slowly, "like you had an ordinary dream."

"No." The word came out in another groan. "Brenn, I . . . I may have made a terrible mistake."

Chapter 14
Great Hall

pavillon en air
brass instruments' bells are to be directed upward

"Show me," Brennen said gently.

She buried her head against his chest, clinging to him as his presence filled her, comforting, seeking, observing. Safe in his arms, she watched the dream unwind again. Meanwhile, more accusations rattled through her mind. Her self-absorbed whining at Hesed while Brennen faced the Shuhr at Three Zed. Her eagerness to accept the Assembly's invitation, and rub noble noses in her new status, even before Brennen's people conceived the entrapment mission. Even her hope to wear Netaia's colors at Three Zed, supposedly for Netaia's honor.

Our humility before the One, Brennen had said. He'd been trying to tell her this. Pride still dominated her mental habits. If only it weren't such a long Path from the first sheltered steps to actually arriving!

When the dream ended again, she gripped Brennen tightly, still terrified by her self-imposed height.

"What can I do?" she asked, knowing there was no easy answer.

"What do you believe you should do?" His arms pulled her closer, chest to chest, until her chin rested on his shoulder.

"I don't know. Yes, I do," she realized. "I have to pray."

"I will, too."

Clinging to Brennen, she begged the Infinite for wisdom, for direction. Should she retreat, after all? Fly back to Hesed, resign her new rank ignominiously, and cancel the ceremony? That would be the ultimate death of her pride. She could never show her face on Netaia again.

No. She must not back down. Brennen needed that information. They must take a Shuhr. . . .

And couldn't that be done some other way? Danton's people, accompanied by plainclothes Sentinels, had fanned out across Citangelo—but they had turned up nothing.

Quieting her mind, she waited for an answer.

It came softly.

She could not save Netaia. Only the Electorate could do that . . . but she had offered to serve the Federacy. She had also sworn to Burkenhamn that she would serve Netaia, and she must keep those promises. At least, she had to try. The Singer would bring success or failure and show her the consequences of stepping out in pride. *I shatter the proud heart. . . .*

Do what you wish, she prayed, clenching her hands behind Brennen's back. She felt the pulse in the side of his warm neck. *But don't, I beg you, don't let Brennen suffer. Or Kiel, or Kinnor. Spare my loved ones. Everything I have . . . it's yours. Take my life, or my self-absorbed happiness. I will try to serve you.*

She pulled away from Brennen.

He kept one hand on her shoulder. "We're going ahead, aren't we?"

She nodded miserably. "Maybe He'll be merciful. Maybe I've repented in the nick of time."

" 'We are called to a higher standard,' " he quoted solemnly. "And, Mari, we'll have the biggest guard force Citangelo ever saw. He didn't tell you the Shuhr would actually take either of us."

"No." She stared into darkness. "If I backed out now, that would be the ultimate insult to the Assembly, the Electorate . . . to Netaia itself. Not to mention Governor Danton, and the Three Zed situation—"

"I didn't say you should back out. I think you're right. We have to go ahead, and we've been warned that if anything happens, it will be a natural consequence of what we've already done. Both of us. You aren't here alone. The real price, Mari—the final debt—is paid for us."

"I understand." . . . *I think*. For all her intellectual assent, she still flinched away from accepting someone else's atonement.

Brennen rolled away from her, sliding off the bed.

"Where are you going?"

His answer came out of the darkness. "I'm going to spend the rest of the night praying. Get your rest."

A vigil? Good idea. Excellent idea. She wished she'd thought of it first.

She rolled off the bed and onto her knees beside him. She could think of only one thing the Shuhr might do that would utterly break her proud heart.

Please, she begged. *Don't let them take Brennen!*

Some hours later, she stumbled out of the bedroom bleary-eyed. After a minute of shuffling through duffels, she picked out a simple dark blue outfit to carry into the freshing room. Halfway through her vigil, she'd found her recall pad, loaded the Soldane University simulation program, and run two more projections through the complex equations. Sure enough, Governor Danton could count on another half year of peace if she went through with the ceremony, whether it ended in celebration or disaster. Then, struck by a horrible thought, she ran a different chain of events. Sure enough, a Shuhr attack would also stave off civil war—but probably destroy Netaia.

Surely that wasn't your plan, she reflected. *Surely we were right to come back.*

From the adjoining cubicle, she heard percolating sounds. Brennen was already in the other vaporbath.

According to her Path instructor, acting out of pride was the spiritual equivalent of proclaiming that she was her own little goddess, her own holy Power.

I thought I'd shaken loose from them!

Fear came straight from the Adversary, though. She counterattacked with an Adoration she'd memorized before leaving Hesed.

Do battle with those who attack me.
Rise up for my help, and let them be ashamed,
Drive them off with your mighty weapons.
My soul shall rejoice in your salvation.
Who is mighty like you, rich with mercy?
Who delivers the weary, and binds up their wounds?
Clothe my enemies with shame and dishonor,
But let those who love me shout joyfully,
"Exalt the One, who defends His beloved!"

That calmed her. Live or die, they remained in the Singer's hands. Nothing could touch her, or Brennen, without His permission. *His sovereignty*, Master Dabarrah had said, *cannot operate independently of His love.*

I'm only your servant now, she prayed, and this time, she felt a difference. There was no thrill in the thought of confirmation now. She must trust the Singer . . . today like every day . . . but today, it would be much harder than usual.

Two minutes with a hot brush dried her hair. Tressers at the Hall would worry it into a style of their choice. Her physical person was only raw material to be costumed.

During their swift ride across town in an armored base car, she fought an unseen battle. Her imagination roiled, suggesting possible consequences. Death, injury. Catastrophe. A sprung trap, with no one caught inside.

She fought back: *Exalt the One, who defends His beloved!*

Streamers hung from buildings, draping them in gold and Angelo scarlet. Netaians loved pageantry.

She sent off one last frightened prayer. *Take me, if there has to be a sacrifice, like long ago in your temple. He could survive without me, but . . .*

She glanced sidelong at Shel, imagining herself six years from today, still recovering.

Brenn murmured, "You're all right, Mari?"

Staring ahead, Firebird could see his reflection in a panel that separated them from Uri and a base driver—the fine chin, the dark eyebrows framing his blue eyes. He pressed a finger against the scar on his cheekbone. Outside, the air was cold and still, a typical winter morning. Knots of people stood on street corners.

"Yes," she answered. She would not give in to fear. "Are you?"

He said, "Yes." She couldn't tell if he too was struggling.

After confirmation, and before tonight's ball, she was expected to bestow charitable gifts from her new allowance. Giving away as much Angelo money as possible seemed a worthwhile goal . . . and finding an architect. She'd meant to do that, anyway. Rogonin would be into the Angelo accounts soon, if he wasn't already.

As Port Road dead-ended on Capitol, she spotted a long line of huddled forms along the roadside, people who'd slept beside the street anticipating the traditional motorcade back to the palace.

Sadly, she wouldn't see them again. There would be a decoy car in that motorcade. She and Brennen would be flown over by Federate shuttle.

The golden cube with its ice white columns loomed ahead. She felt Brennen's dread at the sight of it, and this time, she couldn't steady him.

The Shuhr wanted him dead, not her. He was the Carabohd heir. To them, she was just a distraction.

She caught a flicker reflecting off his eyes as he glanced at her. He must've caught her worry, because instantly his dread changed to a slow, relaxed drone she recognized from Chapter worship. He'd gone beyond reciting Adorations to focusing on the Singer himself and praising Him.

She should do the same. In the Adorations, praise led to deliverance and victory.

And victory—eternal victory—had been guaranteed.

The car whisked them to the blockhouse. Black-uniformed city Enforcers escorted them through the tunnel. At a turning near the main gravity lifts, Brennen's escort urged him forward while Firebird's Enforcer waved her to the right. "I'll be a little while," Brennen said, and he walked on with Uri.

Ten meters along that corridor, the man in black opened a door. Firebird pushed through, followed step for step by Shel. Two women who'd been sitting on a bench scrambled to rise and half bow.

Now Firebird was only a player on a magnificent set, and she might as well try to enjoy what she'd come here to do. Everything lay in the Singer's hands. She must trust Him, put on confidence—that was allowed, when pride wasn't!—and walk open-eyed onto the trap's trip plate. Governor Danton's people, Thyrica's people, and even Citangelo's Enforcers couldn't catch Micahel if she and Brennen didn't lure him out.

But maybe she still could try one thing.

She turned to the nearest servitor. "I need to get a message to First Lord Erwin." She dictated her request one more time, this time as a flat refusal. She would not accept the Powers' blessing.

Then she moved toward a table piled with pressboard boxes. "All right. Where do we start?"

"With this, evidently." One woman held up a shimmering silver-white garment. "Compliments of His Excellency, the Governor."

The body armor she'd requested! She reached for it. "Decorative, don't you think?"

"He asked if you would return it undamaged."

"He sent one of these over for Brennen, didn't he?"

"I don't know, my lady."

"Have someone check. Please."

Another servitor was dispatched while Firebird submitted to undressing. The first woman went for her hair while the second slipped soft, cold, shimmering armor up her legs and arms and down her chest. It covered her body from ankles and wrists to a wide V neckline that she guessed matched her regalia, barely exposing her collarbone. "I've never seen anything like it, my lady. The Federates have wonderful technology."

"Yes, they do." Firebird had never seen anything like it, either.

An hour passed. She relaxed in the cloth-of-gold undertunic, washed down a roll with hot cruinn, and let the women arrange her hair, apply makeup, and finally dress her. She wore Brennen's chain long today, hiding the medallion low but determined not to take it off. Considering how little she'd slept, she felt thoroughly awake. Two more times, she sent servitors with messages for First Lord Erwin. Nothing came back.

The older woman held the crimson train in place for the younger to pin with shoulder brooches. This was truly Firebird's last chance to gracefully back down. She reviewed her choices, weighing the risk they were taking against the hope of capturing Micahel Shirak or his comrades—if even a Shuhr who could blur his face to a mob was overconfident enough to walk into a building full of Federate guards! Brennen might as well still be a Master Sentinel, for all the Shuhr's chance of striking undetected.

But Brennen had said that an ES 97 Master could detect epsilon-energy uses that a room full of 32s or 50s might miss, so maybe a Hall full of guards wouldn't keep Micahel home today. Plainly, the Shuhr had waited for this moment.

Her hands shook as a servitor slipped a house signet ring onto her right hand. The women had the good grace not to ask if she was feeling all right. They knew now that there was a threat of disruption. Shel remained by the door in an attentive stance, her Sentinel midnight blue a shock in these surroundings.

More shocks like that one would be reassuring.

I trust you. You only. Yes, Brennen's obedience at Three Zed cost him terribly—but the Singer preserved his life. He'd accomplished his real purposes.

Let us serve you today, too.

Rogonin would probably watch on tri-D from the North Hall. She doubted he'd miss a chance to wear his robes of office. He valued pageantry as much as any other elector. The high-commoners who chose to attend in the North Hall's safety would still get their eyes full of electoral finery.

"Perhaps my lady would like a final chance at the freshing room?" asked the older woman.

Firebird pushed up a golden sleeve and checked tiny lights on her wristband. Two hours had passed since their arrival. Brennen had said he'd be only a little while. She hoped nothing had gone wrong with security details.

She took her smallest duffel with her, and after taking care of her most pressing business, she pulled out Brennen's old leather wrist sheath. The undertunic's sleeve was tight, but she buckled on the sheath and slipped in her night-black dagger. Also from the duffel, she pulled out Tel's tiny blazer. She checked its charge and slid it into a deep undertunic pocket. This would take a little maneuvering to draw, but she practiced, avoiding the gown's side ties and hitting that inner pocket, where she was expected to keep only a cloth for dabbing at tears of sincere emotion.

She paused in front of the mirror. What a costume, all scarlet and gold. As she slipped back out through the freshing room door, the heavy regalia steadied her stride.

To her relief, she sensed Brennen nearby. It was a splendid stranger she saw, though, standing with Uri just inside the dressing room. Could this be Brennen Caldwell, who never wore more decoration on his uniform than a Sentinel star and the Federate slash?

Over a magnificent sapphire blue dress tunic brocaded in pearl white thread, two wide black belts crossed each other at his waist. On one belt he openly wore a holstered blazer, handgrip exposed. A dress rapier, basket handled with its blade hidden in a long silver-trimmed sheath, hung at his left hip. Midnight blue trousers vanished into supple, high black boots. At his collar, to her relief, she saw a thin rim of silver-white fabric like the body armor Governor Danton had sent her.

"My lord consort," she murmured, dropping a half curtsey. "Pray, would you grant me the first dance tonight?"

He glanced down and touched the sword hilt. "I think this part of the costume was created for sound effects." He jingled its harness. "The blade is sharp, though." He smiled faintly. She knew how he felt about bladed weapons since Three Zed.

She eyed his high boots. "You'll be able to run, at least," she said. Ruefully, she tugged her scarlet gown. "If I leave Netaia without a tri-D of you looking like that, it won't be for want of trying."

His tense smile relaxed into something more sincere. He strode closer and took her in his arms. She felt his crystace, solid and hard through his left sleeve. "The grounds have been sealed and searched, and everyone who arrives is searched, too. There's a good chance they'll have him before we walk out into the aisle."

She kissed the side of his neck. "Brenn, we could still back out. If you want to, I will."

"No," he said firmly. "For Kiel and Kinnor's sake, we will take down these murderers." Ignoring the dressers and both their bodyguards, he kissed her deeply. He had told her that before Three Zed, before Veroh, he enjoyed the challenge of hazardous missions. She'd complicated his life . . . for the better, she hoped.

To Firebird's satisfaction, the door guards admitted a tri-D man half a minute later. For fifteen minutes she struck poses, several of them with Brennen. If Rogonin had ordered portraits done now, instead of later, he probably planned his own interruption for the ceremony.

The Federates were ready.

An electoral policeman slipped in, holding the door with one half-gloved hand. "Any need to delay, my lady?"

"No," she said in a firm voice. "I'm ready. . . . Almost," she added after the redjacket left her dressing room. "Kiss me once more. Please?"

He took her in his arms and held gently, kissing her eyes with his stare before touching her lips. She felt a gentle quest-pulse assure him of her decision. Then a wash of smoky-sweet calm started beneath her consciousness and welled upward until all doubt dropped away.

"Thank you," she whispered.

"I want you standing tall."

"Me? Tall?"

He leaned down and pressed his smooth cheek to hers. "You, Firebird Mari. Show them you were born for this, whether or not they let you claim it. You can demonstrate that without pride. Anything less would be false humility." He looked left, then right. "Uri? Shel? Ready?"

"Yes," said Shel. Firebird saw Uri nod at the corner of her vision.

Brennen held the door open, and they rode the lift together. In the long narthex, the procession was forming. A redjacket led her to her place in line, behind six skirted heralds. His red coat looked drab against the rich scarlet train Firebird's dresser carried, draped over one arm.

Shel and Uri stepped back to stand flanking Brennen. Slowly, the line moved forward. Heads approached an archway ahead, then disappeared. This morning, she couldn't hear the organum from back here. A nave full of bodies deadened its acoustics.

She stepped along the narthex. On both sides of the entry, waiting for the procession to pass, stood men and women in midnight blue, her honor guard. Now she could see that Brennen's task force had raised a glasteel arch, turning the aisle into a long, clear security tunnel. She still felt uncannily calm, steadied by Brennen's epsilon blessing.

She edged forward again. Now she could hear ceremonial music swell out of the nave. She'd despised many of Netaia's formalities as a child, but never its music. A commissioned composer could push for drama at the confirmation of an heir or heiress. The swell of the Hall's massive organum wall, brass and string banks pealing together, reminded her of a Song she'd heard once, in a vision . . . though not nearly as grand as that had been. Firebird had attended services in the Great Hall whenever her duties required it, and watched tri-Ds of her mother's coronation, and—of course—attended Phoena's confirmation.

Odd that she'd seen no tri-Ds of Carradee's coronation. She must ask a palace staffer to send over a copy.

And where was Carradee's portrait?

Still no one hurried up with word that they'd found an intruder.

The glasteel arch opened to her. She moved into position and stepped onto the main aisle. She paused, looking down its scarlet shortweave carpet toward the sanctum steps. *Here I am, Shirak. Show yourself.*

The Assembly stood.

Chapter 15

Sanctum

tira tutti
use the full organ; pull out all stops

Guard my heart, Singer. Protect me from pride. Feeling like a character in a myth, Firebird followed her golden-skirted heralds into the aisle. They raised their horns and answered the organum's peal of chords with a harmonized blast.

Then she walked the aisle.

She wouldn't stumble. She'd rehearsed her lines. There would be cues, too. The aisle seemed a kilometer long. Maybe it was. She let her feet follow the music and glanced side to side, through the glasteel, past security posts, into a blur of faces. High-commoners in their finery stood next to the low—and even servitors—in their cheapside best, for the first time in the Hall's history. What a gesture to offer the Federacy, a truly unifying event.

Step on, measured and slow. Had the Shuhr gotten an agent inside after all? She felt Brennen behind her and guessed he, Uri, and Shel walked in cadence, scanning the hall with their epsilon senses. Nearer the sanctum, but short of the now-perilous electors' boxes, several sashed nobles held cock-hats like Tel's against their chests. She spotted Tel between a black-coated Enforcer and his bodyguard, Paudan.

She didn't see one empty seat.

First Lord Erwin stood at the broad steps' right, dressed in his white ceremonial robes. To her surprise, he clutched the rod of regency across his chest. *Rogonin's presence by proxy*, she realized.

He wouldn't be any friendlier.

Maybe Micahel, seeing their security arrangements, was waiting for the motorcade, larger crowds, and easier escape routes.

She wouldn't be in that palace car, though. She let herself relax slightly as she mounted the steps. Smoke drifted down from a censer, acrid and invigorating. A half circle of motley faces grinned down from the electors' seats. She couldn't help grinning back. Then she hastily composed her face. Who, she wondered, had selected the people to sit up here? Maybe the first arrivals were given that option, or Hall staff chose them at random. She hoped the Netaians hadn't minded *too* much when Federate guards searched them.

With a final crescendo, the march theme ended on three crashing chords. She stood on the trap's trip plate. She could almost feel the winding of springs.

She spoke her lines in a satisfyingly firm voice, substitutions and all. Near the end of First Lord Erwin's speech, his words nudged her out of the overwhelming spell of organum music. "And you shall consider yourself at the mercy of your people," he called in a theatrical, subtronically altered bass-baritone, "should they call upon you to assume the throne. Will you stand ready to serve, should the high calling to which you are now declared an heiress ever fall to you?"

Firebird glanced at the redjacket who stood behind the gowned ceremonials director, guarding the tiara that gleamed with square-cut rubies. Never the throne. Not unless all twenty-six electors changed their minds about her.

But she gave the ritual reply, knowing that even modified, it legally bound her. "I hope to serve Netaia's people," she called in a clear voice.

Frowning severely, he nodded. The director reached around for the tiara. A servitor at each side of Firebird offered an arm, and they steadied her against the costume's weight as she knelt. First Lord Erwin slid the tiara above her ears. "Let us then invoke the Powers that you shall represent," he said.

He'd made a small change in his own lines, adding *that you shall represent.* Firebird jerked her head up. "No," she said loudly. "Lord Erwin, I will not—"

As if he hadn't heard, he droned on. "Fill this your servant, O Strength . . ."

The servitors had backed away, so Firebird couldn't even stand up to make her objections heard. She could only glare and refuse to listen. Instead, she thought ahead to her Naming. *Not something horrible, like*

Indomitability. Please make it Mari. Brennen's boots shone on her right, Shel's low shoes on her left.

Maybe by now, Danton's people had caught Micahel or another infiltrator—outside. That would be better than her happiest dream.

The tiara's weight forced her balance forward.

She tuned back in to Baron Erwin for a moment. He'd gotten past Resolve to Authority. Two Powers to go. Firebird strained to look up, but she couldn't see the tiara's diamond drop.

Erwin's voice droned on. "Let this woman show your face to all the worlds, Mighty Indomitability . . . and Pride, let yours be the Power that fills her spirit and mind." He raised his head, then gave a quick, self-satisfied nod.

Like a meteor burning down from the sky, something drove into Firebird's shoulder.

Brennen flung her toward the nearest wall before pain even registered. Fiery pressure tore through the muscles near her neck and deep into her chest. As from a distance, she heard shouts.

Brennen fell to his knees and seized hold of her shoulder. Mixed with the gentler heat of his access, she felt his horror.

Past Brennen, she thought she saw First Lord Erwin—someone, anyway, a white blur trying to shout orders. Tel dashed up the steps to stand behind Brennen, his own small blazer already drawn. Then a midnight blue cordon blocked her view.

So this was how it felt to be shot. *Catch him,* she begged, more of a plea than a prayer. *Catch him! He's here!* "It . . . burns," she told Brennen, reaching into her side pocket for that square of cloth tissue, "but—"

"Don't talk unless you have to." He still knelt, closing his eyes. Uri crouched beside him, covering his efforts. Firebird hoped he was remembering to look helpless. *The media's here, Brenn!* She felt a deep drain on his nervous system. When he opened his eyes, his cheeks looked pale, his scar dark. "It's an explosive projectile."

Uri nodded grimly.

She objected, "But it didn't exp—"

He seized the cloth and pressed it firmly against the top of her shoulder, close to her neck. The pressure made her gasp. "Shuhr work. It has both a shield and a timer."

Tel dropped down beside him. "Timer?"

Brennen glanced sharply at Tel and told him, "It's lodged in her upper lungs. They—" She felt the resonance vanish as he blocked fear from her perception. "It's designed to explode well after impact, and the mechanism is epsilon shielded. But they made sure I'd be able to count it down if I weren't really disabled."

Inhaling was agony. Exhaling was worse. "How long?" she asked.

"Just under five minutes," said Uri. He stood over Brennen, shielding them both with his broad back.

Tel sprang to his feet. "That's barely long enough to get her out the south door. What can we do?"

She felt queerly clearheaded, possibly from the acrid incense, maybe from adrenaline—or whatever Brennen had done to her alpha matrix before the processional—or maybe from the realization that pride had put her here.

She lay still, staring up at the men, not daring to move for fear she'd set off the . . . the tiny . . .

There was a bomb in her chest?

The gown's broad neckline and her bowed head had given the sniper a clear shot from above, despite Danton's body armor. And cruelly, he'd waited for the end of the Powers' blessing.

"Dig it out with a crystace." She looked down, coughing. Shiny blood pooled below her shoulder on the red Hall carpet. As she watched, another stream trickled down to spill over the step.

"That would kill you," Brennen said.

She had to ask, "Five minutes?"

Brennen's chin firmed. "Four. Uri, can you move it?" He shut his eyes again. She watched Uri raise a hand, felt something tug deep inside her. She gritted her teeth to keep from crying out.

Uri's hand shook. "It won't come cleanly. It's expanded in the tissue. No one can command it out without bringing most of your lung with it."

From between two other Sentinels guarding the foot of the steps, Dr. Zoagrem rushed forward. "Caldwell. How bad is it?"

"She's conscious." Brennen clenched her shoulder. Anguish started to fray the edges of his control, even his shielding. Several Sentinels stood aiming their weapons upward.

Another shot fell from the ceiling. Brennen twisted aside, flinging his arms wide. A tiny dart drove into the carpet between them, pinning Firebird's train to the floor.

They'd set a trap, too! They wanted Brennen—not dead but alive, and crippled by bereavement shock.

Her quest-pulse would accomplish nothing. "Fusion," she gasped to Brennen. "Can I help you? Is there something we can do—unless—" They'd been ordered not to use fusion energy in public, but . . . but the Mighty Singer knew she wanted to live! She felt almost giddy with relief that they didn't want Brenn dead after all. His guards would keep the Shuhr from seizing him. These consequences of her pride were hers to bear . . . except . . . *Oh, Singer, he'll suffer if I die.* She glanced at Shel, then back to Brennen.

Zoagrem pushed something against her shoulder. The sting made her gasp.

Brennen's stare refocused onto some unknown distance. Fusing energies could kill her this time, since she was already wounded—but if they did nothing, she would die. Absolutely.

"No time to experiment," he said. "We'll have just one chance." He touched her temple. "*Can* you turn?"

Doubt sickened her. She'd almost failed to turn under pressure at Three Zed. And could Brennen think clearly? She couldn't. He must choose between her life and his orders, but unless she survived, he couldn't use fusion to strike at Three Zed.

She clenched her teeth. "Don't . . . if there's a funeral, Brenn, don't let them invoke the Powers. Please."

"Never," he declared.

Shel, who'd been speaking over an interlink, hurried up. "Forgive me, Brennen, this is asinine, but His Grace insists the crown be removed."

The ruby half circlet mustn't be damaged. Firebird reached up, but she couldn't raise her right arm far enough. Shel carefully slid off the tiara as Firebird released the belt of emblems.

Zoagrem held the stinging substance against her shoulder. A Sentinel shouted orders.

Catch him, she pleaded silently, *trap him up there—just don't let him get away!* She heard more shouting out in the nave.

It took less than one of the minutes she had left to beg the Singer to care for Kinnor and Kiel. Her head swirled with disconnected thought, as if she already lay halfway Across into the Singer's world. "What are you going to try?" she whispered.

Brennen's inner shields were fully in place, and that frightened her worse than anything else. "Commanding it out, unless . . . no, there isn't any alternative. It'll wound you, but Zoagrem's here, and Uri or Shel can put you in t-sleep until we get back to base. If I get it out, though, the projectile will explode here on the dais." He wiped his mouth with one arm. "Uri, have Tel and Dr. Zed move away."

Neither budged. Tel stood between Brennen and Paudan while Zoagrem fumbled in his case. She wondered if Codex newsmen were moving into balcony position for spectacular, grisly imagery.

Brennen had trouble remote-moving objects. Even using fusion, *could* he—

"Brenn. Brenn," she said, and this time, inhaling deeply made her grunt.

"What, Mari?" He bent close to her lips. Glints in his eyes made a blurred, fiery dance in her vision.

"Could you . . . instead of trying to move it, could you make a field, a shield . . . around it? To try and absorb the . . . explosion?"

He looked at the time lights on his wrist, then back into her eyes, projecting controlled assurance that wobbled with each of his heartbeats. "Is that what you want me to try?"

"I don't know," she moaned, and then she regained control. If this was death, she didn't want Brennen remembering her weak and frightened. "Yes," she said. "Try it. Thank you, Brenn."

"By the Word, I love you." He turned his head. "Zoagrem. Give her something for pain."

She scarcely felt the jab. Hypnotized, she watched time lights change on Brennen's wrist. Twenty seconds. Fifteen. She gathered herself for the effort and felt him do the same.

He clutched her hand.

As she groped for her carrier, she felt Brennen breaching to access. Energies fused. With all the strength left to her, she clung to his point of presence, hiding from death with Brennen's strength. He would not let her see it.

Tel couldn't believe this was happening. Shel ran along the sanctum steps, shouting and shoving people away. Another pair of Sentinels tried to fire toward the traceries, but their weapons kept malfunctioning.

Did it only take one Shuhr to render them all helpless?

Paudan seized Tel's arm and pulled him down the steps to crouch behind a golden anointing font. *Ten*, Tel counted to himself. *Oh, please. Seven . . .*

Then a second tiny dart dropped from the ceiling, striking Brennen's neck, near his hairline.

"No!" Tel cried, leaping forward. As he batted off the dart, a golden figure plunged out of the tracery into the pews. Midnight blue figures converged on him from three directions as several small explosions started people screaming again.

Tel only had eyes for Firebird.

Her legs convulsed. Brennen drew up straighter, then crumpled across her. Zoagrem plunged forward and attended to Firebird. Tel pulled Brennen's shoulder up. The Sentinel's sapphire blue sleeve was soaked in blood. Tel couldn't look down any farther. Another center of shouting and scuffling erupted near the south door.

Brennen's eyes barely opened as he pushed up to crouch. Shel Mattason hurried to his side.

"No pulse." Zoagrem reached into his case for another injection ampule. "Did you . . . could you contain the—?"

Caldwell exhaled, shaking. "Not completely."

Tel looked now. Where he'd feared to see her torn open, she lay unconscious . . . no, Zoagrem said her heart had stopped. Dead? Her eyes rolled upward. Her lips had drawn back, showing her teeth.

Zoagrem pressed the ampule to her shoulder, watching his scanner. "It's trying to beat and can't. The sinoatrial node must have been destroyed, and Powers only know how much heart and lung."

Caldwell rubbed his mouth with one sleeve again. This time the sleeve left a bloody stripe across his chin. "Shel," he managed, "I've lost my turn. Put her in t-sleep. Hurry." Then he collapsed.

Tel turned around. To his horror, the golden figure came on, seemingly striding a meter in the air—leaping along pew backs, mowing down guards and spectators with a projectile gun. No one else's weapon seemed to be firing. The intruder wore a cloth-of-gold hooded skinsuit, his face and hands glimmered, and even his eyes gleamed the unnatural shade. Netaians scattered, trampling those who had already fallen.

Midnight blue figures fought the fleeing crowd, trying to reach the gold man with their crystaces. On the sanctum, the Caldwells' bodyguards crouched close to their fallen charges. Zoagrem shouted orders to arriving medical aides.

The golden figure leaped down into the open space in front of the sanctum.

Well, if he's got some way to freeze our blazers—

Tel drew his dress sword and stepped into his path, determined to buy Firebird two more seconds of life if he could do nothing more. For the second time, he looked down the sights of someone else's weapon—

Then popping noises erupted from several directions. As Paudan charged, the gold man changed course, headed for the south door. Tel lost him in the crowd.

Distant sirens wailed.

Terza watched live tri-D coverage over her father's servo table in the apartment across town. An aerial shot followed an evac van speeding up Port Road toward the Federate base.

She doubted Caldwell was in it. An atmospheric shuttle idled on the roof, ready to transfer Micahel's prisoner to their transport ship.

A tone sounded, indicating the security garage had been breached. Two crewers were downlevel, guarding that entry. Another sat between Terza and her father, while two others readied the shuttle.

She stepped away from the servo table. At any moment, she would see her child's gene-father.

To her horror, she did think of her hypothetical daughter as a child—no morula, no embryo, none of those comfortable, distant terminologies. The cells growing, dividing, and (by now) differentiating inside her were the building blocks of a life.

She wanted to shriek, to deny the change in her soul. Instead, she buried it behind her deepest shields. Few of the unbound ever bonded to any other. Under Testing Director Polar, she'd been taught how to evade pair bonding; otherwise, it was an inevitable consequence of sexual liaison. But Terza had formed a bond of exactly that sort, the kind breakable only by death.

Her father also stood, and he stepped toward the lounge area.

Micahel swaggered through the rear entry alone.

Modabah blocked his son's path. *What happened*? His question, freely broadcast, echoed through Terza's mind.

She's dead, came the answer, *but I couldn't get to him.* Micahel stalked to the table, took Terza's vacated chair, and sat down.

Dead, Terza reflected. The woman was gone, and Brennen Caldwell would be half dead with bereavement shock. Evidently he *was* in that evac van, riding beside whatever remained of his mate.

Then would Modabah send Terza onto the base to draw Caldwell out? She dreaded what Talumah might do to her mind, preparing her and protecting her compatriots.

Affiliated News still blared over the tri-D set, playing and replaying key moments from the interrupted ceremony. Micahel fell silent, watching. Terza looked over his shoulder. Modabah rubbed his chin.

The Angelo woman knelt. Close-up, headshot—she blinked once as the tiara was set on her head, then stared forward.

At least she died a princess. Or did she? She'd worn the tiara, but they never made the official proclamation.

As if it mattered now. In slow motion, the projectile tore into her flesh. It seemed to take her several seconds to gasp and tumble out of closeup range. The field widened to show her lying prone, her supporters dropping to their knees.

"See that?" Micahel demanded aloud. "That was a marksman's shot. The explosion killed her. I darted Caldwell, but I couldn't get to him. He won't show himself, won't move, for days or weeks. In that much time, we can easily infiltrate the base and take him. Easily. We'll own the RIA technology and then the Federacy. All that with one shot."

Hearing the defensiveness in his voice, Terza avoided looking at him or their father.

The image played once more. Terza leaned closer, still surprised to see so little blood. The image shifted, showing a scuffle near one of the hall's side doors. She recognized Ard Talumah, costumed as a nobleman, clearing a path for her brother's escape.

"They haven't announced her death," Modabah said gruffly.

Micahel raised his chin. *What's keeping them?* he wondered without shielding.

Their father sat back down, settling onto the last vacant servo chair. "Official announcements require protocol here. Or she might not be dead."

Micahel laughed. *Not this time.*

The security tone sounded again. This time, Ard Talumah slipped through the inner door, clothed in celebratory scarlet. A nobleman's blue sash completed his costume. He touched his forehead in salute and sent, *Congratulations, Micahel.*

Your disruptor grid worked, Micahel sent with a magnanimous sweep of both arms. *I got into position before they closed the hall for security, set up the grid, and stayed behind my own personal shields.*

Polar had excellent shields. Obviously, you studied with him. And skinsuit armor looks good on you. Ard Talumah poured himself a drink. "Look, there you go." He pointed back to the tri-D image.

Terza watched Micahel flee in miniature, saw Federate guards close in at the south door. This time, she spotted Talumah sooner. "Why didn't you just stay up there?" she asked Micahel.

He shrugged. "And miss this?" He stepped closer to the tri-D. "I changed clothing down in the tunnel, and then we separated—blended into the crowd. I looked a Sentinel straight in the eye and ducked a sorry excuse for an epsilon probe. It was almost too easy."

Terza managed to smile.

The replay shifted to real-time. As the evac van vanished into a tunnel on base, an announcer tolled the names of dead Netaians.

She only half listened. On the sanctum steps, there simply had not been enough blood, if that projectile had exploded.

A new face appeared center-screen, the sandy-haired Federate governor. "Not Rogonin." Micahel turned to Talumah. "He must be opening old wine."

"I have an update on Second Commander Firebird Angelo Caldwell's condition," Danton began.

Terza felt Micahel's alarm. *No! An announcement! You want to make an announcement!*

Modabah glanced his direction and said, "Hush."

Danton hadn't stopped speaking. ". . . lodged in lung tissue, four centimeters from the heart." Another picture replaced Danton's face. Diagnostic imagery of a ruined lung roused Micahel's pride, and he let everyone in the room feel it. He had placed the cartridge perfectly. But—

"Her chest should've exploded," he protested. "You gave me a defective cartridge—"

"Shh," said Modabah and Talumah.

". . . Caldwell evidently was able to partially contain the explosion. Again, Lady Firebird Angelo Caldwell has been rushed to Citangelo's Federate military base, where she remains in critical condition. . . ."

"*Contain* the explosion?" Talumah demanded.

Terza stared.

Modabah straightened his stooped back, sitting as tall as he could. "Then Caldwell is no ES 32. They falsified college records. Harris must be a Master, too. Or Mattason. They must have linked. And obviously, you missed him with that drug dart."

"It hit his neck. Left side, back." Micahel picked up a writing stylus, broke it in half, then broke each half again. "He couldn't have contained that much physical force. Not even a Master could do that."

"There was something else," said Talumah. "I was less than twenty meters away. Someone did expend energy."

Modabah craned his neck. "Why didn't you say something?"

Talumah raised his glass. "I only now realized it was epsilon power. I thought it was a blast wave from the explosion. I felt it as a physical force. It was huge, enormous."

"The RIA technology?" Modabah suggested. "Shef'th," he swore, "have they already learned to miniaturize it?"

"I don't know." Ard Talumah drained his drink, then yanked off his blue sash.

Modabah steepled his fingers. *We need to get onto that base*, he subvocalized slowly, *before Caldwell can get off it.* He turned to the wide-eyed lackey next to Terza. *Get every operative on world here, in this room*, he ordered. *Tomorrow morning, before six hundred.*

Then his glance rested on Terza, and she lowered her eyes.

Five hours had passed since the shooting. Brennen stared down at his bond mate's pale face. She lay propped against a large pillow, and a slender tube drained fluid from her chest. Beneath the microfiber blanket he'd raised to cover her, her torso was bruised from neckline to hip. Meds had clamped a regenerative field source over the cauterized new suture that crossed her ribs. Arching from one side of the bed to the other, its green-and-white surface was interrupted only by a control panel and a series of monitor lights. Besides hastening the cardiac muscle's self-repair, it would speed thoracic healing: the torn muscles, the microbreaks in her ribs. She was already well beyond physical danger, but if they hadn't achieved fusion before that dart hit him, she would be dead.

The small bruise on the back of his neck was his only injury. Ultradialysis had cleared the dart's dose of blocking drugs from his system even before Mari emerged from reconstructive surgery.

A twisted mass of scorched metal fragments and several grams of spent explosive had been extricated from her chest cavity before the base surgeons repaired her inner wounds. She was expected to recover quickly, but Micahel's slug-thrower and the resultant pandemonium had killed sixteen Netaians. Twenty-eight more lay seriously wounded. According to Uri, a second Shuhr had hidden in the crowd near the south door, dropping his camouflage only when it looked as if his partner might be taken. No one saw them leave the Hall, though Federate and Netaian security—working together, one small miracle in the midst of these failures—had kept the grounds sealed and released spectators in small groups after weapons inspectors cleared them. Grim-faced Sentinels, sensitive to any flicker of epsilon-energy use, backed up the inspectors.

A miniaturized field projector, found smashed in the overhead tracery, was suspected of disrupting all the energy blazers.

How had he gotten in past security?

Brennen exhaled heavily. *Was this the cost of our pride, Holy One?* Sixteen Netaian lives, two Sentinels among the seriously wounded . . .

And empty hands.

He stared down again, assuring himself that Mari was only sleeping off a surgical anesthetic. Her chest rose and fell against the bridgelike field generator. She would have been ripped in two if that dart had hit him one second sooner, preventing their fusion.

In hindsight, maybe he could have penetrated the device and defused it. Maybe he could have spared her some of this. Could have . . . but how?

Standing beside him, Zoagrem shook his head. "That injection series she took yesterday gives us another advantage. Her lungs started regenerating almost instantly after penetration. Pulmonary damage will be minimal."

"But her heart . . ." Brennen trailed off.

He didn't have to drop shields to see Zoagrem's satisfaction. "The cardiac nerves have been replaced. Parts of the right atrium and ventricle temporarily lost contractile ability, but the surgical team had them beating again within the hour." He frowned. "There's been considerable thoracic trauma, though."

Psychic trauma, too, though the Netaian couldn't see that. Brennen had sensed the breaks that smashed across her alpha matrix as fusion energy coursed through her at the moment that should've been her death. Maybe the alpha-matrix trauma was what kept scarring her ayin.

And the assassins had escaped. *Bedim them!* Had Micahel Shirak chosen to dress in gold because of Brennen's fears, or was that just a coincidence?

"She's a fighter," said Zoagrem. "Always has been." The palace med glanced nervously over his shoulder as someone walked down the base infirmary hall. "In a day, we'll have a more specific prognosis. But I wouldn't worry about her long-term chance of recovery."

Not unless the Shuhr penetrated this base! The Federates were absolutely right to fear those people. His own kindred lived under so many restrictions that no one could have guessed—until the Shuhr showed them—what they might have become.

Brennen sensed someone else at the door behind him. He looked around to see the infirmary administrator, a broad-chested man whose cleanly shaved head gleamed under hallway lights. "An announcement must be made," he told Brennen. "Governor Danton insists you approve the wording."

Reading the recall pad, a common media release detailing his Mari's near-death, he shuddered. "Strike this," he said, pointing to a suggestion that he had helped her survive. That must not be publicized. "If I could have helped her, she wouldn't be here. She would be . . . with me," he realized. "On a dance floor."

Chapter 16
Survival

molto rubato

taking great liberties with tempo, as expression demands

Firebird blinked up at an institutional white ceiling. The upper half of her bed was tilted to make breathing easier, but the humming metal-and-composite arch of medical machinery wedged her down. She could move her arms, but not far. She'd been medically dead for a quarter of an hour.

The Shuhr had almost taken her—and Brennen had recognized the golden face in newsnet broadcasts. Micahel was there, himself. But he'd gotten away!

Though the "news" was now eight hours old, all three nets were still playing and replaying the shooting from every angle imaginable. Brennen had looked princely, poised. Elegant.

Why hadn't the guards looked up? Or had they, and had Micahel Shirak shielded himself from sight? They now knew Shuhr could blur their faces in an observer's vision. Was that how he got past the exit screening?

The small woman above the tri-D projector fell. A scarlet train wrapped her like a shroud. Blood pooled beneath her. Close-up, freeze frame: It had been a master sniper's shot, missing both collarbone and shoulder blade to penetrate her chest.

Nauseated, she waved off the set. The ragged entry wound in her shoulder burned under a layer of biotape.

She couldn't as easily wave the sniper's image out of her mind. At Trinn Hill, his face had been blackened. This time, it glimmered with gilt.

Firebird groaned, shifting on the pillow. Pain blocks made her restless. So did the notion of lying here while the regen field accelerated her recovery.

But if she checked out of regen therapy, she'd have no chance of being cleared to fly combat at Three Zed—if ever they could get a Shuhr in custody.

Dear Singer, she sighed, *thank you for taking us out of there alive. Deliver my people from the threat of war.*

But, my Lord, will you stop at nothing to keep me from dancing with Brennen? She sighed, hoping the Singer wouldn't think that irreverent. She'd been taught to be honest in prayer.

She felt dead from hip to neck, due to the pain blocks. She wished she'd struggled up off her knees and challenged First Lord Erwin about that blessing, right there in the sanctum. She nearly had died, with those words almost the last ones she heard. From now on, she would be more outspoken about her faith.

And on the subject of speaking . . . though Firebird had sworn no one would ever use the title, netters were calling her "Princess."

Not for long! They could call her "Commander," if they had to call her anything. Her shallow, half-pretended nonchalance toward that high gilt chair had turned to real aversion. She reached toward a call button, then fell back on her pillow. It hurt to raise her arm.

He'd gotten away. Anna Dabarrah was right—she should've stayed at Hesed with her babies.

Sixteen Netaians were dead. She wanted justice for them, not revenge on the one who had done it. Something inside her had changed . . . no, the shift went even deeper. Something had died. Pride, maybe.

Half a dozen more Netaians might die before morning. She could never compensate their families for that loss, not even if she'd inherited the entire Angelo fortune instead of a token allowance.

Near midnight, Brennen squeezed her hand, relieved to find it warmer than before. She scowled and struggled to shift under the humming regen projector.

From a pocket in his wide belt, Brennen pulled the bird-of-prey medallion on its chain, its wings swept back almost to touch each other.

One of the surgeons had brought it out to him. He no longer cared if it was gold, silver, or lead.

"How do you feel?" he asked.

"You of all people don't need to ask," she muttered.

He did feel her frustration and remorse, and even some of her numbness came through as a vague dampening of sensation. He dropped the medallion on her bedside table, carefully coiling the chain in a spiral.

She added, "I'm sorry. I make a rotten invalid. How soon can I get back in the flight simulator?"

"Not today, Mari." She *must* be fit to fly before they could get to Three Zed—but were all their hopes built on a false assumption? Maybe the Shuhr were genuinely untouchable.

"It could be close, couldn't it?" There was a plaintive note in her voice.

"Your medics have planned a regimen. You've got to stick to it." Regen time, a gradual increase in physical activity, and a return to sim training had all been mapped out, hour by hour. "You need twelve days, minimum." Or she'd be a liability, not an asset, at Three Zed. Assuming those were his orders.

"Like a limpet mine," she declared. "And thank the One for onboard gravidics. Without those, I'd be grounded for good."

"There's one man I want to ground for good." He touched the pocket recorder he'd added to his belt. "Danton sent out some of our currently unemployed infiltrators on surveillance teams. They'll find him. One of the Sentinels at the Hall did let him leave."

"I don't understand. Did the guard remember him later?"

Brennen nodded. "That implies that the Shuhr can cause temporary amnesia, besides their permanent memory blocks." *One more ability we never suspected.* "But we finally have Micahel's alpha-matrix profile. He's detectable now, if he turns up in public."

"And how did he get in?"

"It looks," Brennen said, "as if he'd been in position for some time, possibly in t-sleep. No one sensed him there."

She sighed. "What about your cover? Your epsilon rating, the fusion . . ."

"I think it held. I want to go check, though, if—"

"Please stay." She reached toward his hand, and he saw how the effort made her wince. "I was afraid you would die in there. I can't imagine why he aimed for me instead of you."

But Brennen had been trained to notice deception. He saw it plainly now.

"I can," he said grimly, "and so can you. RIA. They want me alive, just like we want one of them." He reached for her hand. Her proud heart really had been broken—literally—but someone, somewhere, had covered her with prayer. "Promise me you'll rest and not fight the regen arch or demand to watch Rogonin's version of the news."

The sensations radiating from her reminded him of a trapped animal, panicked and unable to stop struggling. She stared straight ahead when she said, "I promise."

He laid a hand on her forehead and stroked her alpha matrix, in the tender way only he could calm her. Eyeing the humming arch, he wished such technology could've repaired his own injuries. Certain tissues, such as cardiac muscle, responded with amazing speed to regen therapy.

But the mind was more than nerve cells and electrical impulses. No physical device could repair what he'd done at Three Zed.

He glared at the bird-of-prey medallion, willing it to rise on the bedside table. The chain barely rustled. Even that effort made his temples ache.

Too tired, he reminded himself. He, too, needed sleep.

"Please read me an Adoration," she mumbled. "I left my *Mattah* back at our quarters."

He didn't want to wave on a light, and anyway, he'd been meditating on one Adoration for most of the last ten hours, praying that if this truly was the time to strike Three Zed, that divine call would come. " 'The Holy One,' " he quoted, " 'long-suffering and just, will one day release His vengeance. If the wicked will not repent, He will sharpen His sword. He has prepared for himself deadly weapons. . . .' "

Firebird smiled faintly.

Another woman sat up late, watching a rebroadcast. From a bedroom in her father's apartment, Terza Shirak stared into the space over a media block. Her eyes fixed on the small, handsome figure in sapphire blue. He knelt with his eyes closed in concentration, then fell prostrate across the woman who ought to be dead.

She'd give a hundred Federate gilds, a thousand, to know what he'd done. Once, he'd been rated ES 97. *Would his gene-daughter inherit that carrier strength?* Terza wondered. But no Master Sentinel, regardless of potential or training, could have defeated that exploding shell, so well lodged.

This must have been a demonstration of the Sentinels' RIA technology. She wondered when Tallis would announce that.

Sighing, she turned away from the screen.

With that kind of power . . .

Alarmed by the thought that whizzed through her mind, she raised her inner shields and trapped it for future consideration. She glanced at her door, then extended a quest-pulse through it.

The others had gone out, undoubtedly assembling their forces. Now they must penetrate a military base. Impossible by nongifted standards, but Terza didn't doubt they would succeed.

She let the thought rise again.

A man with abilities like Caldwell's, assisted by RIA technology, might—might—be able to stand even against her father and brother. Might be able to shelter one woman's attempt to escape from the Shuhr.

There. She'd thought it at last. Escape . . . and she'd called her own people *enemy*, by using the Sentinels' word. In their ancient common tongue, *Shuhr* meant foe, adversary.

Squeezing her eyes shut, Terza gripped the edge of her bunk. Unknown by her consciousness, the urge to escape had grown stronger while she held it down under her inner shields. Stronger, and more complex. To live free on Thyrica, where her daughter might have the casual happiness Terza never knew . . . where she might grow strong in the wind and sun, instead of banks of lights . . . on a world where the most severe penalty for weakness was the denial of training, not immediate death. . . .

She'd had one friend as a little child. One of the few light-haired youngsters at Cahal, Caira always let Terza choose games and usually let her win. When the first competence evaluations were given, Caira vanished.

Terza's stomach fluttered. She hadn't eaten in hours. She reached for a tin of fruit biscuits she'd stashed beside her bed.

When they sent her to the base, they would watch-link her mind in such a way that she could bring others inside the link, so Modabah or Talumah could observe and control her. She didn't dare wonder if her inner shields might give her some defense against that strategy.

Adiyn had said that they wanted the child she carried—for breeding stock. He'd talked mockingly about creating antimessiahs, using Caldwell's genes.

Terza couldn't move openly, but for his own child's sake, Brennen Caldwell might help her escape. That had been compassion she'd seen in him . . . plain, raw grief . . . as he knelt above his fallen bond mate.

A bond mate Terza never would be, but her child carried his essence in every cell.

She shut her eyes and cursed pregnancy hormones.

Well past midnight, Brennen lay awake on a cot that base staff had wedged into Firebird's room. Shel had only left this door when Brennen lay down and Uri took over.

She *would* recover, he reminded himself. He'd sent reassuring coded messages to Dabarrah and Carradee via the first messenger ship leaving Netaia. For the first time, though, he doubted the wisdom of bringing her to Three Zed. They hadn't taken a prisoner yet. The strike might be delayed indefinitely. He had to hope so, for her sake.

On the other hand, every day they delayed gave the Shuhr more time to attack other worlds—and get RIA technology.

At least Danton's watchers in low-common neighborhoods were sending good news. For the moment, Citangelo's people had united in concern and in anger that the same Shuhr who cratered Sunton had struck in Citangelo. They were in no mood to throw off the electors. For the moment, they were blaming neither Firebird nor the Sentinels for drawing an attack. Some were even demanding a stronger Federate presence.

One newsnet report, though, quoted rumors that Firebird had died, and the Federacy was covering up. Brennen guessed that was an attempt to draw her out into a vulnerable position, so Micahel Shirak might try again.

Not here, Brennen vowed. *Holy One, salvage this situation. You can use even our mistakes for a greater good.*

This base could withstand a siege by conventional weaponry, but not for long. How long could it hold back the Shuhr?

At least none of the most disquieting reports would reach her. Danton's people had scrambled Codex on her set.

He shifted on his cot, unwilling to look away. When he closed his eyes, he saw her crimson blood. She slept restlessly, but at least she slept.

So this was His Grace the Regent, Muirnen Rogonin.

A dim winter's sunrise filtered into the sovereign's day office through its east window. As Terza followed Talumah and Micahel down three carpeted steps onto an inlaid wooden floor, she wondered if he depended on props, such as the five translucent world globes suspended over this sunken floor, or the elevated platform on which his desk stood, to command respect. He was neither attractive nor wise-eyed, and though his vanity implant created a youthful illusion, overconsumption was his obvious weakness.

With Firebird gone from the palace, the ten-plus epsilon presences had also vanished. Muirnen Rogonin would never know that his rival's presence had protected him—briefly—from his real enemies. Today marked the end of his volitional independence.

Micahel walked across an inlaid sun, complete with solar prominences, that had been created in some gold-grained wood. He stepped up to desk level and reintroduced himself and Talumah, then presented Terza.

On cue, she stepped forward. "I bring my father's greeting," she said, as ordered. "He is Modabah Shirak, hereditary head of all the unbound starbred."

In Rogonin's terms, that made her royalty. He raised his head. "What is your title, then, as his daughter?"

"No title is necessary."

"Then I am to call you. . . ?"

"Terza. Terza Shirak."

He glanced at Micahel. "Are you . . ." He flicked a finger back and forth. "Related?"

"Distantly," Micahel answered, and Terza spotted disdain in the narrowing of his eyes.

Disquieted, she looked away.

"Very well, Terza," said the regent. "Sit down. Tell me more."

One of his attendants pushed a chair away from the wall at one end of the platform, and she sat down across from him. A minute ago, he'd been openly suspicious. Now he meant to flatter her.

Talumah remained standing beside her, under one of the five globes. She'd been told that they stood for Netaia, two other settled worlds in this system, and its two buffer systems. "Our people," he said, "wish to establish an observation post in this residence." Terza felt a flicker of protest, then the counterflicker as Talumah smoothed away Rogonin's objection and went on speaking. "We are disappointed, of course, that Lady Firebird survived our attack yesterday."

"Disappointed?" Rogonin's cheeks flushed. "You killed sixteen of my subjects. That is inexcusable, unforgivable—"

In that moment, Talumah thrust a breaching probe deep into the regent's alpha matrix. Terza felt the backflash. Rogonin sat motionless, wide-eyed, clutching both arms of his throne-chair. Talumah worked swiftly, manipulating Rogonin's will exactly as he'd mind-altered Princess Phoena.

Exactly as he would manipulate her if they discovered her secret hope.

The silence lasted ten minutes, and Micahel kept his stare on Ragonion's attendants. Then Terza felt echoes of epsilon activity fade away. Rogonin's contorted face relaxed. He drew a deep breath.

Memory block firmly in place, she understood.

"We now wish," said Talumah, "to penetrate the Federate military base. Help us only a little, and we will eliminate your Federate overseers."

Rogonin spread his hands. "Gladly. Tell me how."

Micahel stepped toward the long desk's other end. "We want to take the base in two stages, probably an hour apart. First, it is still crucial to kill Lady Firebird and take General Caldwell prisoner. We still assume you would not regret losing *that* subject."

The regent straightened in his gilt-crusted chair, clasping fleshy hands. "No. I would also be pleased to see the lord consort gone, permanently. Terza," he continued, looking back at her, "tell me, and the secret will go no further. What really happened to the young queen whom I serve as regent? Carradee's daughter, Iarla Second."

She glanced up at Micahel, who was deeper inside their father's confidences.

Go ahead and answer, he sent. *This is one secret he'll keep.*

She turned back to the regent. "Iarla and her sister are dead, Your Grace."

He inhaled slowly, smiling. "Tell me more."

Disgusted by his delight in child murder, Terza used her inmost shields. "Step forward, Talumah." The taller man made a mocking half bow to the regent. "My co-worker," Terza said, "intercepted a Federate shuttle carrying them to the Inisi system. He destroyed it as it reentered normal space." She didn't tell him about the tissue specimens preserved in her laboratory, nor her supervisor's interest in the Casvah genetic line.

Casvah. A thought struck hard. What if . . . what if it were *Firebird* whose epsilon potential saved them yesterday? Or maybe, some psychic union of the Casvah line with the Carabohds? If so, then those Casvah specimens in Terza's laboratory could have the same potential. They might give her people the powers that had just saved Firebird from certain death.

Talumah stared down over her shoulder. She felt his epsilon probe lick up that thought. He raised one eyebrow, radiating pleasure. *Yes*, he sent, *that is possible!*

"And then?" Rogonin asked Micahel. "What about your second stage?"

Enraptured by his own destructive fantasies, Micahel seemed to have missed Terza's exchange with Talumah. "We will destroy Citangelo Occupation Base," he said, "just as we hit Sunton on Thyrica."

Rogonin's fleshy face turned pale. "Yes, we heard about Sunton . . . but . . . Citangelo . . ."

"This time," Talumah said slowly, and Terza felt the calming overlay, "we will not take out the entire city. There is enough distance between the base and this district that the finer homes will be spared."

"How soon will you strike?" Rogonin asked, clenching the arms of his chair. "I want my family sent out of danger."

"There is no danger." Micahel spread his hands.

"How . . . soon?" Terza felt the effort that question cost Rogonin. His will was strong to be able to question them at all.

"As soon as you can give us ships capable of this kind of attack. Sooner, I think, than Lady . . . *Princess* Firebird," Micahel taunted, "and her lord consort can leave the base. She may not be dead, but she shouldn't be moved."

"Excellent." Rogonin finally succumbed, touching a desk control that lowered the large, central globe to just over head-high. Now Terza recognized the coastlines of Netaia's North and South continents. Another flick of his finger created a glowing zone on the globe. An enlargement of the glowing area focused over his right shoulder, on a projection panel she'd mistaken for a wall. "The spaceport district," explained the regent, "is badly in need of urban renewal."

Micahel smiled slowly. Terza choked on the urge to tell Rogonin that his spaceport district, if Micahel got several warhead-loaded ships through, would be the rubble-strewn deep spot of an uninhabitable crater.

"Regarding your first stage," he said, "I have a suggestion. First Marshal Devair Burkenhamn of the Netaian Planetary Navy has gone over into Lady Firebird's camp. I saw them speaking at my daughter's presentation ball, and he just reinstated her into the Planetary Navy. With a promotion," he added, frowning.

"So we heard," said Talumah.

Rogonin nodded. "Since she has reason to trust him . . ."

Terza plainly felt his last struggle for independence. Then he blurted the words, "Could your people use him as an assassin? He lives out in the city, but he works on base."

Terza raised one eyebrow. Ard Talumah wouldn't have planted that suggestion but commanded Rogonin to serve them with full loyalty and his favorite "impossible" ideas.

For all Micahel's murderous skills, Modabah seemed reluctant to let him penetrate the base at ground level. So he would send in Burkenhamn—and Terza.

"That bears consideration," Talumah said slowly.

Rogonin stared down at Terza. "Are you all right, my dear? You look pallid."

"Your Grace is a fine strategist," she said stiffly.

"Obviously, I have employed fine agents." Rogonin spoke firmly now, his alpha matrix reorienting to its newly imposed loyalty. He called up another map projection. "For your second stage, I suggest using Sitree Air Base. I can give you access codes. You can get other information when you . . . when we interview Marshal Burkenhamn."

"Excellent," said Micahel.

Terza looked aside, at Talumah. He paid Rogonin's props no attention at all. She could almost feel his mind racing.

Casvah-Angelo and Carabohd-Caldwell, Terza reflected again. Casvah and any Ehretan line, maybe. The Angelo woman might be key to their victory, after all. Firebird . . . and Terza's child, to get them to Caldwell.

INTERLUDE 6

Second Lieutenant Aril Maggard dropped into her seat on *Babb*'s crowded bridge and entered another tick mark at one corner of her com console. They had been eighteen days in Inisi space and found no trace of the little girls' shuttle. Curious by nature, Aril had studied the Federate register between watches. She guessed she'd learned more about Netaia's customs and its noble families than most other Federates knew about their home worlds.

With this much time gone, though, hope had faded. The diplomatic runner's supplies would have run out some time ago. Aril's best remaining hopes were to see a footnote entered in Netaia's history . . . or better still, to go back to Lenguad and get on with her life.

She really would prefer someone else found them now, if they were in Inisi space.

The salvage ship lurched as *Babb*'s pilot fired braking thrusters. "Almost on sector," he announced.

Aril activated her scanners and leaned back, stretching.

An hour later, the shift's first *ping* brought her upright. The second curled her forward over the scanning screen. "Debris," she called. "Metallic, irregular. Considerable mass."

Major Dunn leaned over her shoulder and ordered, "Block the

quadrant and rescan. Transponder check and mass estimate."

"Transponder check and mass estimate, aye." Aril stroked her controls, first defining a scan volume, then collecting data. She read off a mass figure, then craned her neck to look up at Major Dunn. "Transponder confirm, ma'am." This was the missing shuttle.

Could they still be alive?

The officer frowned. "Check life signs."

Aril had already flicked another scanner. A red light glimmered on her board. "Negative, Major." She said it calmly, but her chest went tight. She had several young nieces and nephews.

Maybe they'd gotten away in a rescue pod.

Major Dunn took the command seat. "Helm, take us closer. Scanners, spotlight whatever there is to see. Com, call Inisi base. I'm afraid we may have found them."

Minutes later, Aril's neck and shoulders ached from sitting in one position, staring, waiting to activate the big lights. At last, she switched them on.

The underside of a Tallan courier appeared, rotating slowly. Even from this angle, Aril could see that several steering units had been blown off. "Confirm battle damage," she said. She'd seen this before. It had never affected her quite so deeply.

"Match speed and rotation," the major ordered.

On the main screen, a long, gaping tear with metal and composite hull curled back from its edges drifted into view. The cockpit had taken a direct hit. Aril stayed at her post while two salvage workers donned extravehicular suits and exited the main lock, carrying rescue bags and remote imaging equipment. She touched a control that split the main screen. It continued to display the damaged courier's exterior but added a view from the salvage team's imager.

Avoiding the tear, they approached the main lock.

It hung open.

"This ship has been boarded since impact," said a young male voice on the cabin speakers. The image on Aril's screen bumped and shifted as the imager jiggled, then floated steadily inward. The powerless shuttle had naturally lost all gravidics. "Crew of six on station, no life signs," the voice said dispassionately. He didn't swing his imager around to show bodies. His partner would be taking those recordings, using a different instrument. "Significant toxic residues on the bulkheads."

Aril tried to comfort herself with the fact that there'd been no accident. No mishap would be blamed on Federate ground crews. "Shuhr," she whispered. The fiends! She brushed moisture off one cheek.

"Look for a private compartment," Major Dunn directed.

The image floated up a short corridor. The first starboard hatch hung open, damaged. Aril's chest tightened again as she spotted a soft, brown stuffed animal—some domestic Netaian creature—floating in a corner between bulkheads. This had been a child's private cabin.

"They're not here," the male voice concluded several minutes later.

"Rescue pods fired?" Major Dunn asked.

"Negative."

What could the Shuhr have done with two small children? Aril wondered. The ship had been boarded. Were they kidnapped? Acting on a hunch, she activated one of her other scanners.

Something cold seemed to settle on her chest and shoulders. "Biological debris," she announced. "Eighty meters aft, drifting."

Major Dunn relayed that report. The salvage crew exited the shuttle, and on the main screen, Aril saw the faint red glow of EV suits' steering units.

The remote image remained trained on the starfield.

"Yes," the voice said softly, angrily. "We've found them."

"Com, inform Inisi base." Major Dunn sounded weary. "Tell them to notify Hesed and the Netaian Electorate."

Aril did a quick mental calculation. Because of the relative distances to Hesed and Netaia, Carradee would receive the news first.

Chapter 17
Bequest

intermezzo, piu agitato
interlude, slightly agitated

Tel pressed the CT earpiece in tightly, then cupped a hand over it. "Yes, Solicitor Merriam, I remember you." The elderly man was the sovereign's legal counsel. "Could you speak louder?"

"I'm sorry, no," said the husky voice. "The regency has been monitoring my office for days. I'm not certain my home is clean. It's urgent I speak with Firebird, but the base is allowing no one through. Can you have her contact me immediately?"

Barely awake and less than half dressed, Tel leaned against one wall of his spacious wood-paneled bedroom and peered at a clock. What time was it—six, maybe seven hundred? "I will try, but I was unable to get through myself. The base is taking no chances." The implications—that Shuhr agents might find and influence him so that he might harm Firebird—were chilling. Still, he had plenty of loyal bodyguards now. He felt safe enough.

"It regards Carradee's will." Merriam's voice—or was it even Merriam?—dropped until Tel strained to catch words. "I am leaving the city for my own safety. I will drop certain documents by Your Highness's estate in half an hour. You must see them delivered."

The connection went dead. Through a force-screened window drifted the song of an awakened bird. Tel replaced the earpiece in its uteh-wood box, then slipped on a pair of warm house shoes. If these documents were genuine, then by the urgency in Merriam's voice, Tel guessed they would cause a sensation—and bring Rogonin's redjackets to his door.

Alarmed on all counts, he picked up the earpiece again and put through a call to base. He still couldn't persuade the staff to let him speak with Firebird—no one wanted to wake her—but Caldwell's bodyguard, Uri Harris, intercepted his attempt.

Tel liked Lieutenant Colonel Harris, who moved and spoke with upper-class grace and self-confidence. "If you could reach my estate in twenty minutes," Tel said, "there will either be extremely important documents delivered that are meant for Firebird, or else an attempt on my life." As he spoke, he stared up at the portrait over his bed. His late wife wore orange, which represented Excellence in Netaia's symbology. Heir-named *Eschelle* for *Excellence*, she had always called that "her own" Power.

The imperious tilt of her head balanced the grace with which she clasped her long fingers. She'd sat willingly, letting him adore her on canvas.

To his chagrin, this morning he could look at that portrait without longing for her. She'd brought Netaia to the Shuhr's attention. Because of that, they threatened to take the world—and they nearly killed Firebird yesterday.

"If this is real," he told Harris, "and if His Grace at the palace is watching the solicitor's home, I will not be secure with those documents in my hands. Please come and take them."

"I can't leave my post," said the Sentinel, "but I can send another courier. She'll be in uniform, with my personal clearance code."

"Again," ordered Modabah.

One of the ship's crew who'd brought them to Netaia toggled a control. Over the media block, the familiar tableau appeared: Firebird Caldwell knelt at center stage with her Sentinel beside her.

The projectile drove her to the floor. Caldwell all but collapsed.

"Not yet," said Talumah. "Keep going. . . ."

Terza watched Talumah watch the tri-D. His eyes fell half shut. The miniature figures huddled—

"Now," Talumah exclaimed. The crewman froze the image.

But they're just lying there, Terza said.

Modabah occupied the largest chair. He brandished a recall pad. "Listen to this." He read off several paragraphs couched in self-assured prose that reminded her of Dru Polar. "Polar's research," Modabah explained, confirming her guess. "Just before his death, he was working with the idea of fusing two epsilon carriers, one artificially repolarized to an unusual conformation. His theory was that joining two such carriers would release a flood of energy. He called his theory 'antipodal fusion.' "

Micahel spoke first. "Do you suppose Caldwell stole Polar's idea and perfected it? This looks like—"

"How did you say it felt, Talumah?" Modabah demanded.

"Like an explosion of pure energy."

Modabah flung the recall pad against the wall. "That's what they're doing. Caldwell and Firebird, somehow. The Angelos have been isolated here for over a century. There must have been a mutation. Something altered their epsilon potential."

"Kill them," declared Micahel. "Separate them first. Then we can kill them both."

Modabah slicked back his hair with both hands. "We still could take him and use him. But yes, finish her. If she has that kind of epsilon carrier, and she inherited it, then he couldn't do this with anyone else—except Carradee, the one who abdicated."

She would've taken a vanity implant, Terza pointed out. *Her ayin is probably destroyed.*

"Good, Terza," said her father.

It was the first time he'd ever praised her.

Ard Talumah turned his back on the tri-D image, crossing his arms over his chest. "So nothing has changed. Kill her, dart him, and grab."

Modabah scowled. "Something has changed," he insisted. "If our assumption about the Angelo line is wrong, then other Sentinels might be learning this technique. They've undoubtedly studied whatever it is these two have been doing. We can't give them one more day."

"Yes," Micahel hissed. "Hit Thyrica. Take down the college. And I tell you, Hesed can be attacked. All we need is one Thyrian ship with RIA technology—"

"We've tried. They're guarding those ships too closely. Take an order," Modabah called to the crewman, who pulled his own recall pad off his belt. Modabah rocked forward on his chair, clasping both hands. "This is for Adiyn, by fastest courier."

The crewman nodded.

"Adiyn," said Modabah. "Mobilize. Deploy to Tallis," he stressed, glaring at his son. "To the capital city, Castille. I want a crater twice as deep as Micahel left at Sunton."

One side of Micahel's mouth quirked upward.

Modabah gripped air with one hand. "Make it look like a Sentinel attack—use the Procyel-Tallis approach vector, and transmit from Thyrica that Tallis's inaction after Sunton could not be tolerated. Turn them on the Sentinels at all cost."

Terza quivered behind her deep shields, staggered by the loss of life he was ordering.

"Second order," said Modabah. "Those Casvah gene specimens could be priceless. Get them into the deep vault under the main chamber. I will follow close behind this message, as soon as Caldwell can be taken. End message." He glared at the crewman. "Get moving."

Then he turned to his son. "The third order is for you. Get on your way to Sitree. I'll transmit specific orders as soon as we have Burkenhamn. Get three fighters. Heavy ones, long-range. Load up, stand out, and await orders. As soon as we take the Angelo woman down and Caldwell out, demolish that base. Pick two pilots from the settlements. You know the drill."

To Terza's surprise, Micahel didn't seem delighted by his assignment. He stood cracking his knuckles. "For once," he muttered, "just once, I would like to be present when Caldwell is brought in. He is mine. So is Burkenhamn, after he roughed me up at that ball."

Terza watched her father hesitate. After all, one day Micahel would lead the unbound. He had the right to take this generation of Carabohds. . . .

"I can't promise you Burkenhamn," Modabah said. "But I will say this. No one will kill Caldwell until you arrive."

Firebird woke herself midmorning, thrashing, trying in her sleep to find some position that eased the main weight of that field generator off her chest. It was only twenty centimeters wide and ten thick, with rounded edges, but after just one day, she'd started to think of it as an instrument of torture. It hummed incessantly, not quite a true pitch. She also had a new, nagging itch at her left wrist. The base's chief med, a Tallan named Adamm Hancock, had secured a life-signs cuff. She would be wearing that little bracelet, too snug to be removed, until the surgeons pronounced her fit to fly.

She felt stronger already. Something else had changed, too, back at the sanctum. Along with her pride, that asphyxiating fear . . . for Brenn, for herself . . . had vanished. There remained terrors to be faced, but she couldn't bring herself to care. Mightier hands than hers, moved by a wiser will and a richer love, controlled her destiny. It was obvious now.

She just wished she felt stronger yet—and more comfortable.

The door slid open, and Shel slipped into her room.

"Where's Brenn?" Firebird asked.

"Uri says he's been up since two hundred. I don't think either of them slept. May I ease you?"

"Yes, thank you."

Shel walked over and locked stares with her. Nauseating otherness swept across Firebird's alpha matrix, but it leveled peaks of discomfort. "Thank you," she repeated.

Though the deep, infuriating itch faded, the generator's weight still tormented her. According to her regimen, in a few hours she could get up for a while. That couldn't happen soon enough. "Did they find any more traces of Shirak overnight?"

Shel took the bedside chair, leaning away from her hip-holstered blazer. "He left a few skin and hair cells on the overhead beam. They took a full DNA tracing and cross-checked the Netaian medical database. That only proved he was offworld. *His* people don't publish referents. Nothing else on the search. Rogonin insists the palace is cooperating, but we have doubts."

Firebird nodded. She did, too.

Shel slipped out.

Only a few minutes later, there was a quick rapping on the door. Firebird straightened her hair over her shoulders and called, "Come."

Uri and Shel pressed through together, along with a third Sentinel Firebird had met yesterday on guard shift, Lieutenant Rachil Mercell. Slender with short brown hair, she'd sat and talked music, describing herself as a lapsed brass player.

Uri held a sealed message cylinder under his elbow. "We've safed this," he said, sounding slightly less composed than usual, a little more tenor than baritone. "Lieutenant Mercell picked it up at the Tellai estate, with instructions from an older gentleman to greet you in the name of Solicitor Merriam."

"Merriam's afraid." Lieutenant Mercell stood against the door. "I've applied to Governor Danton for his protection."

Startled, Firebird forgot where she lay and tried to sit up straighter. The field generator held her down. "Did Solicitor Merriam say what this is?"

"Not to me," the lieutenant said.

Firebird thumbed the seal, and the cylinder's halves fell apart. She fumbled out several sheets of rolled parchment. The smallest, in Tel's hand, dropped free. "I believe you need to know," she read aloud, "that the Ceremonials Committee turned down your request. Your heir name is Domita." *Not Mari*, she reflected, *but at least they shortened Indomitability.* Two years ago, she had hoped to be remembered for indomitably facing her wastling fate.

She eyed the other sheets. "These look like original documents," she began, then she realized, "They are. Heatsealed." She turned over the loose roll. It was illegal to break a heatseal unless authorized, but above the seal was printed, "Firebird Elsbeth Angelo, upon her Confirmation as an heiress of the House."

That looked like Carradee's scribing.

She punctured the seal with one thumbnail. "Testament Upon Renunciation of the Throne," she read aloud. Then, sobered by the realization that these documents were vital family property, she scanned the top page.

By the time she started reading the second, her heart thumped under the field generator and the life-signs cuff gave off a pale green light. The Angelo fortune—the entire wealth of Netaia's most powerful family—was to be placed under her administration, if she were ever confirmed as the heiress.

No wonder Solicitor Merriam feared for his life. She couldn't waste a minute. She could accomplish something for Netaia right here in the infirmary, and pride had nothing to do with it. Carrie had arranged this even before leaving for Hesed. She'd kept it secret, too, and explained why . . . right there in the fifteenth clause. "So that no one might accuse Firebird, now or ever, of monetary motivation in accepting confirmation."

That explained Carrie's delight over her decision to come back here, though. She'd practically shoved Firebird up the shuttle's boarding ramp.

"Uri," said Firebird, "is there a legal consul on base authorized to access civilian programming?"

"I don't know."

"I need to speak with one right away. And can you access him, to make sure he's not under Rogonin's influence?"

"That depends. We're only allowed use of our abilities—"

Under strictly controlled circumstances, she chorused mentally as he spoke. "All right," she said. "This solicitor is about to be asked to do several things. He must have Tel Tellai-Angelo authorized on these documents as my Netaian representative—and executor, if necessary," she added, determined that whether she lived or died, Muirnen Rogonin would no longer leverage the Angelo fortune.

Her voice rose with excitement. "I also need documents of incorporation, so that moneys I now control can be distributed without certain parties' knowledge or interference. I mean to use Angelo resources to end the electors' stranglehold on Netaia's economy, Uri. Is that circumstance enough?"

She saw a hint of Brennen in Uri's half smile. Second cousins, weren't they? "I believe it is," he said. Then he added in a teasing tone, "Commander Caldwell. I'll send down breakfast, too." He left with Lieutenant Mercell. Shel stayed at the door.

Firebird stared at the far wall. Tel must examine the family portfolio—no, first he would have to *find* it—it was probably at Merriam's office and might have been stolen.

She could withdraw enough funds to build a Chapter house, too, and bring non-Sentinel Path instructors to Citangelo.

Smiling, she shut her eyes and relaxed against the field generator. What *was* the pitch it had hummed all night? Not quite a C-sharp, but a sharp C-natural . . .

Another idea rose to tantalize her. All her life, she'd wished she could be remembered as a patron of musical arts. It would have been lovely to establish a conservatory scholarship in perpetuity. Or an orchestra . . . she'd always wanted to found a new orchestra. This one could be dedicated to diverse programming.

Could be. She couldn't afford to think in those terms yet. Resting her recall pad against the regen arc, she keyed up her list of official charities, side by side with a compilation of Netaian industries that had cooperated with Governor Danton.

Muirnen Rogonin made a chopping motion with one hand, and his servitor hastily waved off the media link, choking out the irritating new song. He wished it hadn't taken his people three days to recognize its deadliness and how far such songs might travel before they were stopped.

But now he had a prisoner.

She stood on the inlaid petitioners' floor below his desk, wearing a baggy, unflattering low-common dress and wrist restraints. Her left eye twitched above a floral tattoo.

"Clareen Chesterson," he said slowly. "If you will cooperate, this interview will be far less uncomfortable."

She adjusted her stance, straddling an inlaid inner-world orbit. "I have nothing to say, Your Grace. I have done nothing wrong."

Rogonin raised one eyebrow. "Is that so? I have here," he said, raising one sheet of hard copy, "testimony of a subtronic trace. A transmission was sent from Prince Tel's residence to yours on the twenty-third of this month. Again," he said, sliding another sheet to lie on top of the first, "a high-commoner willing to swear he saw you the next day, going into Tellai's town apartment less than an hour before Lady Firebird entered."

"That has nothing to do with Your Grace's accusation."

"I think it has." He popped a mint under his tongue to cool and burn and soothe him. "Here is another testimony, stating that you were seen entering the Tellai estate on two other occasions. Prince Tel is known for unconventional monarchist views."

"That has nothing to do with me, Your Grace."

"Is that so?" His new friends had warned him that if she'd collaborated, the Sentinels would have voice-commanded her, making her truly unable to reveal information, even under pharmaceutical or physical persuasion.

Here she stood, though, an instigator of the Federatization he feared.

He regretted that harsh steps were necessary. He dreaded the purge that must come. It soiled his regency, it soiled his House, but for Netaia's sake, he would not back down. He would build new prisons with the Angelo moneys he still leveraged, as regent. . . .

From behind her, near the Coper Rebellion mural, Talumah purred, "She is afraid, when you question her."

Her head whirled toward the voice, and she stared—either at Talumah or the mural, worked in jewel dust over a translucent screen.

"Give us what we want." Rogonin rose out of the day office's chair. "Identify Lady Firebird as the writer of that vile, juvenile ditty. If you do, we will free you. If not—" He laced his fingers across his midsection. "You will vanish from Citangelo."

Clareen Chesterson clenched her crossed hands. She gritted her teeth, looking as if she wished she could rip off her wrist restraints and jump him.

Hinnana Prison was full of the likes of her. He also had detention facilities at Sander Hill Station and under the palace. As of yesterday, he also had new allies who surely could convince her to confess.

"Talumah, escort our musical guest downlevel. Send Burkenhamn in on your way out."

Terza sat in the dank new downlevel observation post, a long, thin chamber between storerooms, stuffed with eavesdropping gear the crew members had brought from Three Zed. She tugged a sleeve of her awkward House Guard uniform. It rode up her arm with a will of its own, instead of following her motions like sensible clothing.

Micahel was headed southwest by superspeed commercial transport, and Talumah was uplevel with the regent. Momentarily alone, she wondered if Talumah had already altered her alpha matrix, either shipboard or since she arrived here. Her father had a reputation for making plans within plans. Maybe her upbringing included subtle pushes toward rebellion.

Or was this growing urge to escape simply the unstable Shirak personality, as her old supervisor Juddis Adiyn called it? Tallis was doomed, the Federacy about to fall.

Think in one straight line! she commanded herself—*escape!* Modabah Shirak might guess that his daughter could try to defect. Or, more sinister, he might be pushing her toward defection. If her alpha matrix had been twisted, she wouldn't remember. That also was standard procedure.

Maybe she, too, was being maneuvered into position to destroy Brennen Caldwell's bond mate, without her knowledge or consent.

She covered her abdomen with both hands. If she killed Lady Firebird, Caldwell would never—never—help her escape.

But she had to get to him, even if that was exactly her father's intention.

Out in the north corridor, footsteps passed. Terza peered through the storage room in time to see Talumah pass, escorting a manacled woman.

Netaia's seizure was beginning.

Outside, it was cold midmorning. Muirnen Rogonin stood behind his day desk and listened to Devair Burkenhamn abase himself. The marshal stood at the flaming, inlaid sun's center, at rigid attention. "Your Grace," he concluded, "I am oath-bound to come to you in time of conflict. You called, so I must offer my services."

Here was one more traitor to Netaia's lasting grandeur . . . but this traitor would be of use. No Sentinel would have dared to put voice-command on First Marshal Burkenhamn, the way they got to Clareen Chesterson. Behind Burkenhamn, almost invisible against the older mural—of Conura First's victory over the outsystem invaders—stood another one of Rogonin's new House Guards. Rogonin returned the man's slight smile. Burkenhamn—with his size and strength, and Firebird's trust—would make an ideal assassin.

He returned his attention to the beefy marshal, who looked rather like a target standing at the center of all those inlaid orbits. "Thank you for your timely arrival. I assume this is a difficult gesture for you to make." *You still want her back in the palace, don't you, Burkenhamn? She'll be there, all right. Lying in state, thanks to you.* "I want you to deliver messages to the occupation governor and Commander Angelo."

Burkenhamn barely inclined his massive upper body.

"First, you will need a strategic briefing." He beckoned another one of his new employees away from his post by the east window. They had promised him Burkenhamn would remember nothing from what they were about to do, except having been brought to their new observation post. Rogonin did not want Netaians carrying memories of their foul treatment. Burkenhamn's suicide would be honorable, too. Rogonin would slip him a dagger in custody after they arrested him for murdering Firebird.

CHAPTER 18

BURKENHAMN

tutti
for the whole ensemble

Ard Talumah called Terza into the south storage room. "Look over what I've done," he ordered. "I need to send Micahel some intelligence." Then he stepped out.

Lying unconscious on a dusty, marble-topped table, Devair Burkenhamn looked like a monument carved from stone. Terza focused for access, probed for the breach Talumah had left, and slipped through.

Twisted threads of Burkenhamn's alpha matrix, linked with recently inserted suggestions, showed how subtly Talumah had blocked the memory of interrogation, preparing the marshal to return to full consciousness only when taken inside their observation post. Deep beneath Burkenhamn's consciousness, bird's-nest knots of thought and emotion would be Talumah's preparation for betrayal, murder, and finally suicide.

Talumah was a master.

Again, she wondered—had he already done this to her? Shipboard, or just moments ago, between her arrival in the storeroom and her first glimpse of Burkenhamn? Talumah could have rethreaded her entire alpha matrix after calling her in, and she would remember only the sensation. She turned inside herself, trying to see if anything felt different.

She found it only when she slipped behind her secret shield. Talumah had prepared her, too, for the attack. Trembling, she made sure Talumah really had left her and Burkenhamn alone. To be absolutely safe, she raised her inmost shields once more. Then she examined the preparatory locus in Burkenhamn's alpha matrix, where Talumah had subverted volition at the deepest possible points. As terrified as she was, not knowing exactly what Talumah had just done to her, she knew she must try to thwart Firebird's murder. That was the only way she could get Caldwell's sympathy and help.

With utmost care, because this kind of work wasn't her specialty, Terza loosened the critical locus like a knot. She didn't dare do more. If Talumah caught her meddling, her father would take her alpha matrix apart thread by thread, then blast her out the nearest airlock. This effort would be her signature, her proof to Caldwell that she'd tried, at least, to circumvent their murderous plans.

She could do nothing for herself. She only hoped Caldwell still was capable of detecting what she'd just done to Burkenhamn.

But did she really want to defect? What would it accomplish, what would it prove?

In that one reluctant thought, Terza found her own proof. Her father must've once wanted to plant her among the Federates, maybe to assassinate Caldwell. Now he had other plans for her. He'd ordered Talumah to create new doubts as to whether she wanted to defect.

Then Talumah would have watch-linked her already. The transport that brought them here surely carried the requisite gear. Talumah and Modabah would be able to monitor all her uppermost, unshielded thoughts.

All right, Father. She formed the words clearly, desperately glad she'd shielded herself before tampering with Burkenhamn's alpha matrix. *I am not deceived, but I will serve you.*

Carefully controlling all further thought, she shook back her hair, straightened the uncomfortable sleeves once more, and shut off the restraint table's immobilizing field. She angled a hand to use voice-command. "Open your eyes and sit up."

The monument shook itself. Burkenhamn rose, staring, his eyes processing only enough information for physical function. She dusted the back of his cobalt blue uniform with her crimson sleeve, then nudged him toward the observation post. Talumah sat finishing a late, elegant-looking cold lunch. *Yours, Talumah,* she subvocalized.

Talumah grasped the unseeing marshal's elbow. "Inside, large one," he ordered. Then he subvocalized to Terza, *Satisfied?*

She nodded.

Today, Talumah sent, *we show Caldwell that his God has a short reach.*

Burkenhamn revived all in a moment, bending forward to stare at the nearest bluescreen. The post had three visual monitors, one currently showing the palace's north grounds, another displaying airspace over Citangelo. The third was blank.

Crooking one finger for Terza to follow, Talumah glided toward the opposite door. The storeroom that accessed this post from the north corridor was piled haphazardly with clear-wrapped uniforms in black, gold, and scarlet, moved out of the inmost room to make room for surveillance gear.

He handed her a recall pad. *The rest of your orders.* Then he slipped back out.

She sent the door shut, then touched the ON button and read.

> Burkenhamn will be quick—a simple strangulation, a blow to the head, break her neck, anything—but it must be his doing, not yours. Do not interfere.
>
> Once that is accomplished, you and Talumah will still have Burkenhamn as hostage for a safe exit. Deliver our ultimatum to Danton. Caldwell will be experiencing bereavement shock. He may be entirely without control. Again, be quick. Dart him. Drag or carry him toward the main gate. We'll pick you up.

Yes, Father. Again Terza formed words with deliberate care. Behind her innermost shields, she wished Talumah weren't coming. Sending her alone onto the Federate military base would be foolish, though, even with new subliminal orders to leave the base. Her father was no fool.

The vision of Ard Talumah as a malformed embryo flitted across her mind. She dismissed it hastily and read on.

> I'm ordering Danton to withdraw all forces from these systems. Instantly. He is granted his personnel's lives, but he must leave all matériel. Micahel is prepping two crewmen for the clean-up mission. Don't worry—we'll be far out on the plains in less than three hours, before Micahel can get back.
>
> Bring Burkenhamn out with Caldwell if you can, but don't delay for Burkenhamn's sake. Only Rogonin cares if the marshal is killed on the base or if he suicides. Rogonin is cooperating fully.

Terza stared at the device. *Well planned, Father*, she thought hard.

If Caldwell cannot be drugged, the second threat to be leveled against him will of course involve the fetus. If you leave the base without him, it will be flayed and dismembered at a viable stage, and the remains delivered personally into his hands. The procedure will be transcorded for general Federate consumption. If he has already lost a bond mate, I don't think he'll resist this threat.

Once more, do not delay. You must not be on base in three hours.

The message ended.

Nauseated, Terza squeezed the OFF panel. She frowned, covering another shielded reflection with surface gratitude. She should be thankful that Modabah meant to get her out of Citangelo before Micahel sent in his suicide pilots. Did he know—did he guess that her heart, betrayed by the workings of her own body, really had chosen against him?

He couldn't think otherwise. He'd just threatened to abort, torture, and callously dispose of her child. Short weeks ago, she had destroyed human embryos with no more remorse than he showed now.

Excellent, Father. I am ready. We will defeat the Federates from our new base on Netaia. I would like a rural estate, south of here, near a river.

She dropped the recall pad onto a clothing stack, then strode back to the inner door.

"Ah," Ard Talumah said when she emerged into the observation post. "Here is our other escort, Marshal Burkenhamn. Terza," he added in a clipped, authoritarian voice. "The marshal is to deliver messages to Governor Danton and Commander Angelo Caldwell. We will see that he passes safely onto the base *and safely returns.* We are his Netaian escort, from families he knows well."

"Sir." Terza dipped her head to Burkenhamn. "I am at your disposal."

This is for you. Talumah dangled a lens-shaped tri-D pickup, swinging like a lavaliere on a short golden chain. *A gift from His Grace. He wants a recording of Firebird's demise.*

Then he slipped her a silvery injector. She made sure it was sheathed before pocketing it. She spotted a standard dart pistol tucked into Talumah's belt.

Well planned, Father. Well planned.

Talumah led out, his long face pointed confidently forward. *Here we come, speaker-god. Stop us if you can.*

Terza followed Burkenhamn up the north corridor, then out an echoing white tunnel to palace garages. The heavy lavaliere lens pressed against her breastbone. The Netaian marshal slid behind the driver's seat of a palace groundcar as easily as a smaller man might move. His strength had to be tremendous.

Talumah joined him in front. Terza took the place behind Talumah, determined not to watch him too closely. They emerged near the spear-tipped gates and accelerated down into Citangelo. The city streaked past under a winter blue, late-afternoon sky.

Deep behind her shields, she let the thought rise: At the surface, she no longer wanted her freedom. But how deeply could her father affect her will? Somewhere in Modabah's web of counterplans, did he want Ard Talumah disposed of? And if so, why?

Did the law-bound Sentinels live like this? she wondered, still hiding her thoughts—each one suspecting all others? Or was their propaganda based on truth, and did their allegiance to a higher cause make them a truly different people?

Her daughter had little chance of reaching maturity if she returned to Three Zed. She would probably be aborted anyway, or euthanized, and her cells cloned as breeding stock. Yet the hereditary abilities of Modabah Shirak and Brennen Caldwell could've made that child great for either side. A treasure had been thrust into Terza's hands.

She would guard that treasure if it cost her life. If the Federacy's new weapons might be used to turn the Golden City, like Sunton, into dust and rubble, then her child must not be there.

She thought of her lifetime's work—all those genetic samples—and Three Zed's armory, its records, its Ehretan artifacts—the treasures stolen from Federate worlds—must they be destroyed? Could she carry that burden?

She clenched one hand. *Of course not, Father.*

Automatically braked by central guidance at the end of city-controlled roadway, the car slowed. Ahead, Terza saw massive energy-fence walls. She loosened her blazer in its holster.

Two Federate watchmen guarded each side of the base's tall main gate. Behind them, a fifth man sat half shielded on the gunner's seat of a huge new energy projector. A man in midnight blue stepped to Burkenhamn's side of the car, followed by one in Verohan pale blue.

Burkenhamn opened his windscreen to answer. "I need to speak with Governor Danton." He handed out an ID disk. "You may tell him I'm here."

A gust of breeze lifted the Sentinel's dark blond hair. He stared at the Netaian officer, then glanced in Terza's direction.

"My aides," Burkenhamn declared.

Terza slipped complacency into the suspicious Verohan's midbrain, letting Talumah deal with the Thyrian. He'd proved he could deceive Sentinels when he escaped the Hall of Charity.

The Sentinel rested his left hand on Burkenhamn's door. "One moment." He lifted a tiny subtronic device, backed away, and spoke rapidly. Terza caught the word *Burkenhamn*.

Then they waited. Terza might have dashed past the guards to a cluster of gray buildings beyond the perimeter, but that energy projector looked capable of ground-to-air defense. It wasn't something she wanted to tackle.

The Sentinel removed his headset. "I'm to accompany you. Unlock a rear door, please."

Danton probably realized Burkenhamn was in danger, even on base. Terza rested her hand near her blazer as the Thyrian slid in.

Half a meter separated her legs from those of someone who had been raised to kill her kind on sight. She mustn't provoke the Sentinel, not this time. She must not make enemies.

Burkenhamn steered the vehicle toward the L-shaped main building.

Brennen reentered the base's command center after a quick break. Several Sentinels that had been withdrawn from palace infiltration stood at guard posts. He was pleased to see Firebird reclining in a mobility chair, studying the tri-D well with Governor Danton.

She glanced up at Brennen. "I'm barely moving. *Largo*," she joked feebly. "We're drawing up an evacuation plan for Citangelo's civilian population."

This was her transitional day, slowly working up to walking again. Brennen turned to Danton. "Any word from Marshal Burkenhamn?"

"On his way. Just passed the gate."

Burkenhamn saluted a quartet of door guards, two of whom stepped forward as he approached. "I must speak with Governor Danton," he said calmly. "Direct me, please."

One in Tallan gray saluted again. "Follow me, Marshal."

Terza came behind Talumah and Burkenhamn, and though Terza was taller, the Sentinel guard paced her step for step. The other Federate guard followed.

How many minutes might I have to live? she wondered, down deep. Then she thrust the thought aside and pointedly recited, *Get the drugs into Caldwell. Cover Burkenhamn while he kills Firebird. Get Caldwell off base.*

Well planned, Father.

Their Tallan guide led down a soft-tiled hall, past doors on the left and right, all closed. The guide's home world, Tallis, would be struck—probably within fifteen days. Terza wondered if he had family.

Ahead, double doors stood open, guarded on both sides. Terza touched the tri-D pickup around her neck. Now it would record, though it wouldn't transmit, so far as she knew. Netaian transcorders were larger and heavier than this.

Striding in, staying on Burkenhamn's left, she took in the instrument panels, display monitors, and other accouterments of military power. Half a dozen Federate staff stood or sat at various stations, flanked by several uniformed Sentinels, undoubtedly the ones withdrawn from the palace—

Her sweeping glance snagged at the sight of a man she recognized from Three Zed. Caldwell had a slightly squared face, with one cheek faintly scarred and alert-looking blue eyes. He stood beside the Federate governor, near a tri-D well. His epsilon savor was plainly muted, weaker than she'd imagined. He wasn't as tall as she'd pictured him, either . . . nowhere near as tall as her brother. Slim shouldered, he retained the presence that had carried authority—but without the hard, arrogant edge that marked Three Zed's leaders.

Burkenhamn saluted the Federate governor, then looked aside.

And there *she* sat: Firebird Angelo Caldwell, white medical coveralls bringing out the flame in her hair. Her face looked flushed.

There they were together, her daughter's gene-father and the mother of the only children he ever would acknowledge—his prophesied heirs, miraculously safe at sanctuary.

Burkenhamn saw Firebird, too. Smiling, he strode toward her mobility chair as Talumah palmed his dart pistol. Terza felt Talumah gloating, taking mental aim at Caldwell, measuring his range. Burkenhamn picked up speed as he crossed the room.

"Marshal." The Angelo woman smiled warmly. "We needed to talk with you about—" Welcome faded from her face. It would have been easy to let Burkenhamn reach her. Easy, and right—

From behind her inmost shields, Terza brought up the cry, "Stop him!" Against common sense, against all sense of loyalty, she leveled her blazer at Talumah's back and kept one eye on Burkenhamn. "Caldwell!" she forced out the words. "He's under command to kill her!"

Burkenhamn lunged. Firebird flung herself off the mobility chair. A cleft-chinned woman Sentinel sprang toward Burkenhamn. In the same instant, Talumah pivoted.

Terza shot him in the chest.

Firebird landed hard and rolled over with impressive speed for someone so recently and severely wounded. *Pain blocks*, Terza guessed, *and regen therapy*—

The Sentinel woman landed a flying kick on Burkenhamn's left hip, knocking him aside. She hit the floor in a tuck, somersaulted, then lashed out again from a crouch. Caldwell and another Sentinel closed in on the big Netaian, raising their hands to use voice-command. Two guards in mismatched Federate uniforms caught Burkenhamn's arms.

Other men and women scattered. Terza opened both palms and extended her arms. Her hands trembled with self-reproach. Her blazer hit the soft tile, bounced once, then lay still. She fixed her stare on Brennen Caldwell's eerily blue eyes, holding it there even when someone seized her right shoulder from behind and pressed something hard against the base of her skull. "Don't move," said a woman's voice. Other hands fumbled at her belt, then patted her down. Someone pulled the lavaliere pickup over her head.

She drew a deep breath, smelling charred fabric and flesh. Talumah's flesh.

I'm sorry, Father. There are things even I have to do. Good-bye.

A Sentinel knelt beside Firebird, supporting the small woman in a sitting position. The female guard who'd intercepted Burkenhamn stood over them, brandishing a blazer. The room quieted. Controllers and com techs returned to their stools and sat motionless. Burkenhamn blinked as his mismatched guards helped him stand up.

Caldwell stepped in front of his bond mate, defensive fury in his eyes. Did he realize how narrowly she'd just escaped assassination . . . again? Finely muscled, he moved well, and the savor of his presence had an uncanny peace. When he stopped two meters away, she dropped her shields in submissive greeting.

His dark eyebrows arched. She felt him focus the remnants of his epsilon shield. She waited, passive but tingling in every nerve, for a thrust of mind-access.

"Who are you?" he demanded.

The voice, too, surprised her. It wasn't as deep as she remembered from Polar's interrogation files. Did Caldwell sense nothing? Her desire, her intentions, her . . . the state of her body?

Three med assistants in yellow tunics dashed through the door, pulling a medical litter. One knelt beside Ard Talumah, touched a hand to his chest wound, then shook his head at Occupation Governor Danton, who hung back between two big-muscled Carolinians.

Other meds helped Firebird back into her reclined mobility chair, where she kept her eyes trained on her bond mate.

"Who are you?" Caldwell repeated. "Who is he? Why did you kill him?"

She wondered what Juddis Adiyn saw at this moment on the shebiyl, back on Three Zed. Surely a dozen possible futures snaked off from this nexus. Her voice shook when she answered, "My name is Terza Shirak."

His eyes widened.

"I am asking . . . requesting asylum. I believe your people hoped to take a prisoner, just as mine did. Guarantee my safety, and my memories are at your disposal." Was she really saying this?

He stared, and still she felt no probe. Maybe he thought she was insane, or illogical, or hurried over the brink of competence.

"Asylum?" came a feminine voice from behind him.

Caldwell stepped aside, glancing down.

That had been Firebird's voice. Her bodyguard remained close, holding that blazer.

The weapon Terza couldn't see pressed hard at the base of her neck. Still shieldless, she felt Firebird's curiosity and gratitude mingled with suspicion. Neither she nor Caldwell accepted Terza's plea . . . yet. Terza would have scorned them if they had so quickly.

Terza indicated Talumah with a flick of her eyes. One of the meds unfurled a body bag over him. "His name is Ard Talumah," she said. "I killed him because he would've killed me, once he understood that I mean to defect. Believe that or not, as you will. But I am not acting under orders now. I am breaking them."

Firebird pursed her lips and raised her chin.

"He deserved to die," Terza said softly, pitching her voice so that only Firebird and Caldwell would hear clearly. "He mind-altered Burkenhamn to kill you. He also murdered your nieces. The Angelo girls."

Firebird's eyes narrowed as if she remembered something. "Talumah," she muttered. "Cassia Talumah's brother?"

"The same." Cassia, who died when this pair escaped Three Zed, must have bragged about Ard's attack. "I have something else to tell you." She focused on Caldwell again. "It will be better if you hear it alone."

He barely shook his head, perhaps distracted by a second burst of unshielded realization from his bond mate. Carradee gone, then Phoena, and now Carradee's heiresses—

"You have every reason to suspect treachery," Terza said softly. "I am almost certainly watch-linked. I'm also sure my alpha matrix was manipulated. And one other thing has been done to me. To my body. I am—I was—a genetics technician. The plan was to lure you in."

To Terza's satisfaction, Firebird glanced directly at Terza's belly. Again, comprehension burst out of her. Naturally, the woman would understand first. She was a mother and a bond mate. She stretched out one hand toward Caldwell.

He leaned down, letting her whisper into his ear. His stare whipped toward Firebird, then back to Terza in horror and . . . was that hope?

I want the child to live, she projected, using minimal carrier strength. There were other Sentinels present. *That's why I'm defecting. I'll tell you everything I know or have been led to believe. But then you must find a way to see that I can't harm you, or else the tragedy will have only begun. They want you.*

The governor stepped forward, sandy hair dangling across his eyebrows. "Do you know this woman, General Caldwell?"

"No." He tilted his head back, exhaling slowly, his every movement caution. "But I know her family."

"Not—" the governor began.

Caldwell nodded curtly.

Again, Terza felt faintly nauseous.

One of Burkenhamn's guards held the lavaliere pickup. He pointed it back at her, and she spotted her own injector in his other hand. "Would you submit to blocking drugs, Terza Shirak?"

She bit her lip. Blocking drugs might break the watch-link, but they could also damage her child's neural system. She held her breath, wondering if Caldwell would let that fetus be mentally crippled, to render Terza harmless. If so, he was more like his *shuhr* than she'd thought. "I will submit," she said, letting Caldwell feel her anxiety, "if General Caldwell orders drugs."

The hostility in him dimmed. Maybe he hoped she might be genuine. He flicked one hand, and the pressure against her skull eased off. "Go with Sentinel Mercell, Terza. She will make you comfortable. I'll follow as soon as I can."

The guard behind Terza grasped her elbow.

"Lieutenant Mercell," Caldwell added.

The Sentinel woman turned around.

"No drugs," he said. "That is an order."

Esme Rogonin sat at table, clutching a cloth serviette in her lap as she silently finished her soup. Her father had actually invited one of his mercenaries to dine with them. Esme was trying—vainly, she feared—to hide her disgust. This was the father of that sniper who nearly killed Lady Firebird, eating Netaian food in the palace's most elegant private dining room! Until this hour, Esme had been able to pretend that her father hadn't collaborated to commit murder.

And something was terribly wrong with her father. In place of his usually regal manner, he was cordial—even effervescent—with the intruder and his aides. Esme had warned her mother, who was visiting the

Parkai estate, by CT link. Duchess Liona had dispatched a driver to pick up Esme and her other children, but he had not arrived. Maybe the mercenaries wanted hostages.

It *was* odd for all four Rogonin children, heirs and wastlings, to eat together. Beyond Esme at table, her young brother Kelsen catapulted bits of food at Lady Diamond, the youngest. Thank the Powers, Esme could still pass for fourteen. She made a point of slouching, looking intimidated. If they thought of her as a child, they might not consider her a threat.

"Until this incident," said the oddly stooped chief mercenary, "we had no idea how dangerous Firebird is. I guarantee that she will commit no further treachery."

Esme kept her fork moving. Her father laughed merrily, and his guest watched him . . . instead of his eldest daughter. A good thing, because if they really could read people's emotions, her horror might attract attention.

What would her life be like as heiress to a seized throne, controlled by offworld interests? It was clear to her, if not to her father, that these people were about to grab all Netaia. Did she have to choose between collaborating with these murderous "unbound" or with Prince Tel's Federate friends?

She never, never could take a warning to the Federates. That would betray all she believed. But Prince Tel had pricked her conscience at the ball, talking about wastlings, and motives, and . . . and her little brother and sister. Her father's actions today were *wrong.*

She shivered over her hot soup.

INTERLUDE 7

Carradee woke up wreathed in a strange feeling of peace. She checked the time—three hundred forty. For a while, she listened gratefully to the soft hum of Daithi's spinal regen apparatus and his slow, steady breathing. Then she rolled out of her bed toward the twins' chamber. A small luma glimmered there, and a watch-keeping sekiyr lay on the bed between warming cots. Her nephews slept peacefully. Tonight she plainly saw Brennen in Kinnor's relaxed expression. That was unusual, but she knew an Angelo from a Caldwell.

Silently she dressed. She couldn't have said why. She slipped out of the medical suite and walked onto the waterside pavement. A pale turquoise band rimmed the vast pool, shadowed by islands and square stepping-stones but casting enough light to walk by.

She followed a stepping-stone path to an island and sank onto a stone bench. There, she gazed into the water until memories came: Iarlet tottering onto her feet and then, seemingly only a day or two later, dashing naked out onto the palace balcony. Kessaree shrieking with laughter at her sister's facemaking. Iarlet explaining soberly why she would not, could not, wear the same-colored skinshirt two days in a row.

It felt good to weep.

Half an hour later, Master Jenner strode out onto the stepping-stones, and Carradee knew what he must tell her. She was as ready to hear it as a mother ever could be. She'd cried herself dry.

"They have found your girls' bodies," he said as they sank back onto the bench, "and the wreckage of their shuttle. It was attacked, Carradee. I am sorry. They were . . . murdered. We should receive more details soon."

She shook her head. "They are with Him," she murmured. "They are safe. No one can hurt them now. But pray for me, Master. And for Daithi."

"Shall we move the twins from your suite, to give you time to grieve your daughters?"

"No!" Carradee cried.

Chapter 19
Orders

prestissimo
as quickly as possible

Firebird's pulse pounded as she sat and watched the tall, pale woman walk out. Signs of early pregnancy—the full, high breasts, the barely darkened mask across her cheeks—were there for any observant woman to read. Terza Shirak's statement, "The plan was to lure you in," told her the rest of the story.

Could anyone call this Brennen's child, since he had no role in its conception?

At least Terza was trying to see that no one found out except Brennen and herself. Firebird tried to imagine Brennen's eyes, Brennen's personality . . . Brennen's abilities . . . imprinted on a baby that wasn't hers, too. They knew that the Shuhr carried on the Ehretan tradition of genetic research. They'd discussed the possibility that his cells might have been cloned. Now ramifications were occurring to her that she hadn't considered. Especially . . .

Was the child genetically Terza's, too? A Caldwell-Shirak? *Mighty Singer, what is this?* Her arms and shoulders still trembled with her body's reaction to danger. She hadn't lost her maternal instincts, either—she wanted to rush home and grab Kiel and Kinnor, to never let them out of her sight again.

Terza's other revelation, alone, would have stunned her. Cassia Talumah had told the truth when she claimed her brother "brought in tissue samples" from Iarlet and Kessaree. If that man, Terza's victim, really killed them, then . . .

Poor Carrie!

Then Firebird's promise in the Hall of Charity could shackle her to a gilt chair and the weight of a world. She no longer wanted that, not even as a reformer.

Mighty Singer, send me back to Hesed, to my children, my new life. I was wrong to try to return to this.

Then she thought of the ice miner and thousands of other commoners struggling for a share of Netaia's prosperity. She thought of monstrous Hinnana Prison and wondered how many children's parents languished inside.

Singer, what do I do?

She knew one answer from Path instruction: Commit this day to His will and live it. She would be grateful for specific guidance, though.

Brennen looked in her direction, and his lips tightened again. She could almost read his thoughts: *You shouldn't have been here.* His next glance was at Burkenhamn. The big marshal stood motionless, covering his face with both hands. Governor Danton leaned against the tri-D well, staying close to his guards.

Surely he hadn't heard Terza's revelations.

"You have your prisoner," said Danton. "Finally. Who's your strongest Sentinel here?"

"Firebird's bodyguard, Major Mattason, has the highest ES rating." Brennen said it without hesitating. "But Lieutenant Colonel Harris is better qualified for access interrogation, and even before he begins, I have orders to open." He raised an eyebrow to Uri. "Marshal Burkenhamn," Brennen added, extending a hand, "my sincere apologies. You must not doubt what the Shuhr woman said about her compatriots planting that suggestion."

"Not at all." Burkenhamn cleared gravel from his voice. "I felt it as she shouted. I deeply wanted to kill Commander Angelo, whom I respect."

"Commander *Caldwell*," she murmured.

Burkenhamn didn't seem to hear. "And it . . . still . . ."

Burkenhamn's guards seized his arms, but he threw them off. Shel stepped toward him, blocking Firebird's view. Uri hissed a word of command.

The marshal came no closer. Firebird saw only his legs, working as if he were trying to walk in mud. "Not my doing," he muttered. "Help me, Sentinel."

"Gladly," said Brennen. "And I need one thing from you, sir. I need a set of orders, for Second Commander . . . Caldwell," he said after a moment's hesitation. "I need her to report to me, for the duration of an upcoming operation."

"Yours," said Burkenhamn.

Shel stepped aside, but not far, and she kept her blazer ready. Now Firebird had a clear view of her marshal and the anguish on his lined face. "Commander," he said, "report to Field General Caldwell for the duration of operation . . ." He broke off, glancing at Brennen. Getting no response, he turned back to Firebird. "You will remain under General Caldwell's orders until he dismisses you back to me."

Chain of command wasn't so different from palace nod-and-bow, really. Firebird raised her right arm stiffly, touched one eyebrow, and murmured, "Y'sir."

Brennen glanced to one side. The Sentinel at Burkenhamn's right shoulder nudged the big man's arm. "Come with me, Marshal." Two more Sentinels followed him out, through a different door from the one the Shuhr woman's guards used.

Brennen's glare softened, and Firebird felt his concern. "Commander," he said, "your first order is back to sick bay. Your exercise interval ended five minutes ago. I'll join you there," he added.

Her medical aide drew out a hand controller for her mobility chair. Firebird still heard her pulse thudding in her ears. She raised her wrist and saw that the cardiac monitor's display had gone red, into the danger zone . . . as if that would surprise anyone. She felt aged, decrepit—

And bitterly resentful, that the Shuhr used Marshal Burkenhamn against her. Once again, her new rank and honor nearly led to tragedy. *I see your point, Mighty Singer. I get the message. Enough!*

As the aide steered her back up the corridors, her thoughts fled to Hesed House. *Poor Carradee! Who will tell her she has no daughters?*

Brennen waited until she'd passed out of the range where they could share each other's feelings, then clenched a fist. This situation wasn't developing remotely as he'd anticipated.

Glancing around, he beckoned the nearest remaining Sentinel . . . not Uri, who couldn't leave him, but the next closest. "Lieutenant Cowan?"

The young man with the blond beard hustled forward.

"In my quarters, on my work desk. Sealed message roll. Meet me outside sick bay with it."

One more Sentinel left the command center. It was becoming almost private in here. . . .

Then he sensed a tracking tech's alarm from over near the tri-D well. "Sir." The woman stared at him, not the governor. "Messenger ship outbound, heading six-one-two point one-two. Refuses to ID."

Brennen hurried to the three-dimensional cylinder that represented space within the primary Netaian system. Green spheres were planets, silver dots meant satellites, and gold pinpoints represented friendly ships.

The tracking tech pointed toward a gold pinpoint streaking outsystem. According to characters displayed alongside, the ship was a DS212 Brumbee messenger, launched from the NPN's Arctica Base, accelerating too quickly for any hope of intercept.

"On that vector," Brennen said softly, "it could be headed for Tallis, or Caroli—or Three Zed." That system lay north-spinward of Caroli. Shuhr agents here could be reporting on events in the Hall of Charity.

What had they concluded?

"Keep trying to reach him by DeepScan," said Governor Danton. "If there's any other unscheduled activity, either on or offworld, notify General Caldwell and myself."

Medical supervisor Adamm Hancock's dark eyes and sharp chin framed a frown as he tucked a microfiber blanket around Firebird's legs and chest, bathing her in warmth. She started to relax. "You're supposed to be working back up to walking," he said, "not trying to get killed."

Her cubicle's door slid open. Brennen stepped in, clutching the silvery message roll down at his side.

"Thank you," Firebird told Med Hancock. "I really didn't plan—"

"Of course not."

"May we have a few minutes alone?" she asked. Over her chest, the regen arc felt oddly warm, almost comforting.

"Ten minutes, General," said the medic. "Then I'm going to sedate her. That'll put her back on schedule."

"Excellent," Brennen answered.

Hancock scurried out. After the door slid shut again, Firebird raised a hand. Brennen seized and stroked it. "You're cold," he said.

"You're warm. Open your orders."

"I will, as soon as I've cleared you to hear them." He set down the message roll to pull the new pocket recorder off his belt, thumb it on, and recite date and time. Then, "Second Commander Firebird Angelo Caldwell, Netaian Planetary Navy, now under my orders, hereby designated my forward attack subcommander." He returned the tiny recorder to its place, then thumbed the cylinder's security seal and twisted the halves apart. "Breathe, Mari," he murmured.

She hadn't realized she was holding her breath. She took a deep, slow breath. Then another.

He unrolled the sheaf carefully. His eyes flicked left and right several times. "Operation Yidah," he read softly. "We're . . . hmm." He frowned.

"What, Brenn?" she demanded.

His displeasure came through strongly. "We're to take off, with prisoner, and interrogate en route to a rendezvous point north-spinward of Caroli."

Hastily, she calculated travel time against her retraining schedule. She could do it—barely—if they really were headed to Three Zed. " 'Yidah' sounds Ehretan," she said.

"It is," he murmured, still scanning. "It's one of those prime words with half a dozen meanings. Various uses of the hand—to throw a stone, cast out, offer praise . . ." He lowered the roll, widening his eyes. "Or thanksgiving. Or to bemoan."

"The hand," she said softly. "A sword in His hand."

He shook his head as if to clear it. "We'll leave today. You'll have ten days en route, and that doesn't give you any leeway at all. I'm ordering you to stick with that schedule."

"I will." Firebird knew which system "ten days en route" indicated. "Then we are ordered to Three Zed."

"Of course." He curled the sheets between his hands and slipped them back into the message roll. "As directly as possible. No devious attack vector, no warning. The Federacy wants us to burn it to bare rock."

Her breath caught. This went further than she had expected. Clearly, the Federates were so terrorized by the Shuhr's destruction of an entire city, and by their uncontrolled use of epsilon talents, that they felt this was justified. Even Brennen's people had been warned that they would be called to this task one day.

"But is there a discretionary provision?" she asked. That holy call still had not come.

He shook his head, washing her with a dizzying mixture of reluctance, eagerness, anger, and pity. "Even if our force is wiped out, the Holy One always keeps a remnant alive. Only sixty-two of the faithful survived Ehret—Mattah and his family, their friends, and the orphans."

"Then at worst, Kiel and Kinnor will be part of the next remnant," she murmured. He'd obviously thought this through.

"They sent a roster of ships and personnel waiting to rendezvous with us." He ran a hand over his hair. "My first job is to get a transport with a full med suite, and a secure room to hold . . . Terza."

"Quickly," she said. "Once they know she defected, they're likely to throw everything at this base."

She still felt his uneasiness. He leaned down and brushed her lips with his. He smelled of kass. "By the time you come out of sedation, we're likely to be en route. Is there anything you need to accomplish first?"

"Yes. I've still got some business for Tel." There had to be some way she could disinherit herself. But when Terza's news about Iarlet and Kessaree reached Netaia from other sources, the electors would have to either acclaim a new monarch or else give the crown to Rogonin.

"Finish it," he said, and his eyes softened. He'd probably guessed half of the thoughts that just blasted through her mind. "You're prone, you're under regen. I'll hold off the med for a few minutes."

He sent a sick-bay aide for her recall pad as he left. When the aide returned, Firebird dictated a new will, with orders for copies to be sent to Hesed, the Netaian Electorate, and Prince Tel. If she died at Three Zed, Tel was to distribute whatever remained of her allowance to Kinnor and Kiel, pending their confirmation as heirs. If by some miracle Carradee conceived again, he was to petition the Electorate to restore the throne to Carradee's line. Three days ago, she wouldn't have requested that. *Dying does change a person. . . .*

Finally, she outlined her plan to reconfigure the Angelo portfolio to support eventual covenance with the Federacy. Effective immediately, Tel was to divest her of hidebound, nobility-based trade and industry, using the family wealth to support offworld trade and programs that would strengthen the common classes.

If he hurried, they might prevent civil war after all.

In the two hours estimated to convert the Luxian diplomatic transport *Sapphira* for his needs, Brennen had to do two days' work. The heavily armored, adequately armed transport had been assigned to the Luxian ambassadors, Comete and Cometesse Remelard. Brennen's message roll did include a *commandeer* order from Regional command, and on seeing it, the mustachioed comete instantly relinquished claim to his ship. Danton's top engineer went to work, removing most of its comforts to make room for additional quarters and converting an inner cargo hold to a reasonably comfortable brig.

With work teams dispatched, Brennen paused in a secure room off the corridor and reread his orders, trying to commit all salient points to memory. Even after all the Shuhr had done to his family, and to the rest of the Whorl, he did not want to command such a brutal operation without divine confirmation. This could also be the end of Special Operations as a significant group if his force was defeated. Most of the rest of Special Ops, and Thyrica's Alert Forces, waited at the rendezvous.

Please confirm this, he begged. *Send us with your blessing, or else show me I must disobey Federate orders again. You know I will obey either call. The Federacy is afraid, but you are above fear. We all live by your unconscionable grace and mercy.*

He'd given up his chance at the Federate High command by disobeying an order he couldn't follow in clear conscience. He would do that again, if necessary, to save Sentinel lives. That would mean a permanent dismissal from Federate service. At least.

Firebird was the last Angelo, though. The Electorate would undoubtedly call her back to Netaia. He was willing to serve wherever the Holy One sent them. If only he knew . . . clearly . . .

He waited more than a minute, resting his forehead on clenched hands.

Nothing came.

Then he would have to wrestle with his conscience en route. Meanwhile, he did have orders.

Most of an hour later, he and two other Sentinels were testing epsilon-fielded locks on the new brig's windowed door and every other escape route, logical and illogical. He'd also arranged for Terza to be watched clock-around from a guard station just outside the brig and by in-cabin monitors. Only the One knew what other compulsions her people had put on her, besides the watch-link.

As he stepped through the crew lounge, past a triple bunk that workers were bolting to a bulkhead, the door to his own forward quarters slid open. Shel stepped away from the hatch and stood aside. Two med attendants came steering a medical litter up the port passway. Firebird lay on the litter, unconscious under the regen arch. He lingered at the hatchway, watching the meds squeeze alongside a newly installed forward berth in his cabin. Marks on the deck and bulkhead showed where other furnishings had been removed.

"I want medical monitors at my bridge station," he said, eyeing her face. A faint flush warmed her cheeks, and those delicate features never quite relaxed, but carried a hint of her determined spirit. He wanted to protect her, not take her to—

"Installing them next, sir." The meds raised the green-and-white arch, rolled his bond mate onto the new berth, then set about installing the arch in its new position. "Barely room to swing this aside, sir."

"We'll manage," he told them. *For five days, until we get to the rendezvous point and aboard a bigger ship.*

Back out in the passway, Sentinel pilots hauled duffels into assigned cabins, singles reconfigured as doubles. *Sapphira*'s redundant life-support suites would support them, and he wanted every combat-trained Sentinel on board to crew RIA ships. According to his orders, he would command the attack cruiser *North Ice*, the fighter-carrier *Weatherway*, and their complement of RIA-equipped scouts, bombers, and fighters.

He flexed his hands and stepped onto the bridge. Pilot, nav, shields, and sensor/com officers were already there, running preflight checks, cross-programming the escorts' navigating computers.

A tone sounded on *Sapphira*'s com board. The Sentinel running checks touched a tile. "*Sapphira*, Lieutenant Mercell at Sensors."

Danton's voice came through clearly. "If General Caldwell's on board, send him back to the command center. All haste."

"On my way," Brennen called, already jogging.

Lee Danton gestured toward a wall screen. "We're getting a picture from . . ." He stared a question at the nearest controller, whose headset dangled from one ear.

"Satellite outsystem, sir."

The governor frowned, drawing his eyebrows down almost to touch at center. "We've got an unauthorized rollout at Sitree Air Base."

Brennen eyed the screen. Sitree was twelve hundred klicks west-southwest of Citangelo. Well within striking range, three long-range fighters had been rolled out of their hangars and were being serviced.

"According to Sitree Command, they're being fueled and fitted by Marshal Burkenhamn's order," said the controller, "but Burkenhamn insists the order didn't originate in his office. Not that he can remember."

"The Shuhr could've had him authorize any number of things." Brennen cast a glance around the command center. "Sir, you'd better go to full alert."

"Gambrel Base is scrambling regular crews to fighters," Governor Danton assured him. "But how many ships did the Shuhr throw at Sunton?"

Brennen silently raised three fingers.

Danton touched his collar mike. As he called for a second-stage alert, Brennen sprinted back into the corridor.

Tel Tellai glared at a tri-D image. He couldn't believe this Codex propaganda! Firebird, dead by Burkenhamn's hand? And Caldwell, sheltering a woman who carried his child?

Ridiculous.

". . . as proof Caldwell's treachery started months ago," the Codex commentator intoned, "proving again that Netaia's former lieutenant governor has been a covert leader of the Federacy's attempt to enslave the Netaian systems. His Grace the Regent is in emergency session with the Electorate, considering a declaration of war. A further announcement is anticipated at any moment."

Another electoral meeting, called without him—illegal!

Tel strode across his study and poured a glass of mitana, an edenfruit liqueur. Rogonin's loyal commentator had to be lying. Surely Devair Burkenhamn hadn't killed Firebird, not after all she had survived at the Hall of Charity.

He sent a servitor to bring his remote CT link, then tried to ring the base. Again he was told Firebird could not be reached.

So he paced his portrait-lined library. Caldwell never would have been unfaithful, any more than Firebird could have been. Yet the unknowing Netaian would react with savage insistence that the Angelo dynasty had been cuckolded.

Another face appeared over the projector, again no spokesman, but Lee Danton himself. Sipping the perfumy liqueur, Tel stalked back to his media block. According to Danton, Rogonin's announcement was proof of the regent's treachery, not Caldwell's. Firebird was not dead, he insisted. Burkenhamn had been sent to the Federate base, ordered by Rogonin's mercenaries—there was some confusion on that point—to murder Firebird. The offworld woman had been impregnated against her will with cells cultured from an unidentified donor's skin, using a well-known *in vitro* technique. She had been granted asylum.

Had Shuhr agents told Rogonin's office that the unwilling "donor" was Caldwell? It was possible. He'd been their prisoner.

My fault. Tel passed a hand over his eyes. *And Phoena's.*

Additional imagery followed. It appeared to have been recorded inside a military base, and the image bounced as if it had been made with some kind of hidden equipment. Even now, certain panels were obviously blurred for transmission. There was Burkenhamn, pressing toward Firebird. She looked considerably less pale than Tel might have expected. A garbled shout from behind the pickup brought in guards. Sentinel Mattason made a spectacular flying intercept. Two Federates seized the huge marshal. Imagery shifted to show a tall, black-haired woman with a strikingly sharp chin leaving the room under guard. "Bravo!" shouted Tel.

"Lady Firebird took no further injury and is resting comfortably. We return you to scheduled programming," said an unprofessional voice, some tech maybe, at the Codex studio.

Tel shoved his liqueur aside, rang for cruinn and sank onto his most comfortable lounger, pondering his next move in an increasingly dangerous field game.

His footman broke into his thoughts. "Prince Tel, the Countess Esmerield and Duke of Kenhing are here."

Tel sprang to his feet.

The slender dark blond woman swept past his servitor, wearing thrown-on clothing. Her hair and face were lovely for not having been coifed or shaded. "Dismiss your servitor," she ordered, panting. Kenhing followed several paces behind her. Immaculately dressed in dark green, he looked startlingly like his brother Daithi. It had to be his hair, waving slightly out of control, that emphasized the resemblance.

Kenhing had seemed mildly sympathetic to Firebird's cause, back in the electoral chamber. Still, he wore his dagger. Tel clasped a little blazer deep in his pocket. He nodded over Esme's shoulder at his footman, who stalked out. Tel's hidden security staff could defend him against this pair, although if Esme had come from the palace, Shuhr "mercenaries" might have tampered with her, just as they had obviously brainset Burkenhamn. "What is it?" he asked, willing her to be sincere. "Kenhing, I thought you were in an emergency meeting."

"It ended half an hour ago."

Esme glanced around his library, at the volumes his fathers had collected and the portraits he'd purchased and painted. "Prince Tel, something is wrong with Father. He isn't acting at all like himself."

"We have also been assured," the duke said stiffly, "that Citangelo Base is about to be destroyed by our new so-called allies. Allies the Electorate did not call to Netaia, nor were we consulted about allying ourselves with them."

"Allies that Governor Danton just accused of setting Marshal Burkenhamn against Lady Firebird?" Tel demanded, clenching his pocketed blazer. "Allies who destroyed a city on Thyrica?"

Kenhing frowned. "We're in danger, Tellai."

Tel stepped closer. "Why did you come to me?"

"My staff tells me you recently raised a security force—"

"And you're Lady Firebird's friend," Esme interrupted.

"You want me to rescue your father." Tel stared down the countess, loathing the idea.

One heartbeat later, he guessed this was exactly how Caldwell had felt, four months ago when Tel asked him to rescue Phoena. The realization wrenched his gut.

Esme tilted her chin. The redness in her eyes brought out their green fire. "I know Father treated you shabbily. Please help us anyway. They'll destroy Citangelo, and he won't listen to reason."

Kenhing raised one hand as if in entreaty, but he seemed reluctant to lift it too far. "Tellai, I never would tell you this, except that I need you to trust me . . ." Trailing off, he glanced at Esme.

She straightened her shoulders. "I can be trusted with secrets, too, Kenhing."

The duke tucked his thumbs into his belt. "You will recall that my wastling brother Alef vanished some years ago. Lady Firebird was suspected of involvement."

Tel raised his head. "And?"

"She *was* involved, Tellai. I overheard a conversation. This is the first time I have ever mentioned it. I never incriminated her, nor Lord Bowman, when the incident was investigated. There are times to look the other way and times when we must act. Tonight, we have no choice." Straightening his tunic, he added, "Esme says there is talk of leveling your estate."

Tel whirled toward the countess. "Who said this?"

"Father's mercenary." Esme glanced from Tel to Kenhing. "Moda Shirak, or whatever his name is. The man with the cruel eyes. You're right, Kenhing. If Alef is alive somewhere, I don't care. In fact, I'm glad."

Esme had seen Micahel's infamous father? Tel wondered what kind of fears she'd been living under, with Shuhr haunting the palace.

Save Rogonin?

Save Phoena? Brennen hadn't scorned him but had gone to Three Zed. If Brennen could go to that planet, Tel might dare step into an occupied palace.

He ran his fingers through his hair. If the Shuhr threatened his own estate, he must not risk his servitors making multiple trips into the countryside, trying to save possessions.

But he must alert Danton. He'd seen what the Shuhr did to Sunton.

"Thank you," he told them both. "We won't have much time."

Her cheeks flushed. "Do you think you can do anything?"

"I will try." He motioned Kenhing and Esme to a lounger.

He rang for Paudan, gave a few orders, then paused to think. Firebird had finally admitted that Sentinels had infiltrated palace staff. Had they all left the grounds when she and Caldwell moved out?

Yes. If Shuhr were there now, all Sentinels had left. Maybe he could enlist a few of them at the Federate base. He could disguise them in Tellai livery.

He called the base again. "This is Tellai," he told the man who answered. "I need to speak with any one of the Sentinels. This is a Shuhr-related emergency."

Chapter 20
TRAITORS

precipitando
rushing, impetuous

Terza sat in a close, bare cell with the familiar dull scent of recycled air, watched by two keen-eyed Sentinels. Grim thoughts taunted her. *You thought he would value you. Already you've been ignored. They don't want you at all. He doesn't want your daughter, either. Traitor. Useless traitor. Do away with yourself, quickly.*

At least they'd let her change out of that uncomfortable palace uniform.

The door opened. Her guards saluted someone in the hall.

Caldwell stepped inside, followed closely by the Sentinel she'd identified as his bodyguard. "I apologize that we haven't been able to speak with you sooner, Terza," he said. "We're going to move you. Since you believe you might be watch-linked, we're going to ask you to wear a sensory hood set to an entertainment display. You could help us by concentrating on it."

There was a presence to that man, an empathy, that was utterly different from anyone she'd ever known. She would've expected a former captive to be angrier, more vengeful.

A third Sentinel steered a mobility chair into the room. On its seat was a hood like ones she'd seen used for personal recreation. It had an eyepiece, earphones, and sensory pads on both sides of the nose.

She helped them adjust it for comfort, then took a seat on the mobility chair. When they switched on the hood, the eyepiece went opaque. Instead of her bare holding cell, she saw the view from an open-air mountaintop, a jagged horizon that seemed to stretch on forever. Pale blue sky darkened to azure overhead, and there was a scent of woodsmoke and . . . was that intoxicatingly sweet odor wildflowers?

"We just lost your sister," said a voice in Micahel Shirak's flight helmet.

"What do you mean, lost her?" he demanded, dancing on his rudder panels. *Just a little closer, Federate . . .*

He had penetrated Sitree Base with six of his father's voice-commanded lackeys. Only two had fighter experience. He sent the other four, loaded with incendiaries, into the other hangars. Four black smoke plumes rose behind him.

Evidently Sitree Base already had two fighters out on patrol. One was hot on his tail.

"Watch-link's still functioning," said his father's voice. "But they put a sensory hood on her. She's cooperating with them."

"*Can* she? Really?" Micahel sneered.

Modabah probably was in the new observation post under the palace's central public zone. "We've been trying to trigger suicide. So far, she's resisting. I'm not sure how. As long as we have her in link range, we can keep trying. But the sensory hood could mean they're taking her shipboard. If so, they could be headed—"

"To Three Zed," Micahel interrupted, firewalling his throttle as his left wingmate blasted the second pursuer. Caldwell, taking off with Terza, couldn't beat Modabah's messenger to Three Zed, not even if he launched quickly . . . but he might give Micahel a close race.

He wouldn't leave Netaia's atmosphere at all if Micahel got to Citangelo in time.

He vectored east, followed by his wingmates. They had taken off in three armored HF-class fighters, fully fueled and warhead-loaded. That weighted them for the deepest possible penetration at Citangelo.

"I'm turning you loose," said his father's voice. "We'll have to break a second-rate captive to get that RIA information. Crater Citangelo Base. Kill them both . . . what?"

The helmet voice became an unintelligible buzz. Micahel cruised east, accelerating over the midland corridor's irrigation grid, leaving a roiling wake of turbulence in thin clouds.

Modabah's voice came back. "Lift-off," he exclaimed. "One armored transport and four fighter escorts just cleared Citangelo. Cancel the base attack. Engage that transport. You're authorized to destroy, Micahel. I wash my hands."

Micahel shifted his hand on the Netaian fighter's control stick, arming a missile. From this range, his beyond-visuals couldn't pick up Caldwell's launch plume—but no transport could outrun heavy fighters. Not far.

The winter sun dropped in the southwest as the Angelo footman Tel knew as Paskel opened a side gate of the palace grounds. "I don't think the Shuhr have been here long enough to find all entry points," he murmured, "and we put down remote surveillance, but that might not last."

"Only gardeners use this gate," Tel said, waving Esme, Kenhing, and a column of liveried men and women through the vine-draped arch. Five Sentinels had appeared at his estate twelve minutes after he called the base. He reinforced them with ten armed Netaians. "We expected to need Esme's personal codes to open this."

One Sentinel, Thurl Hoston, had warned him: Either they would surprise the Shuhr agents, in which case this would seem all too easy or they would be taken captive and subjected to terrible violations. Tel had given all his new guards the option of backing down. Two did.

As Tel walked, he glanced up at the private wing's dark windows. So Firebird really had gotten Alef Drake offworld. He should've known! She had amazing courage.

The next time he was at Hesed, he would ask her permission to tell Alef's brother Daithi, Carradee's husband, what she had done.

Paskel shook his head, huffing as he kept up. His tight curls looked limp and sweaty. "The sensors on this side of the main building should remain down for six more minutes," he said. He pumped his arms as if jogging. "Palace staff is in turmoil. We're accustomed to taking orders from nobility, but something plainly has happened to the regent. The countess"—he nodded respectfully toward Esme—"left a message with her personal girl, which I intercepted. We lacked a leader, Prince Tel. Thank you for coming."

Tel glanced aside at Kenhing, who walked with his chief guard, Paudan. Kenhing might have sheltered Firebird's old offense, but obviously, he didn't dare to take responsibility this afternoon.

The footman, Paskel, halted the group at the edge of the grove of drooping evergreens. Tel checked the time lights at his wrist. They had four minutes to get inside.

Paskel strode up the lawn, up the colonnade steps, and spoke to a sentry. The crimson-liveried House Guard, sworn to defend the Angelo family, marched with Paskel to one of the huge white columns. He vanished behind it, and did not reappear.

Evidently the invaders hadn't yet taken time to mind-bend palace servitors. No wonder Paskel and the others had rallied around Esme. The sentry probably had agreed to turn his back.

Sure enough, Paskel peered around the column and flicked his fingers.

The group sprinted almost to the colonnade, then slipped in through a small side door. Paskel led down granite stairs into a corridor. "We need your Sentinels now," he murmured. "Stay on this side of the first door. That's the next surveillance zone."

Tel waved the Thyrians forward. Paskel was right—within a room's width or so, the Shuhr could detect other minds. Only the five Sentinels could shield their approach from the invaders and hope to surprise them.

Almost indistinguishable from Tel's own employees, all wearing black and indigo now, the other Sentinels crowded around Sentinel Hoston. "The intruders set up an observation post," Paskel explained. "Behind the fourth door on the left there is a storeroom. Behind that is a long chamber, directly below the palace's communication office. They tapped in between levels."

"Any other way out?" Hoston asked.

"Yes." Paskel pantomimed a long, invisible swath in the air. "The inner chamber can also be accessed by way of a second storeroom behind it, which connects with the next corridor south."

"We'll split up." Hoston looked hard at Tel. "Send your people to the next corridor. Paskel, can you show them the right door?"

The big servitor nodded. To Tel's surprise, he slid a blazer out of his white cummerbund.

Sentinel Hoston eyed Kenhing and Esme. "If we don't make it through that second door into the chamber, be ready for a violent counterattack. Noncombatants should wait in the stairwell." He raised a blazer, then donned a breath mask. "We're going to use gas." His voice came muffled through the mask. "Stay well back until we signal."

Tel nodded, wanting to help storm the chamber but knowing that was as unrealistic as when he'd wanted to enter Three Zed with Firebird. He didn't have the strength—epsilon, physical, or emotional—to carry a fight to this enemy.

Paskel led the Netaians toward the second passway, then the Sentinels moved out. As they passed the first door, Tel pulled a deep breath.

Twenty meters down the corridor, the Sentinels filed through a door on the left and out of sight.

Something touched Tel's hand. He looked into Esme's wide green eyes and turned his hand to grip hers. "Countess, you should be in the stairwell. We both should. Those people are professionals."

As they backed into shelter, she didn't pull her hand away. "Do you think they can—"

He heard three blazer shots, then scuffling noises. Finally, a *whump*. Full of dread, he tugged her back several more paces. The Sentinels would've warned them if that gas might spread, wouldn't they? Some chemicals broke down or dissipated quickly—

He peered out. One Sentinel reappeared at the door, slightly disheveled, her mask in one hand. She beckoned.

Tel led Esme and Kenhing through the uniform storeroom into a long, narrow chamber haphazardly crowded with subtronic gear, including three live observation screens and several unreadable consoles. The woman who'd waved them inside busied herself assisting another, who bent over someone leaning against the wall. It was Hoston, the senior Sentinel.

Paskel peered in from the south storeroom. "I can call for a staff med." He raised one hand. Tel spotted an interlink curled between his plump fingers.

Tel started to say, "Yes—"

"No." Hoston coughed, then explained, "There were only two of them down here. There must be more uplevel. Don't attract attention. We have biotape and topicals. It's . . ." He winced as his partner applied something to his chest, maybe a painkiller. "Just burned skin," he managed.

Esme backed out of the chamber, looking pale. "Stay with her," Tel murmured to one of his own men. "Don't let her tip them off."

The security guard nodded and followed her out.

"Look." An older Sentinel pointed. "That console was made by a Carolinian manufacturer." He moved his hand. "This display is from Inisi. That sensor array is Bishdan."

"Stolen," another Sentinel explained to Tel and Paskel. "Those are all Federate worlds that supply Regional command, Tallis."

Kenhing squeezed in alongside Tel. "Is that proof?" he demanded. "Proof of collaboration, admissible in electoral court?"

"Maybe not, but this certainly is." The Sentinel raised one of several recall pads. Tel squinted at the display. He couldn't read a word.

"Ehretan," the Sentinel explained. "That is our holy tongue of worship. Evidently *they* use it as their primary language. We have common ancestors. And that," he said slowly, "constitutes proof. So do these epsilon-fielded devices." He gestured toward the door. "If we hadn't caught this pair unaware, they would have sealed the room, and none of us could have gotten in."

Too easy, Tel heard in his mind. It had been their only chance of success.

Kenhing turned aside. "Wait," he exclaimed. He picked up another recall pad and passed it along. "How many of these did they leave lying around?"

Sentinel Hoston drew out a cloth square, took the recall pad inside it, and thumbed it on. His fingers tightened on its edges. "This is even better. These are orders to someone who accompanied Burkenhamn to the base." He read phrases that put ice water in Tel's veins. " 'Burkenhamn will be quick—a simple strangulation, a blow to the head—break her neck . . . but it must be his doing, not yours. Do not interfere. . . .' " The Sentinel trailed off. "This is next: 'Micahel is prepping two crewmen for the clean-up mission. Don't worry—we'll be far out on the plains in less than three hours—' "

"I've called Citangelo authorities and suggested evacuation," Tel interrupted.

The Sentinel glanced up at him. "Well done. I'll call this in, too. But here is the incrimination. 'Rogonin is cooperating fully.' " As Hoston's glance traveled down the screen, other Sentinels wheeled around and stared down at him. Tel wondered what Hoston had found. Something had brought up such a strong emotional reaction that he couldn't hide it, despite that infamous Sentinel emotional control.

Hoston pocketed the recall pad, though, so Tel refrained from asking further questions. Another Sentinel steadied Hoston on his feet.

"Will we recognize the Shuhr who are here?" Tel asked. "We mustn't harm innocent bystanders."

Paskel slid several thin tiles, printed with images, from inside his cutaway coat. "We've been using a camera recorder when we can. Several of our guests seem to constitute a core group. This appears to be the woman who defected." He laid a tile on the nearest console.

Tel had never appreciated servitors' cleverness or ubiquity quite as much as he did today. The dark-haired woman on the tile did look familiar from newsnet broadcasts.

So did the next image. It was the man she had killed on base.

The third image made his hands clench. "That's Shirak," he exclaimed softly. "Micahel Shirak, the assassin. I last saw him in gold." He passed the image to Hoston.

"Just so," said Paskel. "But he seems to answer to this one." He laid down the final image. The man resembled Micahel, somewhat older, with the same cleft chin and dark hair. "They call him Modabah, or Eldest. According to my sentry, he was down here for a little while, but he didn't stay long. He's with Rogonin in the main level private dining room." The big Netaian glanced up and north.

Moda, Esme had called him. *The man with the cruel eyes.*

Again the Sentinels exchanged glances.

Kenhing squared his shoulders, laying one hand on his dagger. "With this chamber secured, we should be able to get up there. Paskel, is the entire staff with you?"

"No." Paskel adjusted his cummerbund. "There are a few who can't imagine disloyalty in His Grace."

"Look," exclaimed one of Tel's own.

Tel glanced up. On one of the observation screens, several gleaming objects accelerated away from Netaia. Four small darts escorted a larger, blunted craft. Out of the west came a second flight, three darts pursuing the first group.

"Caldwell?" Tel demanded.

The Sentinel bent toward the console. He fiddled with controls, enlarging the image. Numbers scrolled across the monitor. "Probably.

The others are Netaian heavy fighters. Origin looks like Sitree."

"Friendlies?" Kenhing asked.

"No!" Tel exclaimed. "That would be Micahel—he was to prep two crewmen for the clean-up mission! They're on their way here—"

"No," Hoston said, drawing a blazer to check its charge. "Citangelo isn't in any danger if Micahel has General Caldwell in sight."

"They're closing," the man at Sensors announced. "According to calcs, they won't reach intercept range before we can slip, unless they haven't fully accelerated yet."

Brennen answered, "I suspect they have." A suite of monitors enclosed his raised chair on *Sapphira*'s small command deck. The heavy Netaian fighters drew steadily closer on his aft screen. He had no doubt who was on board. He hated to run from Micahel, but this time he couldn't turn back and fight.

Unfortunately, even if *Sapphira* escaped being shot down, its northspinward heading would leave Micahel no doubt of his destination. Those long-range fighters were slip capable, and Micahel wouldn't lose precious hours decelerating to rendezvous with a Thyrian battle group. Unless Brennen's pilot coaxed more acceleration out of *Sapphira*, Micahel would beat the Sentinel force to Three Zed.

From the previous messenger, the DS-212 launched from Arctica Base, Three Zed's defenders might even know exactly what threatened them. Shirak's home forces could have time to mount a fierce resistance, doubling or even tripling their fielding staff, even though Micahel might report that Brennen was coming with only this small force.

Brennen touched a com panel. "Engineering, can we safely exceed maximum normal speed? How long, and by how much?"

"I'll calculate and get back to you, sir."

"Push it while you calculate," Brennen ordered.

"Preparing to slip," Shields announced from the next seat over.

The slip-shields took hold. Brennen let himself relax slightly. Micahel wouldn't have time to catch them on this end of the slip.

The odd vibrational sensation nudged Terza out of her induced alpine reverie. At the same instant, a heaviness—something like her father's epsilon presence—slipped away from her. Along with it went all thought of suicide.

She had been taken shipboard, then, and they'd just escaped watch-link range. Shutting her eyes against the magnificent upworld view, she turned deep inside to hide behind her inner shields again. Was she free?

No. From this vantage, examining her own alpha matrix, she still sensed something unstable. She might be clear of watch-link, but Talumah had performed deep epsilon tampering, and she could do nothing to counteract it.

Then she hoped these people had locked her down securely. They'd promised they would do everything in their power to free her.

In the next moment, she knew where she was bound, and what her captors would want from her en route. Of course they meant to destroy Three Zed! They wouldn't take her to Tallis or Thyrica, and certainly not to their own fortress world. She'd faced that fact once today—what her defection could mean to others—but that had been under her father's compulsion. She had no emotional tie to anyone left in the Golden City.

Traitor! The accusation blasted through her mind anyway, from no source but her own stricken conscience.

She pressed her palm to the warm place below her belt. *This is for you*, she thought at her child. *It's the only way you ever will be safe.*

And, she realized, it was also for the Netaians—and others—that Juddis Adiyn would have infected with gene-modifying organisms.

On the observation screen in front of Tel, the blunted craft vanished, followed almost instantly by its escorts.

"They're away," murmured one Sentinel.

"Headed back to Hesed House, I'll guess," Tel said, doubly relieved. Caldwell had escaped, and Citangelo wouldn't be turned to a crater.

The two nearest Sentinels stared at each other, obviously speaking mentally. One said, "I hope so."

Hoston spoke up from the floor. "Don't frighten Countess Esme, but it's vital to get Rogonin in custody. He can be released from whatever they've done to him if he lets us try."

Tel remembered Firebird's assurances and Caldwell's self-restraint, proving that Sentinels could only use their gifts under special circumstances. "I understand," he said. "So you won't . . . dispatch him . . . without giving him that chance?"

"Not if there's any way to save him."

Tel rejoined Esme in the corridor, seizing her hand again. Her fingers felt cold between his. "Esme," he said, "listen. You were right. Your father is not himself. These intruders are Shuhr, and they've done things to his mind."

"Obviously," she snapped.

Tel didn't take offense. A frightened daughter would tend to snap. He glanced pointedly over his shoulder. "The Sentinels have promised me they will try to heal him—"

"Don't promise him," she demanded, glaring into the storeroom. "Promise me. You have no idea what a leap this is, trusting Sentinels."

Whatever they did behind his back, it must've satisfied her. She gripped his arm with her other hand.

"I promise, too," Tel said. "I will not harm your father." He drew his little blazer out of that deep pocket.

Esme nodded solemnly.

Hoston stepped toward the door. Now Tel saw that his livery jacket was burned open, low on the left side of his chest. Pale pink biotape showed through the gap.

The group followed Paskel up another service stairwell, placing feet softly, shifting weight carefully. With the observation post put down, there was less worry about being spotted, but "less" worry wasn't little enough for Tel.

He thought instead of the man with Rogonin. Modabah Shirak was probably the one who had ordered Firebird killed at the Hall of Charity. More than likely, he watched Phoena die. Tel didn't doubt he had the emotional strength to kill *that* man, if given a chance.

The Sentinel behind him must've picked up his determination or else spotted his small personal blazer. He nudged Tel's arm, silently offering a Federate service model butt-first. It looked twice as powerful as Tel's own, but Tel shook his head. He didn't want his life depending on an unfamiliar weapon.

The Sentinel returned his spare to an odd-shaped holster.

At the landing nearest the main-level kitchens, one more part of the palace Tel never had thought to see, the senior Sentinel halted the group again. "Have your people pair off with us," Hoston directed. "We'll have to hope we can shield your minds, so they won't sense us coming as we get close."

Tel passed the order down the line, then stepped closer to Hoston. Six of his own, unpaired, fell back.

Again he thought of Hoston's warning. This must seem utterly simple, or they had little hope of succeeding. The slightest alarm or mishap could doom them.

Tel and Hoston emerged shoulder to shoulder at one edge of a kitchen. Clattering noises covered their footfalls. A large man supervising kitchen machinery stared, wiping his hands on a floury towel. He barely nodded to Paskel, eyes wide, lips firmed.

Tel spotted a closed-down service window, where higher-ranking servitors out in the dining area would bring spent dishes to this crew for sterilization. He waved the others back. Hoston stayed at his elbow, breathing quickly but quietly. Tel edged closer to the window. The other four Sentinels, paired with four of Tel's guards, hurried to the main door. Tel's people held blazers. So did two Sentinels. The others drew silvery handgrips out of sleeve sheaths—their ceremonial crystaces, Tel realized.

Footsteps approached on the window's other side. Tel raised his blazer, steadied his elbows against the windowbar, and waited. He would have only one chance. The instant they saw him, they would attack.

Simplicity or failure, the quickest of surgical strikes or slow death. He would rather die here than live on a Netaia ruled by Shuhr.

The service window blinked like an eye, and Tel glimpsed the private hall. Several plainclothes men and women stood along the walls. Beneath a jeweled chandelier, two men sat at the table's near end. Tel recognized Rogonin's broad back. He knew the other man from the tile-image—Modabah Shirak.

In that moment, the intruder raised his head. Evidently Tel's escort couldn't shield his disgust.

Modabah would warn the others! Tel squeezed his trigger and held it down, pumping out three energy bursts.

Shirak toppled with a patch of his scalp smoking.

"Go!" exclaimed a voice behind Tel. Tellai-liveried Sentinels and Netaians spilled into the dining hall. Tel let the blazer fall from his hand, staring at that smoking hair. His gorge rose. He rushed to the corner, gripped the sterilizer's edges, and emptied the contents of his stomach. He vaguely heard shouts, eerie humming noises that had to be crystaces, the sharp crack of furniture and the duller sound of bodies falling.

By the time he turned back to the private hall, guards stood at every exit—his own guards, joined by several kitchen staff wielding knives and other kitchen tools. Bodies strewed the parquet floor. Six wore Tellai livery, and Tel cringed at the sight. Rogonin stood beside his chair under the chandelier. Scorch marks spotted the ceiling and walls.

He hurried out into the hall. "Call your med, Paskel," he ordered.

"On his way." The footman coolly covered one fallen Shuhr with his blazer.

I'd never make a soldier. He'd told Firebird and Brennen that months ago. Now he knew how true it was.

He joined Kenhing at the long table's near end. Rogonin spotted Tel and laughed shortly.

"Your Grace," Tel said, "I have the dubious honor of asking you to submit to arrest."

"Arrest?" As Esme suggested, Rogonin had a giddy light in his eyes, a defiant lift to one eyebrow. Even during the fracas back at Hunter Height, Rogonin had always maintained some dignity. "I'm a sovereign head of state," he declared. "You can't arrest me."

Tel drew up as tall as he could. "The sovereign answers to the Electorate, Your Grace, and there are several electoral charges that must be brought against you."

"What charges?" Rogonin put out a fleshy hand and grabbed the back of a chair. "In desperate times like these, strong leaders take stern measures."

A gilded entry opened. Three medical staff hurried in.

"First," Tel said, trying to sound firm and self-assured, "a charge of sedition against the noble house that you serve as regent. You have tried, consistently and illegally, to discredit and disempower House Angelo."

Rogonin laughed sharply. "The traitors deserve to be discredited. Every one of them—except young Iarla, of course." His lips curled in a smile. "And I don't think Her Majesty will be found soon."

Something like a cold hand gripped Tel's emptied stomach. "Do you know that for certain?"

"Of course not—"

"He's lying," said a voice behind Tel.

Aghast, Tel turned his head slightly. One of the Sentinels frowned at the regent. "He knows."

Rogonin had known Carradee's daughters would not be found, and he'd done nothing? That was treason! "What else did your . . . guests . . . tell you?" Angry now, Tel gestured toward the nearest body. Two servitors and a Sentinel crouched over it, draping it with kitchen towels.

"I am not on trial," Rogonin growled. "I only asked to hear what trumped-up charges you think you can bring against me. Speak carefully, Tellai. You too can be accused. So can you, Drake."

Tel exchanged dark glances with Kenhing. "Second charge," said Tel. "Subverting electoral procedures, by excluding House Tellai from two known electoral sessions, and probably others."

Kenhing spoke up. "That is an indictable offense," he added, "though not as serious. The Sentinel just accused you of the highest treason, Rogonin, and complicity with murder. Have you nothing to say?"

Rogonin lowered himself into his chair, then pushed the remains of his meal aside. "You're in on the uprising, too, Kenhing?" He laced his fingers across his stomach. "Go on."

Rogonin hadn't denied the charge! "Finally," Tel said, clenching his own hands in dark fury, "you will be charged with collaboration with offworld enemies of the Netaian state. The evidence is overwhelming, Your Grace." He looked pointedly at the nearest body—his own recruit!—and then laid Paskel's tiles on the table. "These individuals brought outworld gear into the palace and established an observation post downlevel. Much of it can be identified by world of origin. Some of it plainly—plainly, Your Grace—originated on Three Zed. This evidence also implicates you in the second attempt on Firebird's life, as well as a pending attack on Citangelo. On the people you are sworn to serve, Rogonin."

Rogonin's left cheek twitched. "You would have to convince twenty-six electors, Tellai."

Kenhing stepped forward. "I'm convinced. I don't think there will be any difficulty with the rest of them. You will be charged, Rogonin. You are plainly guilty. And if you're implicated in Iarla and Kessaree's disappearance, even by Sentinels, I will—"

"Traitors," Rogonin cried, clenching a fist. "Have you no idea what the Federatization of Netaia would mean? Workers displaced, commerce and government disrupted. Common influences taking over all arts and media, low elements ruling our schools, poisoning our children—"

Tel leaned both hands on the table, facing the regent. "Sir," he said sharply. He must try to show mercy.

Rogonin shut his mouth.

"Sir, these so-called guests of yours tampered with your mind. Let these Sentinels help you. They say they can undo Shuhr mind-work, but they will do nothing you will not allow."

Rogonin straightened. "Tell that to Caldwell," he barked. "He forced mind-access on me." He lowered his voice. "Who brought these creatures into my home? Wait—I think I know. Esmerield looked furtive at supper."

Tel flicked a glance toward the kitchens, where Esme hung back, hidden from view but not out of earshot. "She wants to see you healed, Your Grace. She loves you dearly."

"And she shows it this way?" Rogonin sprang to his feet, tipping his chair.

Tel backed away from the table. All around the room, liveried men and women stepped forward, brandishing whatever weapons they held.

Kenhing stood his ground. "If you refuse their help, Rogonin, and frankly I wouldn't blame you, then you will stand trial . . . and we *will* allow Sentinels to give evidence, if there is a charge concerning Her Majesty Iarla and Princess Kessaree—or any damage to Citangelo, including the Federate base." From the scabbard on his belt, he drew his shining dress dagger. He laid it on the table. "Or there is the traditional recourse, sir."

Rogonin glowered at Kenhing. Tel didn't expect him to let any Sentinel into his mind—but if he had only two choices, then for Esme's sake, Tel had to hope—

Then he thought of Firebird and all this man had done to her. To those adorable daughters of Carradee's. He wanted to see this man dead.

Kenhing stood stiffly. "Regardless of your choice, we will abide by the electors' designation of a new regent. Muirnen Rogonin, you are to be praised for your service to Netaia. On behalf of the Electorate, I thank you. But your service to this council has ended."

Two years ago, Tel had heard First Lord Erwin read those words over Firebird as she knelt between two redjackets. Geis orders, requiring her to seek a noble death.

"If you would prefer not to stand trial," Tel said softly, "I can send in your children to say their farewells. But the Sentinels are willing to help you."

Rogonin touched the dagger's hilt. "Traitors," he muttered, "in my own house. Leave this room, all of you." He opened his fleshy hand and seized the dagger.

INTERLUDE 8

Jenner Dabarrah, master of the Sentinels' sanctuary, wryly raised an eyebrow at Carradee. Seated on a bench in his medical office, within earshot of the reflecting pool's continual rippling and splashing, he crossed his long arms. "I did offer," he said gently. "Mazo Syndrome is treatable."

Carradee smiled. That syndrome, diagnosed in Firebird and treated on Thyrica, had kept the Angelo women from bearing male children and proved their kinship with the other Ehretan descendants. "Yes," Carradee answered. She reached aside to her husband's mobility chair and squeezed his hand. Yesterday, Daithi had taken a few hesitant steps out on one of the reflecting pool's green islands, where kirka trees were dropping their bud sheaths, revealing sticky, pale green needles. She could smell the fragrant sap from here.

New life was flowing in them all—

"Thank you, Master Jenner," she said. "We were grateful for your offer, and maybe we were foolish not to ask for treatment before we tried to conceive, but we are not disappointed. Nothing and no one will ever take Iarlet or Kessie's place, but we will be delighted to hold another daughter." *Thank you most of all, Eternal Speaker. I promise you, we will raise her to honor you.*

"Congratulations, then." Master Dabarrah rocked to his feet, stepped forward, and gripped Daithi's other hand. "You will have the very best of care."

Daithi's smile showed most of his teeth.

Carradee squeezed his hand even tighter. Let the gossips theorize about his chances of recovery now!

CHAPTER 21

CAPTIVE AND CONQUEROR

modulation
change of key

After Brennen checked on Firebird, he paused in the forward crew lounge to collect his thoughts. Shel sat watching her charge sleep. *Sapphira* was stable on course, and Engineering assured him it could run at fifteen percent past normal max for at least one shipboard day, pushing their acceleration well into military standards. The Luxian government had invested in an overengineered ship.

Uri emerged from the medical suite, where Terza had just been moved, again wearing her sensory hood. "Hancock's finishing a physical exam," Uri murmured. "Shouldn't take long."

Brennen nodded, listening to the soft drone of engines and ventilators. Twenty-four souls had squeezed on board, and he'd scheduled most of them for at least one daily watch on guard. Terza must be constantly observed by at least two Sentinels.

Uri took four steps back up the corridor, peered into the med suite, then beckoned.

Guide us, Holy One, Brennen prayed.

Uri settled on one of three stools alongside Terza's cot. Another guard sat near her feet. Over her head, a row of instruments gleamed with life signs. The corner readout indicated that a restraining field had been activated.

Med Adamm Hancock stood beneath the instruments, crowded against the inner bulkhead. His ash gray uniform looked rumpled from the hurry to board and launch. "Good general health," he told Brennen. "Mid first-trimester pregnant, as you said, with a female fetus. Are you sure you don't want me to administer a blocking drug?"

Brennen took the stool between Uri and the guard. Dispersing his shields, he felt a whirlpool of sensations—Terza's reluctance, chased by suspicion, anger, and dread.

"No drugs," he repeated. "If the child is in any danger, alert us."

The med nodded.

Brennen watched Terza's eyes for any sign of deception. "Is the child yours, too? Or a monoclone?" A male could have a monoclonal daughter if gene techs used two X-gametes.

"She is mine," Terza whispered.

Brennen exhaled, disgusted by their cruelty to her. "Sentinel Harris will breach," he said. "I'm sure you know I've been disabled."

"So we've been told," she said, "but no one believes it anymore. Not after . . ."

After several seconds, Brennen asked, "After what?"

"The Hall of Charity." She stared straight up. "She's alive. Unless that was *her* doing."

"How could it be?" Brennen demanded. He opened fully to Uri and sensed the gentle probe Uri was passing over Terza's alpha matrix, looking for natural flaws. It was easier and kinder to breach for interrogation that way, and this time it was also safer. Only the One knew what she might do by reflex if provoked.

"Polar's research," she answered.

Brennen frowned. "I don't recall much of Polar's research. I remember nearly nothing that happened at Three Zed."

"You'll see, then," she said, closing her eyes. "You know I was watch-linked. We're out of range, but I don't know what else was done to me."

More cruelty! No wonder the woman defected.

"Talumah probably placed other traps for you," she continued. "He is a master. But he never found my inner shields. I've kept them secret from everyone. I'll open them to you. If you stay inside that perimeter, you're probably safe."

"Thank you," Brennen murmured. Some Sentinels also had inner shields, but a skilled interrogator could find and break them.

Uri leaned away from her and drew a deep breath. Brennen took a moment to compose himself, too.

"There are already a number of rough breaches," Uri muttered.

"Surprise." Terza's bitterness came through strongly.

Brennen winced, observing, *Shirak, you may have doomed your own world by treating her this way.*

Uri leaned forward again. "Look this way, please," he said. "Can you open those shields?"

Brennen felt him stroke aside her bitterness and doubt, entering her alpha matrix on his first modulated thrust. She stared bleakly at Uri's eyes. As Uri maintained the breach, Brennen sent a follow-on probe. He swept gingerly over her surface emotional state, confirming her intention to leave her people, a motive so powerful that even their newer countercompulsion hadn't stopped her. Then he penetrated her memory and confirmed her claim to that hated name.

He saw how the girl-child was created and implanted, and he confirmed that the gamete carried his genes. This was a laboratory child, conceived not in love but in cold calculation—but his child nonetheless. Aware of Uri's intimate presence, he internalized Terza's shame, and how it intensified her latent wish to escape.

He'd felt the savor of Shuhr before, but that time he'd been the subject under scrutiny. Terza did not resist as he and Uri studied her personality. Now he sensed the shields, a protective secondary matrix surrounding his probe. They were unbelievably dense. On the Ehretan Scale of a theoretical hundred, this woman probably blasted off any cap. 110, 115?

The ones who'd done this to her were just as powerful. Her impulse to leave them was consistent with lifelong lines of character and intention. She'd always struggled with the demands placed on her. Her single desire now was to save the child she'd been forced to carry.

She had fixated on him, particularly. Once, she'd hoped to help Micahel kill him.

Her people did fear him. Some of them had started to seriously consider the prophecies given by Ehretan shamarrs. Respect for those prophecies had shaped so much of Brennen's life that it startled him to realize the Shuhr were just starting to believe.

And they did want him alive. Any Shuhr who destroyed him now would suffer excruciating consequences.

He sensed a call from Uri and drifted across her alpha matrix to recent memory.

Eldest Modabah Shirak had ordered Tallis attacked, in response to their suspicions about himself and Firebird. The order had gone out on the DS-212 messenger ship that was racing along, two hours ahead of *Sapphira*. They did suspect the Casvah mutation, and that it gave rise to exceptional power in the Angelo line.

Tempted to rush to the command deck, Brennen clung to his stool. He could not warn Tallis from slip-state. Instead, he double-checked their conclusions about the Angelo line. Terza had made the intuitive leap herself.

He couldn't fault her for observing and analyzing events. He probed deeper along that line of thought, into the complex web of long-term memory. The Shuhr did mean to seize other worlds, ostensibly to offer physical immortality. Wealthy Netaia would be first. . . .

In a laboratory, she'd seen evidence of Netaia's ruling family and its members' fates. The four-year-old queen and her sister were dead, just as she claimed. And Phoena . . . he'd forgotten watching her die, but his captors had taunted him about having failed to save her. Now Brennen saw her current status. Hideously crippled, skeletal muscles torn loose from their attachment points, she was incurable even by Shuhr technology, alive only by medical convention. Her physical brain could not recover. Held in cold stasis, at least she was not suffering.

Chilled, Brennen abandoned that thread and went deeper yet, beneath Terza's memory, to see if anything could be read at depth. Down here, the asphyxiating otherness of her core personality stole his breath, and he knew this was making her excruciatingly uncomfortable, too.

Studying the layer at depth, he found knots of suggestion—sabotage, deception, murder—a minefield strung with trip threads. Touching any locus at this depth would activate a deep, treacherous programming that would override any other intention, whether or not she truly hoped to escape. Neither he nor Uri had the skills to help her. Only psi-medical masters like Dabarrah or Spieth might make her safe.

Brennen pulled back, for her sake as much as his own. His chest ached with pity. His ancestors had created the skills that had allowed all this. His own people would have turned to domination just as surely as hers, without the Codes holding them back.

How many other Shuhr had doubts like Terza's?

Not many, maybe. She let him examine her inner shields at depth, where they arose. Now he understood how she'd hidden the compassionate side of her nature in order to escape Polar's vicious culling processes. Behind those shields he found a woman he could respect.

He withdrew for a moment, tiring. He would have a daughter. A half sister for Kiel and Kinnor. *Guide us*, he pleaded again. *Can I destroy her people in good conscience?*

As if in response, his epsilon carrier flickered out.

He opened his eyes, afraid Terza had attacked him. She reclined on the cot. Hancock attended to the flickering life-signs board, and Uri sat with eyes closed. Only the guard raised his head, catching Brennen's glance. Nothing seemed to have changed. . . .

Then he felt a nudge at the edge of awareness. This Voice never shouted but waited to be heard.

Brennen shut his eyes again. *Yes?* he asked urgently. *Yes?*

The Voice spoke in darkness this time, without giving him visual cues. *Take comfort in this*, Brennen heard. *There are no innocents in that city. Its iniquity is complete. Destroy them completely. You shall be a sword in my hand.*

The confirmation he'd wanted—the assurance he craved! He was free to attack evil in good conscience.

But . . .

Holy One, I am inadequate. Please restore what I was before. Crippled like this, I cannot serve you well.

The Voice answered, *I am strong when you are weak. Only in seeming death will you begin to live.*

Seeming death? In *Dabar*, that Ehretan term referred to physical death, which his people euphemistically called "the passage Across." *Is that my own call, then? To die at Three Zed after all? Show me, if I can bear it.*

He felt a deep love, a weight of eternal humor and terrifying sovereignty. Whether from the Holy One or his own imagination, he pictured the debris left from a terrible space battle. Pieces of a Thyrian Light-Five fighter tumbled, blasted open to space. He recognized a dead-on missile hit. *Even then*, said the Voice, *I will not forsake you. You are never alone.*

Brennen gulped air, naked before the Eternal. He remembered Mari's dream-vision, and the pronouncement that had been made over her, as the specter of wreckage drifted through his mind. Out of respect for the Presence, he strangled his terror of darkness and enclosed spaces and his very real, very human fear of dying. Of course the Holy One would not forsake him, even in physical death. But he'd hoped . . .

He could create other hopes. *I'll go wherever you lead*, he responded, *but please send Mari home to be a mother to our sons. Spare her from grief. Sustain her in your mercy.*

I will be all things to her, answered the Voice.

Terza had easily distinguished Lieutenant Colonel Harris's brisk, efficient probe from Caldwell's. Caldwell had a depth, an earnestness that settled the nausea of mind-access. After Caldwell's presence vanished, Harris withdrew almost immediately. She stared at them both, dissipating her own shields. Harris's confusion was easy to read and understand, but whatever was happening to Caldwell, it was nothing she'd seen before.

After several seconds, he opened his eyes, startling her. From this angle, there seemed to be a light behind his irises . . . an afterimage of something incomprehensible, something supernatural.

He moved his head, and the light vanished.

Maybe it was a reflection from the overhead panels.

"Are you all right?" Uri asked urgently.

Brennen nodded, though he felt more stunned than comforted. He wished he hadn't asked to be shown. Maybe his death would change the Federacy's attitudes toward his kindred. It was not necessary to understand, only to accept the holy call, and its cost—just as he'd gone to Three Zed. *You're certain I can bear this*? he prayed. "We're called," he murmured. "He . . . spoke to me."

Uri sat up straight, smiling as he lowered his eyebrows fiercely. "Was there more?"

"Not . . . yet. Go on," Brennen urged, to distract Uri. "We need to map Three Zed and find out how they mean to attack."

Uri adjusted his stance. "Terza," he said firmly.

The Shuhr woman's stare focused on Brennen just a little longer, long enough for him to understand that she'd seen something she couldn't comprehend.

Then she squinted at Uri again.

Brennen managed a turn. He felt Uri breach with one efficient probe. Piggybacking again, he drifted alongside Uri into a deep, golden city . . .

And he recognized it.

The nugget-textured corridors, the magnificent central chamber, the ancestors' hall . . . he knew them. Without hesitating, he led up a northbound corridor to the fielding station. They had not taken him there, but he'd heard them refer to it. *This way*, he cued Uri.

An instant later, Uri seemed to be peering over his shoulder. *How did you know?* Uri subvocalized.

Brennen whispered, "I remember." Again he pulled out of access. Had the Eternal One granted his prayer, restoring everything he'd been? He spotted a writing stylus beside Hancock's elbow. His hand shook as he focused epsilon energy, then willed the stylus to rise.

It rolled, but it didn't lift.

He clenched his hand and dropped it in his lap. He'd received the confirmation he wanted, and an assurance that his attack would not kill the innocent alongside the guilty. Now he remembered that no children lived in the Golden City. They were raised in outlying settlements. His other memories from that place would be vital for the upcoming attack.

He did remember Polar's research now. He understood Terza's reference. He knew why pulsing red lights carried the terror of Three Zed: His cell door had been ringed with them.

He also remembered Phoena Angelo, writhing out her life in a pale yellow gown, sprawled on the glassy floor of a chamber full of exotic artworks. He recalled the unsettling temblors that had felt like distant explosions.

Rejoining Uri, now he saw areas where he had not been admitted. Terza knew little about its military sites, as he would expect, but enough to show heavy bombers where to strike. Enough that he and Mari should be able to find the fielding operators and blast them with fusion energy.

Uri pressed a final query, and now Brennen saw their abominable plans for Netaia, including the deliberate infection of every Netaian with gene-altering viral agents.

Tallis was in a more conventional danger.

Plainly, it was time to strike. Destroying the Shuhr stronghold would prevent both tragedies.

Uri rocked back on his stool, away from Terza. "Enough," he said. "Terza, unless there are other things you want to show us, we are finished."

She blinked, and Brennen sensed her surprise. "I thought you would take it all," she muttered. "Not just the colony, but my mind, my memories."

"Those belong to you," said Brennen. "We never take more than necessary." Now he recalled one other interrogation, when he *had* been ordered to go deep, to capture the Netaian mindset. Federate needs had led to the fulfillment of his own almost two years ago. That memory warmed the cold chill that had settled on him. "We serve a God of mercy," he added.

"So I hear," muttered Terza.

Uri raised his head, glancing up sharply.

Maybe he shouldn't have said that much. Terza hadn't asked any relevant question. *If I said too much, forgive me.* But in his urge to show mercy, Terza was the nearest in need. She'd done everything in her power to help them. *Accept that as her service to you, Holy One. Give her grace to receive you.*

"Pray for me, then," she muttered. "For my . . . for your child."

Stunned, he rested one hand on her shoulder and let the words come. "Show Terza and this child that mercy, Holy One. If Terza is a danger to herself or to us, protect us all by your power. Dispel her fears with your glory. So let it be." He barely pressed down on her shoulder, a reassuring gesture.

Terza lay motionless, clenching one hand over her chest as if seizing a new sensation. Her lips quivered. *So that*, she subvocalized, *is what faith feels like.*

Firebird pulled out of sedation by stages. First she sensed the deep contentment of lying in Brennen's presence. Gradually she became aware of a steady thrumming.

She opened her eyes. Brennen sat on the carpet beside her bunk, leaning against a richly embossed bulkhead, studying a recall pad. He finished making a notation with one finger, then reached up and laid the pad on the pillow of a second, luxuriously deep cot. "Good morning, Princess," he said softly.

"Don't call me that." She kept all venom out of her voice, though. The long, deep sleep had left her feeling extraordinarily refreshed. "Looks like you found quite a ship—" Or was this sense of peace something she felt in Brennen? "What is it?" she murmured. "What happened?"

He carefully released the humming arch and helped her sit upright. "I hardly know where to start."

That brought her fully awake. She stretched, careful not to twist her spine. "Then go from the middle. What happened?"

He told her about mind-accessing Terza, then about hearing the Voice again.

"The call your people have waited for?" she asked, laying a hand on his forearm. "What a relief! Now you can be certain."

"Yes. I made an announcement in the crew lounge. I wish you could've seen the change in attitudes. The new determination, the humility. And there's more." He looked directly into her eyes. "I have my memory back."

"That's why you feel different," she whispered. "You feel . . . complete again." Trying to will her pulse rate down, she leaned against him. "How did it happen? What did you do?"

"Only what I've been doing since Three Zed. I asked. This time, the answer wasn't 'wait for my time.' " His voice fell several notes down the scale. "My other abilities didn't come back, though. And He . . . didn't promise either of us would survive."

"Has He ever promised that?" she asked gently. She caught a faint feeling, almost a scent of mastered fear.

Brennen shook his head. "Only that in His country, we would be cleansed and restored. Remade as we should have been."

"With all our atonements made."

His eyebrows knit. "Mari, we don't make our own atonements."

"I know." She clenched her hands into fists on her lap. "But all you went through at Three Zed, doesn't that count for something? What I'm going through now?"

Brennen hesitated. Her Path instructor had explained this. *He* had explained it. Sometimes, she even seemed to understand.

But she'd been raised to believe she must sacrifice herself, and that her own actions must balance her shortcomings. Her willingness to give everything, her determination to serve at all cost . . . those were laudable, but . . . *Holy One, how can I make her understand that you will pay the price for what is inside her?* She'd learned so much . . . and at least the nagging notion of making her own atonement no longer roused her Angelo pride.

"He refines us, tests us, disciplines us. Sometimes He even lets the Adversary use pain, Mari. But we do not make our own atonement. You seemed to understand that, not long ago."

She spread her hands. "I can recite everything they taught me back on Thyrica. But this . . . idea that I have to do it myself, it keeps bubbling up out of my past, and I latch on."

"Don't give up," he murmured, twisting around so he could face her. His lips pressed against hers, warm and strong. Then came the smoky-sweet sense at the back of her mind . . . and it carried the memory of all the trials they'd shared, this time as *he* remembered them. She sensed the way her mental cry of grief over Veroh had sparked his eager curiosity, and she rejoiced in the way that his determination to see her recruited, possibly even converted, had been completed. Their sweet wilderness flight at Tallis, when she leaped off a mountainside into his arms . . . now she felt the passion he'd barely controlled at the time and his ecstasy in its consummation at their pair bonding. In memory, she stood inside his skin to face Phoena's death squad at Hunter Height, and then at the moment when Master Spieth told them they would be parents. She felt his anguished pride in the insane moments when Kiel and Kinnor emerged, and a regret almost as deep as his faith when they parted at Hesed House, as he left for Three Zed.

Truly, he was back! He leaned deeper into the kiss, tangling his fingers into her hair. She raised one arm to slide it around his shoulders, and a jolt of pain made her pull away.

It was only a little jolt, though. She was substantially better. With exquisite care, he helped her to her feet. "Ready to walk a bit?" he asked.

Before coming to the palace this morning, Tel had checked on Clareen Chesterson. Rescued from detention by two servitors, she was back at her own apartment. She'd answered his CT call in high spirits, assuring him she had enough song ideas to last into the next year.

A high-toned bell called the Electorate to order and broke off his thoughts. He stood beside the gold-rimmed table and then watched as a redjacket escorted Bennett Drake, Duke of Kenhing, to the gilt chair at the table's head. Newly sworn as regent, Kenhing held his silver rod along his forearm, close to his chest. Like Tel, he wore three narrow black wristbands. Esme Rogonin, her cheeks pale and her eyes red above her long purple mourning gown, held her head high. Her mother had declined to attend.

Kenhing took his new place. The electors seated themselves.

"Our first order of business," Kenhing said, "is to acknowledge Esmerield Rogonin as Duchess of Claighbro, head of House Rogonin. Our sincere condolences, Duchess. Your father's death was honorable."

"Thank you," she said gravely. "The holy Powers have surely received him into bliss, along with Iarla Second and Princess Kessaree." There was no bliss in her eyes, though, or on her trembling lips. Tel ached for her. Rogonin's allegedly honorable suicide was utterly unnecessary, just like the deaths of so many wastlings, but it had saved House Rogonin the humiliation of an ugly, protracted trial.

Yesterday, Netaia had added mourning bands for Iarla and Kessaree.

Kenhing—regent for whom?—touched Tel's arm. "Prince Tel," he said, looking up the table. "You asked to speak before we deal with the issue of succession."

Tel knew what they expected him to propose. Count Wellan Bowman already was glaring.

Tel laid both hands on the table and pressed slowly back to his feet. "First, my respects and congratulations to Your Grace." He turned to Esme and softened his voice. "My sympathies as well to you, Duchess." He paused, giving them place if they cared to respond.

Esme looked away.

"There are," Tel continued, resting one hand on the table, "unconfirmed reports that Second Commander Angelo Caldwell and General Caldwell are en route to Three Zed, the stronghold of those offworlders who brought this tragedy on House Rogonin. We are hearing rumors of an impending attack."

Young Duke Stroud Parkai swept out his arms. "We could lose House Angelo!"

"No," Tel said firmly. "For one thing, I witnessed her sons' birth. They do exist, under protection at the Sentinels' sanctuary world. They are in deadly danger if they go anywhere else, as long as the Caldwells' enemies have the power to strike."

Several sad stares turned to frowns. They'd never liked the idea of bringing an offworlder's sons into the palace.

"I urge you to . . . to pray," he said carefully, avoiding the customary *petition the Powers*, "for Firebird's safe return. Meanwhile, noble electors, I have received a communiqué from the Sentinels' sanctuary world, Procyel II. You may recall that Carradee and Daithi took up residence at Hesed House there. Daithi has been treated for his injuries."

He fingered the ends of his gold-fringed sash. "Noble electors," he repeated softly, "I have just been informed that Her Former Majesty Carradee is pregnant again. Before Lady Firebird left Netaia, she asked me to propose that the throne be restored to Carradee's line if Carradee conceived." He hadn't contested Firebird's instructions. He'd thought this was impossible.

Esme Rogonin tilted her chin. Winton Stele pushed away from the table, smiling broadly. Kenhing's sober frown faded. "Has Carradee given the child a name?" called the regent.

Tel nodded. "She has. Her third daughter will be Rinnah Elsbeth." *Rinnah*, a small blue Netaian songbird, was also the Ehretan word for *Adoration*, according to Carradee's communiqué. He shook his head. "I do suggest, for the sake of stability and a more rapid return to status quo government, that we acclaim Firebird instead."

"I would second that proposal," said Kenhing.

Reshn Parkai, Baron of Sylva and DeTar, gripped his writing stylus in a hammy fist. "A convicted criminal, the mother of a mind-crawler's heirs? When we could acclaim an innocent, pure-blooded Netaian?"

"Technically," said Count Quinton Gellison, "Firebird was not confirmed as an heiress. The ceremony was interrupted before that point."

"Rinnah Elsbeth," Tel answered the count, "has not been confirmed either."

Valora Erwin scowled. "Better a known monarch now, a woman who was raised among us, than a someday unknown who will probably grow up on the Sentinels' fortress world."

Tel clasped his hands on the tabletop as the argument heated up around him. This session would probably last far into the night. At one corner of his vision, Esme Rogonin stared in his direction.

He opened his hands, spreading his fingers in a diminutive shrug.

Esme smiled faintly.

CHAPTER 22

STORM'S EYE

allegro malinconico
fast, melancholy

Walking steadily, Firebird followed Uri across a docking tube onto the Thyrian battle cruiser *North Ice.* During her rest intervals, she'd spent hours developing a new visualization to help her stay conscious during epsilon fusion. Brennen had insisted they not try it—yet. From time to time, she caught a new depth, almost a desperation, in the small, kindly gestures he always made. There were hints, too, that he was shielding something from her.

She thought she knew what that was. If he'd been called to destroy the Golden City, his sense of duty had to be struggling with his compassion. Any trained soldier had doubtful moments, and he'd just regained memories of that place and its people. They must be haunting him, she guessed.

They probably ought to be haunting her. Terza had turned from Shuhr ways. Weren't others capable of changing?

"She's different," Brenn had explained. "Most Shuhr children with her disposition are culled in training—killed by their teachers. Either that, or they aren't admitted to train in the Golden City."

Firebird stepped onto the other ship's deck. A woman who appeared to be in her mid-forties, wearing midnight blue and a Sentinel's star, saluted Brennen. "Wing Colonel Janith Keeson, General. I relinquish *North Ice* to your command."

Brennen also saluted. "Colonel, I return *North Ice* to you with thanks. Carry on."

Sentinel Janith Keeson wore her chestnut hair short and curly, and her cheeks bulged like pink snow-apples. She turned to one of the few crewers in the docking bay who didn't wear midnight blue, and she gave a hand signal. Orders passed out of earshot, up the passway and onto a transpeaker system. "Shamarr Dickin sends greetings and a blessing," she added.

Firebird smiled at this news from Brenn's spiritual father.

"There's one important development," Brennen said. "We're called. The Holy One has ordered us to strike Three Zed. There's no longer any question of following the Federate order."

"That's a relief." Colonel Keeson broke a smile, but it quickly faded. Firebird had wanted to see a Sentinel react to this news, and evidently the thrill of following a divine call didn't last long. Next came the sobriety of taking up holy responsibility.

Colonel Keeson stepped briskly up the corridor, and Firebird matched her pace. Under regen, her bruises had faded, muscles knit, and the last nerves were regenerating—though her ribs and spine still ached.

"How quickly can you secure and accelerate for Three Zed?" Brennen asked the colonel. "We're racing an advance scout."

Sentinel Keeson halted beside a wall console and called a string of orders. "How quickly can you prepare for acceleration, sir?" she asked.

Minutes later, Firebird sank onto another bunk, raised her arms as a new set of medics clamped down the regen arch, and then lay listening to the drive engines' pitch rise. Around her private cubicle, the meds anchored everything that was loose. "War is always like this," said Shel. "Weeks of boredom punctuated by minutes of panic, when only solid training means survival."

"Netaia has a similar saying." Brennen had assured her that *North Ice* would have flight simulator booths, and that her assigned Light-Five fighter would have an onboard sim-override program. She must be at her peak for this mission.

Brennen stepped into the small, private cubicle half an hour later, after gravidic compensators restabilized the deck. "Thank you, Shel," he said solemnly. "I relieve you."

The bodyguard slipped out.

"We sent a messenger to Tallis," Brennen said, standing close, "and general alerts to the Second Division. Terza's on her way to Hesed, under guard. There's no need to keep her in harm's way any longer."

"Good," Firebird murmured.

He laid a hand on her forehead. "Colonel Keeson just gave me more good news. When Alert Forces heard that Burkenhamn recommissioned you, they refitted a full-powered Light-Five for you with RIA and remote-pilot capacity. We're as well-equipped as we could hope."

"Good," she said again. Actually, as badly as she wanted to start her onboard sim training, she was scheduled to rest now. "Help me sleep." She shut her eyes. . . .

When she opened them next, Brennen had gone. A dark-haired woman had taken his place—a slender woman with keen dark eyes and a strong, shapely nose. Firebird knew that face. "Ellet," she exclaimed, tensing. Once, the Sentinel woman had been determined to claim Brennen for herself. Ellet had eventually pair bonded Brennen's friend Damalcon Dardy, though Brennen never adequately explained how *that* came about.

"I won't stay," Ellet said softly. "I only wanted to wish you well. To congratulate you on your new rank, and your survival. You're a tough woman to kill, Commander." Ellet barely smiled. She looked hesitant, unsure how she would be received.

Firebird couldn't resent Ellet any longer. "Coming from you," she answered, "that's a compliment."

Ellet's smile spread to her eyes, crinkling the skin around them. "I didn't just come with compliments." She slid a stool close to Firebird's narrow bunk. "I came to apologize. Firebird, I have been blind to your humanity. I owe you a debt, and I must ask for your forgiveness."

Marriage had certainly changed Ellet! Firebird could've easily gloated, but what would that accomplish? She was finally rid of pride . . . temporarily, she guessed. She would postpone its return as long as possible. She raised her arm, and Ellet clasped her hand. "Thank you, Ellet. What's your job here? Where's Damalcon?"

"I'm military historian for Colonel Keeson. Damalcon's on board the carrier *Weatherway*, and I transshipped over as soon as you arrived. He'll command the second flight, the heavy bombers."

"It's good to have you on board," Firebird said. This five-day slip might be Ellet's first separation. "Look me up if you get lonely."

Ellet Dardy raised an eyebrow. "You put me to shame," she said.

After Ellet left, Firebird checked the time. She had to spend another half hour prone, and she couldn't waste it. She must learn to stay conscious after achieving fusion with Brennen. He'd said that fusion stayed with him for as long as he could hold a turn, like keeping all mental circuits hyperactivated. If she could keep from fading out, then maybe she could actually do things with it, beyond simply setting off the explosion.

Brennen was probably on the command deck or down at Engineering. He'd spent most of his time on board *Sapphira* in one of those places. Struggling against the regen projector, Firebird loaded an off-white audio rod into a player Brenn's engineers had attached to the healing arch. Soft strains of a Netaian *largo* sprang up around her, amplified by net-cloth speakers draped over her pillow.

Before Ellet showed up, she'd been dreaming. Some kind of energy storm had descended on Hesed, and she'd cowered inside, protecting her babies with her arms and her body.

That dream, she'd be glad to forget.

Then she reconsidered. She'd run out of logical ways to visualize and control fusion. What about seeing it as an energy storm? Medical Master Spieth had warned, months ago, that if she played the wrong games with her epsilon carrier, she could go mad—but she would shortly face a fielding team that used madness as one of its weapons. She needed to stand against it somehow.

Pushing her head into the deep pillow, she tried to set the dream firmly in mind. The slow, somber bass line of the *largo* gave her a rhythmic framework.

Next, she imagined touching her epsilon carrier to Brennen's, and then she envisioned their fusion as a gale blasting over and through her imaginary wall. She heard its howl, smelled on the wind the warm-incense scent of Brennen's access—but hotter, fiercer, wilder—

Yes. She could imagine that.

She had no way of knowing if the image would give her any control, though. Not until she and Brennen actually tried it.

Now she must hit the simulators!

She rang for a med attendant.

The second slip passed too quickly for Brennen. *North Ice* and its carrier escort, *Weatherway*, hauled every fighter, bomber, or scout Thyrica had equipped with RIA equipment. Six light fighters were reserved in *North Ice*'s hangar-bay for Day Flight, the first attack wave. He'd ordered both ships' engineers to link the fighters' threat-assessor displays to firing overrides, going beyond standard ID procedure to actually prevent pilots from targeting friendly ships. That was one of the chief dangers of flying a group into a fielding defense. If engineers could make that impossible, Three Zed's defenders would have to fall back on direct mental attacks—amplifying enemy pilots' terrors or trying to induce madness. Those risks were sobering enough without destroying his own support group.

Another danger drove him to complete this project. If the vision he'd seen, the missile-blasted Light-Five, proved accurate—if he was destined to die at Three Zed—then he would do everything in his power to keep the Shuhr fielding team from voice-commanding Mari to fire that fateful missile.

Two days out from Three Zed, Firebird shook off drowsiness and tried to sit up.

Brennen stood over her. Last night, he'd reported on his other subcommanders' planning session. Sending a field general into combat flew in the face of all rules of engagement, but no other Sentinel would dare to fuse carriers with her.

So Day Flight, including her and Brennen, would launch the moment *North Ice* dropped slip-shields. Protected by their overlapped slip and particle shields, they would fly into fielding and RIA range. Brennen would initiate fusion by quest-pulsing to her, then try to overload the fielding site's circuits with fusion energy. They would have the combined power of two RIA ships, and if fusion left her unconscious, then her modified Light-Five could be flown out by a remote pilot while Night Flight—Dardy's heavy bombers—dropped their payloads.

Another Sentinel had volunteered to fly lead in Day Flight, where the enemy surely assumed Brennen would be. Firebird had to respect that man's courage. She prayed he would be spared.

"It's time we ran our own simulation," she told Brennen firmly. "High time."

"I'm afraid so." He reached toward a bulkhead. "I'll send Shel for a med, in case."

She had explained her new visualization. "Maybe focusing on the storm image will give me enough conscious time to fly out of the thick of things," she said. "You could press your attack while I pull out far enough to feel safe about activating the fighter's recovery cycle. I really don't want to use the remote pilot."

"I wouldn't either." He sank down beside her on the bunk and asked, "Are you ready?"

Firebird pressed her eyes shut, visualizing the wall, the carrier, the storm. "Ready," she whispered.

Brennen reached inside himself for his epsilon carrier. As he focused for access, he felt her carrier flicker, as if she'd been mildly dosed with blocking drugs. Twice, he tried to grasp and fuse with it. Twice, it blinked out of existence.

Had their fusion at the Hall of Charity damaged the ayin complex in her brain? She had managed to turn several times since then, but this was not a good sign.

Her eyes came open, dark and serious. "I can't turn," she exclaimed.

"Sickness or injury does sometimes affect us in unpredictable ways," he said. "We'll try again later."

After Brennen left, Firebird sat clenching her fists. Master Jenner had said that repeated fusion could scar her physical epsilon center beyond the ability to function—eventually.

Not before Three Zed! she prayed—but she hated the flaming darkness inside her. For all Shamarr Dickin's assurance that she was not actually using evil, but only seeing it clearly, she dreaded watching it spark the evil inside others . . . watching the evil, empowered by fusion, destroy them.

Brenn had been right all along. Epsilon talent carried responsibilities that no thinking person would want.

She hurried downship to her simulator.

A messenger ship's arrival called Juddis Adiyn away from his gene laboratory. Without waiting to hear progress reports from Netaia, he had ordered an accelerated primary fertilization program, enough to make a serious start at synthesizing enough genetic material to modify

Netaia's next generation. Gametes were almost ready to be combined.

From his own rounded gold corridor, a gravity lift carried him up to the City's communication center, where he had a clear view of a bleak sunset. This courier should bring word of Firebird's demise and General Caldwell's captivity—or possibly his death. On the shebiyl, Adiyn saw him nowhere in the future. There should be no more Carabohd heirs until those twins grew up, unless his own lab produced them—but the shebiyl did sometimes shift, showing him the only safe course in the cruel nick of time. In those moments it seemed like a living evil, just as the Sentinels claimed.

Under the only sizable viewing dome in the City, he seated himself at a secure station, as the DS-212 pilot requested. He activated its sonic shield. "Acting Eldest Adiyn," he said into the transceiver. "What couldn't you send over general frequencies?"

"They failed." From the messenger's reproachful voice, Adiyn pictured a grimace. "Firebird survived. Caldwell appears to have saved her, and there's suspicion that they may have perfected an antipodal fusion technique. Reference Polar's research, if you don't recall—"

"I remember that project," Adiyn interrupted.

"Shirak orders immediate mobilization. Hit Tallis. Now."

"Slow down, slow down." People who hadn't reached their first century thought everything had to be finished now . . . or sooner. The shebiyl would tell him what must be done and when. "What exactly is the worry?"

"That Caldwell and his lady," said the irritated voice, "with the fusion ability Polar predicted, *plus* the RIA technology the Federacy just announced, could strike here. We would have no defense against that. Terza thought of the fusion idea. Maybe from a mutation in the Casvah line."

Adiyn rubbed his chin. "Our agents on Thyrica have turned up some RIA data. Its range is still finite, no more than a fielding team's." And yet—

Though RIA technology could explain how Caldwell and the lady got through the City's fielding net before, no theory adequately explained the power that blasted Dru Polar into the underground generator chamber's stone floor.

And what about Harcourt Terrell, killed under watch-link when he attacked Lady Firebird? The link supervisor, Arac Nahazh, was unfortunately dead. They would never know what killed Terrell. But definitely, there was more afoot than RIA development.

For years, his people had planned to set the Federacy against its Sentinel defenders. In the Shiraks' absence, Adiyn had continued the vital raids, relieving the Federacy of another half dozen fighters, two military transports, and even a small cruiser. Parked here in orbit, they could be sent against Tallis with only hours' warning, along a vector that would make it look as if the attack originated from a Sentinel world. The colony's commander-in-chief continued to conscript and train pilots out of the settlements. Adiyn wished the suicide-compulsion sessions weren't necessary, but weighed against humankind's immortality, already-limited lives had little value.

He had also sent signals to deep-cover agents on several worlds, including Thyrica. Those agents would trumpet to the Federacy that the Sentinels, with their terrifying new technology, must bear the responsibility for any further Sunton-style attack. Maybe nongifted Thyrians would respond to his own attack at Tallis by leveling the Sentinel College.

But what about this other development? He rubbed his chin. "What happened? How did they miss her?"

"I've transmitted a tri-D sequence, recorded off newsnet coverage."

Adiyn touched a control. "I see the file. And Terza?"

The messenger's hesitation prepared him for bad news. "Talumah's last set of subconscious commands appears to have failed. Her original orders kicked in, and she defected to them . . . by the old plan."

Against a new compulsion? The girl's Shirak genes had proved stronger than he suspected, stronger than the submissive maternal line that Modabah had ordered when he had her conceived.

Or was this a matter of human will—and did the girl have rogue epsilon talents? "Her deep linkages should remain," said Adiyn. "We have an agent among them now."

"Whether the old sabotage orders will activate, we won't know until potentially too late. But it's clear now that they were trying to trap one of us just as surely as we tried to get Caldwell for a full mind-access strip. Shirak wants you on highest alert."

Adiyn would do nothing without checking the shebiyl and the most likely paths the future would take. "Report to the communication center as soon as you're down," he said.

The courier signed off. Adiyn fed the burst-transmitted tri-D file to the secure booth's media block. As he watched, he smiled at the secondary explosions, minor—but noisy—charges Micahel must have planted around the nave, coordinated cues blaring that Firebird was about to die. As always, Micahel displayed a gift for showmanship.

But plainly, something unprecedented had happened on that carpeted stage. He shut down the projection unit and waved off all lights.

Terza! At least she'd left them with the idea that a Casvah mutation—not the Caldwell family at all!—produced whatever enabled Firebird to survive at that Netaian altar. This probably had destroyed Dru Polar, and Terrell as well.

Then they had a second formidable enemy. He must not underestimate Firebird again. He had already cloned breeder cells from the other Casvah-Angelo specimens. He would fertilize them immediately. Epsilon abilities usually matured at around twelve years old, but multiple ayin and hormone treatments could push epsilon maturity forward at the cost of other brain functions. In less than a year, he might produce laboratory creatures who could be epsilon-manipulated, but who could scarcely be called human.

Polar's offspring, he decided. Polar's strength, matched with the Casvah mutation. "Casvah, the vessel, a cup full of death," he'd called Phoena.

Polar and Phoena, then?

In the booth's darkness, he reached outside himself for the elusive shebiyl.

Firebird perched on the edge of her bunk in that narrow private cubicle. Medic Hancock returned his instruments to their case. Brennen stood behind him, leaning against a bulkhead, arms crossed over his chest. Shel stood just outside the door, with only her left arm and shoulder visible.

"Lady Firebird," Hancock said, glowering, "you've done an excellent job of sticking to your regimen, but under any other circumstances, I would not even consider releasing you to combat status."

"I understand," she said. "Under any other circumstances, I might have second thoughts, too. But I'm ready."

Hancock exhaled sharply, pulled a hand tool from his tunic pocket, and applied the tool to her wrist monitor. It fell free.

Firebird watched her medic leave. The countdown to drop point had begun. In twelve hours, *North Ice* would reenter normal space in the Zed system.

Brennen sat down beside her on the cot.

"Everything's under control, then?" she asked.

"Planned, replanned, and backed up with fail-safes," he said, running a hand over his face.

She felt his uneasiness. "I wish there were another way to end this threat, too," she said.

"No one is utterly evil." Brennen clasped his hands between his knees. "The One made us all. The same Ehretans who changed their genes changed ours."

"Is it harder," she asked gently, "now that you remember the place?"

"Yes and no. I was not treated well. But not all of them were as evil as . . . the ones who kept me in custody."

She nodded, staring across at the door, a meter away. "And the bioweapons?"

He'd mentioned flash-frozen cultures, organisms that destroyed all remnants of life on Ehret.

"That," he said, "is the best reason to burn it down to bare rock. But they are exiles, too."

"They made themselves exiles. They declared the war, and they ended it with those bioweapons."

"But they also honor the memory of Ehret. Better than we do, in some ways."

"Not the ways that count."

"No," he admitted. "Their greatest pride is in rebellion. They want to make themselves into a higher species, something immortal in the flesh. That would be a terrible fate . . . to exist forever in a life that's tainted, growing more and more tainted ourselves."

"Or else stronger?" she suggested.

"Maybe. And when I think of the people who would love to see their artifacts—"

"That we're about to destroy."

"If we can." He said it like a sigh. "I would pray, if I knew I would survive this, that this will not haunt me the rest of my life."

A touch of that mysterious dread came through, and she seized one of his hands. "What have you seen that you still haven't told me?" she demanded.

For several minutes she felt the low rumble that meant he was struggling with his thoughts. She felt a faint engine vibration, too, and she breathed the acid tang of disinfected air. She edged sideways until her leg pressed against his.

"I saw a fighter," he said quietly. "My ship, though I'm not sure how I knew it was mine. It was in pieces. It looked as if it'd taken a missile hit."

She resisted the downward pull of his dread. "That wasn't necessarily a vision, Brenn. We often dream about our worst fears."

He gripped her hand. "I was not asleep. But you're right. And for decades, the shamarrs have told us that if we refused to pick up the sword when He called, then our enemies would slaughter millions. I can't wait for them to strike Tallis or Netaia." He reached over, twining both hands around the base of her neck. "What have we lived for, Mari . . . ourselves, our pleasures, our own wills and dreams? If I live for you, and you for me, we exist only for ourselves."

In this mood, he seemed utterly strange . . . yet he had always been vaguely alien, though he was half of herself. "I know," she murmured.

He massaged the back of her neck. "Whatever happens, it will be the highest good. Mari, if anything happens to me, I want you to be prepared. Tell Master Dabarrah I was told, 'It is time. Destroy my enemies.' He'll understand. He'll ease your grief, and Kinnor and Kiel will give you a thousand reasons to live."

"Tell him yourself," she murmured. *Didn't you order him to lead the fight, Mighty Singer?* "I'll be there with you." She craned her neck to kiss him, then let her mind go blank, her body limp, as they relaxed together on the cot. She concentrated on the warmth of his body. He wouldn't die out there in the cold. *Singer, he has done everything you asked him. You have no reason to punish him, and you've already disciplined me.*

He caressed her throat, then her jaw line, her lips. They'd hardly had an hour alone since her injury. She wondered how many other vital things they'd put off for "one day."

Life was a promise that had to break . . . break free of the physical, of space and of time. Tonight, she lay with her bond mate.

She slapped the cubicle's privacy control. The door slid shut.

Spent and unable to speculate any further, she pressed her head against Brennen's chest. His heart beat a strong, slow rhythm beneath her ear.

All her horizons slowly receded. It had been a spectacular hour. But in that Brennen-place at the back of her mind, she felt a certainty that tormented him cruelly. Whether or not they survived, this was the end of a part of their lives. If she didn't want a crown anymore, how did he feel about leading a holy war? *If there's some way to show mercy, spare him this*, she prayed. Then she drew a deep breath and raised her head. "Lock me down again, Brenn. We have eleven hours, and I'm entitled to one more regen session."

She rearranged her clothing, and then he clamped the field generator in place. He covered the humming arch with a pillow and rested his head on it. Waves of his drowsiness washed over her, dragging her down with her weary lover into unmeasured depths.

Chapter 23

SWORD'S POINT

furiant
a lively dance with frequently shifting accents

A deceleration alarm blasted Firebird awake. Brennen rolled off the bunk and released the healing arch. "It's time," he said softly, plucking his midnight blue tunic off a wall hangar. "Ten minutes to hard decel. Three hours to launch."

"Wait," she said. Closing her eyes, she envisioned the wall and pressed through, touching her epsilon carrier as smoothly as she'd ever done.

"Good," he murmured, closing the last clasp.

She seized his arm and pulled him into an embrace.

"I hate to see you risk this," he said. "I may not be able to ride your wing back in."

"I might be able to stay conscious."

"Do whatever is necessary. You must," he said, drawing back far enough to pierce her with the brilliance of his eyes, "no matter what happens. I will not build false dreams, and I won't run from what must be done."

"I won't either," she said firmly. "Take this." She fumbled with the little medallion's chain. "Wear it and think of me. And remember Tarance—"

"No," he said, and once again, she felt his lingering abhorrence of gold objects. "I gave it to you. Better grab a holdfast."

As the second decel alarm sounded, she seized a bulkhead loop with one hand and grabbed Brennen with the other.

As the cruiser started its stiff deceleration toward the Zed system, inertia momentarily pushed her toward the bulkhead. Something rattled inside a nearby storage bin.

Then Brennen pushed away. "See you shortly," he murmured.

Brenn had shown her where to find the uniform locker Burkenhamn had sent. In the cubicle's adjoining freshing room, after a fast vapor-bath, she slipped into Netaian cobalt blue for the first time since . . . since not long after her capture by Federates, at Veroh.

A new insignia over her breast startled her: the gold-edged Fedorate slash. Like Burkenhamm, she was now Federate personnel.

Excellent.

Before closing her collar, she gingerly touched the ragged red entry-wound scar on her shoulder, then the fading surgical line across her chest. Both wounds were too deep for biotape to prevent scarring. "I owe the Shuhr for these scars," she told Shel's reflection in the mirror.

One inner pocket felt lumpy. She fished inside and pulled out the gold three-moon insignia of her new rank. An unfamiliar theater clip separated itself from the pair of three-moons. Veroh? she wondered. Was Netaia issuing theater clips for that disaster?

If so, she'd earned the insignia. She laid the clip and the three-moons back inside the locker, hoping she would survive to wear them on a noncombat occasion.

The quartermaster had included a hair catch. Hastily, she made a tail at the nape of her neck, then clipped the long gloves to her belt. At the bottom of the duffel was a heavy gray life suit and pilot's helmet.

Those were donned just this side of the cockpit. Carrying them, she walked up to the bridge.

She found Brennen there, conferring with his other subcommanders. *North Ice*, a light cruiser, had a large scan/sensor station and four transceivers, one inboard and three for command purposes. Between one subcommander's chair—occupied by Brennen at the moment—and the sensor station, engineers had moved one of the sim stations and linked it to Firebird's fighter controls, so that a remote pilot could steer her out of danger if fusion left her unconscious.

She hung back, leaning against a bulkhead while she waited for Brennen to finish. Threat axes, refuel procedures, med evacuations . . . as he'd said, every plan had been laid with excruciating attention to detail. He hadn't had any more time to dress than she had, but his jaw was clean and beardless, the line of it firm and straight.

She listened intently, glad for Brennen's steady nerves. If she ever wrote another clairsa piece for him, she must capture the tension of this moment, his calm acceptance of a pressure no one else understood . . . and the wisp of light red-brown hair that stuck out from having been slept on crookedly.

She spotted Ellet Dardy sitting at a bank of transcorders, uniformed as crisply as ever, ready to record and transmit the history they would make today. Ellet saluted, and Firebird returned the gesture.

Uri stood behind Brennen, still at his post. Brennen straightened his shoulders and reached for the subcommanders' hands in turn, finishing with Colonel Keeson. "Go with the One, General," she said.

"And you," he answered. Then he looked at Firebird.

He was her commanding officer now. She pushed off the bulkhead and saluted.

"Hangar-bay one," he said.

She embraced Shel. "Thank you," she murmured, then hurried out, leaving Shel on the bridge.

Uri also stayed behind. Their duties had ended.

Three men and a woman, the rest of Day Flight, stood in a briefing room near the hangar-bay's lift door. All carried life suits and helmets. Beyond a long window, crewers scurried through the bay, readying the fightercraft, performing final checks. Firebird sniffed an odor of ozone and fuel.

Brennen gathered his flight team around the table for final instructions. "There's some risk," he said, "of erratic asteroids in this vicinity. Watch for debris."

The man closest to Firebird—Major Hannes Dickin, a nephew of the shamarr—held his head erect. Since he had volunteered to fly the lead position, that would make him the Shuhr's number one target. She wondered if they could remote-manipulate orbiting rocks.

"To approach closely enough to strike," Brennen said, "we have to enter fielding range. Commander Caldwell, you will fly slot and hang back, since you are at greatest risk from fielding attack."

She nodded.

"We will remain within maximum shield-overlap range," Brennen went on, "take one pass at the fielding unit pinpointed on our targeting displays, and egress. Night Flight will follow three minutes behind us."

The woman beside Brennen tapped one finger against her helmet. Firebird wasn't the only nervous one.

"We have to destroy the fielding site," Brennen said. "If Day Flight fails, the operation fails. If you survive an aborted attempt, try to recover on *North Ice* before it accelerates outsystem for Tallis."

"Speaking for all of us, I think," said the stocky man on Brennen's other side, "I don't expect to have that problem, sir."

Firebird raised her head. That was a more typical pilot's attitude, a firm denial that anything might strike his particular craft, no matter how exotic the enemy's technology. She usually heard it after the mission, though . . . not beforehand.

Brennen smiled and kept talking. "Automatic recovery cycles and fire overrides are to be preactivated immediately after launch. If you find yourself acting irrationally, surrender operation of your ship. It will set a reasonably evasive course."

His voice softened. "One more thing. In an environment defended by fielding technology, any pilot who ends up extravehicular will be vulnerable to accentuating attack. Even at Hesed, we use that."

He'd discussed this with her privately. In a fielding zone, an EV pilot's fear and disorientation could be amplified by the Shuhr's coordinated, projected mental powers. This defense caused madness in ninety-nine percent of cases, even at Hesed. The Shuhr might have found ways to make that defense even crueler.

"Therefore, any pilot who goes EV will be moved to the second triage category for later recovery," Brennen continued. "Your EV unit has oxygen for more than an hour, but here, it will be kinder to let events take their course."

Simply falling asleep in the cold . . . Firebird had to agree. It wouldn't be such a terrible way to make the Crossing.

Was that what he foresaw?

No . . . he had described a missile hit. He'd said nothing about EV—

"Other questions?" Brennen stared at each pilot for several seconds. Firebird felt him send pulses of epsilon energy, and she guessed he was reinforcing the others' confidence. When he looked at her, her fears did drop away.

He dismissed the group, but she felt him urge her to linger. As soon as the others had left the briefing room, he broke uniform etiquette. He embraced her, one arm pinning her head to his chest, the other arm clenching her waist. She struggled to free her head, then thrust up her chin.

As he kissed her, the scent at the back of her mind intensified, as if he were pushing himself deeply into her memory in the last few seconds remaining to them. Emptied and panting, she shut her mouth as he drew back.

Neither spoke.

Firebird walked out into the main bay, then followed a crewer toward one of the small swept-wing fighters. The crewer halted beside a blocky starter unit and helped her into her depressurization suit. Proof against hard vacuum, with dozens of sealed inner compartments, the life suit would inflate automatically if she lost cabin pressure.

Why bother, she wondered, *if going EV means madness and death?* She'd trained in a life suit, though. She had always trained the way she meant to fight. It was the only way to survive.

She glanced up at the Light-Five fighter. She'd spent hours simming in this cockpit, first with an instructor and then alone. The fighter was nimble and well shielded. The RIA add-on system's energy demands limited its weaponry, but she did have four programmable missiles and excellent gravidics. She rounded it hastily, sliding her gloved hands along the little ship's smooth surface. Somewhere farther down the row, Brennen was checking out another such RIA fighter, but without remote-pilot capability.

Minding the connectors that dangled from her suit, she climbed aboard. Crewers fastened her in. In the seconds that took, she focused her thoughts beyond today, beyond her lifetime. If Brennen turned out to be the Carabohd descendant who wiped out the nest of evil, then obviously, the rest of the prophecies remained to be fulfilled by Kiel or Kinnor or their descendants. *All the Mighty Singer's power, in human form!* Maybe seen from a human perspective, stuck in the flow of time, the body of prophecy was something like a series of mountain ranges, with nearby peaks obscuring the distant ones. Only when you arrived at the first summit could you see that the second range was still far off . . .

Or something like that. She pulled at each of her suit-to-ship umbilicals and all five harness points, checked that they were secure, then turned thumb-up to her chief.

From far down the row, she sensed a call at the back of her mind. She stretched her neck to peer over the closest fighter's fuselage and spotted a helmeted figure looking her way.

She saluted him.

He touched one gloved finger to his helmet over his lips.

There were few things more useless, Shel Mattason decided, than a bodyguard whose employer was going out into battle.

Colonel Keeson had assigned her and Uri to bridge security, pending their reassignment to retrieval detail, post-combat. Really, both posts were gifts, excuses to observe. She sat on her assigned stool, following the glimmering break indicator's countdown to final decel. In her breast pocket was a heatsealed letter like many she'd carried before. This one was from Firebird, to be opened only if she and Brennen were both killed. Uri carried a similar packet. She almost hoped that if one of the Caldwells died today, both of them died.

She glanced around. Actually, they all might.

A Carolinian veteran of the Netaian campaign sat at the modified flight simulator, ready to override Firebird's flight controls and bring her back.

A com officer's voice rose. "One minute to drop point, at mark. Three, two, one. Mark."

Shel pressed her palms against her thighs.

Firebird pulled her splayed-finger RIA array over both ears, then stretched on her pilot's cap. Finally, she tipped her head into her helmet as the cockpit bubble dropped.

Her in-suit transceiver was already live. Brennen's tenor voice rose over a drone of more distant voices to call off final checks. His Federate terminology was significantly different from the orders in which she'd drilled, years before—but she'd used her sim time to reprogram her expectations. Brennen clipped out, "Day Leader, generator check."

"Two, check," she heard. "Three, check." She waited her turn, then answered, "Six, check."

Her seat vibrated as the engines lit. She scanned cockpit lights.

When cued again, she answered, "Propulsion, shielding, go. Weaponry, countermeasures, go. All go, sir."

"Run-up," Brennen ordered the flight. "Full brake and throttle."

Firebird applied brake to the Thyrian craft, then gradually, she pushed throttle power fully forward. Still racing that Shuhr messenger—not to mention Micahel and his escorts—they must do everything at full speed, including launch. It would be a loose formation, with no dependence on cross-programming. Night Flight, on board *Weatherway*, would launch just as loose.

"Throttle check," said Brennen's voice in her ear.

She'd flown a personal fightercraft with him aboard over a year ago. She wished momentarily that she might ride out with him now, in a two-person trainer.

But that might not have done the job. They needed the power and versatility of two RIA systems.

She answered in her turn, then laid one hand on the brake lever. Seconds passed. Her heart thudded. She glanced down for her life-signs cuff, but it was gone now. Lights in the hangar-bay winked off. Ahead of her position, a force barrier shimmered with the chaos of quasi-orthogonal space.

"On my mark," said Brennen's voice, "brake release."

Go with us, Mighty Singer!

The shimmer grew brighter.

Seated in the communication bubble on the Golden City's south arc, Juddis Adiyn wrestled with the shebiyl. He had foreseen an attack, and that his forces were needed here before he sent any to Tallis. All probabilities showed strongly in Three Zed's favor today. Along several possible streams, he saw himself as Eldest of Three Zed colony. The Shiraks would not like that, but without his assistance, their line would die out anyway. His leadership might be best for the unbound starbred.

His reclined seat faced the transparent viewing bubble. On it, dozens of reflective display zones showed data, translucent against the backdrop of space. It had been a long day, and unless he'd read the shebiyl wrong, it would end well. At stations around him, other ranking officers called off orders. Adiyn had served some time in both fielding and command stations, so he knew battle language. The noise kept wresting his mind off the shebiyl. Tonight, he had the disquieting sense that something larger and more powerful than himself was controlling all paths of the future.

Someone shouted. He glanced at the overhead arc. A slip zone sprang into existence, entering the system not far from a cluster of asteroids, remnants of the colony's original defense. It showed on the arc of space like a set of concentric circles, dark red brightening to crimson at center, in the western sky.

Even closer in, three small ships—crewed by pilots who obviously knew where those asteroids would be—dropped slip-shields as they decelerated into normal space. "ID incoming," Adiyn shouted. "All of them."

Friend-foe analyzers whirred. New data appeared beside the red circles. "Polovia 85-B light cruiser," called a voice, "Thyrian. Also Thyrian, Polovia 277 fighter-carrier. Fighter bay opening."

Had Onar Ketaz's fearful illusion been a genuine glimpse of the shebiyl, after all? Uneasy, he demanded, "ID on the other three."

"Believe they're Netaian—" the voice started.

"Three Zed," shouted a static-charged voice over a room speaker. "Who's commanding?"

Adiyn recognized Micahel Shirak's voice. "Netaian fighter," he answered sternly, "this is Three Zed, Juddis Adiyn commanding. Micahel, what are you—"

"Listen to me." Micahel did not lower his voice or slow down. "Firebird Caldwell is in one of those incoming bogeys. She and Caldwell *have* learned to fuse carriers, just like Polar tried to do it. All the rest is only a diversion. Kill her, and Caldwell is helpless—and they can't use fusion against us. That order is from Modabah himself."

Commander-in-chief Ketaz relayed it into his link.

Polar, Adiyn reflected, would have objected. He would've liked to snatch the Angelo woman and conduct experiments—but Polar was dead, maybe at her hands. To Adiyn, her research value was genetic, and he already possessed cells from that strain.

There was also the possibility of recovering samples from her body. It should freeze quickly in space.

"Particle shielding down," announced a voice.

Firebird forced herself to go limp.

Drop point shivered the cruiser.

"Mark," Brennen called.

Firebird released her brake and hurtled forward along the hardened deck, through the collapsing shield barrier, and then out into starry space. Thrust compressed her insides against her spine. In the seconds before her head-up panel lit with route/risk data, she double-checked her position, starboard and aft of Brennen, and locked temporary tracking on the heat of lead pilot Dickin's engines.

For one instant, a spectral calm flooded her. Her husband sat on that gleaming engine at ten hundred low. He lived, and that was reality. His vision was only that—a vision, a glimpse, a chance to face down the worst possible outcome.

That was all the time she had for thinking. "Recovery cycles," she heard inside her helmet. The Zed star's arc shrank, falling behind the near planet's cratered horizon.

Next, she heard, "Firing control overrides."

She preactivated both cycles, then took a firm grasp on stick and throttle, each knurled knob solid and assuring through the life suit's gloves. If she let go of either for ten seconds, the recovery cycle would steer her back to *North Ice* and its pickup crews—or elsewhere, at the remote pilot's discretion. At least she'd be in voice contact with him.

Thrust made every move a struggle, even though she'd regained her strength. She checked energy shields again. Particle and slip both gave steady readouts.

Speckles appeared on her display. Four—five—six Shuhr defenders blinked into existence on one side of the targeted peak. The Shuhr commanders hadn't ordered blackout. Amber lights ringed the colony, presenting a beckoning target.

She recognized that symmetrical mountain.

From a northerly launch point came twelve, thirteen more defenders. Brennen hadn't guessed how many stolen ships Three Zed could command. *There just aren't that many Shuhr*, he'd said.

They would soon know.

"Four mark," said Brennen's voice.

Four minutes since launch? At this speed, anything might happen. She wished she'd had longer to tell Brennen good-bye. Illogically, she wished they were back at Esme's ball. She might never finish that dance with him.

As the cratered surface grew closer, blotting out thousands of stars every second, she realized that last complaint wasn't true. Here and now, she danced with Brennen in a realm where few mortals knew the music.

CHAPTER 24

DEATH GRIP

martele
forcefully

Brennen settled into awareness of surrounding space, as represented by six tiny screens on his console. Out here the claustrophobia didn't bother him nearly as much as it had in the hangar-bay . . . and no one could call the grand starfield *dark*. He pushed his vision of death deep into memory, where it wouldn't interfere with this mission. In less than a minute he would send a quest-pulse through the RIA apparatus to Firebird's craft, and link, and then would come the energy storm. Then he must strike.

He'd made his peace, first with fear and then with regret. At least he felt assured that the Shuhr would not take him alive.

At eleven hundred high, relative to his heading, several more engines burned to life, up in orbit—stolen Federate ships, activating against his force. His scanners showed two fielding satellites below.

"Six, lead," he directed his transceiver. "Mari, thirty seconds to range. Check pre-engagement on your recovery cycle."

"Pre-engaged," she answered.

"And the remote override." If only he could have done more, to protect her from fielding—

A new voice reverberated through his headset. "Thyrian battle group," it said, "break off. We have a hostage. Phoena Angelo is still here, and she is alive."

Firebird's throat constricted. Brennen had seen Phoena die . . . or was that another one of their deceptions?

No, he'd shown her the memory. She flicked a transceiver switch and transmitted privately, "Brenn, she may be alive, but only artificially.

There's no hope for her recovery after what they did to her." The equation of right and wrong, justice and mercy, and the moral calculations that allowed this attack at all balanced only when Phoena's chance for survival—mindless—was discounted.

Still, Firebird was glad she wasn't in a Night Flight bomber loaded with incendiaries. *Singer*, she pleaded, *if she's finally about to meet you, show her how vast your mercy is.*

Brennen recognized Adiyn's voice. Now that he remembered the geneticist, he realized that Adiyn might be the Sentinels' truest enemy, the strongest and most stable Shuhr leader, skilled at mind tampering and steeped in *keshef*—sorcery. He transmitted back, "I am sorry, Mari—"

Then a foreign presence brushed his awareness. Hostile, inquiring, it probed deftly through his epsilon shields for his private fears. It echoed oddly, like multiple presences.

Fielding range! It was a Shuhr team. Quickly, before they could debilitate Mari, he focused to quest-pulse to her.

A missile-lock alarm pierced his attention.

Only part of their fielding attack, he told himself, *playing on my fears*—but he also glanced at his screens.

From eight hundred high, three Netaian heavy fighters closed on Day Flight. "Double shields," called Hannes Dickin, at lead.

The Netaian fighters trained their targeting lasers on Dickin, then poured energy into his slip-shields. As the trio passed, Dickin's ship exploded in a globe of debris.

There was no time to think, and grieving had to come later. Brennen activated his RIA unit, plunged into the RIA accord, and probed the lead bogey.

Its pilot must have expected exactly that attack. Like hooks driving into his mind, another presence attached itself to him. He tried to drive it off but couldn't.

Watch-link!

Welcome back, Carabohd. The words tore into his head. *I didn't think you'd be stupid enough to put yourself at lead. Where is she?*

The masquerade was over. Using all the epsilon strength he could muster, Brennen tried disrupting Micahel's consciousness with the sharpest possible probe.

Micahel only plunged deeper.

"There—that one!"

One Thyrian fighter started flashing on Juddis Adiyn's master board, as well as on the arc overhead. There she was, at slot position—the only real risk to them. He activated all communication frequencies, even Federate DeepScan. Let *them* hear this, too.

"All forces, bogey now designated FC on your targeting computer is Firebird Caldwell. Reconfigure targeting priorities. She dies first."

At the instant Firebird heard that, her controls went berserk. She wrenched stick and throttle in all directions. Nothing happened externally, but the nausea of mind-access threaded into her like ethereal tentacles. The fielding team probed deep.

"Activate remote," she transmitted, no longer reluctant. That pilot should be able to pull her back just far enough. As soon as Brennen got off a quest-pulse—

The nausea turned to a stab of pure terror. Out of her console came a hollow, silvery spike, aimed straight for her chest. It drove into her life suit, burrowing deeper to skewer her—

Only the fielding, she screamed to herself. *It's an illusion!* But they had found her irrational fear.

Next came sounds—screeching voices, instruments discordant and out of tune . . . and a vivid memory.

. . . Flailing frantically, she struggled against a much larger Phoena, who stood with both arms wrapped around Firebird's waist. Firebird had to be . . . three, four years old? A seemingly huge young man, dressed in natrusilk and velvette, grabbed for her flailing arms. His free hand held two injectors. . . .

Ignoring a host of needles and spikes now driving up out of her front and side panels, she managed a turn. She stretched out through the RIA unit and felt Brennen's ship, still in range. She tried to steady herself on his presence, blocking out everything her lying senses could shriek at her—the piercing, the cacophony. *Now*, she pleaded. He must quest-pulse, must initiate fusion.

It's no use. The leering young heir's lips moved, an ethereal face floating midcockpit. *You are about to die. But you can end it quickly, and suffer less.*

They must have found out about her odd epsilon carrier—

The voice dropped in pitch. *Yes. You are a freak, a mutant. Now that we know you, we can destroy you.* More needle-sharp illusions threaded through her life suit, burning in from all angles. More tone clusters of half and quarter and third steps whanged into her mind, exploding like sonic warheads, a hideous crescendo.

She tried reciting an Adoration, the way Brennen had beaten his new fears, but she could concentrate only on the metal horrors impaling her, pumping vile substances into her body. They were right . . . they would destroy her . . . poison her . . . deafen her. . . .

No! They would not! She felt her ship decelerate. She prayed that was the remote pilot, vectoring her out of fielding range.

Where was Brennen's quest pulse?

They had her, and Brennen saw nothing else. Decelerating, her fighter started to drop toward the planet's surface. Her remote-pilot connection was plainly defunct, overridden by the fielding team.

Now his fears pounced out of hiding—now, when he was most tempted to rely only on his abilities and not on his deeper anchor. He struggled against the watch-link. He knew who sat at the controls of that Netaian heavy-fighter. Micahel kept up a running attack, sending deeper and more vicious probes, distracting him. He could not focus a quest-pulse.

On his threat board, Micahel's heavy-fighter gleamed momentarily. Micahel was arming a missile.

Brennen gripped his stick, keyed over from ground-attack to dogfighting mode, and fired off a laser volley. It went wide. Micahel's missile streaked away, locked on Firebird's decelerating Light-Five.

The stabbing cut off, and he sensed his enemy's glee. *Watch, Carabohd. Watch her die.*

Finally free to go to quest-pulse, he saw nothing but one accelerating missile. He launched a pair of decoys, but an instant later, he comprehended the geometry of the situation. The decoys would fall short. She couldn't escape.

Now, Holy One. Now I see.

He fired all his remaining missiles at Micahel, lightening his ship. Then he shoved his throttle full-forward.

Firebird clenched her eyes shut, trying not to see the horrors she plainly felt. Through her RIA unit, she sensed Brennen getting closer again.

Maybe he couldn't quest-pulse. Their fielding team might have gotten a stronger lock on him. Surely Terza didn't know everything about their defenses.

She slitted one eye open. Beyond the silvery web of illusion, Shuhr fighters converged on her fore screen. Squadron mates' calls to Brennen echoed in her ears.

Her missile-lock alarm wailed. She wrenched her stick aside, evading. Through the RIA system, she sensed another strong presence. *Micahel?* she challenged him.

Greetings to you as well, Lady Firebird. Hail and farewell.

Brennen had meant to reach out for her, then strike. For some reason, he couldn't.

But Firebird had learned to quest-pulse. Letting her hands and feet control the fighter, she turned inward. This time, she resisted the impulse to shut her eyes and concentrate. Through doubled vision, she saw two worlds. She flailed along her lichen-painted wall even as the missile appeared on her aft screen, glowing red-orange. She held to her inner course and breached the wall. She thrust energy at it and focused her little energy surge. Then she fed that energy into the RIA system and directed it toward Brennen's presence.

Fusion!

Now, Brennen! Strike!

Light washed out her eyesight. It was an illusion, the onset of psychic shock. She flailed for her stick and seized it, but it didn't respond—and the cabin's interior seemed to be dimming. She was losing all sense of Brennen's location.

Take them down, Brenn—I'll wait for you in His country!

Surrounded by her own energy storm, she felt the shudder and tumble of impact, felt blazing heat wrap around her and burn deep. As she flew against her flight harness, Micahel Shirak laughed. A second impact blasted beneath her, pushing her seat into her thighs.

Had she gone EV? She focused on the outer world again. To her shock, she still plunged toward the light-rimmed city, strapped into her own Light-Five. On her aft screen, the remains of another Thyrian fighter tumbled wildly.

Those sensations had been Brennen's, not hers! She'd caught them through RIA, through fusion, and the pair bond itself. What had he done? Had he accelerated into the vector between Micahel's ship and her own—and taken the missile meant for her?

Strike, Mari. His words came through the RIA link, overlaid with the same kind of fielding-induced terror. *Take it down, take it down!*

Then *he* was EV! Aghast, she squeezed her eyes shut. A shrieking, howling gale surrounded her point of consciousness, but she found she could hold her turn. Her knotted, twisted epsilon carrier flared with unaccustomed energy. To grip it was holding fire. She wrenched energy through the breach in her inner wall and dove back out into the visualized energy storm for her splayed-finger RIA arrays.

A surging sense of hugeness meant she had reactivated RIA. Instantly, she flung energy—guided the storm—and rode with it toward Brennen and the circling Netaian craft. In her senses, the attacker gleamed with black lightning.

Micahel Shirak watched the biggest piece of Caldwell's ship tumble toward a cluster of asteroids. He savored Firebird's terror . . . and Caldwell's, as Three Zed's fielding team lashed out to shred the Sentinel's sanity and quench his life. Micahel's cockpit glimmered under battle-red striplights.

They both had only moments to live . . . and he'd done it himself. He had destroyed the last adult Carabohd, spinning off in his pitiful EV suit—and now he would take down the freak bond mate. Linked to her through their vaunted RIA system and his own watch-link on the dying Sentinel, Micahel thrust outward to batter her with epsilon power. His hands worked stick and throttle, vectoring closer. He armed another missile for the *coup de grace.*

He tore into her alpha matrix. His abhorrent otherness gagged her. She fled the cruel spikes and screaming disharmonies, drawing his presence inward. The pursuing storm swirled in, blasting her stony wall to rubble. As Shirak thrust through her mind, she clung to her twisted, flaming carrier, far less painful than the fielding attack. She felt him dive for its deadly darkness, evil drawn to evil.

Micahel's crimson cockpit lights turned black and burst into flame. Black fire surrounded him, hungering to consume him. . . .

Black fire? A part of him, only a glimmer, refused to believe.

. . . Gouts of flame licked into him, singing audibly, whizzing and whining, exulting in suffering and death. . . .

He fought the blackness and its searing pain. No one had ever breached his defenses like this. He struggled inside his own shields, trying to loose himself from Firebird Angelo.

The mutation! Was *this* what killed Dru Polar?

Before he could fire his second missile, his alpha matrix ripped. Streaks of blinding light drove from all angles into his center of inner vision. His epsilon carrier ruptured, flinging energy out against the blinding streaks. At the back of his head, down his spine, and then through every nerve of his body, ganglions withered in fiery heat.

He plummeted toward the planet.

Brennen flew wildly toward open space, curled by his inflated EV suit into a fetal tuck. The blast that blew him from the ship had distracted him from his turn. He'd lost fusion energy, and Micahel still held him in watch-link. He sensed Mari's fall into her own flaming darkness as the Shuhr fielding team amplified that heat to scalding torment. Gasping, he plunged down inside himself. He had only one defense against fear: his own focused dependence.

Mighty One, destroy my enemies.
In you is truth, and life forever—

The watch-link dissolved in a burst of agony as Micahel lost consciousness, but the fielding techs kept on pressing their attack. No human mind could endure this.

Three Zed's surface spun crazily. His enemies amplified that sensation, too. Bile rose in his throat.

Save me by your mercy,

Cradle my loved ones in your mighty hands.

He glimpsed the rest of Day Flight, engaging Shuhr fighters as Mari's ship plunged toward Three Zed, followed by Micahel's.

I will be with that remnant.
I will refine and test them as meteor steel
And make them a sword in my hand. . . .

Focusing any original thought was a struggle now. *Catch and hold her, Holy One. Hold her. Keep her.* In his mind's eye he saw Kinnor and Kiel. *And them*, he managed. *And . . . Terza's daughter.*

Then he let his mind tumble into the remembered hymn.

. . . Where you are the light, and there is no darkness at all.

Fresh terror blasted through him. What if it all was a lie, a figment of desperate human imagination?

No darkness at all.

No Eternal Speaker. No reason to be dying. No country to Cross to.

No darkness at all.

He had been a fool. Now he would die . . . insane . . . for nothing.

No darkness at all. . . .

Firebird couldn't sense Brennen any longer, but Master Dabarrah had told her she'd know if pair bonding ever were broken.

This anguish must be something else. Must! She screamed and pounded her console. . . .

And then steadied herself. She was conscious after fusion, for the first time. She had to do this alone.

She refocused her mind's eye, thrusting the energy storm outside the ruins of her imagined wall. Massive spasms wrenched her chest. More long, silvery spikes drove into her forearms and up her calves.

"General?" someone else called in her headset. "Caldwell, come in. Come in, General."

She knew Brennen couldn't answer. The only transmitter in an EV unit was the rescue transponder, calibrated to an identifying frequency—for retrieval.

He'd given the triage order himself.

Infuriated, she fell into the fielding team's mental hold. She felt it tighten on her soul. This time, she deliberately did to them what she'd done to Harcourt Terrell, to Cassia, and to Micahel. If evil called to the Shuhr, she would call them deep. Let evil rise out of her tainted heart—and let it claim them! Anything at all to stop them from destroying Brennen.

The energy storm swirled around her, and she had the sensation that she couldn't slip out of her turn if she wanted to. Micahel had blasted down the wall. Black flames licked up, and a fire burned in the middle of her head.

"Remote pilot," she muttered, "you have firing control. I'm so close. Will my missiles launch?" Ground side guns fired up at her. On her targeting display, the fielding site flashed rapidly. She had it in range. She recognized a toothy crag near the entry she'd used before. Her fighter lurched as all four missiles fired simultaneously. As they accelerated, she plummeted behind them.

Seemingly in another world, she felt the fielding techs plunge deeper into her mind, stabbing as they came. She poured vengeful fury into the RIA link, pulling them in as all her other senses expanded, exploded, diffused. Focusing desperately on the task, unsure how Brennen would've accomplished it, she brushed aside their incinerated epsilon shields, traced the power lines that connected their flickering mental input with . . .

There. The fielding station's main energy banks.

As she poured fusion energy through the RIA unit, she felt the first of the fielding operators die. Her missiles pierced the mountainside. A moment's explosion burned after-images on her brain. Out of sheer instinct, she wrenched her stick aside.

The fighter responded this time. The spiked silver mesh in her cabin evaporated. "Fielding down," she shouted into the interlink. "Night Flight, go in!" Compared with the Shuhr cacophony, the cackle of transceiver voices sounded like music.

Then she spotted Micahel's Netaian fighter. It kept falling, following her previous trajectory. Micahel might be dead on board, but his heavy-fighter was about to hit his own city.

Justice! But she didn't care. Brennen . . . was he alive, was he sane? Where had the blast sent him?

As if a fuse had burned down, the fire in her head exploded, wiping out all thought . . . and all awareness of Brennen.

The bond link was gone.

She collapsed across her flight controls.

Micahel groped back up to an agonized consciousness. He got an eye open, but no other part of his body responded. He recognized his trajectory. He couldn't work his hands. He couldn't pull out of his own suicide dive. Like one of his own voice-commanded pilots, he was headed straight into the target, accelerating.

The tightness in his chest surged out in a scream.

Shel glanced aside. Ellet Dardy sat at station, tears streaming down her cheeks. Uri remained at stiff attention.

"Remote pilot," barked Colonel Keeson. "Full override. She's gone unconscious. Her signs are critical. Get her out of there."

Like every other Sentinel who could see Firebird's life signs, Shel understood. Firebird was falling into bereavement shock.

Brennen was lost. For his sake, she hoped the blast had knocked him unconscious before the fielding team could torment him to death.

Behind Shirak's hijacked Netaian fighter, Night Flight dropped toward Three Zed. Thyrian bombers flew a steady course between their fighter escorts.

Juddis Adiyn stood over a tracking console, cursing under his breath as Micahel's fighter hit the city. The horizon flashed. The ground shook.

"Particle shielding holds," a voice announced. "Ninety-two percent of impact energy absorbed by planet's surface."

Adiyn pushed up from his console. Naturally, the colony's powerful defenses had drained most of Micahel's momentum away from the city itself. Caldwell was gone, but the Angelo woman vectored out and away. Adiyn reached toward his transceiver to alert the larger ships.

Then without any effort on his part, the shebiyl thrust itself into his mind. All of its stream-like paths unraveled like a vast web, flickering wildly—and then twined again, this time into a swift, unstoppable river of fire and light. A single figure straddled time's flow, robed in billowing, blinding white robes. He raised his left hand in imperious challenge. His right hand gripped a glimmering sword, poised to strike. His face was too brilliant to see.

Beneath Adiyn's feet, a throaty rumble answered the impact of Micahel's fall. The shebiyl faded and dissolved.

Adiyn tried to cry out a warning, but the ground shook again. Voices around him cut off in midsentence. He grabbed the console with hands that were suddenly slick with sweat.

There was one second's silence.

Chapter 25

His Hand

senza fiato
without breath

Shel stared at the monitor screens. Firebird's ship vectored back, escorted by three Day Flight pilots. Brennen's body had tumbled out of sensor range. Fragments of Micahel's heavy fighter rolled out across Three Zed's basaltic surface.

Abruptly, the Golden City's amber external lights went dark.

Shel glanced over at Sensors, a fortyish woman in Tallan ash gray. "That impact shouldn't have knocked out the main generator," Shel said. Brennen had described that obsidian generator chamber, protected underground. . . .

"No, but it triggered a ground quake," Sensors answered. "Big one, getting bigger."

And those lights had probably been on auxiliary power.

Sensors gasped. *North Ice*'s boards painted a superheated plume rising into the mountain from beneath. "Magma," shouted Sensors. "No, it's gaseous!"

In front of Shel's eyes, the Golden City dissolved in a haze of scarlet dust, expanding like a bubble. Then it imploded, collapsing in on itself. Waves of blue lightning played back and forth over Three Zed's surface. A second blast sent fighter-sized globs of molten metal and stone into space. A glowing cloud of superheated air and ash flowed out along the planet's basaltic plain.

Shel shook her head, stunned. Basaltic lava didn't explode like this on a dry world. Either Three Zed was a geological oddity, or else the Shuhr had created an unstable situation. . . . *Or is it your wrath, after all, that destroys them?*

Colonel Keeson was already shouting orders. "Night Flight, all bombers, pull back. Fighters, break off. Pursue the ships they've launched."

Shel glanced down at Ellet, who was still working furiously over her transcorder, though tears spilled down her cheeks. Shel brushed her own cheek and realized it was wet, too. On screen, the ash cloud continued to flow away from the ruined city.

A flight of Shuhr fighters vanished. "Tallis vector," called Sensors.

Shel wiped her cheeks with both palms. Brennen had warned Tallis. Regional command would be on full alert.

On another display, the aft fuselage of Brennen's fighter spun toward a rogue asteroid cluster. Uri stared, setting his jaw.

Shel shut her eyes, not wanting to see the impact. His EV transponder had been sending for several minutes—but Firebird's life signs already told her everything she did not want to know.

Torment seared Firebird from her throat to her groin, and sweat rolled off her forehead. Someone bumped her, reaching into her Light-Five's cockpit. In the next instant, she recognized a crewer unhooking connectors. Brilliant light flooded the hangar-bay.

Her remote pilot had brought her back to *North Ice*, unconscious. Either the crewers had bumped her awake, or else the lights and fresh air roused her. Like the dying vibrations from a huge bell, her senses still rang with fusion energy. All of her senses except the bond-link to Brennen . . .

"No," she shrieked, "no!" She clutched the nearest arm.

"Don't move," she heard in her helmet. Someone pushed something hard against her shoulder. It stung. "Please, Firebird."

These were meds, then, not crewers, and they'd just hit her with a stimulant. Two more stood by with a heavy stretcher unit.

Pain throttled her, grief and fury so exquisitely compounded she could think of nothing else. She tumbled without caring how hard or far she fell. Someone, something, pulled her legs and torso straight and bound her to a flat surface. Something squeezed her upper arms.

Nauseating otherness flooded through her. Swallowing hard, she opened her eyes to see Shel's face. It bobbed as the Sentinel walked alongside her. "What was his vector?" Firebird cried. "Maybe he's alive, maybe he's still out there—" Talking drove new knives of pain into her chest.

The nausea intensified as Shel probed deeper. The Sentinel laid a hand on her arm. "Oh, Firebird, be strong. I'm so sorry. This is bereavement shock." Shel turned aside, speaking to a med in a yellow tunic. "I've been through this."

"No," Firebird groaned, "no, he can't be—"

Couldn't he? He had accelerated directly into that missile's path. Wouldn't she rather he'd crossed into the Speaker's country . . . than that he survived out there, deranged and terrorized?

And this time, she had deliberately used the evil inside her—wielded it like a weapon, instead of letting the evil ones be drawn in—

Forgive me, she pleaded, *forgive and cleanse me. Oh, Singer—*

"Be calm," muttered a med alongside her, "be strong, Commander. We'll help you." They propelled her around a corner into a passway.

Shel kept up, one hand gripping Firebird's shoulder. The tender gesture raked Firebird's agony into red-hot fire. "Firebird, I've been there. I remember. I won't leave you."

The meds transferred her again, this time from the litter onto one more sickbay unit. Another field projector dropped over her chest. Two meds clamped it down, binding her to a life she despised, if this really was bereavement shock—if Brennen was gone, and she'd done such an abhorrent thing.

Another med swept a translucent mask toward her face. "You have to rest," he said.

"Let me go!"

The vapors flooding her lungs smelled of Hesed House. "Breathe deeply," ordered the med.

She felt herself relax. The pain's knife-edge dulled. Her head started to clear.

He'd put himself in harm's way, dying in her place. . . .

It wasn't atonement, not the way Path instructors described it. But clearly, he had saved her with his own life—while she plunged into evil, fouling his sacrifice.

"He shouldn't have," she managed. It sounded and felt like a groan.

She barely felt Shel pull away.

"Major Mattason, this is Colonel Keeson."

Shel slipped out of Firebird's sickbay cubicle and raised her interlink. "Mattason here. Go ahead, Colonel." She glanced back into the cubicle. Firebird thrashed on her cot, plainly in the deepest throes of bereavement shock, her mental and emotional savor burning with loss.

"General Caldwell's ship impacted one of those asteroids. His EV transponder was still active when he tumbled out of range, but our people gave his final vector a thorough sweep and found no life signs. Other damaged fighters are sending positive signs. I'm sure you understand."

Shel's hand tightened on the interlink. "Yes. Yes, I do." *Welcome him home, Holy One. We will miss him terribly.*

"I'm sorry, Major Mattason. There are many other wounded to rescue. That's taking all our resources."

Shel slumped, wondering what Uri was feeling, as Brennen's personal guard. He'd already transshipped to *Weatherway*, ordered by Colonel Keeson to report to the battle group's chaplain. "I understand, Colonel. I'll tell her."

She slipped back into the cubicle and checked Firebird's monitor board. Plainly, she'd suffered a deep mental injury that endangered all her life functions. *We need to get her to Hesed*, Shel observed, *with the other bereaved.*

"Shel," Firebird pleaded, seizing her arm with both hands. Plainly, she'd heard some of that conversation. "Shel, if anyone could've survived that attack, he could. He might be in t-sleep. He could—" Her eyes widened, and Shel sensed her panic.

Shel turned around. A muscular young med advanced, brandishing a sub-Q injector. "I'll put her down," he said. "She'll kill herself if she doesn't rest."

Firebird's body arched against the field projector with terrorized strength. "No," she shrieked. "Shel, help! The Shuhr . . . the fielding . . . it was Phoena all along! Phoena and one of the other heirs—"

They play on our greatest fears. Firebird was making no sense, but Shel guessed how the Shuhr had tormented her. She thrust herself between Firebird and the med. "Wait," she said. "The woman is phobic. Let me talk to her."

"Shel, please." Firebird tried to grab her hand again, missed, then wedged both hands under the regen arch. "Aren't there med runners coming in with the wounded? Or isn't there some kind of a courier ship? Let me into one. Let me go out. I'm fit. I can fly. I have to see him. I must."

Shel shook her head. "Firebird," she murmured, "there's no need. And you're *not* fit. No one can think rationally in fresh bereavement shock. I couldn't. What would you accomplish out there? The forces will recover all the dead before we leave." There. She'd said it. Dead.

The med laid down his injector. "Please, Lady Firebird. You must rest. A retrieval crew will bring him to you. You've been through torments, and in your present state, stress could literally kill you."

"I wouldn't care," Firebird muttered.

Shel frowned. "You have to care. You have children. Brennen just gave you, and them, everything that was in his power. Don't throw that away as if it meant nothing."

Firebird tried once more to push the regen arch off her chest by bodily strength and adrenaline. Then she collapsed, surrendering.

Shel was right. If she couldn't accept Brennen's last gift, then she spurned him. Besides fouling his sacrifice, she called it valueless. . . .

She couldn't tell Shel what she'd done, though. She couldn't stop pleading. "Shel, Brennen survived so much at Three Zed. Couldn't he have lived through this?"

"I might have hoped so, when he was an ES 97." The tall Sentinel's chin lifted. "But Firebird, remember. Dying EV is just fainting in the cold. He wouldn't have wanted to survive mindless. Give him up to the Holy One."

Firebird envisioned his deep eyes blank, his dancer's body nerveless. "Master Jenner could help him," she managed, though she knew this was wrongheaded thinking. "Even if the Shuhr damaged his mind, even if . . ." She shivered. "Even if they destroyed it, I'd gladly spend the rest of my life taking care of him." *Just as Carradee will gladly care for Daithi. Let me atone for what I did, Mighty Singer.* "I'd make him happy," she promised.

Shel shook her head. "Firebird," she murmured, "he's gone."

"Then let me help bring back what's left," Firebird whispered.

Shel's eyes narrowed. She glanced over at the med, up at the life-signs display, and then to Firebird's surprise, she dropped to a crouch and gripped Firebird's hand. "Listen. Colonel Keeson did assign Uri and me to retrieval. There is a courier, and I'm cleared to use it if necessary. If you need . . ." She cleared her throat. "They wouldn't let me go back out for Wald. I never saw his body. Do you understand?"

"Yes," Firebird gasped, though she didn't.

Shel frowned. "Search-and-rescue has right-of-way over retrieval. We may have to wait for them to get a ship."

She understood that.

Shel's eyebrows arched. "And you mustn't hope he's physically alive. Let go. Think of him, not yourself."

"I'm trying," Firebird managed, but she could think of only one thing. Whatever remained of her bond mate, she must take him home to Hesed.

Most of an hour later, Firebird slumped against the little courier craft's starboard bulkhead and tried not to shiver. Stars seemed to quiver around her. Clearly, something was wrong with her senses. It could be bereavement shock. It could, but until she saw . . . until she was certain . . .

She shut her eyes and made one more promise. *Mighty Singer, I deserve nothing from you. If we can find him alive and whole, I'll give you the rest of my life in service. I'll serve wherever you send me.*

Just as at Hunter Height, though, it didn't feel right to bargain with the Almighty. She let go of all her pretended claims. *Truly, I owe you a life. One way or the other, it's yours.*

It always was, she realized.

Flying along Brennen's last known vector, far out of the search area, they finally got a weak transponder signal. It took several more minutes on thrusters to home in on the tumbling shape of an inflated EV suit. The pale gray curl brightened and dimmed as it rotated in the Zed star's feeble light.

"Four minutes to close approach," Shel murmured.

The stars kept shimmering. Firebird squeezed her eyes shut. There would be no way to go on, raising her children alone, except by accepting Brennen's sacrifice. She tried imagining him in the Singer's country, strong and whole, shining with new light.

Actually, that wasn't hard to imagine. *Bless him, Mighty Singer. Bathe him in your magnificent music. He has longed for that all his life. Give him back all he lost, down in the Golden City. And give me peace*, she finished weakly, *with whatever we find here.*

Really, she hadn't diminished his sacrifice at all.

Shel glanced aside. Firebird sat slump shouldered, her brown eyes dulled by pain medication—when they opened at all. She hadn't spoken since they launched. Shel hadn't mentioned the shivering. She remembered bereavement, with its mental and physical disorientation. Watching Firebird, Shel realized how far she had come, herself—how much she'd recovered.

Something old, hard, and cold seemed to be melting in her heart. Wald, long safe with the Speaker, would have understood what she was doing. Until Firebird saw Brennen's body, she would cling to false hope. She needed the assurance that Shel had been denied, the sense she had done all that she could, trying to save him.

Please, Holy One. Let us find that he went to you peacefully.

Shel matched her course with the spinning body, then slowly decelerated. The life suit didn't look as if it had been badly holed. *He probably did suffer, then*, she realized bleakly. The Shuhr must have tormented him.

Firebird roused. "Hurry," she whispered.

Shel took her time. At least Firebird would be able to see him here, against the chill beauty of space.

She activated the courier's low-power catchfield and tugged him closer. She and Firebird had both slipped into extravehicular suits on board *North Ice.* Now she pulled the umbilicals from her chest plate, attached a temp tank, and slipped a furled rescue bag over her shoulder.

Firebird disconnected too, and Shel didn't try to stop her. Instead, she double-checked Firebird's temp tank, shut down their ship's gravidics, and then helped Firebird steer herself into the airlock. As its outer hatch opened, Shel tethered to the dull gray exterior. Firebird followed, moving weakly, like a half-charged automaton.

Shel caught his stiffly inflated arm. His faceplate was dark. She tried a quest-pulse and felt nothing.

She clenched and unclenched her hands, relieved for Brennen's sake, agonized for Firebird's. *Thank you*, she managed to pray.

"What can I do?" Firebird's interlink voice quavered.

"Anchor yourself to the hull and hold my waist so I don't spin," Shel directed. She wrestled the unwieldy life suit into her crinkly, reflective rescue bag, following standard procedure. Firebird hit the bag's pressurization control the moment Shel sealed it. It inflated swiftly, and then Shel towed the weightless bag back into the runner's airlock. She helped Firebird inside, then secured the silvery bag on one of the med runner's cots. Then she reactivated gravidics. Her feet settled to deck.

Firebird had already broken the bag's seal. She peeled it back, then wrenched off Brennen's flight helmet. Only his upper face showed behind his breath mask. Shel exhaled, deeply relieved. She saw not pain but an uncanny peace, his eyes and forehead relaxed.

Firebird pulled off her own helmet. Shel suspected the truth was finally sinking in.

Determined to play the comforter's role, Shel drew a deep breath. "If that's only tardema-sleep, I'll bring him up in a few seconds. But . . . Firebird . . . if I do, you have to be ready for the worst you can possibly imagine. If he's mindless, he could be violent. He might attack us both."

Firebird set her chin. "I understand."

"We can see he didn't suffer at the end." Shel groped behind his neck, found and toggled the deflation switch. The shape shrank to human size. She didn't bother to snug the restraint straps. Instead, she let herself fall into the standard rescue drill. She eyed the med runner's compartments, locating everything she might need for survivable injuries. She turned inward for her carrier, pausing to pray, *Holy One, have mercy on them both.* Then she stretched out an epsilon probe.

Firebird silenced all thought and emotion, trying to sense any change in Brennen. Where the pair bond had been at the back of her mind, she felt only a burned-out vacancy.

Maybe Shel was right. To be past all pain . . .

"Brenn," she murmured. She drew his breath mask away, shuddering as she touched his pale cheek. There was the scar where Phoena had kicked him. She brushed back a strand of light brown hair.

She laid her head on his still chest and shut her eyes. *Thank you, Mighty One. For all you gave us. For almost two years—*

"Firebird," Shel said softly, "I'm afraid—wait—"

Beneath Firebird's ear, Brennen inhaled hoarsely.

"Brenn," she gasped. Her pulse accelerated.

He struggled weakly against the cot's loose security bonds.

Looking horror-struck, Shel lunged forward. "Brennen, lie still," she ordered. "Brennen, can you hear me? Do you understand?"

Firebird seized both of his hands. She still felt nothing back at the Brennen-place in her mind.

What had she done? Because of her selfishness, would he live out his days mindless at Hesed House?

"Lie still," Shel repeated. "Brennen, lie still. You've been EV."

Brennen gasped. His right hand tightened on Firebird's, but his left hand hung limp. He tried to pull it away. "Shel," he said in a ragged voice, "bless you. Did you . . ." He coughed, then managed, "Did you rescue Mari, too?"

Brennen stared up through a medical scanner at Adamm Hancock. Every bone and muscle ached—except in his splinted left arm, both of his shoulders, and his neck. Pain blocks were in place.

Hancock eyed his scanner. "Headache gone?"

Brennen nodded cautiously.

The med finally smiled. "Your fluids are giving normal readings again. Six or seven hours on regen and you'll be free to go, but don't hesitate to call if the headache comes back. We'll fuse that fracture as soon as the swelling goes down."

Mari sat beside Shel on the next cot over, dangling her legs and watching Hancock finish. Pain lines still creased her forehead and cut between her eyes. He could see her worry, but even to him, at short range, the pair bond felt like a ghost of what it had been. Her symptoms—neural paroxysm, unfathomable grief, change in life signs—all indicated genuine bereavement shock.

Sanctuary Master Dabarrah would be able to tell them what had happened to her. For now, he could only thank Shel for showing such deep empathy toward her—and bringing him in before his EV suit's resources ran out.

He managed to smile at them both. Finally, he understood why the One had let him be weakened at Three Zed. His months of fighting irrational fears had taught him to fall completely into the Holy One's power. That strength had held against the fielding attack when his own strength would have shattered. Instead of destroying his own sanity resisting their attack, he'd slipped peacefully into tardema-sleep.

Meds and their assistants bustled around him. He'd asked Uri to stay on *Weatherway* and help debrief returning pilots. A memorial tonight would honor Hannes Dickin and the others killed.

Hearing footsteps, he opened his eyes. Colonel Keeson stepped into his line of sight. He touched his forehead to return her salute, cleared his throat, and asked, "What's the downside status?"

Colonel Keeson took a parade-rest stance at the foot of his cot. "The main city is utterly destroyed, full of magma and gas. Four small domes, which they call settlements, have asked to surrender. I need your authorization to answer. May I accept?"

At the edge of his vision, Firebird straightened her back. He saw fierce joy in her wide eyes and firm lips, and in the determined set of her eyebrows, even if he could not feel it in her mind.

The Holy One had spared his forces from having to slaughter their own kinsmen by destroying the Golden City. Would He not spare them from slaughtering the less guilty?

Brennen covered his face with both hands. *Lord of mercy, let this be the end. The city is burned to bare rock, as we were ordered. Your hand swept their power away. You spared us from—*

Yes. His answer came promptly. *You have finished. Well done, my child.*

"Yes," he told Colonel Keeson. "Accept!"

CHAPTER 26
CODA

calmato
quieted

Master Dabarrah laid his palm over Kinnor's wrinkled forehead. Immediately, the squirming child stopped bellowing and gazed up into the sanctuary master's face. He grabbed for Dabarrah's white-blond hair.

Firebird relaxed, too. "He dove off that chair like he thought he could fly," she explained, frustrated that after all she'd been through, she couldn't catch one leaping infant. Kin would give her heart failure—again—if she didn't keep a close watch.

"I biotaped this precocious little bird six times while you were gone." Dabarrah fingered the side of Kin's head. "You're right—he wants to fly, like his parents. Only a bruise," he assured her. "Not the first, and certainly not the last."

Kinnor struggled to be set down. Firebird looked around the med center, saw nothing dangerous within the little one's reach, and released him on the stone floor. He raised up on both arms and scooted toward the door.

His father caught him, picked him up by his padded hips, and aimed him into the room, toward the white-haired man in torn drillcloth overalls.

Brennen's spiritual father, Shamarr Dickin, had just come in from the gardens. Knowing that this was always his first stop upon arriving from Thyrica, Firebird had sought him out between rows. She'd bent with him over a pair of shovels and made a heartfelt confession. He assured her she had been forgiven the moment she asked for mercy, and that no one would blame her for the way she took down the Shuhr fielding team.

Now he crouched and held out both hands, beckoning Kinnor.

"Since we are all here, Jenner," he said, "tell me the prognosis on this little one's parents."

Firebird edged closer to Brennen. These secrets couldn't be kept for long. Already, Brennen's masquerade had been exposed in Federate circles. Word would return quickly to Netaia, too. A messenger ship was decelerating toward the Hesed Valley with Tel Tellai on board, the only Netaian elector who could be allowed inside Hesed's fielding net.

Firebird had a terrible new respect for fielding technology.

Master Jenner opened a long hand in her direction and told the Shamarr, "Firebird's ayin is completely gone. Prolonged fusion scarred it through. She can no longer even turn."

—Visualization or no visualization! Micahel's blast of power and the repeated kills had damaged that tiny brain complex irreparably. She would do no more fusion killing, and there would be no further temptation to use evil against evil.

As Master Jenner explained it, the physical injury had traumatized other parts of her brain, combining with the prolonged fusion to disrupt her alpha matrix and interrupt the pair bond, creating genuine bereavement shock. As the trauma diminished, she felt Brennen's emotions again.

The bond had not broken.

"Then fusion," said Shamarr Dickin, "is riskier than we imagined."

Master Jenner answered, "I agree. No one will want to learn to do this, since the danger is so great." As the tall, thin sanctuary master eyed Firebird, a comforting wave of epsilon energy lapped through her mind. She welcomed Dabarrah's consolation, even as she fretted that Kiel or Kinnor might have inherited the reversed-polarity carrier, with its potential power and risk. That wouldn't make itself known for years. Raising that pair to training age would be a daunting job.

"And you, son?" asked the shamarr, eyeing Brennen.

Jenner spread his hands. "Full memory did return while they were en route to Three Zed. I verified that."

Dickin raised a bushy eyebrow. "Then there should be substantial restoration of ES potential."

That's right, Firebird wanted to shout.

Jenner nodded. "I can't perform fine calibration here, but my rough measurements put him nearly at the Master's range again."

The Shamarr took three long steps and wrapped his arms around Brennen. Brennen's hands clapped the shamarr's shoulders. Only someone who knew he'd been injured, Firebird observed, would see the slight stiffness in his left wrist. "I am glad," murmured Dickin, pushing away. "Well done, Brennen. Well done." He eyed Jenner again. "And I hear you have a fourth patient."

"Carradee?" Jenner smiled. "Yes."

Firebird sat down on a long stone bench. "I told Carradee to have Tel announce her pregnancy on Netaia. Kenhing can restore House Angelo to her new daughter. That shows on the simulations as a stabilizing factor, especially now. Without Rogonin in power, the Electorate can take a more long-sighted view."

"And?" asked the Shamarr. "Their reaction?"

Raising her head, Firebird glanced at Brennen. "Tel should be bringing us a report."

"This also looks significant." Shamarr Dickin pulled a message roll out of his dusty coveralls. "Brennen, this is for you. Tallis."

Brennen took it and thumbed the seal. At Tallis, Regional's First Fleet had wiped out the disorganized Shuhr attackers who fled Three Zed. Other Federate ships orbited Three Zed now, controlling all traffic as a committee of Sentinels oversaw the surviving settlements. Assisted by Shuhr survivors, Federate agents were searching the settlements' labs and data banks for bioweapons or gene materials.

Shamarr Dickin had also decreed that this other Ehretan remnant could be proselytized without waiting for inquiries—though already, Shuhr were registering as inquirers. After all, a Caldwell seemed to have done exactly what the holy books prophesied.

Maybe this union of remnants would bring about the true atonement, the new song . . . the Word to Come.

Firebird snatched Kinnor up off the floor and tried to hold him to her shoulder. He squirmed, giving out a groan that started to crescendo. She set him down once more. *It's going to be a battle of wills, isn't it, little one?*

She felt Brennen's shock—faintly—before his eyes registered it.

"What?" she asked softly. Shamarr Dickin hadn't given him the message in privacy, so it had to be news that could be shared.

Brennen raised a rolled scribepaper. "With the insubordination episode struck from your record," he read aloud, "the Federate High command has the honor of requesting that you accept the position of Battlefield Director, Federate Regional command . . . Tallis."

Firebird crossed her arms. Regional command, back on track toward his life's dream! *Thank you, Mighty One!* Tallis's MaxSec tower was no place to raise children, but with her new allowance, she and Brennen might buy a piece of prime land . . . something like the home she'd loved on Trinn Hill, in sight of the city but secure and secluded. She could set up her cultural exchange program right there at the Regional capital.

Brennen had told her, though, that he felt they had other priorities.

"Congratulations, Brenn." She slipped her arm around his waist. "Whether or not you accept it, this is a true honor."

He stared at Shamarr Dickin's eyes. "Yes," he said softly, "but I wonder what I could accomplish at Tallis, with the biggest threat to Federate peace ended."

"There will always be conflict," Firebird argued, glancing to the shamarr for support, "until the Word comes in power."

The white-haired man nodded solemnly.

"And this is your dream," she insisted. "If even the Federate bureaucrats are willing to set you back on track, think twice before turning them down."

"That doesn't compare to the need on Netaia," he reminded her. "Thousands of lives are still at stake." He laid a hand on Firebird's shoulder. "And you gave a solemn promise."

As Shamarr Dickin raised one hand, a shadow fell across the door. Carradee stepped inside, carrying Kiel against her shoulder. "He was looking for his brother," she said. "Is Kinnor going to be all right?"

"He will be, if he ever learns his limits." Relieved by the interruption, Firebird picked up her small explorer, raised her foot onto a wooden chair, and perched Kin on her knee where he could see Kiel. They reached for each other's fingers, communicating on some level that even Master Dabarrah couldn't sense.

Firebird didn't care squill for what she had promised First Lord Erwin, especially after he'd laid the Powers' blessing on her, but she *had* promised the rest of her life in service.

She'd come forward when Netaia needed her, but her desire to be a ruler had died with her pride. Even the desire to single-handedly save her people was utterly gone. In the future, if she could spare any attention from Kinnor and Kiel, she would rather develop her musical gifts than study those Federate simulations—and why should she spend her days sparring with the Netaian Electorate when she was no longer barred from proselytizing?

She was alive only because Brennen offered his life in her place. She was a flawed reflection of the divine image, with no cause to be proud.

She set Kinnor back on the floor and crossed the room, halting in front of the shamarr. "I defer to you, Shamarr Dickin. I owe a life to the One who saved Brennen. Please advise me."

The blue candles on both sides of Hesed's chapter room gave off the aromatic scent of kirka trees. Midday sun shone down through its skylight as Sentinels gathered to hear from Prince Tel. At Master Dabarrah's request, she and Brennen had taken seats in front, off to the left. Brennen looked resplendent in his dress whites. Firebird felt only moderately comfortable in her own pale blue sekiyr's gown. They'd let her keep this, even though all hope to train as a Sentinel was gone. From here, she had a good view of Carradee, who sat next to Daithi's mobility chair at far right. Kiel perched on Aunt Carradee's lap, gazing up at the nearest candle sconce. Kinnor had finally curled up on the bench next to them both.

On the third bench back, Ellet Dardy waited beside her muscular bond mate.

Terza sat behind them with Sanctuary Mistress Anna. Terza's silhouette changed quickly these days. According to Master Jenner, who had healed the deep tampering on Terza's mind, she was as content as anyone could be while grieving so many of her people. Though she spent most of her time closed in her room, she did attend Chapter, and she worked in the gardens. Shamarr Dickin had sought her out as soon as he left the med center. Firebird remembered her nightly in prayer.

Behind Terza, the double doors opened. Tel strode in, dressed in elegant white velvette and carrying a papercase up the center aisle. He stepped lightly. Brennen raised an eyebrow, then bent toward Firebird's ear. "Tel seems pleased with himself," he whispered. "There could be a young lady."

. . . Or else something else that he'd wanted badly, Firebird guessed. Shamarr Dickin's counsel had been gracious but somber. If Tel called her forward, instead of Carradee, then she must accept. Even if she spent the rest of her life wrestling with the electors, she wouldn't face them alone.

Tel mounted the steps and turned toward her. "Lady Firebird," he said, "General, please join me on the platform."

Firebird pushed slowly to her feet and walked forward. *So be it, Brenn.* She felt him follow her, and she steadied herself by staring up at the star on the wall over the altar flame.

Standing beside tall Master Dabarrah, Tel opened his papercase. He plucked out a small, clear presentation box, then a certificate.

A soft, surprised grunt left Firebird's throat, though she tried to hold it back. Netaia's Triple Arrow was the highest military award the Electorate could bestow. *For Valor*, read the certificate.

She took a step backward, to the platform's edge. "Thank you, Your Highness," she said formally, "but the Golden City was destroyed by other forces, and I couldn't have touched its fielding station without Brennen. This was his doing, more than mine. Much more."

Tel reached into his papercase again. "So I've been told," he said. "So for the first time in Netaia's history, General Caldwell, the Electorate has also awarded this honor to an offworld-born recipient."

Brennen stood at relaxed attention as Tel pressed the gold emblem to his dress whites—temporarily, she knew. Sentinels wore only the star. Even Master Sentinels. Surely Shamarr Dickin would give that back, no matter what else Tel announced. Brennen had pioneered a new, spiritual epsilon skill in addition to his recovery.

Firebird stood still as Tel fastened the other emblem near her neckline.

Then Tel stepped to the platform's center, blocking her view of the altar flame. Almost fifty Sentinels and sekiyrra had assembled when Master Jenner called them in.

"Now," he said gravely, "I have been asked to deliver a report from the Netaian Electorate."

Firebird kept her shoulders at a dignified military brace and caught Carradee's glance. Carradee smiled, but Firebird saw a pleading look in her eye.

Tel turned to Carradee and made a dignified half bow. "Majesty, as Firebird requested, the Electorate has acclaimed your daughter, Rinnah, as the next sovereign of the Netaian systems. Kenhing is willing to serve as her regent until she comes of age. It is our hope that you will agree to the acclamation. Will you give your consent?"

Firebird imagined she could feel the weight of a world slide off her shoulders and fall to the red stone floor.

Carradee inclined her head formally. Kiel reached up and snatched a curl of her blond hair. Carradee laughed softly and pulled it away from him. "I consent to the electors' wishes," she said, "as is my duty."

Firebird could barely keep from bouncing on both feet. She seized Brennen's hand instead, and he gripped hers back, flooding her with his own happiness.

Shamarr Dickin rose from the front bench and walked forward, mounting the steps. "Come here," he said kindly, drawing the blue-green vial of anointing oil from his side pocket. "Firebird, Brennen—and you, Carradee. It is time for new blessings."

AUTHOR'S NOTE

Due to circumstances beyond my control (writing fiction is like that), *Crown of Fire* developed a dual theme of pride and atonement. The issue of pride, raised in *Firebird* and continued in *Fusion Fire*, needed closure. Firebird's lifelong desires to excel and to be remembered aren't intrinsically sinful. We are commanded to do all things "heartily, as for the Lord rather than for men" (Colossians 3:23, NASB), which I understand to mean excellently, using all the gifts He gives us. As for Firebird's desire for remembrance—when Mary broke her jar of perfume and anointed Jesus for burial, He said, "what she has done will also be told, in memory of her" (Mark 14:9b, NIV). We can aspire to be remembered for the right reasons.

Pride was always Firebird's temptation, though, and mine. Whenever I do something well just to outshine everyone else, or I insist on getting my way while ignoring someone else's needs, or I refuse to do something that I know God wants, then I set myself up as my own little Power. Fortunately, our merciful God rarely finds it necessary to let the Adversary break our proud hearts quite as dramatically as Micahel shattered Firebird's—or as utterly as the One blasted Three Zed (Adiyn's final vision of the shebiyl is based loosely on Revelation 1:13–16).

I do not feel qualified to deal with such a vital subject as atonement, so I portrayed this seeming death and resurrection as a parable for Firebird's enlightenment, rather than as allegory. At this point in Firebird's story, she understands mercy, her flawed nature, and the necessity of dying to pride and self. In her universe, true atonement lies in the future . . . but she grasps the concept only when Brennen acts it out. His action saves her from being destroyed simply for who she is. Similarly, Christ submitted to death in our place, rescuing us from the inevitable consequences of who we are: His flawed but beloved children, created in the divine image but tainted by our propensity to sin.

Jesus was not miraculously saved from death, though. Even more miraculously, He satisfied the demands of justice and then returned triumphant from death. His resurrection proves the victory. Death has no claim on us, and we too can step out onto a new Path.

Kathy Tyers
Montana
Good Friday, A.D. 2000